A Rooke's Tale
BOOK I

Salvation Taverns

A Rooke's Tale

BOOK I

Salvation Taverns

E.M. GOLDSMITH

*For my cousin, Elizabeth, who kept believing
even when I despaired. And for Ginger, the
best friend a person could ever have.*

*For my daughter, Kate, and her courage that
inspired me to keep going through all the dark
days we traveled.*

For Carly & Bryan who made it all better.

Table of Contents

SUBJUGATED AERDA
THE BOREAL SEA
The R
Primordial Boreal
Aroghotto City
Chazir
The First Empire
Astarte
SMUGGLER'S COVE
Ellyn
Bradamate
THE ACARIAN OCEAN
Jebellen
The Flowery Kingdom
Lesser Faroe
Parthal
The Tombs of Alleyslande
The Razor's Edge
THE DREAD SEA
The R

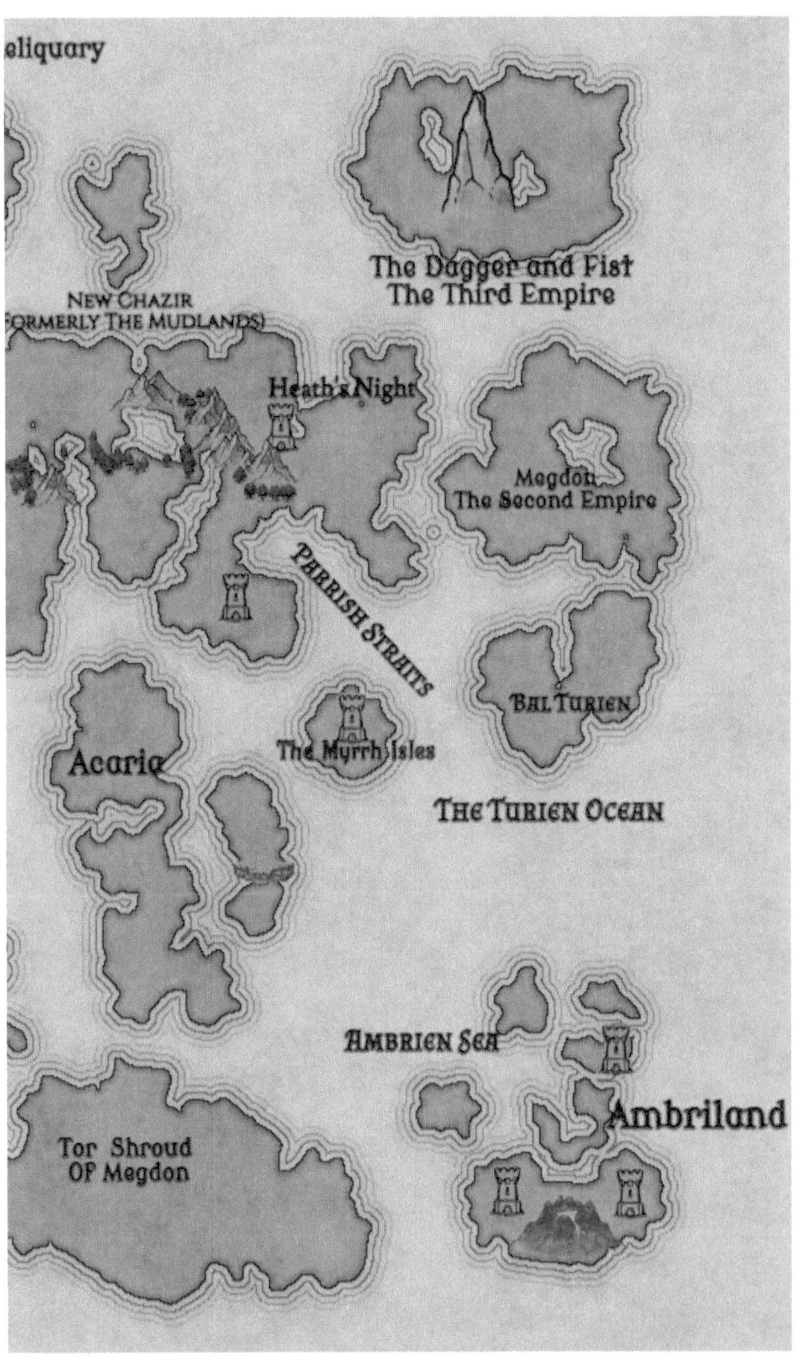
eliquary
The Dagger and Fist
The Third Empire
New Chazir
(Formerly The Mudlands)
Heath's Night
Megdon
The Second Empire
Parrish Straits
Bal Turien
The Myrrh Isles
Acaria
The Turien Ocean
Ambrien Sea
Ambriland
Tor Shroud
Of Megdon

Tavern I:

The Dragon's Neck

Words can change the world. But sometimes it takes a dragon.

Mordecai's Grimoire by Felix Wren of 'Those' Wrens
Preface by Hazel Kyran

The Knight Scrivener

O n his first night back home to The Reliquary from his journey in the Three Empires, Kentigern Dagan Leesh returned to his favorite tavern to find everyone dressed in black. His correspondence home traveled faster than he did. A rooke murdered by an assassin's guild believed to be extinct.

"What was his name?"

The first inevitable question came from the old barkeep, Shanks, sending a hush through The Dragon's Neck. Even the blizzard on the mountainside went quiet for the revelation of the name of the murdered rooke.

"Torres Rushie," Kentigern said and left it there.

A rooke's name could only be recalled after their death, and so a bristle of pain echoed through Kentigern's soul as he offered the true identity of the dead man. His best friend. His responsibility to protect.

He did not need to tell Shanks to fill his mug with dark Boreallean ale. Everyone in The Reliquary knew Kentigern Dagan Leesh both by name and reputation, both scrivener and guardian knight.

"Alright, Kenny?" Shanks asked.

"Can't say I am, Shanks. They butchered him. Made us all watch. Spytes, I am certain. The last kingdom of Acaria is done thanks to them."

"That's not on, mate. Are you sure they were truly Spytes?"

"Had to be. Some like children, all beautiful to the see. Sweet, pretty with soulless eyes and the darkest of weapons. I struck one down and instead of a corpse, black smoke blinded me and killed two others I was trying to protect."

"Was there an odor when these assassins appeared?" a

woman asked, slinking into the pub under the gaze of Shank's giant, horned owl.

"Yes, there was. Unpleasant like sweet piss," Kentigern said, trying to identify the woman from under her hood. She felt full of shadow, as if barely there. A faint scent of roses and wild rivers accompanied her, a view of a world lost below.

"Yes, then those were Spytes. Pity. They are difficult to dispel," the woman said. "You are lucky to be alive, Kentigern Dagan Leesh."

"I am the only one in our party who survived. I ran. Like a coward. In the darkness, I just ran, praying with all that I am that Ta-She spare me. The Rooke's followers were not so fortunate. They were slaughtered down to the smallest child. I could not protect any of them," Kentigern said, not wanting to recall the slaughter but seeing the events flash before his eyes, the trauma fresh like a new wound.

He looked up to ask after the woman but found himself distracted by a rat scurrying away under the bar. The woman disappeared into the crowd of patrons who huddled closer to hear Kentigern's news.

"Shanks, your owl has let its meal get away," Kentigern said.

"Figaro can be a bit fickle about his prey," Shanks said. "Get that rat, you lazy bird. Can't have vermin in my pub. Sorry, Kenny, he's been in a right state. This winter isn't agreeing with him."

"What does that leave us?" a patron asked as the blizzard resumed whistling outside.

The gathered patrons began buzzing.

"Seventeen are ready for their robes, I have heard," one patron said, voicing knowledge freely shared within The Reliquary. "Competing to be granted full ascendency, to trade their names for magic. And there is always that fully robed rooke who trains them. Looks a young man but is supposed to be ancient. He claims he was alive before The Evanescence."

"I have heard he was a thousand years old or more," another patron said. "Keeps to himself mostly."

"He is a few centuries at best and has a full range of apprentices to keep him busy. There are enough ready for the robes and knighthood to be getting on without me," Kentigern said to the gathered patrons. "The people of the empires create theater, books, livelies, and music inspired by tales told by rookes over the centuries. They yearn for the world of the tales they hear. There is no need to send more rookes."

"We cannot leave Spytes to their own devices," Ghita Mist, a mature woman and master puzzler by trade, said. "No doubt the dragons are stirring. I feel it. We must send a new rooke, fully robed. If the dragons awake, we all die."

"There are no dragons, Ghita. Maybe before The Evanescence such creatures lived. There is nothing but the empires and their oppression of their people. No devils or dragons needed. Rotten people are all that The Evanescence left behind," Kentigern said. "Neither the empires nor the Spytes pose danger to The Reliquary. We are happy here, are we not? Why keep asking good men and women to sacrifice their names?"

"For hope's sake," Ghita Mist said. "Life can be better for everyone if our rookes succeed."

"I appreciate you, Ghita. I do," Kentigern said, lifting his mug. He sighed.

"What?" Ghita asked. "What do you want to say?"

"All through recorded history, one thing never changes, Ghita," Kentigern said. "People murder their saviors. This is my home. I will not leave it again. I will ask Mara to marry me and raise a family, far from the people below who will never appreciate what we sacrificed to save them. Let them rot."

He took a long sip of the dark ale, savoring it as the sparks in the over-sized hearth danced to the tune of the little fiddle band.

Kentigern held true to his words. He did not leave again. Fifty-seven years passed. Fewer scriveners and knight guardians volunteered to accompany each new rooke as the next several met the same end as Torres Rushie. Until only the most ancient one remained.

The Reliquary

A plump, black rat soiled the spotless foyer before the great golden doors of The Reliquary's inner sanctum. The Rooke stepped out of the lift, cocked his head at the small creature. It stared back at him, curious yet unafraid.

"Where did you come from?" The Rooke asked. The rat lowered its head, wrapped its tail around its backside without blinking.

The sanctum gleamed despite the presence of the rat; white, polished marble, hand-crafted wooden panels, pristine from floor to the high-arching ceiling. Roses filled silver planters at each side of the grand golden doors, running up the archway. The pleasant aroma cheered The Rooke as he recalled rolling rivers in autumn in the valleys below.

He grinned, thinking of his old friend, Phaedra, and how rats plagued her wherever she went. He looked up, half-expecting to see the mad and eccentric sorceress in whatever woman she happened to be wearing these days.

"You are not the greeting I expected," The Rooke said to the rat. "And I doubt The Relic summoned you. I would be gone were I you. Ghita Mist's cats will make sport of you. And Shank's new owl looked hungry this morning."

The rat said nothing, nor did it move. The Rooke shrugged and continued toward the double, golden doors which swung open to welcome him in.

The Seven Aspects of The Relic stood immutable, same height, same shadowed faces, scarlet robes sashed in gold, same pose of bowed heads with folded-gloved hands, one much as the other. Below them, from behind a long table, their old scrivener handed The Rooke an unraveled scroll with The Relic's command outlined in dark, wet ink.

The Rooke could feel the emotions of The Relic's Aspects

despite the absence of it in their voices and shrouded faces. His death was the least of their worries and not the worst fate The Rooke could think of as he reviewed the quest offered him.

"Can we talk about this?" The Rooke asked the Seven Aspects of The Relic.

"The dragons are stirring," The Relic said in chorus. "If the dragons awake, all will perish in ice and flame."

"There are good people in the empires still," The Rooke said, an empty plea. "Surely, dragons will not blame the people for the ill-deeds of their oppressors?"

"Dragons slumber to the tune of their tales. When their stories cease, when the magic of creation is extinguished in the people of Aerda, they awake," The Relic echoed. "The dragons will destroy this world and replace it with one which respects them."

"That seems a bit harsh," The Rooke said. "Even for dragons. Every child born holds the possibility of creation in their soul. No empire can extinguish that."

"No empire can, but those who create Spytes might. Better they all die than be corrupted in the end," The Relic said in that rolling, united voice, the sound of waves crashing on rocky shores. "Your tales can save them, awake in them possibility. So many lost tales and you must tell all of them in a short time."

"Let's take it one story at a time," The Rooke said.

He took the ancient tome from the grizzled scrivener, Kentigern Dagan Leesh. The book recorded all accounts of past rookes and the tales they had told over the years.

The ancient tome bestowed on The Rooke an odd comfort, the feel of the leather cover, the smell of old velum, the gold-leafed ink. He remembered a youthful scribe at the priory, arms always full of antiquated books, a library with shelves so high that sliding ladders were required to access the tallest rows.

This memory was old, a recollection of the world below, before The Evanescence, before The Subjugation, before his home had fallen to the Infernal Empires and their dark technologies. Back before he had given up his name, before he had earned the red robes of The Rooke. He remembered himself only in dreams and shadows.

"Might we offer you counsel?" The Fourth Aspect, the Master of The Relic, said.

"Will it help me survive this?"

"It will," The Relic said in chorus. "Tell the tales true. Be brutal. Be wise. The people below have extinguished all records of the ice dragon, Tem, and the fire dragon, Phaedra, and their abundant brood. Use the tales of the sorceress with the fire dragon's name to rekindle their wonder."

"What did the last rookes do? The ones who regained their names?"

"They started by trying to warn the people of dragon attacks," The Sixth Aspect said. "Imperial citizens are not afraid of dragons and will not change to avoid them. If the dragons awake, the people below won't live long enough to see them. Tem and Phaedra are too big for the human eye when enraged."

"I believe I knew the sorceress, Phaedra. Back when I was an ordinary man, back when she was learning her magic," The Rooke said. "Will this do any good?"

"What?" the old scrivener said. "That's impossible. The robes have confused your memories with those of the characters of myth and story. The Evanescence was over two centuries ago, and Phaedra came into her magic more than a century before that. I know you are older than me, but you could not be *that* old. You do not look half my age."

"Are you not nearing a century yourself, Kentigern?" The Third Aspect said. "The Reliquary allows extensions to mortal lives and more to our precious rookes."

The Rooke often forgot how alarming his un-aging appearance must be for those who knew him long. He had first encountered Kentigern Dagan Leesh when he had been a newborn brought through a terrible storm to The Reliquary by his rebel mother during the first great war after Subjugation. While Kentigern grew old, white-haired, and wrinkled, The Rooke had shown no outward change, no graying hair, no wrinkles, no fading gait.

"Most will not hear your tales," The Fourth Aspect said. "The empires have made the people below comfortable in their chains, turned their hearts to hatred and indifference, convinced them they do not deserve any better in their lives. They cannot imagine the wonders they might unleash if not for the oppression under which they live."

The Rooke knew The Fourth, the master of the Seven Aspects, better than the others: the voice soothing, melodious, ancient, kind.

Beneath those robes and hoods, all Seven Aspects were distinct creatures, human to the eye but something else underneath the skin. The Rooke had his suspicions. He believed the Seven Aspects would suffer worse than death should the dragons awaken and destroy Aerda. The Relic's Aspects were the kind of ethereal beings that The Icari, the thirteen demonic rulers of Pandemonium, would do anything to entrap in their hell.

"The magic will work," The Rooke said. "And if the sorceress, Phaedra, is still out there somewhere, we will find one another. Her magic is strong, and she has a way with dragons."

"She does know them, indeed. Well enough to understand there is no changing dragons. They are what they are, and they will do as they will. Ordinary people must have their hearts changed, give the dragons a reason to preserve this bit of Creation," The Second Aspect said.

This one was one of poetry and song. Deep in sleep, The Rooke often heard The Second singing a gentle lullaby that could be heard throughout this great colony built inside the mountain.

"Rumors of the sorceress still existed when Torres Rushie went down there in his red robes fifty-seven years ago, before assassins returned his name to him," Scrivener Leesh said. "But that could not be. She would be half a millennium old."

"Phaedra is far older than that, but she can change bodies," The Rooke said. "She is a true sorceress. Mortality is not her weakness. She must stay free of the hell she escaped, not an easy feat if the Spytes still roam the world below."

"The sorceress has no ability to keep the dragons sleeping. You must do that with your tales," The Second Aspect said. "Will you accept this quest, dear Rooke?"

"You speak as if I truly have a choice. I know what is at stake."

He turned his back on The Relic, feeling their eyes glaring down at him. This stone bowl had no echo to it as he trudged across the polished black floor back toward the huge, golden double doors.

"Wait," another of the Aspects called, The First. This Aspect, though tall and slender as the other six, sounded like a young boy on the cusp of manhood. "We have each granted you a companion to accompany you, to help you succeed where others failed. Here, we have made a list."

The Rooke turned, feeling something hot rise in him, anger, fear, or pride, unpleasant, and he struggled to hold his temper. He trudged toward The Relic and took the scrolled list from Scrivener Leesh who had been handed the scroll by The Fourth.

"Who I take and who I leave behind should be my choice. It is my life I am giving…"

"A life you have already given. One we extended," The Fourth said, holding his hands up to stopper the rumblings of the other six. "It is critical that you obey the list. We will not be defied."

"Defied?"

"Six perished because they defied us," The Seventh said. "When we put forth the terms for their success, they ignored us, thinking their magic strong enough to evade Spytes."

"But why did the magic fail?" The Rooke asked. "You must know."

"We were betrayed," The Fifth said. "From within. You know this."

"Yes, I suppose that must have been it. That was my failure," The Rooke said. "I did not believe a descendant of Husk

Grayvesone would ever be so corrupted. But what of the rookes before the betrayal? Did they defy you as well?"

"They did not listen," The Sixth said. "We are the only reason those below still exist at all. We calmed the dragons at the last cataclysm between Evanescence and Subjugation. We kept them sleeping to give those left behind a small chance."

"The methods we used before to calm them are not working anymore. Magic is not enough. How could rookes expect others to listen to them when they would not listen to us or to those to whom they gave their tales?" The Fifth said. "Sometimes the power of the red robe brings out something unpleasant in those we award it to despite their immunity to the demons of The Icari. Humans, even the best among you, are so difficult to judge."

"We are tired, Sir Rooke," The Fourth said. The Rooke heard a twinge of feeling and it struck him to the core. "We have sacrificed everything and more to…"

"To save ourselves. The magic that protects us as well as our sanctuary will be vanquished as the dragons take flight," The Third said, a feminine voice, putting a gloved hand on the sleeve of The Fourth in comfort, in unity. "If we're being honest. If you do not succeed where your compatriots failed, we will be devoured, us and all that live in our protection."

"Your tales can restore that which was lost and cleanse what was corrupted, and Alleysiande might be part of Aerda again. Creation will expand here in this world we have so long sought to cultivate and preserve and in doing so, will enliven possibility in worlds beyond counting," The Fifth said. "You are our last hope. The very last. If you fail…"

"He will not fail," The Fourth said, squeezing the white-gloved hands of The Third and The Fifth. "Out of the hundreds of rookes we have raised in over the millennia spent here, I do believe you are the best of them. You have a good heart, kindness, and compassion that has been crafted in the pain you endured below before Subjugation and in the miraculous choice you made before Evanescence."

"Do you understand?" The First asked, in his soft melodious voice of ancient youth.

The Rooke held his tongue and felt his sorrow rise in his belly, feeling defeated before he had even begun. His choice had been no miracle. It had been despair. He choked his doubt back, found that little spark of magic, tried to remember the world before the Three Empires vanquished the everyday miracles of life and made them common, and at times, unpleasant.

The Rooke repeated bits of the ancient tales to himself and some of the ones yet to be told. He smiled as he pictured the stories in his mind. Phaedra, that wicked and wonderful sorceress, and her mad quest for moments of elation, tiny pricks that tormented The Icari and their legions of demons, kept them at bay.

He would wake shards of pure joy in the people below to protect them from the endless whispers of those who would control them. They would hear his stories, and they would repeat them everywhere. In verse, in song, in fireside tales.

The Aspects

Kentigern watched the doors shut with a thud as a black rat scrambled out behind The Rooke. He felt strange, uncomfortable. In his declining years, he had grown weary of watching so many rookes be sent below to have the ghost of their names returned as they fell, one after the other. Not one rooke had survived since Kentigern failed to protect Torres Rushie. He sighed, already grieving.

He had been friends with this rooke his entire life. Kentigern's mother had been in love with The Rooke some seventy years back. This man, who appeared fifty years his junior, might have been a stepfather had The Rooke not been so damned monastic and broken.

Kentigern turned to crane his neck up at the dais where the Seven Aspects of The Relic stood. He startled. He expected the Aspects to be gone, silently leaving the chamber as was their custom.

"This Rooke is worthy. We could elevate him," The First said in that young man's voice coming from an ageless being.

"We cannot," The Fourth replied. "We are only seven. We are not enough. It would damn us if we tried."

"We are running out of time," The Fifth said, her voice quiet. "Can we not do something about the dragons as before?"

"We do not know why they are stirring," The Sixth said. "The tales continue below. Fowler died amid a coup, but his tales took hold, and the dragons were happy."

"Perhaps, we have waited too long to send a rooke," The Fifth said.

"Three years is like three seconds to a dragon," The Second said. "It is nothing to them."

"I cannot understand why they are so agitated," The Third said. "What is going on?"

"Something beyond our power is waking them. They will not listen to anyone, not even their creator," The Seventh said. "The ice dragon grieves, and the fire dragon is active. The tsunami that wiped out the island, Petit Mourne, her doing."

Kentigern wondered if The Seven Aspects of The Relic realized he was still there. He had never heard them converse privately among themselves. Not like this. He shivered and contemplated sneaking out the side passage although he would have a long hike in the dark to get back to the lifts. He crept toward the side passage.

"Kentigern, stop if you please," The Fourth said. "We require your help."

"Yes?"

"The Rooke's last apprentice is too young," The Third said. "And there are no others. People are sore afraid to take on the mantle of the red robes."

"We must find those willing to sacrifice their names to save this world," The Fourth said.

"We will open the Forge to train new rookes. The library,

the arena, all of it," The Sixth said. "We will undertake their instruction ourselves. We will redouble the efforts of rookes. Send several out at a time as soon as we can."

"If by soon, you mean a century," The Seventh said, scoffing at his brethren.

"Whatever it takes, Seventh," The Fourth said. "We should have done this the moment Torres Rushie died. We forget how fast mortal lives churn, and how easy they are to manipulate now that the barrier between this world and the hell of The Hierarchy is so very thin."

"Opening the mythical forge is a welcome idea," Kentigern said. "How I wished to train there as a boy. My favorite stories are of the Erelahian Knights that came from this place. Is it true? Does it still exist? None of the guardians nor rookes who fell were trained by the Forge. Only this one, if the stories of his age are true, have even seen The Forge of Sentinels."

"His training and his magic will be stronger than the others before him. We did not foresee such magic would be necessary below. We underestimated the corruption, and we did not anticipate the nature of the defilement of this world," The Fourth said. "We will train as many as we can find. In addition to young Thiago."

"Those who become guardians or rookes must be strong. The forge will destroy the weak," The Sixth said.

"I have a few possible candidates in mind," Kentigern said. "Ones who might be trained. There is a puzzler…"

"No," The Second said. "We must explore beyond this sanctuary. Go out into the world and recruit."

"What? I…"

"You can and you will," The Fifth said.

"But if this rooke succeeds? Should we risk such exposure?"

"Only if he is successful will it be necessary for there to be other rookes," The Fourth said.

"We will meet with you and the last remaining knight guardians to discuss this further."

"I will arrange it," Kentigern agreed, scribbling down an

audience appointment in his book. "Many would make fine Knight Guardians. If they were conditioned. We are getting a bit soft here in The Reliquary."

"We will harden them in the Forge," The Second said.

"How will I evaluate people that are practiced at deceit?" Kentigern asked. He had grown to fear the empires and their ways.

"You will know," The Sixth said. "You will feel the hidden magic within them. And Kentigern, we will need you to bring Bracken Grayvesone into the fold. His talent is immense."

"But he betrayed us…"

"He has true Erelahian blood. Others with such heritage disappeared with The Evanescence or were hunted down mercilessly by the empires after Subjugation. We will not yield that man's soul to The Hierarchy of Hell. We will have him back," The Fourth said. "Bring Bracken Grayvesone to us. If we cannot redeem him, we will dispose of him in a way that does not strengthen The Hierarchy's hold on the people below."

Kentigern sighed. He knew better than to argue. He would speak with Mara. His wife always knew what to do. He perked up a little, thinking this would give him an excuse to visit his son, Paul, in the valley below. Perhaps, he could find suitable candidates without having to venture further than Primordial Boreal.

He heard a last whisper from the Aspects as he reached the double doors that would lead him to the lifts.

"Is there any hope?" The Third asked.

"Always. Hope is the nature of chaos," The Fourth said.

"This rooke is no longer the boy who sang away the darkness," The First said. "But his magic is better now. Due to the children we allowed him."

"A cruelty masked in kindness," The Fourth said. "No greater sacrifice has been asked of a rooke before."

"And this is not the first sacrifice we have asked of him," The Fifth said. "What if he refuses finally?"

"Do not even say such a thing," The Fourth said. "He must agree, or we are all doomed."

The Red Quarter

The Rooke pushed his way out of the chamber, refusing to look back. In this mountain fortress, time stood still, years he had spent and taken for granted were coming to an end. Warmth interrupted the chill against his neck, soft with promise of the coming spring in the steamed heat pushed through vents. He dismissed the scurrying rat, hiding in shadows, the same way The Rooke kept his pain and dismay hidden away in dark corners of his mind.

The doors to The Reliquary's Sanctum shut behind him with a dull thud, letting him out in the passageway overlooking snow-covered rocks and crags through tall windows of unbreakable glass. The view stoppered his breath in its beauty.

The Rooke gazed out for a moment, taking in the blue-gray rocks rising like long knives from the deep snow, the trickle of white flakes swirling in the breeze, the clear opening in the clouds to the wooded hills below and further down, a deep green valley waiting for spring to reveal it. Somewhere, in the imperceptible distance, was the sea waiting for him, calling to him with the name he once wore like a shield.

The gears of the lift groaned as the double doors slid apart. He selected the level that would see him home in the eastern part of The Reliquary, far below this sanctum although still far above the tree line. Alone in the lift, he collapsed onto the floor, head in his hands.

The magic of this mountain city combined with his red robes to earn him centuries more of life than he deserved. He felt the steady drop of the lift, down, and down, fast until it jerked to a stop.

The doors opened to an empty, long passageway lit by dull lamps embedded in the stone every ten or so meters. There were no windows here inside the rock of the mountain. The

Rooke stood up and meandered down the passage past six sets of lit, massive, double doors, each a different color. Gray, green, purple, steel blue, orange, and finally the red, marking his quarter.

Once, the Red Quarter had been the most lively of the eastern residential areas, full of curious scholars, scribes, minstrels, philosophers, professors, and bards, all aching to trade their names for a red robe.

The Rooke hated how quiet and somber the place had become in the last half-dozen years. He worried. He was down to his last apprentice, and there was no time to train the boy. He would likely be the last rooke to take these tales below.

He passed doors of empty homes, as he turned right at a fork, another right, and down a staircase into a long and dark, meandering passageway until he came to his own red door at number 42 of the Passage of Songs.

He entered his flat, light flooding out and the comforting sound of the lively chattering of his two adopted sons greeted him as the boys fussed over maps and books.

"Well?" the older boy said, the question needing no further words. The boy looked over his shoulder from the long table where he sat with his smaller brother, who was already scampering toward The Rooke.

"It is as we thought. I have been given the quest," The Rooke said as the younger boy embraced him.

"It's about time. It's been three whole years since the last rooke," Thiago said, all of fifteen and ready to face whatever it took to leave this mountain. He hastily gathered up the books and papers from the table so that they could take their evening meal together.

"We want to come," Kostas, the younger boy, said. He danced a little jig, clapping his hands together in delight at the prospect of adventure. "You'll need a puzzler."

"I will," The Rooke said. "A master puzzler. Are you a master, Kostas?"

"In due course, I shall be. Grandmaster Mist says I have great ability for an eleven-year-old."

"We have been plotting out the best course for us," Thiago said, as he rolled up a map of Aerda, sealing it back into a cylindrical, black carrying case. "If we can evade Spytes…"

"You're coming with me, are you?" The Rooke said, holding up his still-sealed scroll of those who The Relic wished to accompany him. "Only if your names are on this scroll will you accompany me."

"I am your apprentice, father. You have to take me and if I go, we can't leave Kostas behind," Thiago said. "We will see that you do not fall prey to assassins. I have been studying Spytes and their methods since Steven Fowler's name returned to him. Father, you need us."

"I will not be made an orphan," Kostas said. "Even if I never know your proper name. I will not have you die, father. We love you. Thiago and I will protect you."

"One. I can't risk my only living apprentice. Scrivener Leesh, Gareth Gillespie, or Aldo Thierry will help finish your training. Along with The Relic itself. Two. I will not be a father who buries his sons," The Rooke said. "It's going to be dangerous, and I do not think The Relic would risk children."

"We're not afraid," Thiago said. "Father, we want to come. We need to come no matter what that scroll says."

"We shall see."

The Rooke knew the boys heard 'yes' in his words and not the *absolutely not under any circumstances may you accompany me* which he meant. The boys danced about their evening chores, all smiles and questions. It delighted The Rooke to see his young sons so happy and used it to mitigate their disappointment when he denied them with the full sanction of The Relic.

"Wait until we return each summer," Kostas said, ignoring that he might be left here. "We'll have such stories to tell."

"Aye, we will," Thiago said. "And we will see the wonders of the empires for real, their cities of glass and steel, buildings that reach as high as a mountain."

"Not this mountain. Nothing is as big as this mountain. Not in this world," Kostas said.

"Sir, why so thoughtful? Are you not pleased? Not all in the empires is evil," Thiago said. "You know all the best stories, the true tales of this world and the last. The Relic should have sent you years ago and all would be well. Do you not want to tell them to the people below?"

"I do. Of course, I do," The Rooke said as he chopped onions and tomatoes to dress the fish they prepared for their dinner.

"Father, we will be fine," Thiago said. "We can help. We will tell all the stories. The people will believe, and the dragons will dream."

The Rooke grieved that he would not see any he left behind again, not his sons nor all his dear friends. There was only a small window each year when it was possible to leave or return to the mountain unobserved by the imperial spies and assassins. There would be no time between taverns and tales. He took a breath and told himself, one at a time. One step, one day, one tavern, one story at a time.

Tavern II:

The Sorcerer's Cottage

The landscape of Hell is peppered with views of paradise, close but too far to touch. This torment burns at the soul of the damned for all eternity, the view of the possibilities squandered and forever lost.

A Walk in the Abyss by Sabarino Riley,
translated by Hazel Kyran

A Small Adventure

The Rooke could not find sleep as a blizzard grew outside, worrying him as the promised spring seemed to be blotted out in the hours since he met with The Relic. He looked through the circular window of his study; the darkness thick with white snow that was piling up against the mountain, drowning his view of the night.

He would have to brave the depravity that was Sentinel Peake to escape the mountains if he was to leave before summer. A part of his ancient mind called out to Ambriel, the Time Weaver, to grant him the time he would need to bring a future in which his sons might thrive, free of the threat of waking dragons and power-mad emperors.

He heard a shuffling from the common room and rose to find young Kostas wrapped in his old fluffy, blue blanket, scribbling something in a worn notebook marked with the puzzler crest, an old children's book set to one side, *The Oracle and the Monkey.*

That had been his son's favorite, the first book Kostas could read on his own. The boy wore only his sleep shirt, no socks, and thin sack trousers that were in sore need of mending. Kostas loved his grunge and comfort.

"What are you doing there, son?" The Rooke asked.

"Grandmaster Mist set an essay on the truth in a favorite children's book," Kostas said, sticking his tongue in his cheek, a heavy sigh that signaled his discomfort with the assignment. "I've no clue what she means. How is this related to puzzling?"

"Can't say. Puzzle it out," The Rooke said, understanding the assignment but knowing he must let Kostas work it out himself. "Keep at it."

He did not see Thiago but observed signs of his older son's presence. Books decorated the long table, open and scattered.

A worn journal with copious notes in Thiago's precise hand sat abandoned between two unsteady stacks. Typical of curious Thiago, working so hard to not waste a single breath of his young life.

The Rooke suspected Kostas, on the other hand, to be a fortnight behind in his studies.

"I've made tea," Thiago said, appearing from the tiny kitchen with a mug of steaming liquid in his hands. "Ginger tea. We couldn't sleep. Would you like a cuppa?"

"Please. What is all this?" The Rooke asked, running a finger across the spine of the old book.

"Research. *The Ancient Cycles*, historical texts, *The Imperial Canon*, and some of Hazel Kyran's work," Thiago said. "I want to understand all that has been told below by previous rookes and contrast that to what imperials teach as their history."

"Fowler came close to fully awakening the people below," The Rooke said, fingering a copy of Hazel Kyran's translation of Sabarino Riley's *A Walk in the Abyss*.

"I wish Guardian Gillespie would tell me more about how Fowler came to harm," Thiago said. "He just gives me a dark look and shakes his head and changes the subject. And father, he raised his voice to me. He told me I was never to ask you about it."

"He blames me. For Fowler's death. For his wife's death," The Rooke said, wondering if Steven Fowler's journey to the seat of power the defiance to which The Relic referred.

Rooke's tales were meant to be told in pubs, peon dunks, taverns, and commoner inns, not in splendid palaces or manor houses. Kings and things would come to them. Not the other way around.

"It wasn't your fault," Thiago said. "And you don't need to worry, father. I will never do what Bracken Grayvesone did. No woman, no matter how pretty could make me give up our secrets. He let the imperials find his uncle and Fowler, all for lust, a golden sleeve and immeasurable wealth that can buy nothing. I will kill him for what he did…"

"No, you will not. His injustice cannot be undone with revenge," The Rooke said. "And it is in part, my burden. I raised him. I meant to protect him and failed to prepare him. Men's desires are preyed upon below and bring most to ruin. No person is immune. Not you. Not even me. We must hold fast to the greater love that calls us."

"How will we do that?" Thiago asked. "The imperial technology is embedded in all parts of the empire. Religion is outlawed. Most of the best books are banned. Allows the temptation you speak of to be practically unavoidable."

"We will manage," The Rooke said. "Both Gareth and Aldo have contacts below to equip us with the appropriate sleeves. We will blend in until we arrive at each tavern. And I am a full-robed rooke. I do have magic."

"What magic exactly?" Kostas asked. "I don't understand. I've never seen you do anything that seemed like magic."

"Magic isn't all fireballs and illusions," Thiago said.

"Language and music are magic in themselves," The Rooke said. "You are accustomed to it. Magic originates in each of us. That is what a rooke is meant to do, you see. Unlock the magic in each and every person who listens to our tales. In many ways, magic is the great love that calls to us."

"Sounds puzzling to me," Kostas said. "Like finding truth in a children's book. I wish I could do real magic. You know, so I could light the fire without kindling and getting soot all over myself. Or so I could throw Zac Grimm against the wall every time he tells me my puzzling is inadequate. Just because he won all those gaming tournaments in the empires."

The Rooke sipped his tea in the late evening, thinking of all the nights he had spent with his lovely sons, how they had fallen into such a comfortable routine, how this very night, as soon as he arrived home from his audience with The Relic, he had sought that same routine.

"Right. How would you two like to go on an adventure?"

"What do you mean?" Thiago asked.

"Get your cloaks, put on your boots, layer your clothes. It's time I show you how a rooke's magic actually works."

"You mean now?" Kostas asked, his eyes going wide. "It's hours past sundown…"

"Yes, there will not be much sleep tonight, but you two can slog off tomorrow if you like," The Rooke said. "This is important."

"Father, are you feeling alright?" Thiago asked.

"Never better. Get to it. The hourglass empties. Let us go." With that, The Rooke snapped his fingers and their little fire in the hearth went out. Kostas stood gaping, The Rooke giving him a wink.

"How? Was that magic? Did you…father?"

A level of natural caves and tunnels separated the Higher and Lower Reliquary. The ceiling was high, and there were ridges jutting out, some leading to narrow passages too small for a person.

Kostas ran ahead, leaping high trying to grab the ridges above him. The Rooke worried the boy would reach one of those ridges and lift himself up to find himself facing some fantastical and venomous beast or other.

A black rat, very like the one The Rooke had encountered that morning, ghosted along the edge of the tunnel, looking for a place to disappear.

Kostas spied the little rodent, a grin that told his father that the boy was deciding if catching a rat might be fun. A low-lying ridge won the battle for his son's attention. Kostas took a far running start and leapt on high.

He came down in a flurry of gray and white wings, gasping in surprise as an owl dived from above and took the unfortunate rat in its talons. Kostas laughed. Thiago gaped, and The Rooke sighed.

"I did try to warn you," The Rooke said to the rat as it disappeared with the owl above.

"Shanks lets his owl hunt in the caves?" Thiago asked, pretending to be calm. The Rooke spied the alarm in the older boy's eyes but said nothing.

"It has to eat," Kostas said. "My its dark here."

"And cold," Thiago said, pulling his dark scarf up to cover his ears.

"I am so hungry myself. I don't think I'd fancy rat though. Chicken and chips would be great."

"We have already had our supper," Thiago said.

"Yes, but not enough for an adventure."

"There will be food where we are going," The Rooke said.

"Where are we going?" Thiago asked. "We never go to the between levels. Why did we not take the lifts all the way down?"

"Our lift doesn't go to the level we need to reach. This is a shortcut," The Rooke said. "Come on. And mind the rats."

The Rooke sighed. He felt alone in his quest, and for a moment, reconsidered this evening's adventure. What if his magic did not work?

"Keep moving boys."

"More rats there," Kostas said.

"And bats," Thiago said. "In that far cave. I can hear them fluttering about."

"Where? Bats are interesting. They have radar and sometimes they are vampires," Kostas said.

"There is no such thing as vampires," Thiago said. "Not like in those books you and so many of our friends go on and on about. They don't fall in love with humans. If vampires were real, they are demons and evil like ghouls or specters."

"The sorceress, Phaedra, was not evil," Kostas said. "And she came right out of Hell which is why she could resist The Hierarchy of Hell, and people were always falling in love with her. That's what Grandmaster Mist told me, and she knows all about demons."

The boys bantered all the way down to the lift at the end of a long, narrow, and dark tunnel. The Rooke entered with a little apprehension. This lift was ancient, on an old rope, wood, and pulley system that did not merit a feeling of security as it groaned its way down inside the mountain.

The Sorcerer's Cottage was an odd sort of pub near the bottom of The Reliquary. The Rooke arrived late with his sons to find the pub crowded with the heartiest of The Reliquary's artisans and laborers.

The old pub looked well out of place; a country cottage built against a backdrop of dark, carved stone. Life erupted from within, the sound of voices chattering, fiddles and drums playing, glasses clanging, the smell of cooking food, laughter, light of the fire from a large hearth, and flickering sconces hanging from the high ceiling.

The Rooke pushed his sons through the front door, and no sooner had they emerged when the pub burst out in greeting.

"A rooke…"

"Down here?"

"It's been an age…"

"Tell us a tale…"

"Have a pint…"

Tavares and Bittore

The inside rock of the mountain had its own kind of cold. Tavares Flaco thought he would never grow used to it as he shuffled along the cobblestones toward the smell of food and ale. His wife, Bittore, held his hand. Her dark skin gleamed under flickering light. He could hear the happy sounds of music and laughter ahead of them offering relief from the trauma of the past weeks.

Their new quarters felt silent as the grave without the constant hum of the technology to which they had been long accustomed in their lives back in the crowded Chaziri capital of Aroghotto City.

This skyless place inside the mountain felt part of a different world. It had no speeding transports buzzing under their window, no hum of power that generated heat, cold, light, and brought their screens to life with the constant babbling of criers and livelies, distracting them from the true ills of the world around them.

"Are we going the right way?" Bittore asked.

"I think so," Tavares said. "The scavenger said the pub would be round this corner. Aleron and his wife should already be there. I hear people. That's a good sign, yes?"

The Sorcerer's Cottage looked something from a past age. Tavares thought of his grandfather's home in the sunny land of Marlinea, when he had been so small, when his family gathered there for summers at the lake.

The delightful aroma of well-prepared food and rich ale emanated from the stacked stone cottage, matching his memories of a happy childhood. The pub looked mismatched among the cold stone buildings and shelters of the lower Reliquary, as if it should have green gardens, a lake in front with a forest in the background instead of the harsh backdrop of blue rock of this mountain sanctuary.

"Are you certain we don't need credits to buy food here, Tavi?" Bittore asked.

"That's what the scavenger said," Tavares said. "Bitty, we are safe here. And free. Finally. Our sleeves are gone."

His left wrist itched from the surgery that had removed his sleeve monitor from his veins. Bittore did not complain about her surgical wound though she fiddled with the bandage nervously.

"Nothing in this world is free."

"No, nothing is. But we've paid our price," Tavares said. "Come."

Neither mentioned the child he and Bittore sacrificed for the wealth and privilege they enjoyed below. Neither mentioned the guilt they would forever carry for betraying their own families to gain their celebrated status.

That sleeveless beggar outside their opulent flat in Aroghotto

City on a starless night had changed everything. After Bittore's breakdown, he calmed her guilt. The vagrant saw them and knew them. He reminded them of all they had lost, things wealth and status could never buy. He gave them their souls back, a chance for redemption. They left that very night with nothing but the clothes on their backs.

"All to be pretty…" Bittore said, reading his face.

"All to be rich, to be celebrated, to never know hunger or fear," Tavares said, squeezing her hand. "We did what we had to do to survive. Everyone below does it and worse."

"We should have died…"

Tavares would do anything to reverse his wife's bitterness and pain. They would have a life here in this mountain sanctuary that his uncle had told him about when he was a boy, back in his grandfather's cottage that looked like the pub they approached.

"You're not pretty. You're beautiful. All the way through," Tavares said, a whisper in Bittore's ear to her soul. "They can't take that from you because they did not give it to you."

"Do you think it is always so crowded?" Bittore asked. "I mean, look at them all. I had no idea so many had escaped. Had wanted to leave."

They made their way into the crowd. Many sported three scars along their left wrists, indicating they too had their sleeve monitors surgically removed. Tavares smiled. This would be all right.

"Are we dead?" his wife asked as they found a table among the crowd and a server asked them what they wanted as she placed glasses of cool, clean mountain water in front of them.

"No, Bitty. I don't think my surgical wound would itch so if we were dead," Tavares said. "We are newly born."

"My grandmother used to say the only way to escape sin is death."

"She did not mean the Sleeve Imperial Network. Your grandmother was Janusian. It was a tenet of her faith," Tavares said. "Sin had a different meaning then. My uncle was Janusian as well. The empire killed him because of it. He never could keep quiet, the fool."

"My grandmother died when I was so young, and then no one ever talked about her again. Religion being so dangerous and all. My mother and father did not want me to be subjected to it. They only wanted me to be pretty so I could be wealthy. My grandmother wanted more, better. I miss her, Tavi. I loved her. I haven't thought of her for years. It's nice to be able to say that out loud."

"Aleron, over here. We have a table," Tavares called out seeing his rescuers in the crowd. Aleron had arranged their extraction from the Sleeve Imperial Network.

A big, bearded man stepped forward to greet them. "You made it. Good," Aleron Ramses smiled, presenting a robust, dark-skinned, golden-haired woman to them. "This is my wife, Kalare. We are so happy to see you."

The crowd made a sound of joy and began to clap. "What is happening?" Tavares asked.

"A rooke has come. A rooke has come." The crowd chattered and fluttered.

"A true rooke? No, that's impossible," Bittore said.

"There aren't anymore," Tavares said. "My uncle saw one when he was a boy in Marlinea. My uncle witnessed assassins murder that rooke. All the ones that came after all died."

"You're new here. Where did you think rookes came from?" Kalare Ramses said, her smile filled with pure joy. "I hope he will tell a story. He never comes down this low in The Reliquary. He is from the Red Quarter. We live in the Green, close to there. I have been dying to see this ancient rooke. He is the last."

The Rooke in his blood, red robes stood a great distance away, on the far side of the bar, but Tavares and Bittore could see him as if he were right in front of them. This rooke looked young in face, with longish, golden-brown hair, dark skin that looked as if it had known the sun, brilliant green eyes, and a voice that seemed to enchant.

He was tall, lean, scarred, and beautiful. Although, he

appeared a man of no more than forty outwardly, something in his gaze struck Tavares as ancient. The Rooke laughed easily as he took a seat and began to speak.

The Rooke's words transported them into a tale that felt like a memory although it happened in an age that had long been assigned to myth. Alleysiande. Stories from Tavares and Bittore's childhood that were no longer acknowledged in the empire.

The Tale of The Oracle and The Monkey

The sorcerer, Janus, could see there would be more than enough blood to cast any spell at all. His own. He would only have moments before his life abandoned the only body he had ever known. At long last, Hell rendered the divine sorcerer mortal.

The black tower loomed at the borders of Alleysiande, rising out of the wild sea, casting its dark shadow over the enraged crowd that called for the sorcerer's pain.

"I will ask one more time," the torturer said. "Where is your sister?"

"I am Malachi's only son. There is no sister. What are you talking about?"

"We will spare your son and your lover if you give us your sister," the torturer said, repeating the same string of questions for the tenth time.

"Bleed me now for even if I had a sister, I would not tell you. Your magic is no match for mine, you foul, little creature."

"A daughter perhaps? Where is your daughter?"

A twinge of doubt fluttered through the dying sorcerer. He would know, would he not, if there was a daughter? Who had that woman been, the woman that came to him in his dreams while he rotted in the Icarian prison? A dream. Only a dream. He concentrated. He had to cast his spell.

"I don't have a daughter. Who told you such a thing?"

"A sorceress of Malachi must be your sister or your daughter. Tell us. Why endure this?" The torturer asked, genuine confusion on the little man's face.

"Cut me down and this tower will shatter. Cut me down and Alleysiande will be taken away. The Icari of Hell will never have the blessed land of The Erelahians. Will never touch it."

"Alleysiande will be ours. We will find Malachi's sorceress and she will be ours. Die, you meaningless man."

The gory remains of Gareth Janus disappeared as his head hit the top of that black tower which proceeded to crumble and fall, opening a portal to Pandemonium and devouring the souls of all that participated in the foul ritual. Those damned souls would haunt Aerda forever after, even into this day.

On the same day Janus was murdered atop of Shalchar's tower, Imogen Vasilis ran through a burning forest toward the secret cottage she and Janus shared together, holding their infant son, and pushing her nine-year daughter to a full run.

Shadow dragons had appeared in the skies over Alleysiande, destroying the land and its people and their magic. Where the dragons created by the Sentinel Mordecai breathed fire and ice, shadow dragons spewed corruption that sucked magic out of the world until it was gone and they themselves turned to ash.

The great fire dragon, Phaedra, and the immense ice dragon, Tem, hid their progeny in gemstones, distributing their precious treasure among the young children of Alleysiande who had gained their favor. Including little Cassie Vasilis, the daughter of Imogen and her treacherous, late husband, Tiernan Vasilis.

The child, Cassie, held fast to a ruby, a prize worth more than the precious stone it appeared to be. They ran from the shadow dragons and the demon-infested people that pursued them, seeking the protection of the enchanted cottage.

"Not much further," Imogen said. "Don't stop, Cassie, we're close. I know it."

"I can't run. I can't run," Cassie cried, stumbling over root and stone.

Imogen did not answer. She pulled her daughter up by the hand and dragged the child forward, ignoring the girl's cries of terror and pain. They would die if they stopped. This, she knew.

Imogen had seen the Thirteen Black Towers rising to surround Alleysiande from the mountain castle of the Dragon Paradym, shrinking the land, disrupting the magic. The sun, itself, had gone black that morning. This was the end for most. Imogen would not let it be her demise.

The baby dug his only two teeth into Imogen's collarbone. She could feel her son's breath, his rapid, little heartbeat. The babe made not a sound. All around them, the land shook, fires blazed, rocks the size of buildings tumbled from mountains. Imogen could not think. Could not comprehend how she and her children kept going, as her own magic weakened.

At last, the wood opened to the cottage, undisturbed, sun still shining on it, a babbling brook splashing past it, a well-kept garden buzzing with bees and little creatures, gentle and wondrous, a garden faerie still tending the flowers.

The outside world held no sway on the cottage in Malachi's Ring. Still, Imogen could feel the veil that protected the cottage faltering. They would not be able to stay here long.

She opened the door, hoping to be greeted by her lover, thinking he must have escaped. She found only his monkey, Jabber, and the strange, three-eyed man, Liam, who the sorcerer had taken in some centuries back. Liam wept from his two human, blue eyes. His jeweled oracle eye glowed red and angry.

"Where is he…?"

"Dead. They murdered him. But he lives," Liam said. The man, who became younger each year instead of older, was incapable of speaking clearly. Always, his words were riddles and confusion.

Jabber scampered about making excited gestures, holding up

a piece of parchment and fussing at it. Imogen gave her son to Liam and begged him hold the child. She took the parchment, a letter from Janus. It was short.

Flee. Go to the docks. I have opened the way. Follow Liam. Take a ship and get out of Alleysiande. It will fall. Great love calls us - Gareth

"What is this? When did Gareth leave this?"

"Your children, both the child of sorcerer and the child of dragons must be hidden. Must go," Liam said, his voice getting higher and more excited. "Quick before Ambriel, the Time Weaver, returns to the Eternal Kingdom, we must find her and hide your son in time and space so The Icari may not claim him."

Out of the door, the oracle fled, holding Imogen's son, running impossibly fast for a mortal man. The oracle was one of Ambriel's creations and so time and space could be broken by him although Imogen suspected her lover's hand in the magic. She held to his name. Gareth Janus. Few knew the sorcerer's full name.

Few knew his story like Imogen. She screamed in grief. She knew she would never know his embrace again, his quick wit, sharp intellect, and that passion that only Erelahians commanded.

Jabber scampered out the door. This was a small creature, looking part rat as well as monkey. This little creature seemed ordinary to the eye, a variety of fat spider monkey. In truth, Jabber was an extraordinary being. The monkey served as the magical familiar of the great sorcerer, and until Imogen entered his life, Jabber and Liam had been the sorcerer's only companions.

According to all grimoires, this monkey should have died the moment Gareth Janus perished. Imogen noted that as she followed monkey and oracle out the door with her daughter, driven by the smallest sliver of faith.

As they came out of the enchanted part of the forest, they

found themselves at Alleysiande's Outer Ring docks which should have been thousands of leagues away from the cottage. In the harbor, only three of the twelve Erelahian ships remained.

The Swan Song, the ship granted its wood by the great sentinel, Ambriel, had only its captain and a skeleton crew to steer it away. The oracle and the monkey, holding the son of Janus and Imogen, made for that ship. Imogen followed.

"Ambriel's Paradym commanded us to wait for you," the captain said to the oracle.

"No, Imogen, stay," the oracle said. "I must hide the baby in time and space. You can't come. You have the Dragon Paradym's daughter. You are to protect her."

"What, why can't I hide her with my son?"

Her son looked at her, same dark hair as Gareth, wavy like hers, one blue eye like his eyes and one green eye like hers, a perfect combination of her and her beloved. The baby remained calm, holding fast to Liam as if to tell her he would survive and thrive if she let him go. He smiled and cooed, making Imogen's heart yearn to hold the boy one last time.

"You are too old to make this trip," the oracle said. "Your life is too informed to be placed outside of this time and space."

"I want my son."

"Your son will live. He will do his part. Please, Imogen, all will be well in the fullness of time. The sister or daughter of Janus will defeat The Icari and bring Alleysiande back to the world. Now go."

"Gareth and I have been apart since my son's birth. Cassie is the daughter of Tiernan Vasilis, blast him," Imogen said. "Janus has neither sister nor daughter, you mad thing. Give me my son."

"I am sorry I cannot. We will see him safe. He has his own role to play," Liam said. "Please, believe me. I see. I see."

"He needs his mother."

"And so does Cassie."

"Give me my boy."

"He cannot stay in this place and time," Liam said. "Trust me. Trust Janus. He would never hurt you. He loves you. He loves his son. Please. Great love calls you. Can you not feel it, Imogen Hope Vasilis?"

Imogen tried to take her son back. Too late. Jabber and Liam disappeared with her son and the ship, Swan Song. It simply blinked out of sight, out of time, out of space. For a moment, Imogen stood in shock, staring into the blank space in the harbor where her son had been.

Two ships remained.

Many children were boarding a ship called The Agony, the ship of the sentinel, Mordecai, who had made the dragons. Each of the children held in their palm a gemstone, one that held the essence of a hibernating dragon within.

"That's our ship," Cassie said, pulling her mother toward it. "They're taking Phaedra and Tem's children to hide them." Imogen followed the child.

"Do you have a gemstone?" The Agony's captain asked Imogen.

"No, my daughter has one. Let us board."

"I know you," the captain said. "You're the wife of Tiernan Vasilis. He betrayed us."

"And the great fire dragon, Phaedra, ate him. There's nothing left of him for your ire," Imogen replied. "I had nothing to do with that. The fire dragon, Phaedra, wished to promote my daughter as her Paradym. My husband did not approve. In his jealousy, he tried to murder his own daughter, and then he tried to sell her to Bal'Ael, the worst of The Icari. This was years ago. Malachi's only sorcerer, Janus, took us in. I'm sure you heard the rumors."

"You can't board. Only children. Only children with dragon gems. We'll look after your girl."

"No, I can't lose both of my children," Imogen said.

"Most lost everything, even their lives on this terrible day. You still breathe and I will keep your daughter safe."

"We'll go on the last ship."

"She can't leave with the dragon gem," the captain said. "All the gems holding the progeny of the great dragons must be on this ship. She'll have to give the gem to another."

"I don't want to give up my treasure," Cassie said. "It's for both my mother and me. Phaedra gave it to both of us. The fire dragon, herself."

"A gem can only be given to one and only to a child," the captain said. "I don't make the rules."

"It's mine," Cassie said. "I promised I would keep it safe."

"Then you'll have to give up your mother," the captain said. "Choose."

Cassie cried but took her mother's hand and left The Agony to look for another to give her treasure to so that they could stay together.

A skinny girl with blue skin and pitch-black hair stood by herself looking between the final two ships, as if unable to understand which way to turn. These girls were rare even in the time of Alleysiande. Nacharye they were called. Shapeshifters with a peculiar and rare form of dangerous magic.

"Who are you?" Cassie asked. "I did not think there were any more Nacharye in Alleysiande. I thought the sentinel, Errapel, made you all leave years ago."

"She did not. She loves us. Only some were bad, and none as wicked as your father, Cassie Vasilis. I am Jenn Rabican. My parents, my brothers and sisters are all gone. My brothers went on Malachi's ship, Extinction, but the captain refused to let me board because of my blue," the girl said. "I don't know what to do. I don't know what to do. It's not fair."

"Which Ring are you from?"

"The Eastern Rim of Malachi's Ring."

Cassie handed her gem to the stranger. "I know what it is to be blamed for the wrongs done by others. I am sorry for you. My mother loved Janus, Malachi's sorcerer. It was wrong for you to be left behind, and Malachi will be cross with his ship's captain. I trust you. Board Mordecai's ship, The Agony," Cassie said, pointing to the great black ship with the massive dragon figurehead. "This is your ticket. Never lose this gem. Never. I will find you out in the world beyond Alleysiande one day, and you will give it back to me, Jenn Rabican."

"I promise. Thank you. I will do this."

"I am Mordecai's Paradym. And one day I or my descendants will call the dragons from their gemstones."

Ragged survivors were lining up to board the last ship, The Eternity, the ship of the Sentinel Uriel, the Highest of Alleysiande's Twelve Sentinels. Imogen and Cassie approached the ship in a long line of refugees.

"We're full," the quarter master proclaimed as Cassie and Imogen reached the front of the line. "We can take no more."

"We leave them, they die," the captain said. "Come aboard. We will make room. We have enough magic left for this."

Imogen and her daughter found their escape. As Uriel's ship, The Eternity, sailed the horizon, the sea rose up in front of them, a terrible gale blowing. When the waves crested, Alleysiande had disappeared from the landscape. It was no more.

In a single day, Aerda became a paler shade of itself, a lesser world, smaller and mundane, bereft of Alleysiande and the hope it offered.

The First Token

A gentle murmur traveled through the pub as The Rooke took a sip of his warm ale. He sat there, his mind's eye still seeing that empty horizon where the Outer Ring of Alleysiande had once been. He felt a sadness so deep he imagined the pub shook beneath his feet in grief. He had never told that tale before. His son, Kostas, spoke first.

"But the monkey rescued the baby from the oracle, didn't he?" Kostas said, pulling his children's book from his pack and holding it up as if in evidence.

"No. The oracle never stole the baby, not really," The Rooke said. "It is an unfair reputation that Liam earned due to a child's book."

"I never knew the sorcerer was called Gareth. He is always

simply Janus in Hazel Kyran's translation of *The Idylls of Alleysiande*," Thiago said. "Did you make that up, father? Are rookes allowed to just make things up?"

"We can make things up like anyone," The Rooke said. "But I did not make that up. Of course, the sorcerer had a proper name like most."

"You don't," Kostas said.

"I do. I just can't think my name or say it," The Rooke said. "Most called the sorcerer by his surname. It is customary with sorcerers and magicians. Like Phaedra. But she too, at some time, had a full and proper name."

"I don't get it," Kostas said. "What does that even mean?"

"The Erelahians, as the creations of the Twelve Sentinels of Alleysiande are called, are more spirit than flesh," The Rooke said, and a murmur rippled through the crowd.

"Could such beings still be among us?" a dark-skinned, bald man asked, approaching The Rooke. He was a young man, handsome, tall, and lanky with an infectious smile, eyes full of humor and mischief and grief. His left wrist was bandaged, a new rescue.

"Many escaped Alleysiande. Perhaps some of them that perished may have had spirits that lingered in this world. They could have taken new bodies," The Rooke said. "Perhaps, they are still with us, disguised as ordinary people. The empires can only trace blood. They cannot trace souls. Not even The Hierarchy of Hell has that power."

"Not all Erelahians are humanoid," Thiago said. "Dragons are Mordecai's creation."

"Deep spirits that can assume whatever shape they need," The Rooke said, smiling. "For instance, the ice dragon is said to have become a colossal, icy mountain. This mountain, in fact."

"My uncle heard a rooke when he was a boy," the newly rescued man said. "He told of the twelve Sentinels of Alleysiande. He said they abandoned this world for its betrayal of Creation, and they took their creations with them."

"Some say this is so," The Rooke said. "Some say seven

remained. The Wayward. That they disobeyed Ta-She-Serra, the Creator of All, because they believed those who remained after Alleysiande could be saved. That is why we rookes tell our tales."

"You must have great power," the woman with the man said, her wrist also bandaged. "For you scare the empires and its people with your little stories. So much that any true rooke is murdered."

"A well-told story can change everything," The Rooke said. "Even a bad one. False rookes tell tales below to make the people despise one another, to draw them apart, to keep them in line. I tell my stories to enchant, to make people hope, unite, question, inspect, look for a better way, create new and wondrous things."

"There is still love for your tales. Our families remember livelies in which the source was these fabulous rooke tales," the woman said. "They corrupted those wonderful tales in the last decade or two to make them favor the empires."

"My dear wife speaks the truth. I have heard the tales of false rookes. They have names you can say out loud. They wear gold sleeves like my wife and I once did. We can help you, Rooke," the man said. "I am Tavares Flaco. And this is my dear wife, Bittore Rose. We want to reach into your pocket."

The Rooke was taken aback. This was a request he had not expected here in The Reliquary, even in the cold, lower reaches, not from someone who had managed to escape the empires. He spread out his arms to expose the many pockets of the red robes to allow Tavares and Bittore access.

Tavares held forth a token, one that would allow him to hear and to repeat The Rooke's tales no matter how far apart they were. His wife, Bittore, took out a matching token. It was not something The Rooke kept in his pockets by design. His red robes produced them at the request of the worthy.

"Are you sure of this?" The Rooke asked. "This is a great responsibility."

"My wife is amazing at telling stories. She was a thespian as well as a celebrated luminary below. She had great influence there…"

"I influenced people to sell their souls and give their lives to accumulating wealth and bettering their sleeves," Bittore said. "We lost ourselves to it. I seek redemption."

"Well, perhaps you can give those people their souls back with telling of new tales or very old ones," The Rooke said, giving this beautiful woman a wide smile. He saw the light of her soul flickering behind her dark eyes.

"We will do all we can to redeem ourselves," Tavares said. "Perhaps, I will join you on your journey. There are people we left behind who I would rescue."

The Rooke nodded, and smiled at his sons who were enjoying the attentions of the crowd, all curious about the sons of a nameless rooke.

"Come boys. We have a long trip back to our home. We should get some sleep if we can."

Tavern III:

The Looking Glass Cafe

Despite all the darkness, pain, temptation, and despair suffered while wrapped in the mortal coil, salvation can only be found within the breath of life.

The Idylls of Alleysiande, Vol 1 The Time Weaver, author unknown (translated by Hazel Kyran)

Restless Dragons

The Looking Glass Café overlooked sharp mountain cliffs, land that had been cut away from another land millions of years before leaving the gaping sea as a bleeding scar in an ever-changing world.

For years uncounted, The Rooke had been coming to The Looking Glass Cafe three days in every five to break his fast and share a cup of coffee or tea with his three oldest, living friends. The three old men had already claimed a table before the big window where snow swirled lazily in the permanent frost of the high mountain.

Kentigern Dagan Leesh was holding up an old book, the sleeve of his blue robes dusting the scones on the table and arguing some point with the thick-necked Aldo Thierry while the wiry Gareth Gillespie sat back in his chair, a look of wide-eyed disagreement on his face. These men loved their debates, and there was not a topic on which they could not find some point of contention.

Aldo Thierry cursed a greeting to The Rooke and Thiago. "You look a proper shit, both of you," Aldo said.

"Long night," The Rooke said.

"No sleep," Thiago said. "Did you know there was a giant pub at the bottom level of The Reliquary?"

"The Sorcerer's Cottage?" Gareth said. "Rooke, did you take your lads to that dive? Bit young, yeah?"

"We used to sneak down there for proper chippies when we were younger than Kostas," Aldo said.

"And to get Kenny to buy us ale," Gareth said. "We shouldn't have done it. Used to have to discipline my boy for doing the same thing. Simpler times. Can't have been seventy years gone."

"And this is where you took your boys?" Kentigern said, clapping The Rooke on the back.

"My abilities needed polishing. The Sorcerer's Cottage is a place for newly rescued."

"He told a children's tale that frightened everyone in the place. It was epic. Guardian Gillespie, did you know you share the call name of the sorcerer, Janus?" Thiago said.

"Do I? Always assumed Janus was his call name and it was his surname that was missing. Like the sorceress, Phaedra," Gareth said. "Me, I was named for my uncle and grandda. What's this, Rooke?"

"The sorcerer's full name was Gareth Janus," The Rooke said. "Strong coffee. Now. I need it now."

"Can I have some coffee?" Thiago asked. "I could use a lift."

The chair Gareth pulled for Thiago slid from his grasp, toppling over from a vibration that started as a faint tremor and ended with a loud roar and crash. The servers in The Looking Glass Café gasped, a tray of mugs dropped from a young woman's hands and shattered on the stone-tiled floor.

Morning customers cried out in alarm as the place began to shake with another trembling. The Rooke watched through the high window as a piece of the mountain broke off from the high cliff below them and fell into the sea, a sliver in the great distance at the bottom of Tem's Peake.

"Ta-She damn," Gareth said. "You won't be able to wait until summer. The ice dragon is unhappy."

"It's a thaw," Kentigern said. "Don't send everyone into a panic, Gary."

"A thaw? After that blizzard last night, I doubt it," Aldo said. "Can't you feel it?"

"Yes, yes, Kenny," Gareth said in his deep, rumbling voice, assisting in sweeping and mopping up his lost cup of tea. "Early thaw or tired mountain. Nothing another cuppa won't sort."

"Why the red robes?" Aldo asked, helping Thiago put his chair right as The Rooke assisted cleaning up broken mugs. "Kenny, is The Rooke summoned again?"

"Not to my knowledge. The Sanctum is closed today. However, Aldo, you and Gary are called for the morrow," Kentigern said. "Why are you in full dress, dear Rooke?"

"No idea. Might have fallen asleep in them. Didn't have time to think while getting Kostas off this morning," The Rooke said. "What are you three gabbing about?"

"Where you should go first. Will depend on if you go by Sentinel Peake or through the scavenger tunnels," Aldo said. "I say we restore the old traditions. Temple, Talon, the Toenail, onto Dark End of the Rainbow. You'll need to collect some folks this side of the Boreallean Sea to repeat your tales so they can travel easily back here."

"Already sorted. This fellow Tavares Flaco and his wife Bittore Rose…"

"The dragons won't care," Kentigern said. "It's not the tales that matter. It's the people. Their hearts must soften, and here they are sorted. The people of The Reliquary are not enough. Or so The Relic has informed me in no uncertain terms."

"It's worse than when Fowler went down," Aldo said. "Bracken Grayvesone is doing great damage, distorting the tales. Him and that vile woman he ran off with…what was her name?"

"Baroness Teriss Amber. A luminary with both gold sleeve and a minor royal from Acaria," The Rooke said. "And blood kin to one of the Urian betrayers. She has corrupted Bracken."

"He chose to leave his wife and children for that insane woman despite our warnings. He chose to betray Steven Fowler and his own uncle. Did he even realize the first rooke he betrayed was his own kin?" Aldo said. "Anyhow, I will go with you. It's my turn. I will guard you."

"If you happen to be on my list, Aldo. I expect one of the three of you will be," The Rooke said, holding up the sealed scroll.

"You ever going to open that list?" Kentigern asked.

"I am not ready to know whose lives The Relic wishes to sacrifice on my behalf. It can wait another few hours," The Rooke said. "Let's have breakfast while this place still stands."

"The fall of Alleysiande is an ancient tale," Gareth said. "You plan on telling all the tales concerning the fall of Alleysiande?"

"If I were, I started at the end. No, I am going to tell more contemporary tales about the sorceress, Phaedra, and the tale I told at The Sorceress Cottage is part of that story."

"How? Alleysiande fell thousands of years ago. Phaedra was still around at The Evanescence," Kentigern said.

"Scrivener Leesh, do you remember the time before The Evanescence?" Thiago asked, settling himself down next to old Aldo.

"Lad, I am not so old as your father," Kentigern said, a grin across his face that sharply reminded The Rooke of the young man who set out with Torres Rushie almost sixty years ago.

"He was not even born until well after The Subjugation," The Rooke said.

"My parents joined the resistance after The Subjugation. My father was killed for his resistance, and so my mother had to flee her home in The Veiled Pride when she was pregnant with me. I was born at The Temple of the Tail."

"I remember your arrival. The Third Aspect was there as well. I was in terrible grief after The Evanescence," The Rooke said, recalling the red-faced, squalling, ginger-haired infant that had turned into the old man across the table from him. "Up until recently, one aspect and one rooke always came to collect children and babes seeking refuge in The Reliquary. That morning, we were there to collect Torres Rushie and his family. Baby Torres was maybe three weeks old. Your mother had just given birth, half-dead from her journey. Both you and the Rushie family took homes in the Red Quarter. And that did cheer me."

"As a young man, I wished to be a hero like in the tales of rookes and Tower Knights," Kentigern said, stretching back in his chair. "My mother taught me that true heroes are seldom recognized, their names never heard. I thought she was talking about rookes and so I became your apprentice. Then I fell in love."

"Rookes are allowed to marry," Thiago said. "Their families just take the spouse's name, right?"

"I wanted to keep my name for Mara although I worried that I had disappointed my mother when I refused the red robes, and so I became a rooke's guardian. And failed."

"You did not fail. You survived and brought home information to allow The Reliquary to survive. Your mother was proud of you. Anyone who knew her could see how she adored you," The Rooke said.

"It was like losing him twice, you know?"

"Losing who?" The Rooke asked, glancing over one of the books his son had brought with him.

"Torres Rushie, my best mate. After the red robes, I did not remember him as such. I did not know I had ever had a friend called Torres Rushie. He was my friend, the rooke. It's the way the bloody robes work. When he died as the rooke, it was like he died twice. All our childhood, all we shared came flooding back and one body shared the death of two men. It almost undid me."

"And you refused to ever accompany a rooke again?" Thiago asked.

"And now I must again, to pay for my failing," Kentigern said, turning to The Rooke. "The Relic commands I recruit new apprentices, new initiates to train as guardians."

"I am not sorry to hear it, Kenny," The Rooke said, patting his old friend on the shoulder. "I know you fear going below. However, I will be happy for your company, my old friend."

"And I will enjoy hearing your new tales," Kentigern said. "I wish I had heard you last night."

"I have a question," Aldo said. "Whatever did happen to the baby the oracle stole? The children's tale said the monkey left on a ship with the child's mother and sister. They were never heard from again."

"That wasn't it at all," Thiago said. "The monkey and oracle took the baby on Ambriel's ship, The Swan Song. The mother and daughter left on Uriel's ship, The Eternity."

"No one knew what became of that baby for thousands of years as that ship went forward in time," The Rooke said. "As I said, the tale I told is necessary to tell the story of the sorceress, Phaedra."

"Is it? How?"

"It has to do with the demon of Heath's Night…"

"That sounds intriguing," Aldo said, lifting his mug for more hot water for his tea as the serving girl plopped down a fresh plate of eggs, tomatoes, and blood sausage in front of the thick-necked man.

Aleron Ramses

Aleron Ramses saw something of heart break in his wife's eyes. He put his arms around her and the infant she carried, wishing he could split himself in two in order to remain always at her side. He took his son to him as he released her, giving the babe a kiss on the forehead. The baby cooed, happy bubbles at his lips.

"You've only just come home," Kalare said. "And you were nearly killed…"

"You heard The Rooke's tale last night. You felt the magic," Aleron said. "I can make a difference. And our children will be safe here while I venture below."

"I don't wish to be a widow…"

"And I do not wish to blindly turn my back on the world," he said. "Kalare, what good is just cowering in this mountain? We can't leave others to suffer as we did."

"Ali, you've saved so many already," Kalare said. "Is this needful? You have done more rescues than anyone else in The Reliquary. And in such a short time. Can you not leave it to someone else?"

"I promised Tavares and Bittore I would try to rescue…" Aleron said, giving his infant son a squeeze. He lowered his voice and leaned in as he handed baby Lionel back to his wife.

"I have just found out that both Tavi's sister and brother-in-law are dead, and their nephew is missing."

"Oh, Ta-She damned…"

"Kalare, no need to curse. Our daughter will hear," Aleron said, smiling broadly. "I am meeting Tavares and Bittore for breakfast this morning. I have to tell them the sad news."

"You could still have others go after this missing boy. Even Sentinel Peak is perilous for you. Ali, you are a wanted man in the empires. Can we not just stay here and be a family? Have we not earned it?"

"You worry too much, my love," Aleron said. "Ta-She-Serra is with us. The Creator of All will guide us, and we will have a home in the sun one day. Please, have faith. I will see you at supper."

"I believe in you, Ali. I do. I am only frightened. To lose you after all we have sacrificed…"

"You won't. You can't. Great love calls us, and eternity waits for everyone," he said, giving his wife a kiss. His daughter made a disapproving sigh.

"Can you two stop? You're old and I don't want any more babies. My brother cries too much," his eight-year-old daughter said, big brown eyes rolling at him.

"Mendi, come along. You are late for school."

Mendi skipped out the door ahead of her father, adorned in colorful robes, carrying a light pack with her treasures of books, writing pens, paints, and journals. "I want to see my friends," Mendi said. "They are doing art at mid-day. Can I just do school and not have to meet my tutor?"

"You must improve your math and reading," Aleron said, leading his daughter out of the door into the glittering passageway of the Green Quarters. Music played as vendors offered quick grab bites as people made their way toward the lifts to begin their days.

Part of Aleron agreed with his wife. In four years, he had rescued over two hundred people from below. A record for a single rescuer and his team. He wished he could remain here in The Reliquary, exploring all its wonders. It was so free. One could do whatever they wished day in and day out, applying their gifts to their greatest abilities.

Teachers taught. Tailors sewed. Musicians played their lively tunes. Bakers created heavenly treats and bread that could not be matched in the world of Aerda. He and his daughter stopped to partake of one of these glorious treats in the Green Quarter market square near the lifts.

Gardeners grew wondrous flowers, fruits, and vegetables in the magical enclosed greenhouses scattered throughout this mountain retreat. He tossed his daughter an apple to go with her pastry.

Working felt natural and fulfilling. There was no threat of poverty or having a sleeve downgraded. Or being poisoned for 'insurrection' as the empire called it when anyone disagreed with the collective bureaucracy. As happened to Tavares Flaco's unfortunate sister and brother-in-law for the crime of being related to two celebrated citizens who dared to renounce the empires.

"Does it itch?" Mendi asked. "Your scars? Delaney said her mother's scars itch."

"Delaney's mother had her sleeve removed only a month ago. It itches when it is healing," Aleron said. "Your mother's itched for months after. But now we are healed."

"I am so glad you rescued Delaney and her family," Mendi said as they stepped out of the lift into the tram station. Today, it was a good deal fuller than it had been four-years ago. Aleron had a part in that, and this satisfaction made him resolved to continue his rescue missions with his excellent team.

Mendi's tutor, Cymbre Varian, greeted them in the Learning Circles with a bunch of white flowers she presented to Mendi.

"For your family," Cymbre said. "I grew these in my garden. I've never grown anything before. I simply love gardening."

"These are lovely. Ice roses, are they not?" Mendi said, taking a deep breath of the delightful scent.

"Yes, they feel magical to me," Cymbre said. "Ali, I wondered if it would be all right, if after our lessons, Mendi and I could make a vase for these blooms. There's a crafting course in the late afternoon. Mendi thrives when she is creative."

"Yes, please father?" Mendi said. "I would love that. Delaney could come with us."

"That sounds wonderful. Yes, do."

Cymbre was young, barely past twenty, plump and lively. Her scars had healed. Aleron found her on the streets, bleeding to death after having her sleeve illegally removed. The girl told Aleron repeatedly that he had rescued her from Hell.

"Cymbre, you can always live with us. We have a garden," Aleron said. "If you feel too lonely in the Purple Quarters."

"Thank you, Ali," Cymbre said. "But I am happy. I have always wanted my own place. It's like a cottage behind the purple door. And there are other people all around, young people like me who have recently escaped."

"The offer stands. We appreciated you looking after the children last night," Aleron said. "Would you be able to watch them this evening?"

"I can. However, I must tell you that I intend to move to Talon in the valley to see about a job as soon as I can. Teach at the school there," she said, her smile fixed on her face as if she were trying very hard to keep it there. "I miss the sky over my head. Maybe I will meet somebody in the valley and have a family."

"I will come with you to Talon. I could go to school there," Mendi said. "You are my big sister now. I can't wait to make a vase."

"First school," Cymbre said, taking Mendi by the hand. "There is a new teacher, Professor Grimm. After your school, I will fetch you for lunch, and you will deliver your book report to me."

"*The Oracle and the Monkey*. The drawings are so pretty. But the tale is sad, and I don't think it's right. It doesn't make sense to me. It wasn't safe for the baby to stay with his mother. I think the oracle was helping. Not hurting," Mendi said, taking

Cymbre's hand as the two scooted away toward the Learning Circle Café to continue the lessons.

The Reliquary could be confusing to navigate. Even after four years of living there. Aleron got lost a time or two before arriving at The Looking Glass Café where Tavares and Bittore Flaco awaited him. And the same rooke from the night before, telling another fascinating tale.

The Tale of Heath's Night

*I*n the century prior to The Evanescence, the world was falling further into peril, causing soul-destroying pain among mortals. Alleysiande had fallen into myth. While people enjoyed the stories of that wondrous land, they no longer believed in them. In The Fistian Empire, nothing felt magical, and its poorest citizens were left with heart-crushing decisions between survival and oblivion.

Rats filled the alleys and sewers in the little fishing villages that dotted the Razor's Edge between the mountainous Dagger and the hard flatlands of The Fist. None paid any mind to the rodents that flanked the exploits of three children.

Chrysalis, Jesper, and Sid-Jynx Rabican did not fear the rats. Nor the ghost that brought the rodents whenever it was around.

The widowed mother of these children had to make a choice to satisfy her debt to The Fistian Empire. She could sacrifice her children to wyverns so that the beasts would leave the fancy cities ruled by The Fistian Arisea be. She would never know debt or hunger again, and her cup would never run dry of rum. Or she could sell her three young children to Megdonian slavers.

Chrysalis, Jesper, and Sid-Jynx Rabican might be made to work cleaning some noble's house, or they might be sold for perversion. The mother had survived a time in the pleasure houses in the west. It could be done. The children would live. Slavers were more merciful than wyverns. Or so the mother believed.

The eldest daughter, Chrysalis, an imaginative girl with

striped, blue skin, pleaded with her mother to run away. It was impossible to hide the defect of the girl. They could not afford the sugar to keep her skin tanned.

"Phaedra will keep us safe," Chrysalis said to her mother.

"The dragon from the stories that rooke told at the tavern? There are no more dragons, child. No one ever called them back from their gemstones. You are getting too old for such fancies."

"No. She's not a dragon," Chrysalis said. "She only shares a name with the dragon. She's my friend. And she's power-ful. She has magic. Please mother, I don't want to go with the Megdonians. Jesper and Sid-Jynx are too small. Phaedra says she can make us rich and free both. We will have plenty of sugar to hide my blue until I outgrow it. You don't have to do this."

Her mother wept bitterly. She knew if they ran, they would all be slaughtered. It would be worse than sacrificing her babies to wyverns.

The mother sold her children to the slavers and took her bounty to start a new life in another part of the world. She changed her name, married a rich man, had a new family, and never mentioned the three children she sold in her younger years. Not until she confessed to a daughter on her death bed many decades later.

The Megdonian slavers took the three Rabican children to a desolate, abandoned mining village on the edge of The Mudlands on the other side of the Daggera Mountains. This village was called Heath's Night.

At first, it was not so bad. There were other children that joined Chrysalis and her siblings in a small, flat building of stone at the backside of a noisy and stinky tavern. A bigger boy called Luc looked after them for the first few days. He made sure they ate every day. Chrysalis and her siblings were less hungry than they had been with their mother. For a short time.

"Phaedra, something is not right with Luc," Chrysalis said to her spectral friend. Chrysalis saw a gaunt woman, sitting to the right of her, knitting at a patchwork quilt, a ghostly thing that had once been real. Her siblings could sometimes see Phaedra as well. While not afraid, neither Jesper nor Sid-Jynx would speak to the apparition.

"Ghosts are bad," Jesper said to his sister. "Don't talk to her. She should not be here. She should be where the dead go. Mother said the dead don't belong with the living. That's why we never see father anymore."

"She can't go where the dead go," Chrysalis said. "Phaedra is good, and she will help us. We need her to help Luc and the others."

"It is too late for Luc, dear child. These vile men have made him a monster. Echo Horrors hunt for souls here," Phaedra told the girl from the darkness. "These people will hurt you too. Let me help you, and we can free the other children."

Chrysalis learned soon enough that Phaedra's warnings bore heeding. The children were beaten for the smallest disobedience. They were starved into submission. Adults made them do things that were strange and embarrassing. The boy, Luc, did not seem to mind. He dressed as these vile adults liked. Painted his face. Did strange dances. It was all so odd.

Children were bathed and displayed in the town square like they were livestock coming to market. Chrysalis watched children she did not know, ones that were housed elsewhere, be led away from the town-square with collars around their necks behind men and women in fine clothing.

"I hate adults, Phaedra," Chrysalis told her friend. "They all lie. They hurt children. I even hate mother. She said she would visit us, and she never did."

"Not all are like your mother or these human-shaped monsters. I will free you," Phaedra said to Chrysalis. "But I need your body to fight. Let me share your life and your body, Chrysalis. Let us be one."

"How?" Chrysalis asked.

By this time, Chrysalis was sore afraid. She did not know how to protect herself much less the others.

Slavers sent in a fancy man to inspect the children early one morning. Chrysalis hated him, the perfumed smell of him, his grotesquely red lips, the sight of him, his fingers jeweled with rings, chains in gold and silver hanging around his neck, bracelets with shiny trinkets jangling like little bells when he stalked about, exaggerating the sway of his hips. Immediately, Chrysalis felt her skin begin to crawl.

"My sweets. So lovely to see you again," he said, thinking the children must adore him. After all, he gave them sweeties. Chrysalis would never touch candy again. He made it bad. "Go on. Don't be shy. Say hello."

The children murmured their greetings. Chrysalis glared in silence. She never spoke to adults anymore. Only to Phaedra and the other children.

He turned to two of the guards, clamping his hands together, his nails manicured and painted silver to accentuate his wealth, his skin soft like a child, without a sign of heavy work anywhere on him. The men of The Fist looked so different, so rough, and yet they were gentle to children. This man appeared harmless but was not. Chrysalis felt herself screaming inside. She also felt Phaedra lurking about, sharing the same hatred.

"These little girls will fetch a fine price," the man said, referring to Chrysalis and her tiny, four-year old sister, Sid-Jynx, and one other sweet-faced girl. "And this boy…those lips, that rich curly hair. He's beautiful. I might buy him for myself. As a treat. I do think I've earned it."

Jesper looked ready to hit the man as he inspected the seven-year-old. Another boy called Mateo, small but older than Jesper also earned the fancy man's admiration. He was hungry, Chrysalis knew.

"Can I have a treat?" Mateo asked in a meek voice. He was new. He did not know the price for what he wanted.

"Soon, my dear. Very soon. If you are a good boy," The painted man said. He turned to the two men who accompanied him. "These are fine specimens. Perhaps, you did not overpay to free them from their unworthy parents. You have done well. Best children I have seen in years," the painted man said, as he took out a frilly dress from a case he carried at his side. "Now leave me. I will prepare these seven for my clients."

"Help me, Phaedra," Chrysalis said so that only her invisible friend heard.

"Gladly," Phaedra said.

Chrysalis held her shift tight at her knees, tears brimming at the painted man's prodding. This awful human was so intent on this little girl's dirty dress that he did not notice the gathering rats, the cold, or the stench that came with the tear between the mortal world and Pandemonium.

The children sensed a new disturbance exacerbating the terror of their young lives. They squeezed their arms closer about themselves and stepped away. One pointed at the rats running in circles around Chrysalis and her tormentor.

"You must change into a clean dress, Chrysalis, or our clients will be displeased. How will you get fed if the client refuses to pay?" The man held up the frilly frock to Chrysalis's face. "You must show the others what is expected of you. Here, let me help you."

"Do not touch me," Chrysalis said with Phaedra's voice. The man gave her a smile, arrogant, unaware of the powerful being before him.

"You can speak. I knew you could. That is a good girl," the man said, looking delighted. "Now, the dress. We must behave, Chrysalis. You know what happens to naughty girls."

"I am not Chrysalis. I am Phaedra. Back off. I know what you intend to do with this one's brother, you foul man."

The man reached out to force the girl's dress off. Foolish. Phaedra took hold of his arm, her inhuman strength pushing it back, bending it. He let out a high-pitched scream until the bone gave a satisfying crack.

The other children wailed and cried around Chrysalis, none of them aware of the thing that now controlled little Chrysalis. The man flailed about, reaching for a weapon with his good arm.

Phaedra rushed at him and ripped his head clean off.

One child screamed. The others stood in shocked silence or apathy.

"Chrysalis, what did you do?" Mateo asked in a tremulous voice.

"I am Phaedra. I protect Chrysalis and all of you."

The rats frenzied about the corpse of the foul man, feasting as Phaedra claimed the name of her prey, twisting the foul man's soul into one of the rats, causing him to devour his own flesh.

She smiled despite a discomfort in her bowels. Not a human pain. The soul of Chrysalis struggled, digging into Phaedra's essence, trying to regain control of her own body.

The little girl did not know her good fortune. Most creatures of Pandemonium rejoiced in the debauchment of innocence. Phaedra was different. She despised the torment of mortal children. Such depravity grew the power of The Hierarchy of Hell, and Phaedra would not have it.

She had felt the distress of Chrysalis years ago and found her struggling in the dark. She was saving Chrysalis so the child could in turn save her.

"Be calm, child. I will make you strong. Your soul will flare as the sun at its full might."

The soul of Chrysalis felt faint yet sharp and needling. The child's soul merged with Phaedra's own raging spirit. She repeated promises of the light, that one day they would both walk into that shining world of endless creation together. She begged Chrysalis to relent so that they, together, might save the other children. Chrysalis calmed and allowed Phaedra to continue.

Six of the seven children kept a cautious distance while the small Mateo with all his questions, mewled and whimpered, unable to move himself from the headless body of the man who had meant to sell him as a toy for a mortal's perverse pleasure.

A rat ran across the crying boy's feet, and little Sid-Jynx plunged forward to scoop it up. She held it to her like a prize. She sniffed at the rodent.

"Do not eat that, little sister," Phaedra said. Her voice came out a gentle rumble. She felt the hunger of the children. It was loud, palpable, and painful. Phaedra tried to soften her voice, make it mimic Sid-Jynx's big sister. "It will make you sick. I will find you food."

"Chrysalis?" Mateo asked. "How did you make his head fall off like that? Was it magic?"

"I told you, I am Phaedra. Chrysalis has allowed me to have her body so that we might free the rest of you."

"Are you going to kill us?" another small girl asked, face wet with tears. "I don't want to die. I only want to eat."

"No, child," Phaedra said, softening her voice as much as possible, given the rage that had consumed her for untold eons. "I am a protector of children. I will make your life full and good, with food a plenty. We will be an army, a family, and we will shield one another from harm."

The door of the old tavern swung open, and two men entered, one large and armed with a spiked club, the other skinny and oily with a pistol at his belt. Both men were bald, both sporting wyvern brands on their foreheads. These two were foremen, in charge of guarding the children.

"What's going on here? Where is the one that was guarding you?" the big man demanded. "We told you to be silent. We have clients coming to inspect you tonight. If you're good, you'll eat."

Phaedra wondered how they could be so clueless. A moment passed, then two, before realization crossed their faces.

"Children, duck behind that bar, cover your ears, close your eyes," Phaedra said.

Phaedra waited for the children to obey as the men entered the old tavern. She shook a finger at the man with the large club, extending her will and her rage, ripping the face right off the slaver before breaking his bones one by one, cracks and screams with each until his neck snapped.

No light was offered to this man. Phaedra smiled. More rats appeared as the man's corpse fell into an unnatural heap. She pushed it outside for her rodents to feast upon. The oily man took off running, yelling for help.

Phaedra searched the tavern, found a trap door behind the bar. She opened it with her will, breaking the latch.

"Hide in the cellar," Phaedra instructed the children. "There is food. Eat your fill. Do not come out until I return."

She exited the ramshackle tavern into the dirty street of red clay. Dust kicked up under the flesh she held. She surveyed the old, broken buildings of rotting wood, most abandoned, roofs missing, glass broken on the side streets. Old rock-filled mining carts lay forgotten at the edge of her vision. Only here in this square had the buildings been repaired for the slavers and their merchandise.

A woman appeared from the shop across the road. Phaedra remembered too well the torment this woman had inflicted on Chrysalis and the other children. This duplicitous woman had taught the children to submit to their abusers, the correct number of coins to ask for in exchange for certain acts. Foul woman.

Phaedra did not blink an eye or give the woman time to make a sound. Up, up she sent her, bending her like a twig until her neck snapped. Phaedra dropped her at the door of the shop. More rats joined Phaedra's army.

Her newly possessed skin tingled in the barren, hilltop air, dry and relentless. She tasted the thirst of this little girl's body and relished it. She cleared the ramshackle village of slavers, ripping them apart, sending others away screaming.

Phaedra was a step closer to freedom. She stood at the end of the lane where the village sign hung at its gate, hoisting two, flayed slavers up along the crossbeam. To serve as warning. Any who harmed a child or allowed a child to be so exploited in this world would join her army of rats.

"This is not the way," the soul of Chrysalis whispered, retaking control of her own body.

"It is the only way I know," Phaedra said, revealing her true form to the child.

Chrysalis did not step back in horror. Perhaps, the young

girl saw the pale, knitting woman and not the monstrosity The Hierarchy had made of Phaedra.

"I am not sad that these evil people are dead. But such vengeance is not for mortals. Ta-She-Serra teaches that there are better ways," Chrysalis said, a being that was more than a little girl Phaedra realized, feeling the burn of possibility in the place between redemption and damnation. "Let us be the light and not the darkness."

"I will try."

The New Guardians

*T*he Rooke felt cold, yet he wished to strip his red robes from his body. Why did he tell that tale? Did it matter if the sorceress, Phaedra, and the demon of Heath's Night were the same? He looked up at gaping mouths, all silent in the Looking Glass Café. No one said a word for a moment that seemed to drag out for eternity.

He saw Tavares Flaco from the evening before. The tall, lanky man was not smiling this time. He stepped forward, letting the sleeves of his teal robe fall to cover his bandaged wrists. The man's black trousers shown under the robe which was too short for him.

The Rooke stepped back, fearing that this man would give back the token he had taken the night before. An action that would surely upset any sleeping dragon.

"These Rabican children descended from Jenn Rabican, the little girl Cassie Vasilis gave her dragon gem to, yes?" Tavares Flaco said, ending the silence.

"What?" The Rooke said. "Maybe. I don't know. The Fist was filled with Rabicans after the time of Alleysiande. The dragon ship landed at a fishing village at the foot of the Daggera Mountains with the children and their dragon gems. That is why Fistians worshiped dragons. I apologize. That was a terrible story. I am not supposed to tell that kind of story. It will only anger the dragons."

"It is a story that needed telling," Tavares said. The man rubbed his wrists where his sleeve had been. "Those freaks that harm children are everywhere now. And they are protected. Heath's Night still exists and is now the biggest city of Megdon."

"Heath's Night was in The Mudlands," The Rooke said. "It can't be in the same place."

"Megdon claimed the western bit of The Mudlands. The rest is New Chazir," Kentigern said. "This was after the last big war, forty years ago."

"And it is a large city now?" The Rooke asked, wondering how he had lost track of the world below so completely.

"Yes," Tavares said. "And filled with horrible people like the ones in your story. These child molesting monsters are granted celebrated sleeves. They have pretty, green favored ribbons. Only those who speak against them are punished. Phaedra would be welcome. I hope she killed all the slavers of Heath's Night."

"Unfortunately," The Rooke said. "She was not the only demon there wearing a human flesh sack. You say Heath's Night still exists. It was burned to the ground before my robes. Have I been gone so long?"

"It is a giant metropolis," Tavares said. "And oblivious to its history. This tale would never be allowed to be told below. Never."

A big, bearded man who had been sitting with Tavares, stood up, frowning as he surveyed a number of children sitting in the café. The disapproval on the man's face felt justified to The Rooke.

"That was not a good story for this place," he said. "I am Aleron Ramses. Your story remains true only there is no Phaedra to correct those who torment the children."

"It was not like that when Torres Rushie went below…" Kentigern said, rising from his place, looking pale and upset. "There were still so many good people, trying to rebalance the world."

"I wish it were not so," Aleron said, stepping up. "I have

rescued families who refused to share their children with these monsters."

"My wife was one of those children," Tavares said. "Her family allowed it. She was celebrated and given wealth and status."

"Children cannot willingly participate in such depravity," Aldo said, the man going many shades of red. "I will be going with you, Rooke. There is no keeping those dragons asleep if these people continue as they are. No one can dream in Hell."

"I wish to reach into your pocket," Aleron said. "I will be your guardian as those of old. I have rescued more families than any other in this modern time. There are good people below, and despite everything, this world is worth saving."

The Rooke sighed. He would be leading hundreds from the safety of The Reliquary to the perils of the Infernal Empires below if he kept this up. He told himself he would secure his red robes on their hooks until he left for his quest as he spread his arms to expose the robe's pockets.

"This will not be an easy journey," The Rooke said.

Aleron took out a smooth, stone token and smiled. "Do not despair, sir Rooke," he said. "This is what Ta-She-Serra made me for. I would have a world suitable for our children to thrive."

Tavern IV:

The Learning Circle Canteen

Asking a demon its name is pointless. It has no name. It is legion. Should a mortal stumble across such a being, it is best they ignore it. Do not engage, do not speak to it lest it be invited in and the mortal's soul forfeit.

The Spells and Curses of Lecretia by Elfrydah Nix
Translated by Hazel Kyran

The List

A smattering of people followed The Rooke around as he continued his day, all not wanting to miss another tale. He had thought to go back to the Red Quarter to remove his robes. Aldo, Kentigern, and Gareth did not give him the time. Twice more The Reliquary shook as a violent storm grew outside.

"The dragon did not like that tale," The Rooke said, a slight tremor vibrating under his feet. "But it is essential in understanding who Phaedra might truly be."

"If the ice dragon allows you to leave this mountain," Kentigern said.

"I thought you didn't believe in dragons, old boy," Aldo said.

"I do now," Kentigern said. "I wish I didn't. Dragons are not so romantic as tales make of them. I wish they had died like in Hazel Kyran's translation of *The Idylls of Alleysiande*."

"Of course, there are dragons," The Rooke said, giving his friend a steady look. "I have seen many dragons before The Evanescence, both Erelahian dragons and shadow dragons. Come, let's go see what the engineers say about all this shaking."

"And you ought to have a look at that list The Relic gave you," Kentigern said. "You must begin your journey sooner than later."

The Rooke agreed. He shared his list at The Learning Circles with Kentigern, Gareth, and Aldo as they watched The Reliquary's masons gather to discuss repairing damage from the recent quakes.

The First Offers The Rooke his Lost Apprentice

> *The Second Offers The Rooke A Scavenger's*
>   *Nacharye Daughter*
> *The Third Offers The Rooke A Master of*
>   *Games and Puzzles*
> *The Fourth Offers The Rooke A*
>   *Maligned Beggar*
> *The Fifth Offers The Rooke The Gnolgia*
>   *Cartographer*
> *The Sixth Offers The Rooke a Broken Spyte*
> *The Seventh Offers The Rooke a Treasonous*
>   *Bounty Hunter, IPD*

"The Relic has instructed me to bring them Bracken Grayvesone," Kentigern said after a contemplative pause. "I imagine he is the first on the list. The First Aspect always loved that lad. Said he possessed the musical gift of the sentinel, Sandalphon."

"Bracken quit his apprenticeship before he ever began. He was not lost," The Rooke objected. "I expect this list means my son, Thiago. My last apprentice."

"The list reads 'lost' not 'last'. And you did lose Bracken," Kentigern said, a heavy sigh. "I know the script can be difficult to read. It is why they have a scrivener. However, I am certain this reads 'lost'. I can't imagine The Relic would require you bring your children."

"I am not a child," Thiago objected. "And I am going with father whether I am on this list or not."

"It can't be Bracken," The Rooke said, nodding to his son.

"I am not lost, and I do not wish to be last," Thiago said.

"Bracken was still a good man when he lived in the valley," Kentigern said. "He had everything. A family, fame enough, wealth enough, people who loved him true. And he gave it all away for that awful Baroness Teriss Amber. Disgusting.

She took him from a good path in life and put him on the road to oblivion."

"I lost touch with his first wife, Raven, and her twin daughters some years ago," The Rooke said. "Last I heard of the twins, both Rintyre and Carling had passed their IPE-2 exams almost a decade back. Both in good standing with the empires. Not sure what that says about them. I have heard neither speaks to their father anymore. They will be in their late twenties now."

"They have survived," Gareth said. "Raven would have wanted it so. Their mother always insisted on living under the sun despite her misgivings about the empires. She has a tavern in New Chazir."

"Raven always said New Chazir would be restored and become The Mudlands again," Kentigern said. "My son, Paul, visited her right after he got married. You know, he considered moving to New Chazir himself."

"Any guesses on the rest of the list?" The Rooke asked.

"We will ask Ghita. A grandmaster puzzler should be able to help us identify the rest," Kentigern said as The Reliquary shook, and people dropped papers and cups and arms full of things. "Ta-She be damned. You'll have to leave sooner than later."

A woman erupted from one of the lecterns, waving her arms at the alarmed congregate of people.

"This is not a quake," the woman said. "No one panic. That was the masons and engineers re-opening the scavenger tunnels below. It is going well. We have a way back to our supply chain now. I repeat, all is well."

The collective shrug of a trusting people rippled through The Learning Circles as mid-day approached. The Rooke pulled his robe closer to himself, an ear-stinging chill in the air causing him to pull his hood up.

Teachers and parents busied themselves pulling woolen caps down over their children's and their own ears as they entered the main thoroughfare in search of mid-day nourishment as doors swung open around the circle, opening the various lecterns and classrooms for the mid-day break.

Another tremor echoed under The Rooke's feet to signal another of the usual kind of quakes. He thought the dragon less than pleased over the engineer's controlled blast to reopen secret tunnels that connected The Reliquary to the world outside.

"Tell your tale," Kentigern said in his ear, a sharp whisper.

"What tale?"

"I don't care. Something that will appease the damn dragons. This shaking unsettles me."

"Kenny, this isn't a tavern or inn or café…"

"The Learning Circle Canteen is right there, more eat here at mid-day than any other place in The Reliquary, and Aleron is bringing us food and drink," Gareth said.

"The magic will work," Aldo said. "Any place people gather freely for food or drink, to speak freely, to share stories, to hear or play a tune. This will work."

"I wish I had brought my guitar," The Rooke said, sitting down, his back against the wall. He glanced at the sleeves of his robes, blood red. The garment's magic would not allow him to leave his quarters without them. He shivered. The red robes were plenty warm to the air but did nothing to shelter him from the cold dread that filled him. He reached into his pocket and felt the list, free of its seal.

"What happened after the oracle and monkey took the son of Imogen Vasilis and Gareth Janus through time?" Thiago asked. "Do you know?"

"Funny you should ask," The Rooke said, settling himself down. "See if you can spot Janus and Imogen's son in this story. I will continue with Phaedra and what happened in Heath's Night."

The people gathered about him gasped as his tale transported them into The Mudlands before The Evanescence and Subjugation had transformed it into New Chazir. He heard the whispers.

"This is amazing," voices said as they found themselves on an early summer afternoon in a climate where blizzards were rare even in winter.

The Scavenger's Nacharye Daughter

Young Anwyn Finn glared at her mother who grasped her hand too tightly, as if Ani were two instead of twelve. The barkeep tapped his thick fingers on the counter, holding his gaze on her. He was not a large man albeit an imposing one, in black robes, black trousers, a fastidiously tied cravat, under a red scarf as he glared down at her.

Anwyn did not like it. Despite there being few people in the pub to witness her mother's humiliating treatment of her, Anwyn wanted to crawl under a rock and die of embarrassment.

"You apologize to Keeper Shanks," her mother said.

"I will not," Anwyn said. "His owl killed my rat."

"Owls eat rats," her mother said. "Ani, that did not give you the right to steal from Shanks. Besides, you were planning to feed that rat to that awful yellow python."

"Sir Hiss is not awful. He's beautiful and now he's hungry," Anwyn said. "The snake has a right to eat too."

"Hiss was fed. The one species this world will never run short of is rats," her mother said. "And just because you are angry does not give you the right to steal. Ever. We don't steal. We are better people than that, Ani."

"Sorry about your rat, lass," Shanks said. "I just need you to return what you took. I will not be angry."

"I can't," Anwyn said, feeling desperate. "I needed the mustard seed to heal my dog. She lost her leg when on our journey here, and I needed something for Hobble's pain, so I conjured up something. The recipe called for mustard seed. I don't have it anymore."

"Mustard seed?" Shanks looked confused. "That's not what I am talking about."

Anwyn knew all too well what the old barkeep spoke about. She did not care. She was not giving that puzzle box back. Not for anything. It was magic. She knew it. And if she could get it to work, maybe she could go home. Maybe it could make it so she could hide her blue skin forever without needing sugar. She could be an ordinary girl.

Only her mother liked it here in this cold land. Anwyn did not. She hated this mountain fortress. It was a prison. All her friends had earned their proper sleeves, and here she was, cut off from them forever.

She could not believe her mother. They did not need to run. She would have passed her first Imperial Probate Exam. She was not an idiot, even if all her teachers were. She knew how to fool an exam.

"Well, I don't know what you're talking about," Anwyn said. "I took the mustard seed. I broke the little barrel it was in. I tried to fix it, but I couldn't."

"If you said what was taken, Shanks," Anwyn's mother said. "I can get it back for you. I am a scavenger. I can get anything."

"Not this, Mika. Although I appreciate your skills," Shanks said, still gazing at Anwyn. "This item is irreplaceable. And dangerous. Mika, if your daughter has this, you must get it from her and bring it to me straight away."

"Again, Shanks, I have to know what it is," Anwyn's mother said, her voice outgrowing her patience.

"I can't," Shanks said. "It is a matter of security here in The Reliquary. But if young Ani doesn't know what it is, then maybe it was The Rooke's lad who took it."

"Kostas didn't take anything. You leave him alone," Anwyn said. "He didn't even want to come with me. And he's just a little boy. He doesn't know anything."

"He's only a year younger than you," her mother said.

"It's a long year younger, mother," Anwyn said. "Keeper Shanks, I am sorry I broke into your pantry for mustard seed. I won't do it again. Now, mother, dear, can we go? I am hungry and am supposed to meet Kostas for our afternoon puzzling session."

Anwyn loosed herself from her mother's grip and headed toward the exit, head up and back straight. She heard her mother making apologies.

"Not a more deceitful creature in the world than an adolescent girl," Shanks said. "It's like that everywhere. The price of their magic, you see."

Anwyn stopped and turned. She had meant to call him several unpleasant names for his wild generalization before she heard about the magic. Yes. That was true. She had magic, but did other girls? No, no. She was Nacharye. They were not.

"If you change your mind, I can be discreet," Anwyn's mother said to the barkeep. "I will find your missing property. It's what I do."

"I will consider it. I will have to discuss it with The Relic," Shanks said. "And Ani, if you're lying, and I suspect you are, don't ever open it. I doubt you could, but if you do, you will unleash chaos and pain. It's not for you. It's not for any mortal, magic or not."

"What in the world could you have that could do that?" Anwyn's mother sounded angry now. "And if you're lying to scare my child, you will have to reckon with me, Shanks."

"I am not just any mortal," Anwyn said. She saw several rats scampering in the shadows outside the pub, running along the dark curbs that ran into the massive sewer system of The Reliquary. She felt prickling in her skin, like a million sparks bursting inside her veins at once.

It was Anwyn's voice speaking but not her words. She felt that strange presence that had been in her nightmares of late. Maybe it had been the tale The Rooke told this morning. She staggered and rushed away from the pub, heading down a spiraling path, spinning downstairs that went on and on toward the well-lit Learning Circles.

"Ani, wait," her mother said. "Do you know what Shanks is talking about?"

"No," Anwyn said. "He's crazy, mom. And I hate it here. Why can't we go home?"

"We can't," her mother said, her voice soft and her eyes sad, like she might cry. "This is home for now. It is good here, Ani.

Isn't it? We have food and a good house of our own. We don't have to worry about being cast out..."

"No. It's terrible. I will never have a sleeve. All my friends get to go wherever they want, and I will never see them again," Anwyn said. "I hate it. Why are you punishing me like this? It was one mistake. I would never forget again. My skin would never be blue again. I promise I won't mess up again if we can just go home. Please, mom. Let's go home."

"I am not punishing you, Ani," her mother said, voice filled with sorrow that stung Anwyn like a knife, making her tears flow freely. "Is that what you think? You didn't mess up. I did. I didn't properly explain. I didn't want you to be scared. You were a baby, and you grew so fast. You were old enough to understand what would happen if the empire discovered you, but I didn't want to ruin your childhood. You were such a happy child. Know that the whole world is wrong about Nacharye girls. I should have been checking that you were getting your sugar. This is my fault. Be mad at me if you must, but we can't go back. Home doesn't want women like us."

"Neither does The Reliquary," Anwyn said. "Everyone accuses me of being bad here just like Shanks. I am not bad."

"I know that, Ani. I know. It's complicated. Nacharye were once magical. Like in the story about Phaedra and Chrysalis. The empires see women that could hurt them," her mother said. "Let's get something to eat. You'll feel better. We will make it better. Look, that rooke is here. Maybe he'll tell another story."

The Tale of The Urian Pappas

On the same day that Phaedra raged in the village of Heath's Night, Dagan Brude, the Grand Pappa of the Urian Clans, entered the common room of the Damnable Dam Inn, spreading his arms, smiling broadly.

"This will be the day that I die," he said. "Drinks are on me."

People did not know how to take this although they accepted the free drinks and toasted his continued good health. The two younger pappas had distinctly different reactions.

Dagan Brude was getting on in years as people will when given the time. A respectable sixty-three and full of vigor. Young Goolsby Lamb laughed at his mentor, thinking there was some joke here that he did not fully understand.

The even younger apprentice, Sidon Bagwell, newly married with life stretching out its possibility, felt dread at his master's proclamation.

The three Urian pappas had come to the Otter Clan Dam to celebrate the naming of Otter Clan's new clan mother. They had performed all the rituals, Sidon learning this one for the first time.

"You're not going to die, Dagan," Goolsby said. "And I can tell you why…"

"Ah, but I am, my friend," Dagan said, quickly cutting off Goolsby who would talk for ten minutes or more without taking a breath if allowed. "I know it."

"Are you feeling bad?" Sidon asked in his slow drawl. "I am married to a healer. I can have Laynie take a look if you feel sick, Pappa Dagan."

"Pappa Si, I feel more alive than I ever have for this is a great day to embark on a new adventure into dimensions unknown," Dagan said, a Flowery accent still detectable in his words although he had left Jebellen decades ago to join the Urian Clans.

"Why would you say you are going to die today?" Sidon asked.

"Some years back, I happened upon an oracle. He looked a boy of ten or eleven. He had three eyes as oracles do. He proclaimed that on this day that I would die, starting a new and glorious age."

"How much Boreallean ale had you had?" Sidon asked.

"A fair amount. That's not the point. The oracle said today was of paramount importance, a new hope emerging in this world but from a horrifying source."

"Sounds like you were doing some wyvern whisky shots

too," Sidon said. This whole dying idea was nonsense and not like the Grand Pappa at all.

"I did partake too much of such things until that night," Pappa Dagan admitted. "Three days ago, I saw the same oracle. They live backwards which is how they know the future. He was younger, a toddler. He said nothing. He nodded to me, and I remembered that today I will die."

"No," Sidon said. "Oracles are only in stories. Are you over-indulging again? Do we need to talk to your wife?"

Goolsby Lamb began to speak. Shooting out stories about oracles and how they were not what people said they were, and how it was difficult to die in the best of circumstances at an Urian Clan celebration when Uriel's Covenant was renewed and fresh in people's blood.

Goolsby Lamb's words faltered, a unique event, and went silent when the hysterical man from Heath's Night burst into the common room of the inn and asked for a priest. Demons were attacking the village on the hill above The Damnable Dam.

The three Urian pappas followed the hysterical man out of the village, through the gate, across the bridge over the river by the dam, and up the hill toward Heath's Night, a barren old mining town, built on a hill of red dirt with crumbling buildings. The original village had been rich in minerals that had been mined to desolation. Heath's Night looked a scar against the land at the borders of The Mudlands.

Urian pappas had a reputation for being able to dispatch demons and ill-spirits, although from land and houses more than from people. They were not conventional priests, not like this fellow seemed to think. They were counselors for the Urian people, giving guidance on life's troubles.

"We should call for some bhante in the Beaver Clan," Goolsby said. "If there really are demons."

"I know the rituals well enough as do you," Dagan Brude

said. "Sidon has studied them, and we need his eyes. He can see through the veil to see if it is demons that plague Heath's Night."

"Is that the only animal you could find?" Sidon Bagwell asked Goolsby, who held a four-horned sheep at the ready. "We are meant to use pigs."

"Goats are better," Goolsby Lamb said. "Do you think there could be a demon? We haven't seen one in decades this close to The Mudlands?"

"I believe someone went mad. Desperation and poverty often foster disturbances of the mind," Dagan Brude said. "Dirts seldom know the difference between organic madness and demonic possession. Still, considering my pending death, I suspect this will be dangerous, lads."

Dagan Brude, Goolsby Lamb, and Sidon Bagwell did not fully comprehend the horror they were following the ridiculous, little Dirt man into. They saw a child, a fair little girl, sitting cross-legged. Under two swinging, flayed bodies. Dagan held his hand up, turned to the wooly haired Goolsby.

"After we are done here, we will need Phineas Tunvel and the Otter healers, and maybe their fighters," Dagan said. The Grand Pappa turned to the quaking little man. "You said there was only one possessed person. You did not say there had been a battle."

"Yes, there she is. She must have killed everyone," the hysterical man said, pointing at the tiny girl who could be no more than nine years old. "Right there."

"Ah, that's a child," Goolsby said, although the dead bodies swinging in the wind sent a shiver through all three pappas.

"That's no child," the oily man said. "She's a demon."

The child stood and sauntered toward the quartet. She looked half-starved, wearing a dirty shift, and needed a bath. She was covered in blood and dirt, but still as fair a child as there had ever been.

Phaedra, in turn, saw three powerful men who might take her well-earned reward from her. Some kind of priests even if they did not see themselves as such.

"I am no demon," Phaedra said. It was not a lie although to someone wrapped in flesh, the language was limited. There were no words to describe what Pandemonium had made of Phaedra. She had been a woman, untold years ago, in this world or another. She could not tell. Nothing here felt familiar except the breath of life she felt flowing in this body's heart and lungs.

Phaedra's senses tingled with a mixture of latent fear and annoyance. Why had she let that foul, little slaver get away? He had been hurting little boys in the dark reaches of the night. She felt rage building.

The old man with the slaver had a ragged beard and blue eyes with a look of both great kindness and fierceness. He wore an earthen-brown tunic under a blue sleeveless robe, light in weight. These three priests dressed simply and without adornment that she had found on the slavers. She felt love for the old man instantly. He was full of light. He spoke first.

"I am Dagan Brude," he said. "Who are you, child?"

The second priest was a plump man with the curly yellow hair and kindly face, holding the four-horned sheep on a lead.

"I am Goolsby Lamb of the Goat Clan," he said. "Come, girl. We will protect you. What has happened here?"

Then there was the young, dark-haired man with bright, strange, mismatched eyes in blue and green. Phaedra felt power emanating from this man, felt that she knew him. She also feared him.

"Who are you?" Phaedra asked him. "You must be dying to share your name with me as well."

"Dagan, I think our hysterical friend might be right," the young man said. "There is something infesting this child."

Phaedra yearned for a vacation from her eternal torment. She did not relish killing good men, but if they challenged her, what choice would she have? She decided to attempt trickery to avoid the fight. Phaedra fell to her knees and pretended innocence, letting Chrysalis come forward.

"Girl, what's your name," Dagan Brude attempted once more to gain her confidence.

"I am Chrysalis Rabican," she said, the little girl coming forward, pushing Phaedra back. "I am scared. Bad men did bad things to the children here. That man with you did things to the little boys. He did really bad things."

"Child, tell us what happened?" the old priest said. "We are here to help."

"Fool. It's not a child. It's a demon and a liar. That one would not speak to a man before the demon came," the oily man said, shaking like one inflicted with palsy. "I came to you for help. Do you Muddy idiots know nothing? Kill it."

Chrysalis retreated and let Phaedra come forth. That insufferable oily man pulled out his pistol. She reacted. More than she meant to. The priests had moved to stop him, but not fast enough. Phaedra ripped the slaver in two. Her rats appeared in heaps, overwhelming the body sending the three good men into action.

The sheep bleated as Goolsby Lamb dropped his shoulder pack on the ground. The younger priest glared at Phaedra with his mismatched eyes. She felt exposed, and knew this young priest was seeing what lay within. He saw Phaedra's damned form inside the little girl. Impossible. He would not understand.

"I don't see a shadow on the child, but it is clear, she has great power," the old priest said. "This is unusual. Sidon, what are you seeing?"

"There is a demon. A small one, weak and cursed beyond our healing," the young priest said. "Dagan, please, dispatch it. She is grotesque, worse than that roach I crushed this morning."

"I am not. I am Phaedra. I am beautiful. This is Hell's illusion of me. It is only an illusion to keep me trapped. Help me."

"Demon, get out of this child. You are defiling her," the old man said.

"No. I am not a demon. Will you not listen? I will not suffer the debauchment of children at the hands of human-shaped monsters and their perverted, sick desires. They must die. And if you protect such foul wretches, then you too must die."

"You are fallen, beast," Goolsby said, preparing his sheep. "I have the goat ready. Let's be quick."

The exorcism began without the bother of foreplay. Such rudeness. Should these men not get to know her before performing such an intimate act? The old-grayed hair priest pulled out book and symbol and began babbling at her, demanding her name, begging her to leave 'this innocent child'.

Annoyed more than compelled, Phaedra fled from the three men into an abandoned hovel by the gates of Heath's Night, holes in the roof, one side burned out. She threw rocks from a mining cart at the priests, hoping to dissuade their pursuit. Killing these men would not serve her purpose. They did not care nor understand.

"Give me your name, demon," the old priest continued, his voice calm, arrogant, as if he took for granted that he could separate Phaedra from Chrysalis. The two were one. She spat at him and gathered her will.

"I am Phaedra. Do you think I lie? I am Phaedra."

"You are not a dragon," the young priest said. "Give us your true name, demon?"

"Dragons do not have locks on names. I am Phaedra, and I am no demon, you fool men. Leave me be."

The old priest did not bend before her like the others of this desolate village. Light around him burned her with all she had been denied. Phaedra raged against this old man, her will throwing him against a crumbling wall of stone, breaking him.

His spirit flew into that elusive light, leaving a bag of bones crumpled in the mortal world to be consumed by Phaedra's constant company of rats. Phaedra growled in agony and frustration as the old man's spirit reflected the beauty of youth as he disappeared into the light forbidden to her.

"I was beautiful too," Phaedra cried at the light.

"You are beautiful, Phaedra," the old man's spirit called back. "And a new age has begun."

He was gone. Phaedra felt a chill of guilt and discomfort. The old man left her no option. She had to stop him from separating her from the body she had worked so hard to obtain. Phaedra refused to be banished back into Hell. Not this time. She was never going back. Never. She did not belong there.

The old man's companions screamed and cried out. "Dagan!" the man of mismatched eyes said, shaking the corpse of the old man.

"Sidon, Dagan is dead," his ragged, yellow-haired companion said, a voice soft and comforting despite the horror. "We must fight this beast alone. Sidon, do you hear me?"

He ignored Phaedra. She would not have it. She turned on the two remaining priests and their bleating four-horned sheep.

"Goolsby, run, run!" Sidon said, pulling his companion to his feet and taking off at a full sprint.

Phaedra shattered glass and pushed rocks and debris at the two men with her will as she pursued them through dirty streets. They stumbled over the corpses from Phaedra's rampage. The head of a nasty mortal sent soft-spoken Goolsby reeling away as Sidon, so young and fresh-faced, turned to face her.

Blood ran down the face of this comely, young man from a cut above his left eye. He held up the same symbol as the dead priest, a broken onyx tower, and spoke words in a language abhorrent to Phaedra. She did not know the meaning of the tower or the words, but she felt their power.

"Demon, give me your name," Sidon said, repeating a ritual that he could not possibly understand. Phaedra hissed at him.

"I am Phaedra. I am no demon, child of man. Do not stand against me. No more need die in this wretched place. Let me stay, priest-ling. I can reward you."

"Liar. Leave. The Creator of all commands you."

"Does your god not have a name to command me by? Say it, boy! Say the name. You ask mine. I ask for yours and your impotent god."

Goolsby, red-faced and panting, tried to hold the sheep steady while grasping Sidon by the back of his torn robes.

"Sidon, we have to banish the beast into the goat."

"That's not a goat," Phaedra said, a bit confused. She pushed at the sheep, frightened it. The two men could not hold it. The horned animal bucked itself free, its rounded horns knocking Goolsby to the ground.

"Damn you, demon," Sidon said.

"You've lost your beast." Phaedra cackled delight. They could not defeat her.

"Silence!" Sidon said, helping Goolsby back to his feet.

Phaedra had won. They could not separate her now without slaying the child, and these were good men. They would not dare.

"Don't speak to it, Sidon. Have some sense, boy," the sheep-confused priest told the young man, gingerly stepping over a disemboweled corpse.

Rats fed, hundreds of them enjoying the carnage. Phaedra felt a pause of disgust, not at the dead man or rats, but at what that man had done to the children. The light had been offered to this awful man despite all the suffering he wrought. She could not understand it.

"Damn you and your god," Phaedra hissed at the priests. "Did this creator of yours hear the children when they cried out for help? No, I did. I saved them."

"You have no right to deal out death, demon," Sidon said. "Let go of the child. You are fouling a little girl."

"I saved this girl. I am redeeming her. Her soul will have the light, and now her body is mine. I am Phaedra. I am the girl. Do you know what the foul men of this village did? Their damnation was inevitable, even before I came, there were already demons here."

"Remember what Dagan taught you, Sidon. Do not argue morality with a demon," Goolsby said, pulling out his own onyx tower symbol. What was that broken tower? What did it mean? Phaedra had no idea, but it gnawed at her, weakened her.

"Stand back, Goolsby. I am going to banish her," Sidon said with the foolish bravado common in the young.

"We've lost the sacrifice. We can't. Sidon, we need your wife and Phineas. Listen to me, son, for once in your life."

"Goolsby, there's no more time. This child will not survive much longer. Look at how many this monster has slain."

Phaedra laughed at the hapless priests. She could outrun the wind in her half-flesh, half-ethereal form. Goolsby looked horrified. Sidon did not look at her at all.

He rushed her, the fool man, and she tossed him backwards with a push of her hands and a flaring of her will. He came back to his feet in a flash, holding the broken-tower symbol in the one hand and reading from the book in his other. He spoke to her in the language of divinity and creation. It burned like the noon-day sun.

She fought back. "Your name, priest. And the god that you serve?"

"I am Sidon Gale Bagwell."

The name was wrong. Phaedra knew it, but his belief in the name made it powerful. He held up his left wrist which displayed a tattooed bracelet in blue glyphs which Phaedra could not read but made her feel an emotion that shook her to her very essence.

Above the tattooed bracelet, a quiet sea preparing its assault under dark skies emerged in hues of black, brown, and blue as if wind blew within the tattoo that covered the entire forearm of the strange, young man. Phaedra gaped. She had never seen such sorcery before. A tattoo that lived inside the flesh of a man. What was this?

"My graff is called The Eye of the Storm. Leave the flesh of this child and begone. Back into the darkness where you belong," Sidon said. Phaedra steeled herself to attack and flee.

Sidon stepped toward her, leaned in close. Phaedra worked the little hands of the child through his dark hair, down his unshaven face, and around his throat, such heat, such life to hold in her little hands.

Sidon's heart raced at Phaedra's embrace. She could taste his sweet breath on her face. For a flash of second, she ached to kiss this man as a daughter might a father. She hesitated a beat. Then she squeezed using her monstrous strength to snap his neck.

She could not. He whispered the name of the god she had always denied. It echoed inside Phaedra like thunder, rendering her powerless. She tried to grab hold of the priest by the soul, ripping at him, trying to take his name. She could do nothing.

Movement in the rubble disturbed her concentration as a young man crawled out from under the rocks. Phaedra recognized Luc. He looked sorely injured. Had she done that?

"Help me," he begged.

"Do not kill the boy. Luc is hurt like me." Chrysalis said, coming forward at Phaedra's insistence. She turned her attention back to the startled priest.

"We will not harm him," Goolsby said, thinking the child spoke to him. "Sidon, we should bind this child until Phineas and your wife arrive. We'll use purifying wyrms to purge her soul."

"Don't," Chrysalis said, feeling her friend's fear. "Don't. Phaedra is good. She is my friend. We only wish to save the children. They did horrible things to us. Horrible. I promised to look after them. My brother. My sister. They are in the cellar under the tavern. Free them. Help them."

"Child, tell the demon to go," Sidon said, kneeling before her, holding the onyx tower in the other. "You will be safe with us. We will not harm you, but the demon must go. It does not belong with the living."

"Phaedra is not a demon, and she doesn't belong with the dead. She is good. The children. They are so small. Jesper and Sid-Jynx. I am supposed to take care of them. They don't have anyone else. Our mother sold us," Chrysalis said, her tears reflecting immortal grief. "Let Phaedra stay so we can save the children."

It was too late when Phaedra realized that Luc now belonged to a demon who had been summoned by the evil of this place. Luc rose from the rubble, a big knife in his hand. While Chrysalis looked the most precious of small children, not a blemish to her façade, there could be no doubt of this young man's corruption. A demon wore a corpse like a bloodied ball gown.

The two priests screamed, scrambled to their feet to subdue the ghoul. "Stop."

Ghouls move with speed no natural man could muster, and Phaedra was unable to retake full control of Chrysalis in time to save her. This vile creature cut the girl's throat. The pull of oblivion came swiftly to claim Phaedra. Her despair shook the very foundation of the ground below them as the rats raced about her.

"Murderer! Murderer!" Phaedra seethed frustration, the last of her power seizing the demon within the ghoul, dragging it back to Hell.

She screamed threats that no one could hear as the soul of Chrysalis fled from her into the half-light between Pandemonium and dimensions unknown to her. The young pappa, Sidon Bagwell, fell to his knees crying and cursing as he tried to staunch the bloody wound of the child's open throat.

Too late. It was done and Heath's Night was free of the spirit but not of its demons.

Dragon Grumblings

The growing chill in the Learning Circles was not an imagining of The Rooke as he pulled his robes tight. He felt a calmness settle around him. He knew the tales he must tell when he ventured below.

"A new age had begun," he said as those gathered around gaped in silence and rapture. "And such a wondrous age it was, full of wonders."

"There are still wonders, father," Thiago said. "It is still a beautiful world."

"It is nothing as it was. The Evanescence took it all away, left us behind with a shadow of a world," The Rooke said, his memory flaring with all he had squandered, all the possibilities he had missed. "Nothing to defy the demons remained. In the end, a full third of the world's population was gone between The Evanescence and the slaughter that followed. We, who remember, have a solemn duty to restore a better faith, a better way. It is too heavy for me. All of you must do your part, or we will all become rats caught in a terrible trap for all eternity."

"Dagan Brude is my ancestor, a proper Urian pappa," Kentigern said, breaking the uncertain silence. "They're not priests as you would see with Janusian or Serren clerics. Pappas performed the rituals that keep the Urian Covenant, give counsel to people in trouble, but it's not a religion per se. Anyhow, I was named for Dagan Brude."

"Were you?" Gareth asked. "Curious."

"I knew my ancestor died at Heath's Night. I did not know the particulars. Dagan Brude is said to have given rise to an order of exorcists with his death. Rooke, that order still exists at The Temple of the Tail. There is hope, my friend. I have recorded this tale for *The Rooke's Tome*."

"How is that possible, Kenny?" Gareth asked. "Your family should have disappeared at The Evanescence if you were Muddy, and Dagan Brude was a proper Urian."

"He was, but not all the Brude bearns were Urian. My ancestor ran away from home when he was a small lad in the Flowery Kingdom. He started as a novice at The Temple of Tail, thinking he would become bhante. Later, he joined the Dolphin Clan of the Urians. The rest of the Brude family were lessor nobles of some kind. I was born from the line of one of his two sisters. Strange, a lot of my male forbearers from the Brude line ran off to become Muddy or died in childhood. No idea why."

"I think I know," The Rooke said. "But I am too tired to go into it now."

The Rooke's attention was taken as a young girl pulled at her mother to approach him.

"Please, mother. If we reach into his pockets, we can go home," the girl said.

The Rooke stepped back. He did not want children risked. The girl looked no more than eleven or twelve. And she could be younger given that girls developed faster than boys. Then he saw it. The blue behind her ear. Nacharye. She wore a white, collared shirt under a bright red vest with gold buttons, and well-fitted black trousers, tall, laced boots in the style of the empire below.

Her mother wore a scavenger's duster which was all leather and pockets. There was no doubt. He had found The Second Aspect's Nacharye daughter. He sighed, tugged on Kenny's arm, and pointed.

"Hello," The Rooke said as the girl approached. "And who might you be?"

"I am Ani Finn. I can help you. I know I can. I have magic," the girl said. "I know your son, Kostas. We're friends. Both apprentice puzzlers. I want to reach into your pocket."

"Ani, I am not sure this is a good idea," her mother said.

"I am afraid she must," Kentigern said. "Who are you, my dear lady?"

"I am Mika Finn. This is my daughter, Anwyn. She's too young. She doesn't understand," she said. "We have only barely escaped the empire."

"I do understand," Kentigern said as Anwyn pulled a glowing, ruby token from The Rooke's robe that proclaimed her destined to travel The Rooke's Path. "Come with me, both of you. I will explain. Oh, Mika, go ahead and get your token. It might protect you more than you expect."

"And I will meet you all at the Puzzler Octagon this evening," The Rooke said after another half-dozen smooth, stone tokens were distributed. "I am going to take a nap. Thiago, will you wake me an hour before sundown? I want to ask Ghita Mist about the rest of my list. And make sure Kostas has finished his work."

"Sure, father. I am going to the arena to have a kick about with the lads. The Purple Quarter allows me to play with them as there are not enough in Red Quarter to field a proper grassball team."

"The exertion will do you good," The Rooke said. "Enjoy your day. Hopefully, the dragon will be snoring and not stirring for a few hours."

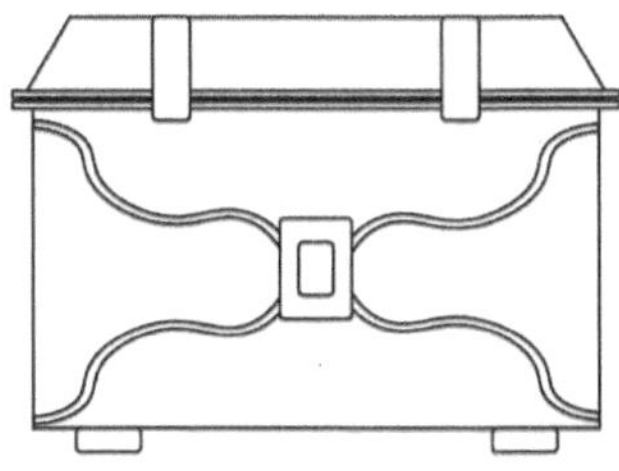

Tavern V:

The Puzzler Pantry

The glyphs on each card of an Idylls & Grimoires deck reads 'El Kal Tal Terra.' Gamers often translate the Asciendien phrase as "What kind of world do you want?" That is incorrect. The proper translation is "What kind of world will you make?"

A Master's Guide to Idylls & Grimoires Cards
By Xherdan Kyran (Forward by his wife, Hazel)

The Octagon

The Rooke arrived at The Puzzler Octagon to find things in absolute chaos. He held the list in vain with no opportunity to get the assistance he had come for.

The puzzler grandmaster raged in her dismay. Few would describe the woman as mild in manner. Ghita Mist was ever the eye of the storm. Today, she was a boat caught in a tempest that she could not control. Her silver-streaked black hair flew out in unkempt angles, her purple-lined, silver robes were untidy from her pulling at them, her cheeks rouged and her violet eyes puffy in panic.

The other gathered puzzlers gave the stout woman wide berth. None of her discomfiture had to do with the series of passing aftershocks that were rocking The Reliquary.

Books had fallen from shelves; papers flew about the room. The stone walls held the great structure steady, and the vibrations of the last aftershock registered as a little more than a foot massage as The Rooke entered the room. He approached the grandmaster, his mind cluttered and confused. Thiago pointed at something.

"Your son," Ghita said, pointing through the crowd of puzzlers and onlookers. "I don't know how this happened, Rooke. Believe me."

"I don't understand," The Rooke said. "Why are you so upset?"

"Father." Thiago took him by the sleeve of his red robe. "Come and see."

Kostas stood shoulder to shoulder with Anwyn Finn. The two children were mechanically putting pieces of a jigsaw puzzle from an open box into place.

At young Anwyn's feet, a small, flat-faced, sharp-eared

dog nestled, happily sleeping in a bed crafted of pillows taken from the cushioned couches situated throughout the Puzzler Octagon. The little pup exhibited no alarm at the crowds or vibrations of the aftershocks or of Ghita Mist's villainous cats, crouched above them in the enclaved bookcases above.

Hex, a skinny black and white cat hissed, tail swinging in displeasure, on the point of pouncing, and Bane, a rotund, tortoise-shell tabby with a face half white, half black glaring from above his sister cat. Several in the crowd stood forward with arms stretched out to hold the gathered masses back. Grandmaster Mist eyed her felines warily.

"Do not touch the children. I think if you disturb them, something bad will happen," a long-haired master puzzler by the name of Zac Grimm warned as he pushed back several novices.

"This will take days," another puzzler said, a young woman in a silver-lined duster called Jeanna. Her father was a professor of music at the Learning Circles. "And they are apprentices. How will they manage? How could they have opened that cube?"

"I thought it was voice activated trick box like I used to get as a kid with a surprise inside. Technology, not magic," Zac said. "I should have taken it from them. I didn't know."

"Zac, this is not your fault. You could not have known," Jeanna said. "You don't know the stories of Alleysiande like we do. This is a puzzle for masters and grandmasters to solve. This is a disaster. If the tales be true and this is what it seems. Two apprentices will not manage. They will die and take us all with them."

"Die? What do you mean die?" Zac said, his voice cracking a bit. "What is going on here?"

The Rooke spied the cube in question. It looked to be made of ancient, polished wood decorated with runes gold and glowing. The top disappeared, leaving no clue as to how. The tiny pieces of the puzzle, all stark white and the same L-shape, filled the cube to the brim.

Tables had been arranged around it so that they would catch any pieces that fell as Kostas and Anwyn reached in to take the next. Already, the tables were covered in blank pieces that only revealed their true shape and color when picked up.

The Rooke could not form the words for questions. Both children were enveloped in some kind of catatonic stasis that made them unaware of those around them. Ghita Mist looked ready to scream or cry or both.

"That, Rooke, is Ambriel's Unbreakable Cube," Ghita Mist said, a wild and implausible claim. "And your son and Ani have managed to open it. We are doomed."

"Oh, the little fool," Thiago said as the long-haired master puzzler gently nudged him away from his younger brother. "How did Kostas even get it? Such a thing belongs in a vault."

"It should have been in the Unapproachable Library. That is where the Muddy Pirates are said to have hidden that vile thing after getting it back from your mad sorceress," Grandmaster Mist said. "That library disappeared at The Evanescence. How could this thing still exist?"

"Phaedra never had it. I remember. She wanted it but she never found it," The Rooke said. "Only, I wonder…"

"She lied to you," Ghita said. "I remember her too, better than you as I have no blood red robes shattering my full memory. She found it in Ambriland when in her early years. She told no one, planning to use it herself."

"How did Anwyn and Kostas get the thing?" Thiago asked.

"When Shanks said he'd been robbed, we thought he meant he had lost some of his Boreallean ale or those gems he thinks no one knows about," Jeanna said. "It wasn't what he meant at all."

"Shanks said it belonged to his sister as if a mortal could claim such a thing. She bequeathed it to him in her will," Grandmaster Mist said, a bitterness touching her words. "He should have told me he had it. He should have told me that was what was missing. I am not the woman I was, and I should have been trusted. Shanks should have known better. I would have protected it, and now it is open. I have no cipher for this puzzle and these children are innocent…"

"Ghita, what makes you think this is Ambriel's Cube?" The Rooke asked, wanting confirmation.

"Just how many magical puzzle boxes do you think there are in the world?" Ghita said. "It has the right runes, and the power. Your son and Anwyn are both catatonic. They have no awareness of where they are or what they are doing, and if you tried to stop them, I suspect both would drop dead on the spot and the puzzle would engulf itself and all in this room in white flame and this Reliquary and all of Primordial Boreal would be destroyed. Isn't that what Hazel Kyran warns us of in her translation of the *Idylls of Alleysiande*?"

"How could The Relic not know of this? They know everything about their Reliquary, all its citizens, all we bring and all we leave behind. They knew about my fake sword and everything," Zac said, catching Hex as the cat leapt from the bookcase, earning himself a scratch. "Damn cat. Bane, don't even think about jumping."

"The Relic knew," Ghita said as she dispatched Bane from the upper shelf and directed him toward the outer sofas of The Octagon. "I will never comprehend those creatures. Why let it be where children could find it? And how did this sister of Shanks get the thing?"

"You questioned Shanks?" The Rooke wanted to ask the old barkeep a few questions himself.

"He was rude about the whole thing. Blamed me when I insisted that he had misplaced whatever it was he was missing. He said it was in his vault in his quarters. Accused me of magicking it out. Clearly, he is wrong, or the children would not have found it. He didn't need to call me a witch."

"Thiago, summon The Relic," The Rooke said. "Tell Scrivener Leesh. He must hurry them."

Boots tied to the knees, mussed long hair of dark auburn, scavenger overalls in black pulled over an ivory woolen tunic, under a multi-pocketed thick leather duster marked Mika Finn as she blew past the gathered crowd into the Puzzler Octagon calling for her daughter.

The Rooke stepped in front of her and explained as best he could.

"Damn, Ani. She said she had not taken it," Mika said, face a furious red. "This is the thing that Shanks wanted back. He said it was dangerous."

The Puzzler Octagon began to shake again. The gathered puzzlers moved to keep things steady around Kostas and Anwyn.

"Damn dragons," Ghita Mist said. "Rooke, tell a damn tale. Make the dragons sleep. We can't have the shaking, or your son and this girl will have us all dead."

A Master of Games and Puzzles

Zac Grimm felt the world spinning away from him. He was not given to hysteria, but this puzzle box. He had always wanted magic to be real. As a child, it was all he dreamed of when playing his games with its pretend sorceries. He reconsidered. Real magic proved terrifying.

When he awoke and left the flat he shared with his father that morning, this was not where he saw things going. He reviewed the day, thinking it might well be his last. He closed his eyes, steeling himself still so that he would not flee. This was his fault. Anwyn and Kostas were kids, and he had been meant to watch out for them.

Zac never did feel the calm everyone else in The Reliquary described. His wrist still itched from the surgery that removed his sleeve monitor. His father was not doing well. Not since his mother's death, and worse in the last few years. His father looked at him with shame in his eyes as Zac made ready to leave that morning.

"Pops, it is fine. I am fine," Zac said. "We are safe here. You are safe…"

"I ruined everything…"

"You didn't. You said what you believed to be true," Zac said. "I have left you soup and bread. You have a class to teach. You remember how to get to the Learning Circles? Go out our door. Go right. Walk about a half mile to those double purple doors. Take the lift to Hub One. It's got a symbol, right? You remember?"

"I like it here…"

"Dad, you agreed you would try the teaching. There are people…"

"I like it here. I will stay here. I will listen to music and read some of these books you brought me. I can read you know."

"I know you can, pops," Zac said, sighing heavily. "You are a great teacher. And you can teach here. Your students loved you."

"I got them killed…"

"They are not dead…"

"They are. They are gone. I am not crazy, son." His father began to weep again. Uncontrollably. "They kill them. Dominick, tiny Will, Benji, Jiao, Esme, Graine, Helena…They killed them all. Little children. Not the stupid ones. The smart ones. They kill them. My best students. I disobeyed the new curriculum so the children would learn to think and be free. I was wrong."

"Dad, I…" Zac never knew what to say. He knew kids that failed their IPE back in his day, nineteen years back when he had been eleven. Yes, things had changed with the implanted sleeves. But not like what his father said. That would be unfathomable. It could not be real.

Zac was still friends with several that did not get sufficient marks on their IPE to continue to university. Had been friends. He supposed he would never see them again. His sleeve was gone and there was no way to contact them.

"There are no IPE exams here. Just teach the kids to read and write. I will be back this evening. I will bring you fish and chips. They're good here. Like true Acarian. Remember when we went to Acaria for that gaming tourna…"

His father was not listening. He had his face in his hands. Zac pulled on his long duster over his short and worn white cotton undershirt. This place was so blasted cold. Nothing like the Broken Fingers in New Chazir where he had lived most of his life. Zac had never seen snow in his home. Here, looking out any window, there was white and blue rock all year long.

"Zacharias, you still get to play games, right?"

"Yes, pops."

"I love you, son. I am so proud of you…"

"I know, dad. And I am not mad at you," Zac said. "Please, go teach that class. It'll be good for you. Let's make the best of this place."

"Tomorrow. I will go out tomorrow."

Zac found Anwyn Finn and Kostas, the boy with no surname because his father called himself nothing but The Rooke, huddled over a gaming table in The Puzzler Pantry arguing.

"What you doing?" he asked, smiling at them. He remembered being a kid. They thought their secrets worth hiding.

"We were getting ready to work on our Idylls & Grimoires deck," Kostas said, deflecting. "We are taking a break."

"Don't worry your pretty, little head about it, Zac," Anwyn said. "Tell Grandmaster Mist you checked on us and we are misbehaving. It's all she will believe anyhow."

"Aw, you think I'm pretty…" Zac said. "C'mon. What are you doing? You look like Grandmaster Mist's cats negotiating to take out your little dog."

"You leave Hobble alone," Anwyn said. The girl was a spitfire. The little dog in question, stretched its three legs as it shifted on the pillows on which it slept. "And if those cats so much as touch Hobble, I'll feed them to my snake."

"I'm surprised your snake hasn't eaten this pup," Zac said, scooting into the bench next to Kostas. He scratched Hobble's head. He liked dogs although he had never kept a pet in his life. His parents had been too chaotic to be around animals when he was growing up, especially after they split up and his mother got sick. Although, his mother had loved horses. She made him learn to ride when he was small. He missed her.

"You can leave now," Kostas said. "You've checked on us. Isn't that why you are here?"

"I have to fully look after you, Curly…"

"Don't call me that," Kostas said.

"I don't mean nothing by it," Zac said. "I am supposed to be playing Idylls & Grimoires with you. You are supposed to be teaching me…"

"You don't like it…"

"Yeah, I do," Zac said. "It's just not the kind of game I usually play. That's all I meant. You know I play SIN games – ones on the sleeve imperial network."

"You would lose the magic of the cards if you tried to put Idylls & Grimoires on SIN," Anwyn said. "I do miss good gaming, but the cards, if they could really be magical…"

"Ani, he's pretty good at puzzles, you know," Kostas said.

This was the start of the trouble. The two looked at each other. Anwyn gave Kostas a seething scowl of disapproval, as if he were revealing some dread secret.

"No," was all Anwyn said, pulling out her I&G cards, the colorful, exquisitely painted cards. There was an undeniable magic in the decks used to play the ancient game.

"What? Is there some puzzle you can't solve? I am big good with puzzles…"

"The way you talk is so weird," Anwyn said.

"Ani, we will never solve it ourselves," Kostas said.

"One second there, Curly. I am not helping you cheat if Grandmaster Mist has set you a challenge."

"No, she hasn't," Anwyn said, now glaring at Kostas full on. "Damn, Kostas. I told you not to tell."

"I didn't tell. I asked you if he might help us. We're getting nowhere."

"What the…what is going on, you two?" Zac asked, feeling a warning rising up in his belly that conflicted with his need to solve every riddle and puzzle, win every game.

"Kostas is wrong. You probably can't help us," Anwyn said.

"It's just a stupid puzzle box. It's ancient. Like what kids played with before SIN. It's only a box."

"I love puzzle boxes," Zac said. "My mom. She used to give them to me for every birthday. Back before SIN games were like they are now. They're not ancient. Some are big time fun."

"Ok, but you can't tell anyone," Anwyn said. "Please, Zac, don't be such an ass."

"Language, missie…."

"Oh, get bent. You talk like that all the time."

"Are you trying to butter me up to get me to help you?" Zac said, smiling at Anwyn's bravado.

She was a little girl. Skinny, pre-pubescent child with a very big mouth. He liked her. The kind of girl he would have hung with when he was that age, all those years ago.

Kostas, on the other hand; that kid was full of mischief, clever, curious, and sweet. And there was no doubt in Zac's mind that Kostas, age eleven, loved young Anwyn Finn down to his very soul. He had seen that before. He had lost friends that way. Girls possessed magic boys never learned.

"Just show him, Ani. What could it hurt?" Kostas said. "I'll make sure he doesn't talk."

Zac laughed, pushing his long, brown hair from his face. "You'll keep me…"

"Don't try me, old Zac. I didn't grow up soft like you. I grew up here," Kostas said.

"You're real tough, Curly. Real tough," Zac said, bemused. "Show me the box."

The small box seemed both ancient and new all at once. A smooth cube about two hands across, not big at all. Just a cube. There were no edges, the seams painted on and marked by leather straps with curvy strokes of gold painted into the box around a square with a small, dark gemstone glowing at its front. Zac took it in his hands and looked it over.

A rat scurried across the floor distracting him as one of the Octagon cats leapt after it. A strange aroma filled the air. Roses and fresh, flowing water in autumn. Zac envisioned river rapids through a forest of deep green, sunlight piercing the needled floor from above, a cool breeze whistling. He pushed the box away.

"This isn't a puzzle box. It's just a painted wood box," Zac said. "Pretty thing. Make a cool decoration."

"It does open," Anwyn said. "See, Kostas, he doesn't know enough to open it. There are runes if you know the Asciendien words."

She whispered "tal terra…" and the gem at the center glowed blue and then went dark.

Zac smiled. "That ain't ancient. It's a SIN puzzle box. It reacts to your voice," he said, feeling confident.

"No, it's magic," Anwyn said. "Here, you try."

"El Kal Tal Terra," Zac said.

"Really? *What kind of world will you make?* That's what you got," Anwyn said, grabbing at the box. "That's the only Asciendien you know because it is on every I&G card. That is not going to do anything…"

"Ah, it worked," Zac said, pointing to the box. The gemstone glowed a bright green, throwing out a dim light across the table. "It should open now."

Ani pushed the gemstone. The puzzle box opened.

Zac witnessed terrible visions as silver light exploded from the box. Cities burning, monsters preying, depraved people roaming in gangs to kill, to rape, to feast across broken landscapes. He saw Hell as his mother used to speak of it when he was a kid, and through the desolation, he saw something impossible. Something miraculous that the word "paradise" did not adequately describe.

He tried to tell The Rooke when he arrived, but all his words went away, and whatever nonsense he said could not help him or the children. He felt a relief when The Rooke began his tale.

Zac saw a small village, cobbled roads, little cottages, each with fox or two frolicking in the gardens. He wished to go there now, away from this cold place with the magic box that would unleash its Hell on the world.

The Tale of Demon Temple Babies

Three years passed in a blissful haze along the Blood Line River in Haniel's Valley in The Mudlands following the horrific events of Heath's Night.

Two foxes regularly attended the Bagwell garden, a respectful number of totem animals for any of the Fox Clan although the children always wished more would come. Jesper and Sid-Jynx felt the neighboring Maule-Finns were stealing a good number of their totem foxes.

In those short three years, few remembered that either Jesper or Sid-Jynx had been adopted, so natural the family seemed to the rest of their clan. It was a happy life although the events of Heath's Night forever haunted Sidon Bagwell.

For a week after the death of Chrysalis Rabican, alongside Goolsby Lamb and Phineas Tunvel, Sidon fought the ghouls and demons left behind until they had no choice but to burn Heath's Night to the ground to purify it.

Two years later, a new settlement of Dirts, as Muddy referred to those who were not Urian, appeared and built a new village on the hill above the dam, hoping to get more from the long-abandoned mines in those hills. As Heath's Night was leagues from Haniel's Valley where the Fox Clan resided, the Bagwells were not fussed.

A nightmare came to Sidon on the night before he became a father for the third time. This felt different than the others. As if it were a memory, something real.

In the dream, a newborn baby cried out, abandoned, and alone in a sea of small monkeys that seemed agitated at the human child's presence. The place appeared to be a temple built around the remains of an old ship.

Sidon felt a disembodied spirit, as he witnessed a three-eyed, young man scurry away from the temple, being chased by hungry ravagers. The monsters all dripping, fanged teeth, torn fur of black and blood, ruined wolves with glowing red eyes stopped their pursuit as if they sensed the spirit Sidon watching them.

The baby in the temple continued to scream. Sidon realized with a haunting certainty that he was that baby, and he was watching the day that Phineas Tunvel, Goolsby Lamb, and Dagan Brude found him thirty-two years ago.

Sidon attempted to escape these visions, even pinched himself, but he could not wake. He watched as Goolsby Lamb, all smiles, cradled the baby and took him away as the night fell.

Ambriel, we know your secret, bitch. We will kill the child of Janus. The Sentinels will be defeated. We will have this world. The very one you sent to defeat us will bring about the fall of the Eternal Kingdom. It is written.

The grim specter hissed in Sidon's mind as he found himself floating above the darkening temple watching the young, three-eyed man climbing into the rubble, searching.

"Jabber? Where are you?"

With that, the specter faced Sidon eye to eye, scythe in hand, ready to strike. And in front of him the image of a woman, terrifying to behold, skeletal, flayed and burned skin, her organs, half-eaten, bursting from her belly, flanked in a scent of roses and wild rivers, stood between him and the blade. She struck with unnatural claws sending the specter reeling back into the darkness.

You will not have my brother, you foul thing. I am Phaedra. I am your end.

"Phaedra, what are you doing?" Sidon called. "I tried to save you..."

Phaedra turned on him, and he recoiled at the light emanating around her, unquenchable, a shield in the darkness. Phaedra hissed at him.

Wake up, you fool, or Hell will take you.

Sidon jerked awake to the sound of something breaking in the kitchens below. Elayne looked annoyed as he emerged from his room.

"You overslept," she said. "I've had a letter from my aunt in Ambriland."

"Does Delilah have a new list of my faults?" Sidon asked. He did not get on with his wife's aunt, a pirate who found Sidon's propensity to become ill at sea a sign of some inner defect, rendering him a poor match for her niece.

"She's built a house for her and her little girl on one of Ambriland's outlier islands. And she has a new ship."

"That's great. She'll be pillaging the empires from sea to shining sea. I wish her luck," Sidon said, pulling on his good, long-sleeved, cotton tunic, the one with only three holes in it. His wife had turned his favorite into cleaning rags when it was more holes than shirt.

"Sidon, she's invited us all to visit her," Elayne said. "And Ambriland is lovely. I've always wanted to visit the tropics."

"It's on the other side of the world. It's so far. And we don't have a ship…"

"We're going. And we will have fun. I command you have fun," Elayne said.

"Laynie. I don't want too. I'm tired," Sidon said, whining the way his children sometimes did.

"If you would sleep properly. Let me mix you up something tonight."

"I had a doozy of a nightmare, didn't I?"

"You did. You still have the nightmares about Phaedra?"

"Intense. She calls me brother in them. I don't know what she means?"

"Sidon, you could easily have a sister," Elayne said. "Maybe she was sacrificed in the temple where you were found as a child…"

"Goolsby, Dagan, and Phineas always insisted I was alone on an altar in that temple apart from all the monkeys. The temple was built around the remains of that ship hundreds of miles inland. When they returned after securing me with Rinsola Bagwell, the temple still remained but the altar was gone. But yes, I suppose I could have a sister or any number of siblings."

"The whole affair is strange. The ship makes more sense than the temple. It is documented that our valley was once a great sea," Elayne said. "Back when the world was bigger and Alleysiande existed."

"I suppose," Sidon said. "Did Saylor Maule-Finn have her baby?"

"It's early yet. A fourth child can come suddenly so I checked on her this morning," Elayne said. "You know something, Sidon, maybe this spirit that calls itself Phaedra thinks you're bhante? That's why it calls you brother? I mean you do tend to dress like a monk who has taken a vow of poverty."

"It's a dream. Just my mind being all crazy."

The couple spoke in hushed whispers so the children would not hear. After receiving their Spawning Graffs, the tattoo bracelets that marked all who joined Uriel's Covenant, it seemed Jesper and Sid-Jynx's memory of Heath's Night disappeared. Or lost its terror. Neither child made inquiries after their dead sister, Chrysalis.

"All these horrors have turned good for us," Laynie said, giving Sidon a quick kiss on his stubbled cheek. "I got a wonderful husband from that cursed temple and two amazing children from Heath's Night."

"They are wonderful, aren't they?" Sidon said, a little grin on his scruffy face, as a cry that was less than wonderful erupted from their kitchen. "And they are more than enough…"

"Mom. Jesper turned me purple," their seven-year-old daughter called out.

"Jesper, have you been doing alchemy in the kitchen?" Elayne said, heading down the dark steps to the little kitchen on the ground floor below their sleeping loft. "I told you not to…"

Sidon followed his wife down the narrow stair into the kitchen to see Jesper lying on his back side, a broken pestle at his hand, and Sid-Jynx pointing at him with a very purple hand, her silky, brown hair striped now in purple. When she turned, Sidon could not decide to laugh or cry. The girl's olive skin had gone entirely violet.

"Why did you take a potion from him?" Sidon asked his daughter.

"He said it was juice."

"It was juice…mostly," Jesper said as the dogs began barking at a knock at the door.

"Did Pappa Lamb teach you this potion?" Sidon asked.

"Mostly," Jesper said.

"Can you reverse this?" Elayne asked, looking exasperated.

"I could but Sid-Jynx broke my pestle."

"We will get you another one. Fix this and Sid-Jynx, stop taking anything that could be a potion from him. He's not going to change. At least you're not covered in itchy spots this time," Sidon said. "Grumble, Rufus, shut up. I can hear the door, you two mutts."

The two dogs, both sizable hounds that threatened to knock Sidon down as he traversed the parlor toward the front door where the knock repeated in more urgency as thunder rumbled outside.

"Don't let the dogs out," Sid-Jynx cried. "They'll scare away our last two totem foxes, and we haven't turned them purple yet."

Sidon ignored his daughter's plea. The dogs needed to be out. In the rain. Away from him. He stomped toward the insistent banging.

"Turning his sister purple. What in the world? He's ten. Ten. And what is Goolsby teaching him? Is there ever a need to turn anyone purple?"

"If this is about one of my patients, get Granville Broomes to go and assess and tell him I will be there shortly. Let me make sure our daughter is not permanently purple first," Elayne called.

"It's not Granville's day. I thought that new intern…"

"Get Granville. Claire is visiting her parents this week at the Bear Clan, remember?"

"I can't keep up with all your apprentices and students," Sidon said but not so Elayne would hear him.

Sidon opened the door mid-knock and found himself face to face with Goolsby Lamb and a host of men.

In his arms, Goolsby held a newborn baby.

With Goolsby, stood the white-haired Phineas Tunvel, an enormous crossbow and battle-axe on his back. Next to Phineas stood his son, Edge, who looked a giant in the group with half his head shaved and the other half with a long lock of braided, golden hair. This was Sidon's oldest friend in all the clans. Edge had been born the week Sidon had been found in the broken temple in Haniel's Valley.

In front of Edge was a tall and slender boy, Edge's twelve-year-old son, Emlyn Tunvel, who had the silkiest and prettiest, yellow long-hair Sidon had ever seen on boy or girl.

"We were hunting," Goolsby said as in way of explanation that explained nothing. "Chasing a goat.."

"A buck," Phineas said.

"A buck goat…"

"Just a buck," Emlyn said as the four entered the house and the dogs escaped out into the rain. The baby gave a little cry with a stretch of arms, opening its eyes to reveal pale blue.

"We found this baby," Phineas said. "In the same place Goolsby, Dagan, and I found you all those years ago when you were newborn, Si."

"Exactly the same place according to my father," Edge said. "Isn't that creepy?"

"Umm…"

"Who is it?" Elayne asked as she appeared in the parlor with Sid-Jynx whose skin had faded from deep violet to soft lavender.

"It's…"

"Laynie, how is your sweet self?" Goolsby said, striding past Sidon and pushing the baby into her arms. "We got you a baby. It's a boy."

"Oh my," Elayne said, nestling the babe close to her. "I have baby's milk, for the new mothers I care for that have trouble breast-feeding. Phineas, do you mind?"

"Not at all dear," Phineas said, carefully placing his weapons in the entry stand where his son and grandson placed theirs, causing a clanking mess. Phineas made his way toward the kitchen. He was a frequent visitor and knew his way around both kitchen and alchemy den.

"Oh mom, can we keep him?" Sid-Jynx said, her eyes lighting up to the size of saucers.

"It's not a puppy," Sidon said, unable to process everything. "We can't…"

"Oh, I think we can," Elayne said. "Let me just message Meagan. She can take over for me for a couple of days. We can borrow a couple of healers from Polecat and Rabbit Clans if needed as we did when Jesper and Sid-Jynx first arrived."

"Laynie! We can't just have a baby. You have to go to Ambriland to visit your aunt."

"That can wait. She can visit us. She can bring little Siobhan. Jesper and Sid-Jynx should know their cousin."

"Laynie, we can't have another baby. We're busy…"

"But this baby is yours," Goolsby said. "Look at his eyes. Blue like Sidon's one blue eye. And we found him…"

"My eye is much darker blue…"

"He's a baby. It'll come darker as he grows older," Edge said. "We found him."

"In the creepy temple ruin that I was found when I was a baby. Was he surrounded by monkeys like I was?"

"There were no monkeys," Emlyn said. "On account of the ravagers. This little potato is lucky he wasn't eaten."

"All of us are," Edge said. "This is great, Sidon. You and I will have kids the same age."

"How is Eugenie? She's due soon, right?" Elayne asked, gently rocking the baby.

"In a month, maybe less now. There's just explosion of babies in the forty clans right now. It's a good thing," Edge said. "My boy and I didn't mean to be gone so long. You should have seen that buck. It was a beauty."

"Like the buck goat we chased when we found you, son," Goolsby said, smiling widely at Sidon as if finding an abandoned baby in a demonic temple a second time to be the greatest thing that had ever happened.

"Is Jesper around?" Emlyn asked.

"He turned me purple," Sid-Jynx said.

"Looks good on you," Emlyn said as if purple girls were a common sort of thing. "I like it. I'd stay purple if I were you. Gives you character."

"You're an idiot," Sid-Jynx said, shaking her head. "Mom, what is the baby's name?"

"This is a trick, isn't it?" Sidon said, searching for explanation other than a second baby being found in a creepy temple in the desolate part of Haniel's Valley.

"I like the name, Trick," Sid-Jynx said.

"He did not mean that as a name," Elayne said.

"But it's a good name. He could be a pirate. Trick Bagwell."

"A pirate would be excellent," Emlyn said in agreement. "C'mon Sid-Jynx, let's go see what Jesper is up to. Maybe we can make you all rainbow colored."

"Or maybe you both could just go jump off a cliff. That would be good. Jesper is going to try and color-coat our fox totems, so we'll know when the Maule-Finns steal them off us," Sid-Jynx said. "At least, Jesper knows the potion works."

"A purple fox? Would look better on a rabbit, no?"

"He could turn your family's totem rabbits purple if you like. Or pink. I don't like pink myself so you could have all the potion for pink."

"Bright orange would be good. All our totem rabbits are brown and there are way too many," Emlyn said. "Mom keeps saying she's going to open a new restaurant that specializes in rabbit stew if they don't quit eating all the strawberries in her garden."

"You're not supposed to eat your totem animals," Sid-Jynx said.

"Not if you are the Fox Clan or the Cobra Clan," Emlyn said. "But what else are rabbits good for but making little rabbits and eating?"

"Run along, children," Elayne said. "Jesper is in the alchemy lab trying to fashion an antidote for his sister."

"I will see you soon, baby brother, Trick," Sid-Jynx said, giving the child a kiss and then scampering off after Emlyn Tunvel, no longer concerned that she was purple.

Sidon secretly feared for Emlyn and Jesper. His daughter was a crafty sort, and he could see the little tendrils of mischief forming in her eyes.

"How long am I to have a purple daughter?" Sidon asked.

"Another hour or so at worst," Elayne said. "If Jesper can't craft an antidote, it wears off on its own."

"Oh, yes that coloring potion I taught Jesper," Goolsby said, clamping his hands together and plopping himself down in Sidon's favorite cushioned chair in the parlor.

"Goolsby, why teach our son a potion to turn someone purple?" Elayne asked.

"It was for the baby goats in The Oasis. Galena likes when they are all bright colors, so I learned it for her. It wasn't meant for people. But I promise it is harmless," Goolsby said. "Now, let me have a look at baby Trick."

"We are not calling our son, Trick. I think we shall call him Liam after my great grandfather and the oracle in that story that Sid-Jynx likes so much," Elayne said, her voice off in dreamland. There would be no reasoning with her. She was in love, and Sidon found himself the father of three.

"Liam Trick Bagwell then," Sidon said, relenting to both girls. He took the baby into his arms, the blue eyes staring at him as if they knew him.

"I like that," Elayne said.

Sidon rubbed his finger along a thin gash on the baby's

forehead, dead center between his eyes. The child fussed at Sidon's touch. "What happened to his forehead?"

"Injured. Maybe a rock," Edge said. "It's healing. We think he's fine."

"There was an earthquake," Phineas said, handing Elayne a goat-nipple bottle. "We won't find any more babies in that temple."

"The shaking started when the ravagers surrounded us," Edge said. "Emlyn heard the baby crying. We didn't hear over all the yodeling of the ravagers. Emlyn climbed into the temple before the earth swallowed it. I thought I'd lost my son and he emerged holding the baby."

"He said he heard the baby crying miles before we got to the temple," Phineas said. "Don't know how he could have. It's why we lost track of the buck."

"Glorious goat," Goolsby Lamb said, dreamingly. "We would have had the best feast."

"It was a buck, Pappa Lamb, a deer, not a goat," Edge said, knowing his protests were useless. Anything with horns was a goat to Goolsby Lamb, the sole member of the Muddy Goat Clan, be it a sheep, a moose, or a unicorn. All were goats. He loved his horned animals.

"Never mind," Phineas said. "And I do not think we should ever pursue that buck again. We are fortunate my grandson can hear the way he does, or this baby would not have survived."

"Wonder how many babies have died in that temple since my dad and Pappa Lamb found Sidon here," Edge said.

"I don't like to think of it," Phineas said. "For once my grandson's defiance was a useful thing."

"We should know better than to ignore Emlyn when he says he hears something," Edge said. "He hears things better than an Igamie Hound."

"And that awful temple was destroyed by an earthquake?" Sidon asked.

"Swallowed entirely. Turned upside down. Good thing too," Edge said. "Think it was one of Moloch's old temples by the symbols we found around it. My dad does not agree. It had to be Icarian, demonic. Pit Beasts everywhere. Not just the ravagers. There were signs of a Fire Snake nest, thrower scorpions, and those giant scarab beetles that eat you alive if you let them swarm. We couldn't get out of there fast enough."

"Laynie," Sidon said, looking at his wife. "How will we keep a baby? We don't have a cradle or anything."

"We have newborn baskets for the babies I deliver. We will set up a nursery in our chamber," Elayne said. "Gentlemen, please help me prepare a room for my new son."

Before Sidon could object, he found himself alone in the parlor with the baby. An uneasy feeling filled him. He looked at the child to see if there were any stain on his soul. He had that gift. Instead, he saw a blinding light for the flash of a second that filled him simultaneously with joy and dread. Sidon blinked himself back to the solid world to find himself confronting something from ancient tales.

The gash on the baby's forehead opened up to reveal a third eye, glowing red and black. Sidon almost dropped the child, standing up and trying to call out when he found himself looking at his seven-year-old daughter standing in the door between the parlor and the front hall. She pointed toward the cushioned chair in which Goolsby Lamb had recently sat.

"Ghost," Sid-Jynx said, simply.

Sidon turned and there she was, a shadow of woman leaning forward as if she had great pain in her belly.

"Phaedra?" Sidon asked.

Brother, I need your help!

"Why do you call me brother?"

And then she was gone, the third eye on the infant's forehead closed, the gash almost invisible. The child's human eyes opened, making little Liam Trick Bagwell seem an ordinary newborn. The baby let out a cry and then another.

"Trick is hungry," Sid-Jynx said. "And so am I."

"The ghost?" Sidon asked his daughter. "You saw her?"

"No, daddy," Sid-Jynx said. "Ghosts don't belong with the living. You have to leave ghosts alone. Remember Chrysalis?"

Kentigern's Dust

"Nope," Zac Grimm said out loud as The Rooke completed his tale. "That's impossible."

"What?" The Rooke asked, feeling confused.

"I heard your tale in The Sorcerer's Cottage the other night. I heard it. You're saying this Sidon Bagwell is the infant son of the mythical sorcerer, Janus, and that Imogen Vasilis girl. That's what you're hinting at, right? And this infant is the oracle. Only he's gotten all the way younger."

"I am not hinting at anything, young man," The Rooke said. "I am telling you a story. To amuse, to lighten the mood on this day of our destruction."

"Yeah, that did not work," Zac said. "That puzzle box – never would believe in this crap. Look at them, making a picture from blank pieces that change shape and shit. And now, magic is real and messed up."

"Is there a question here, Zac?" Thiago said, smiling at the puzzler from New Chazir.

"I wanted magic to be real. I wanted it. But this is no good. This isn't good. Look at them. Like kid shaped zombies."

A picture began to appear on the great table where Kostas and Anwyn worked. The pieces melded together seamlessly as if the two were painting with four hands and one mind. An erupting volcano shadowing a man weighed down by a golden crown.

"A dragon," Zac Grimm whispered. "See there, rising from the volcano in the smoke."

"I know this artwork," The Rooke said, a memory flickered, his or from one of the tales, he could not tell. "The Last King of Ambriland. It's unique. A Bone Master card, you know for playing the game, Idylls & Grimoires."

"What's it mean?" Zac asked.

"It was given to River Swann, and he was the final king of Ambriland," Gareth Gillespie said, slipping in among the gathered puzzlers. "Kenny sent me. He has gone to The Reliquary. He has not been able to summon the Aspects. Aldo is trying to calm Shanks down at the Dragon Neck Pub. Apparently, the children stole this box from him."

"That fool," Mika Finn said. "Shanks would not tell me what had been stolen when he accused my daughter. If he had, this would not be happening."

"Anwyn stole from Shanks?" Ghita Mist opened her mouth in wonder. "How? Anwyn is…"

"Nacharye. She can be invisible for short amounts of time," Mika said. "It is why we had to leave the empires."

"Can Anwyn change her appearance?" Ghita Mist asked.

"Of course, but it's painful so she doesn't do that often. It makes it harder to erase the blue in our skin if you change your appearance frequently," Mika said. "Invisibility is easy and useful. That's why Nacharye are feared and hunted. It makes us effective spies and assassins and scavengers."

"That is why The Fistian Arisea enslaved them for centuries until the Nacharye died out," Thiago said.

"We didn't die out," Mika said. "We simply disappeared. There are a two of us standing right here."

Another few hours passed, people coming and going to see how the picture was coming along and to reach into The Rooke's pockets.

Zac Grimm reached in and pulled a ruby red token. The Rooke sighed.

"Hey, mine is different than the rest. Why?" Zac said, holding up his token.

"It means you will physically follow The Rooke's Path," Gareth said. "I hope you didn't have any big plans, lad."

"The Third Offers The Rooke A Master of Games and Puzzles," The Rooke said, giving Gareth a meaningful look.

He shook his head in resignation as another from his list appeared. He prayed this young man cleverer than his manner of speaking. Still young. Thirty at most. Long, brown hair, skinny, soft, and wearing clothes under his duster that made him look every bit the working class of New Chazir.

"Awesome. But my dad…"

"Leave it, Zac," Ghita Mist said. "He will be able to teach in The Learning Circles, put his natural gifts back to purpose. He will like that after he stops blaming himself for the evil done to his smartest students by the empires."

"I keep telling him that," Zac said. "But he's been sick…"

"We've healers enough, Zac. He will live a while yet. Now, let's see if we can rescue these young puzzlers."

A few hours before midnight, Anwyn slipped in the last piece. She and Kostas backed away from the puzzle and pointed to it, chanting together in old Asciendien. The Rooke attempted to translated.

"The game has begun. When the second Dragon Moon rises, the Archaics will be lost forever. The first is the key to the rest. One clue. One archaic. One curse. That is the rule…price… bargain? Damn, my Asciendien is not what it used to be. I am out of practice."

"The word is pact, father. That is the closest word in Acarian," Thiago said, also taking notes. "How long until the next Dragon Moon? I am not well-versed in astronomy. It occurs when the planet, Irial, aligns with its second moon and our moon and is at a twenty-degree parallel to Aerda's sun…oh, blast, I can't remember."

"How old are you?" Zac Grimm asked.

"Almost sixteen," Thiago said, a defiance in his voice.

"Damn. You're a little genius just like Kostas said."

"My brother said I was a genius?"

"Kid, your brother really worships you," Zac said. "I hope he's ok. I am so sorry, Rooke. I…"

"Zac, it's not your fault. And Thiago, there is a Dragon Moon every twelve years. Next one will be in eight months. I think. Maybe sooner," Ghita Mist said. "I used to pay such attention to the stars, but I have been in this mountain for centuries now. I have forgotten the night's sky. I will confirm this evening."

Thiago scribbled copious notes down in his journal as both Kostas and Anwyn tumbled to the ground, their breath faint, and eyes sealed shut.

Mika Finn charged to her daughter's side as the little dog, Hobble, whined terrible anxiety, limping on his three, squat legs around the little girl, nudging at her with his flat nose, one sharp ear back, the other high on alert.

"How do we wake them?" Mika asked. "There must be some spell."

Grandmaster Mist stuttered, her eyes wide with fear as The Rooke looked to her for answer. He tried to remember the tales of the forging of the Twelve Archaics, the ones that told what they had been. His mind clouded as if some spell were blocking information that he was sure he had known at one time. He mastered himself.

"Rooke, I will help. I'm great at riddles and puzzles. I will make this right," Zac Grimm said. "I figured out the key to open the box. I can figure out how to close it without blowing up the world."

"I appreciate that, lad," The Rooke said. "Stay here and look after the children. Jeanna, get a healer. You lot, come with me. The Relic must sort this."

The cold stone bowl of The Relic chamber felt empty as the full space of the night sky without the Aspects of The Relic there to fill it. The Rooke stood with Mika Finn, Ghita Mist, Thiago, and Gareth Gillespie while Kentigern Dagan Leesh sat at the table below the raised platform.

He glared at The Rooke as if betrayed. The seven ornate daises stood vacant, looking a ruin absent the Aspects. The Rooke had never been in this chamber without being summoned and so had never witnessed it empty.

"Will they be long?" Gareth asked.

"You were not expected," Kentigern said, glancing up from his long desk, without stopping his work. "They will appear if they think your query worth their time. They have things to do, you know."

"Saving all creation is not worth their time?" Ghita Mist said, arms crossed in front of her.

"Time is not worth their time," the graying bronze-haired scrivener said without looking up from the tome he wrote in. "Dust we all are. Dust we will be again."

The Rooke felt his old friend's growing despair from where he stood. Kentigern feared he would fail to protect once more. The Rooke knew. He spoke gently.

"The dust needs an audience," The Rooke said. "My quest will save the Aspects as well..."

"The dust is acknowledged," The Fourth Aspect said from above. The Rooke had not seen the tall, robed, and hooded creature appear, although he sensed a warmth trickling into the cold room.

"My younger son and another child are…"

"We are aware," The Sixth popped into The Rooke's vision as the other five appeared, straightening their robes, standing themselves up straight.

Mika Finn stood bold before The Relic, her anger feeling as dangerous as the quakes that were now assaulting The Reliquary at regular intervals.

"Ah, Mika Finn," The Fourth Aspect said before the woman could speak. "Good, you and your daughter must accompany our Rooke below."

"I can't. I won't," Mika said. "My daughter lies unable to wake."

"The children will wake in time for all preparations to be made," The Sixth Aspect said. "I will see to it."

"We know who you are, Mikhaela Chrysalis Finn," The Seventh Aspect said. "Did you think you could hide it from us?"

"Why would I even try? The actions of my great, great, great, great grandmother have nothing to do with me. She sold her first three children. The world is a cruel place for a woman on her own, even before The Evanescence. It was no easier for me, but I did the right thing. I protected my child. You promised me she would be safe here," Mika said, her voice losing none of its defiance before The Seven. "I know what you are as well, Relic, failures of the past."

The Rooke startled at both her tone and her admission, a distant relative of the children of Heath's Night. That was no coincidence.

With The Relic, what they left to chance went unnamed. They were dangerous and he wondered that Mika did not feel her peril in gazing at them in such anger. He supposed her concern for her daughter overrode her fear of The Relic.

For himself, The Rooke felt The Relic's power emanating from above, that of a booted boy carrying a glass above a hill of ants. A gesture would turn the lot of them into Kentigern's dust if it pleased the gathered Aspects.

"Can you not lure the ice dragon back to sleep to give me more time?" The Rooke said. "I will never make it down the mountain if it falls on me as I travel below."

A deafening roar filled the Inner Sanctum as Aldo Thierry burst through the double doors. "We're under attack…"

"What?" Kentigern said, rising from behind his desk.

"Imperial special forces came from the scavenger tunnels. They are looking for The Red Quarter…they're murdering as they go."

"Scarlet Bans? Here?" The Rooke asked. "Impossible."

"Go to The Dragon Neck. Seventh, take them," The Fourth said. "How did our protections fail?"

"When the engineers blasted the scavenger tunnels back open, it revealed them," Aldo said. "A couple hundred of the blighters."

"My daughter. The children," Mika said, turning to go after them.

"They are awake. They are fine," Aldo said. "Those master puzzlers, Zac and Jeanna, have taken them and the other puzzlers to the Dragon Neck. We have sealed all the double doors and told everyone to stay in their quarters. That big-bearded fellow, Aleron, has amassed several fighting men. The Scarlets are not this high yet, and we are closing the lifts. Follow me."

"Second, go and try and calm the dragon," The Fourth said. "Mika, we have need of your services. Kentigern, make a list of everything The Rooke and his companions will need. Get this scavenger to help you get it all. She can be invisible. Meet in the Dragon Neck. You leave tonight. Shanks will show you the secret path."

Tavern VI:

The Cross-Eyed Hag

Demons are attracted to magic like flies to shit. A powerful sorcerer, trained or not, must learn to contend with the worst of the damned or become one of them.

The Idylls of Alleysiande, Vol VIII. Malachi's Sorcerer
author unknown (translated by Hazel Kyran)

Leaving The Reliquary

Shanks, the barkeep of the Dragon Neck Pub, towered over little Anwyn Finn. His face was red in rage.

"You fool girl," Shanks said as the young girl stood defiant before him. "I warned you and you've doomed us all."

"This has nothing to do with the box," Anwyn said, looking full of venom. "The imperials already knew where the rookes hid. Everyone knows Bracken Grayvesone told them everything. It was your stupid dragon that exposed us, made it unsafe."

"Leave her be, Shanks," Kostas said. "We weren't doing anything wrong. We were solving a puzzle box. We. Are. Puzzlers. That is what we do."

"The box wanted to be opened," Anwyn said. "It wasn't our fault."

"You little arrogant…"

"Choose your next words very carefully, Shanks," Mika Finn said, entering the pub alongside The Rooke. She stepped between the towering keeper and her daughter. "This is nothing to do with Ani. If anyone is at fault, it is you. All you had to do is say what you thought was taken, and she would not have had it."

"The Scarlet Bans did not come out of the cube," The Rooke said. "Shanks, stand down. The box is open, but it is not responsible for this attack. Ambriel's tribulations are far more nuanced."

"Ambriel's Cube is perilous, yes, but it is also hope," The Sixth Aspect said, entering the room with Tavares Flaco and Aleron Ramses, both splattered in blood, panting, exhausted. "The Scarlets are defeated. Our protections are restored for now. We have captured some. Shanks, these gathered here must leave this night."

"Mika, we need your considerable skills. We will need clothes for all these, including Aleron and Tavares. Imperial grays. Plain as you like to make us all but invisible to the imperials below," Kentigern said, taking a scroll and scribbling furiously. "Good walking boots for the lot. Socks, thick and warm."

"You're going, Kenny?" Shanks said, voice softening with compassion. "All right then. But you all, be careful with that wee lass. She looks a pretty thing. But that one is dangerous as fire."

"What of sleeves? We can't go below with scarred wrists," Mika Finn said.

"We have a way of crafting them," Aldo said, plopping down a fat pack, and pulling out a box filled with ribbons, thin strips of various metals, all sorts of straps, tiny screws and pieces, an engraving tool, and a metal cutter. "They'll not know the difference. I can make almost any kind of sleeve at all and connect them to SIN once we are off this mountain."

"Ah, what is going on?" A girl stepped out from the shadows of the bar. "I came here to meet friends and…"

"Cymbre? You shouldn't be here," Aleron said. "I will get you back to your quarters. There has been an incident. You could have been hurt."

"Yeah, I need to go back to my place," Zac Grimm said. "To check on my dad. I need my sword."

"People don't really use swords anymore," The Rooke said.

"Yes, people do, and we must," Aleron said, holding up the broad sword he wielded. "Imperials don't."

Tavares held forth his curved sword. "They forget how useful these weapons are," Tavares said, with a slight smile on his face. "Ali and I are from Marlinea. We trained with these as boys. As sport. Not for battle. But unspoken, we knew that one day we might have to use them to defend ourselves. Our fathers and grandfathers could see what was happening with the empires. Imperials are easy prey if you can get close to them. They are mostly slow, fat, and lazy as the careless hand canons they wield."

"Guardians always use swords, daggers, and sometimes

bows," Kentigern said. He gave Zac a steady look. "You know how to use a sword, lad?"

"I do. Like them two. New Chazir thought the same. My dad loved playing swords with me when I was a kid. Only my sword is not a weapon. It's ceremonial. It was a gift," Zac said. "It's important to me. I don't wish to leave it behind."

"Are you really leaving for Talon directly?" Cymbre asked. "Because I need to get there. I tried to go earlier, but they told me I could not use the scavenger tram because it was blocked and unstable due to the earthquakes."

"We could take her, I think," Aldo said. "We are going that way anyhow, and I think we'll be safe until we cross the Boreallean Sea."

"Do as you will," The Sixth said.

"I will get your things," Mika said. "Including this sword of yours, Zac."

"I need to let Bittore know I am leaving," Tavares Flaco said. "And I'd like a tunic that doesn't have blood all over it."

"Tavares and I will come with you, Mika," Aleron said. "We can both let our wives know what is happening as we gather our things. And we'll need a disguise for Tavares. He is too well known below."

The Sixth had disappeared. The Rooke shook his head. He pulled his robes close about him. "Shanks, is the tunnel to the Sentinel tram undamaged?"

"We'll find out," Shanks said. "When that scavenger returns, you all will follow me. It's a bit of a hike to the tram, a lot of secret doors to keep it hidden."

"I will stay at The Reliquary for the moment," Ghita Mist said. "And find you later, Rooke. You look after my puzzlers. This party is large enough."

"No worries. I will see no harm will come to them," The Rooke said. "Maybe I can find a way to leave them all in Talon which is still defensible against the empire."

"No chance of that," Kentigern said, a whisper only The Rooke could hear. "Zac and Anwyn are on your list."

"Yes, but we are short a good many from the list…"

"They'll turn up," Kentigern said as Kostas and Thiago approached with plates of food.

"I worry about my lads," The Rooke said.

"You could leave your boys with my son and grandchildren in Talon," Kentigern said. "If you want."

"No, Kostas and I are with you, father," Thiago said, overhearing. "Until the end. Nothing will stop us following you."

The tram sped through dark tunnels, over immeasurable caverns, twisting along an overhanging track, diving deeper and deeper down, twisting, and turning through forgotten passages.

Anwyn, Kostas, and Zac Grimm loved the speed and watched out the tram window as the darkness of the inside of the immense mountains sped by them. Thiago slept. The Rooke felt sick. Tavares and Aleron strapped in across from him and Aldo.

"You know, this is a good plan to get you to the valley," Tavares Flaco said, holding tight to the side rails of his seat. "We will be below the tree line, and the weather is not so terrible on this side of Primordial Boreal. It's a short ferry ride from Dream Land to Mal Leshen…"

"No, that is no good. We must avoid Mal Leshen," Mika Finn said. "The rest of the Scarlets will be there looking for rookes. They were hoping to push you out of your hidey hole with that attack. That is clear."

"They succeeded," The Rooke said. "I am pushed out of my home. And there are no more of us."

"We must go to Talon. Mal Leshen is not in our plans. We will go cross country," Kentigern said. "Perhaps our scavenger can ferret us a transport. Or we could walk. In snow-covered hills and through thick icy forests filled with hungry beasts."

"Yes, that would make a great tale," Aldo said, making sure he was secure under his seat's tie-in. "Although, I fear our

Rooke would find it hard to tell his stories from the inside of a pack of hungry wolves or hunting cat."

"Or a giant mountain bear," Mika Finn said. "This was how Anwyn and I tried to come to The Reliquary three years ago. There may not be storybook monsters, but it turns out the giant bears are alive and well and very hungry. I will get us a transport in Dream Land, but first we must survive Sentinel Peak."

The tram came to sudden, jarring stop. A single flickering light hinted at a deep stone cavern that served as the tram station. An usher with a lantern guided the group through a narrow tunnel, up a long staircase through a passage dug in stone.

A door opened onto a dark alley that caused The Rooke to gasp as it led outside into the cold of the mountainous city of Sentinel Peak. The guide signaled the group to stay back as he pushed forward between two close stone buildings.

"Be quick," he said, prompting The Rooke to push Kostas and Thiago in front of him toward a dark street under gathering clouds, empty and running beside dilapidated buildings. They passed a boarded-up passageway with a faded sign hanging over the arch way.

"Everyone, take a screen, attach a sleeve, a ribbon, and put them on," Aldo said. "They all look too new, so try to keep them under your shirts and coats."

The thick-necked man distributed the metal bracelets that mimicked Imperial Sleeves. The Rooke took one of rose gold with a white ribbon, an artisan sleeve. He adjusted his guitar on his back, grateful that Mika had managed to secure it.

The rest sported blue steel acceptable sleeves with white ribbons, marking all the adults as laborers. Thiago, Kostas, and Anwyn were given yellow-ribboned steel probate sleeves, marking them as average as average went for young imperials.

"This isn't going to work for me," Zac Grimm said, holding up his sleeve. "I have never been acceptable. And I'll be recognized here. I won two tournaments here."

"What sleeve did you wear?" Aldo asked.

"Gray despicable ribbon on a notable copper sleeve," Zac

said, grinning with pride. "I was both despicable and notable all at once. It's why I was so popular. Empire disapproved of me. People loved me for the gaming."

"What did you do to be despicable?" Mika Finn asked.

"Lots of things. My mom. She was in debt when she died, and my dad and I refused to pay the debt. My dad said things he wasn't supposed to say out loud, and I defended him. And I told the empire they could…I won't repeat in front of kids."

"That's a first," Anwyn said. "You curse in front of us all the time."

"We don't want you recognized. Let's see what we can do," Aldo said. "Mika, is there a hooded jacket he could wear, something to disguise him in the meantime?"

"We should cut his hair, put some spectacles on him, and he can wear the hood up once outside," Mika said, giving the skinny, young man an appraising look.

"He's known for being ratty," Cymbre Varian said, stepping into the group. "I remember you, Zac. I watched the tournament you won. If you clean him up like Mika said, no one will remember him. He made a game of being despicable."

"I have no hair to cut, and I had great style," Tavares said. "Not many fans of sport here, but still I wore a celebrated sleeve."

"These imperials don't look much at faces. Always it's the sleeves," Aleron said. "If your sleeve is acceptable and not celebrated, I think they will not make the association. Especially if we put a knit cap on you so they can't tell if you are bald."

"Let's move on," Aldo said, giving the guide a nod.

"From here forward, imperial eyes are everywhere," the guide said as he unlatched a door, hidden around a corner, that seemed to cut into the mountain. The Rooke secured his artisan sleeve and pulled tight his gray jacket.

The Rooke remembered a destination meant to teach the world about Alleysiande and its Sentinels. It included parks of entertainments, several universities, the best hospital, and medical facilities to ever exist. The extraordinary campuses of Sentinel Peake were the first to rival Dalmeade's multiple universities and hospitals in the Pre-Evanescent Era.

All the residents of the original Sentinel Peake had disappeared with the Muddy at The Evanescence or were slaughtered by the empires in the bloody years leading to The Subjugation.

For almost a hundred years after, it had been a ghost town. A rich man, inspired by rooke tales, filled with dreams of a better world for his two little girls, decided to breathe life back into the place. He turned it into a destination full of amusements, a ski resort, and a place that celebrated both magic and technology. For a while, it had been good, and many from The Reliquary visited, returning from their holidays with renewed hope. The dragons slept well during those years.

For a brief second, The Rooke could hear the music, the bustle, see the lights into the distance in a time past, filled with stories and amusements to fuel people's imaginations that they might be inspired to restore Alleysiande from the world that remained.

Grief crept upon him as he ventured further into the streets of Sentinel Peake. The imperials left little to remember the original destination. Progress they called it. The imperials disparaged the rich man who tried to restore it. His name forgotten. The Rooke winced. That good man had been taken, body, soul, and legacy by The Hierarchy of Hell.

The Rooke raged at the arrogance of the ones who made this place so mundane, killing its magic. Flickering screens dotted the main thoroughfare, casting its light and shadow over the crowds below, broadcasting adverts to celebrate the Unity Conference in Aroghotto City, how all the world's leaders would be there, and at last Aerda would be one.

The constant buzz of flickering electricity and speeding transports from the tube trains and crowds of people mulling about, looking constantly at their sleeve screens while speaking out loud, to no one visible. None of them noticed The Rooke and his companions nor the ruins around them amid the ghastly hotels and buildings of steel and glass.

"I used to love coming here to Mordecai's Mountain, to the amusement park inside the mountain. Four glorious roller coasters, one in the shape of a dragon where you could pretend you were riding on Tem's back," Kentigern said with a sigh. "My mother used to bring me in the summer when I was a lad. Why did you never go, Rooke? She always invited you."

"Too many ghosts," The Rooke said. "I remember from before The Evanescence when you might be able to ride a true dragon. It could never be that again. I did appreciate the attempt to be true to the magic of that time."

Aldo had them check into The Hotel Sentinel in small groups. This grand hotel, forty stories high, housed a great tavern called The Cross-Eyed Hag, named for a famous pub that had been part of the old Pirate Isles in the Marlinean Straits hundreds of years ago. In the frozen mountains, this pub had an island theme that recalled nothing of the true tavern to The Rooke.

"The food here is pretty good," Zac Grimm said as they gathered that evening. "They used to serve a mean steak. I used to eat a diet that made other people fat."

"Another reason for your despicable standing," Cymbre said, taking a seat next to him at a tall table. "I like steak. Never could afford it."

"Well, I am going to buy you one then," Zac said. "Old man, do these things have credits?"

"They do. And my name is Aldo. Not old man, lad. Credits are unlimited so be careful. Too much spending will alert the gilders, and we don't want them after us."

"Can we play games here?" Anwyn asked. "Do Kostas and I have credits?"

"You do," Aldo said. "But again, remember you are children. Buy chicken and chips. Play the noisy, lit-up games. Behave as imperial children. You can help him with that right, Ani."

"Let's have our dinner and get back to our rooms," The Rooke said. "I find this place uncomfortable."

Thiago

Thiago strapped into the secret tram next to his brother across from Zac Grimm, the girl called Cymbre, and Anwyn Finn. He said nothing of his fears. The tram car reminded him of an egg and felt about as sturdy.

He held fast to the bar that held him in place as the tram lurched forward and started to wind downward, gathering speed as the angle became sharper until it felt like the car was free-falling. He closed his eyes tight and felt more than miles going by. He felt time folding into fractured memory.

Thiago remembered himself a small child, age four, carrying his infant half-brother, hiding in the open along busy streets, not knowing where to go. A vile man stepped out of the shadows, pieces of spun caramel in his greasy palms. He smelled so bad, worse than when baby Kostas required a fresh nappy.

"Pretty boy, is your mother working? I have candy for you. That would be real nice, wouldn't it?"

Thiago did not like sweets. He never had so the temptation did not fool him. He glared.

"Go away," he said. "My father is near. He will cut you."

His father, the one who sired him, was dead. This was the first lie he had ever told. The baby's father had disappeared. His mother was hurt bad. Cut up, not moving. She had yelled at him as bad men attacked. She said to hide, to take the baby and run. He snuck out into a rainy night in streets he had known all his short life, that looked alien in the dark and wet gloom.

The baby was heavy. So heavy. Thiago couldn't run anymore. He did not know what to do. He dragged himself into a crowded shop, one his mother used to bring him to for new socks. He held tight his little brother who fussed and cried.

"Quiet, baby. Be quiet," he begged, as he pushed his way out a back door into a dark alley.

A miracle there. A beggar, black and gray hair dark and curly, tangled beard, wearing rags and old tie-up boots with holes in them. The vagrant smiled at Thiago. The man looked wild and crazy. Thiago wanted to scream.

"No, no. I won't hurt you," the beggar said. Thiago recognized the man. His mother used to give him coins and a blanket. The man would not accept anything else, not even a warm bed to sleep in.

"Imam was nice to you," Thiago said. His language different than it was now.

"Yes, she was, and I will help you. Come. You'll be safe with me. I know a place where you will be safe and loved. It's far, very far, but I can get you there."

Thiago, are you paying attention? This is important. That is the maligned beggar. This quest will not succeed without him. And he has lost his name.

Thiago jerked awake as the tram came to a sudden stop. That voice spoke to him all the time now. Even when he was awake. Always, right before the recent quakes that voice would ask things of him. Impossible things. He clutched his pack of books, his head pounding.

Kostas was smiling at him. "You passed out," Kostas said, pointing at him. "Wow, Thiago."

"Did not. Fell asleep. I was dreaming," Thiago said. "I bet you enjoyed that ride."

"I want to do it again," Kostas said. "Come, turtle brother. Grab that giant shell of books you wear on your back. We're going to play some games."

Thiago did not want to go to The Cross-Eyed Hag, but the others insisted. He followed along. He fell quiet in the crowd. He tended to be more an observer than a participant. He scribbled a few notes about the hotel, how it felt luxurious but corrupt all at once. He glanced at his faux-sleeve and the square-clock-like face that went black unless you spoke into it, and thought how uncomfortable the real ones must be, mounted to trackers implanted in living veins of the wrist.

His father looked paralyzed as they made their way down from their rooms to the tavern for supper. Zac Grimm seemed buoyed, smiling for the first time Thiago could remember.

"Father, is everything all right?"

"I remember another world," his father said. "Come, let's go and see what lies in wait."

The Rooke looked all wrong to Thiago, dressed in gray imperial trousers, a white button up shirt, a long waistcoat on his tall, thin frame. His father looked nothing like him. Or Kostas.

Thiago could not remember the man who sired him. Instead, he recalled a little man, close-cropped dark hair, sharp nose, quick wit, well-tailored clothes, telling him happy things, smiling broadly.

This man who haunted his memories must have been his brother's father. He wondered, not for the first time, why his mother and this man had been murdered. The Rooke, his real father, the man who cared and loved him and Kostas, did not have the answers he wanted.

The Cross-Eyed Hag was immense and took up the entire second floor of the grand hotel in which the entire Rooke's party stayed. It was crowded. Thiago felt relieved. No one seemed to make note of them, given his father did not wear his red robes.

Kostas and Anwyn scooted off after eating their fill, laughing at all the amusements, tables with flashing lights, games that seemed to involve shooting a laser bow at moving targets, tables filled with dice and cards, music booming from above thick with the pounding of artificial drums and a sound that felt to Thiago like a million buzzing crickets that had lost all sense of harmony.

Zac Grimm escorted Cymbre onto the gaming floor. He looked delighted showing her how to play some game that filled a screen in front of them, lots of explosions, weapons, fighting, blood to which both laughed even as they died on screen. Thiago hated these games, wanting to return to the quiet of the rooms above.

He wondered about Cymbre, a pretty but forgettable girl.

Something was off about her. He felt it to his core. She had been a tutor to Kostas this last year, trying to teach him his math. Useless. Kostas could not sit still for long enough to learn figures and formulae.

He watched as Anwyn Finn argued with his little brother about the rules of some imperial game. He thought of going forward and taking her pack that contained that awful puzzle box but stopped short. Gasping at what he saw.

A foul, winged creature, humanoid and naked, hunched over Cymbre Varian, stalking her. He blinked. Only a man, not even looking at the woman who was laughing at Zac's attentions. The figure moved on, casting a shadow under the flashing lights.

"Father…"

"I saw it," his father said. "It's a demon on the hunt. Few see them. It is looking for souls to take so it can be elevated in The Hierarchy. Do not venture out there. If we can see it, it'll know. It will come for us, and we are more vulnerable than those who can't see it."

Thiago followed his father into a quiet, dark place in The Cross-Eyed Hag, tables abandoned in a wide area. This corner of the immense pub appeared dreary, and haunted. Thiago set his books on one of the round tables, looking at the strange rectangular indentations in front of each seat.

"Are you all right, son?" his father asked.

"These are Idylls & Grimoire tables," Thiago said. "Look at them all."

"They have not played Idylls & Grimoires since before The Evanescence," The Rooke said. "This place still has a faint magic, so it is still here. Want to play?"

"What about the demon? We should warn Cymbre," Thiago said.

"It would put us in more danger. It takes months for a demon to devour a soul, and the lass will resist since her monitor has been removed from her wrists. Do not worry," The Rooke said. "Are you sure you don't fancy a game? You have a grand deck."

"You're terrible at I&G," Thiago said, giving the man a faint smile. "If no one plays anymore, and there are no Bone Men to make the cards, why is this area here? Why has it not been replaced with all the flashy lights and automated games?"

"Protected by magic," The Rooke said.

"Why were we attracted to this place then. Should it not have repelled us?"

"This place does not need protecting from us," The Rooke smiled. "You seem to have some innate magic in you, Thiago. I think that is why The Relic insisted I take you on as my apprentice."

"I am not sure I should be your apprentice," Thiago said, sitting down heavily at one of the game tables. "Father, something is wrong with me."

"What do you mean?"

"I think the ice dragon speaks to me when I sleep. Sometimes even when I am awake. Kostas says it is a dream, but father, I know it is more than that," Thiago said. "Am I going mad?"

"No. Though it might be easier if you were," The Rooke said. "It is not surprising that the dragons seek their tales through one who still reads them in their earliest form and happens to be the best apprentice I ever taught."

"You never taught me…"

"Really? Who do you think set you up as a librarian and apprenticed you to The Reliquary's greatest linguist when you were only seven? Why do you think I take you to the Looking Glass Café so often?"

"Right. To learn the languages and the tales. Did the dragons ever speak to you?"

"Not Tem so much. It was always Phaedra with me. The sorceress and the fire dragon both," The Rooke said. "More often, the rookes who came before, reported that Tem whispered to them, begging for tales of pirates and magic, of dragons and Erelahians, of hope and possibility. The Relic said that Phaedra, the fire dragon, only ever spoke to me and Torres Rushie."

"What did the fire dragon say?"

"Let Aerda burn. There are better worlds to save."

"And the sorceress? What did she say?"

"I need more time. Give me more time."

A yell erupted from the lighted part of the pub, crowds watching something obscured from Thiago and his father's view. Uniformed Scarlet Bans were checking sleeves. Aldo's new sleeves would not pass close inspection.

"Father…"

"Relax. We must not panic," The Rooke said. "I will draw our party here. My robes will repel those who would do us harm and attract those who might aid us."

Thiago gasped. The Rooke took a seat on a stage, summoned his red robes, as the entire abandoned area came to life. A bartender appeared as if from thin air. Soft, soothing light illuminated the room, and people flocked into the area, getting drinks, taking seats, and focusing all their attention on The Rooke. Meanwhile, in the modern part of The Cross-Eyed Hag, many remained, taking no notice of the new part of the pub.

"Life is full of grief, terrible loss. Terrible pain. But it is our pain that informs us. It is through pain that we grow, we change, we create, and we learn what it is we truly value," The Rooke said, drawing the crowd in, pushing his magic as far as it could go. "Almost three hundred years ago, there lived a girl called Shanley Rose who tried to lose her grief, her guilt, and correct a wrong by taking a shortcut, by making a bargain with a witch using forbidden magic. She left a hole in the world where a memory should have lived."

The Tale of Shanley Rose's Bargain

Everything was changing. On a fine and warm spring day, six-year-old Trick Bagwell tried to hold onto a memory. He sat in the green garden next to his cottage home. He reflected that it looked a lot like the sorcerer's cottage from his dreams of when he had been the constant companion of Janus. He liked being part of the Muddy Clans. He did not like that he had to be a child. Again.

Little Keile Maule-Finn distracted him. They were the same age, and good friends as much as six-year-olds might be. The bright-eyed little girl held out a hand with food to coerce the fox toward her family's home.

"The fox is purple. It is a Bagwell totem fox," Trick said. "Keile, stop stealing. It's not nice."

"I am not stealing," she said, holding up her left wrist to display her spawning graff, a respectable dark blue for a child their age. "If I was doing something bad, this would go black. I am not. Darling Lavender can decide which garden she likes the best for herself."

"Darling Lavender?"

"I've named her. And she loves me."

"She loves food," Trick said.

He looked at his spawning graff which was burning, yelling at him through his skin, turning from storm blue to raging red, trying to push him into action. He sat on the ground and sighed. It was sad. So sad.

He left the purple fox to follow Keile Maule-Finn into her garden. He did not care about her smug smile. There were plenty of foxes to go around, and he liked ships better anyhow. Although, the Fox Clan was far from the sea.

He sought out his sister, Sid-Jynx, laughing with their older cousin, Siobhan Sage Rose. He closed the white picket gate, and crossed the cobbled road, and walked across the tall grass of the field that separated the village from the Blood Line River. His sister and cousin sat in the newly constructed gazebo by the river with their morning tea. Only when Siobhan and her mother visited was there ever tea.

"Trick, we think we might take Jesper's skiff for a sail on the Blood Line River," Sid-Jynx said. "You want to come?"

"Yes. Only, I can't," Trick said. "I have to make something not happen or we're going to have a terrible time."

"Keile Maule-Finn sneaking our foxes into her garden is not terrible. They always come back," Sid-Jynx said. "Besides, her mom, Saylor, is the Fox Clan Mother. Their burrow is our clan's longhouse so foxes in her garden also belong to everyone in the clan. So, you see, no trouble."

"No. The world is in trouble. Not the foxes. Not just the Fox Clan. But the Urians. They're coming for us."

"Who is coming?" Siobhan asked.

"Demons of The Hierarchy. They really don't like Urians."

"Trick, you are not supposed to be listening to rooke tales at the tavern. Have you been sneaking out of your bed again?" Sid-Jynx said. "Those stories are not for children. You get so scared."

Trick shook his head. He would talk to his father. Sometimes, he could get him to listen. He scampered back into the house in search of solutions. He hated being six and having a child's brain hampering his visions of tomorrow now that he was going forward in time again.

His mother and her Aunt Delilah were tormenting his father over tea. He understood that Aunt Delilah taunted his father because the expressions he made when she poked fun at him amused her.

His aunt looked the pirate she was reputed to be, the way she dressed, the sword she carried, the way she walked. Trick remembered he would be a pirate in the coming years. A famous one. If only he could keep living forward, keep things going the right way. He did not want to live backwards another time. He wanted to grow old and die as ordinary men, and at long last, get back to Alleysiande.

Today was important. He must get his parents and his aunt to listen. He took a deep breath, trying to find a way to say what he must and be believed. Adults did not take what small children said all that seriously.

"Mom, mom," he said, skipping up to give his mother a hug.

"Yes, my darling," his mother said, smiling brightly at him. "Do you want tea?"

"No. I will never want tea. It's terrible," Trick said. "Only, I have a question."

"Tea doesn't always mean bitter-tasting brown water," Aunt Delilah said. "It can mean cake."

"I don't like cake," Trick said. "My question…"

"What is it, nephew?" Aunt Delilah asked, a rare smile across her lips.

"Who is Xante Rose?" he asked.

The rain had stopped to let a rare ray of sun through in Ambriland's rainy season. The heat was terrible. Shanley Rose wished she still enjoyed swimming. She never could again. She stood in the dark hallway of the Rose Manor, fretting over the fitting of her new dress to which she was already late.

Shanley Rose's younger brother, Xante, died five years ago, and her parents blamed her. Everyone did. She heard the whispers. They were all in pity. They claimed that Shanley had been in shock, had drowned her little brother and left him in the pool. She remembered the night differently.

Xante had been two years her younger. His life ended a breath short of his fifth birthday. Shanley and Xante had snuck out of bed for a night swim in Rose Manor's glorious, indoor pool. She had not been able to convince Xante to come to bed once she was tired and filled up on splashing and playing in the lovely, cool water. How he had loved splashing around in that indoor pool. She should not have left him alone.

She had been seven when Xante died. A flicker of anger and frustration buzzed through her. The nanny should have paid better attention to them instead of taking off in the middle of the night. They had both been small children, full of mischief and devoid of any kind of sense. Nannies quit as often as they were fired, and all were warned about her and Xante.

How her father used to laugh at their exploits. Her mother would spit venom and tell her father that he was a terrible influence. Her mother had been pregnant at the time and begged her father to discipline her and Xante. Her father would smile, such a glorious thing Shanley missed. Her mother would melt like ice in the sun when her father gave that impetuous look of amusement and innocence.

Before seven-year-old Shanley could process the loss of one brother, her mother gave birth to Xavier, a few small months after Xante's funeral. Shanley fell in love with baby Xavier, always wanting to hold him and dry his tears.

Now in the room down the hall, Xavier stayed, too sick to leave his bed. Her parents worried that Xavier would not be able to attend school in the autumn due to the peculiar illness that left her brother unable to endure sunlight. A tutor had been hired to ensure Xavier's academic success.

Shanley felt mortified, pleased, and anxious all at once when her parents hired young Husk Grayvesone, an older student from her school, to teach Xavier to read and basic math. It was, in part, Husk's presence that kept Shanley lurking in the hallway. She could not understand it, but she wanted to see Husk whenever he visited, despite the teasing at school.

Husk was an Ambrien with the weird emerald, bejeweled eyes. He had to wear spectacles to see. Still, Shanley found him beautiful with his long, dark hair, his sun-dark skin, and his gentle manner. Husk's patron, The Silver Swann, once known as the Black Swann, recommended him with such fervor that her father immediately hired him.

Husk was in Xavier's room, laughing with her brother. Shanley's classmates made fun of her about having a dirty Ambrien in her house as if there was anything she could do about that. They said of the nine Erelahian races that Ambriens were by far the worst. Her classmates were stupid. There were twelve types of Erelahians which included dragons. She knew all about that kind of thing from books she loved, and her parents disapproved.

Her parents only loved Xavier. And dead Xante. They hated her. She was no good. She was a useless girl. Ugly, unpopular, unable to ever do anything right. Shanley escaped by reading books and living in their pages. She heard all the whispers about her strangeness, about how unfortunate it was that Admiral

Bernard Rose and his lovely wife, Mirror Brude Rose, had such hard lives. Her mother's voice grated on her.

"Shanley, what are you doing?" her mother demanded. "The seamstress is here. I told you to be ready."

"Seamstress?"

"Our summer ball for the end of term. Tell me, you haven't forgotten. I have secured you an escort. Reginald Diamont."

"What? Mother, why do I need an escort? I'm twelve, and the ball is here, in my own house."

"All the girls your age are starting to learn about courting. That means boys and dancing. I know none of the boys at school have asked you, and so to spare you the embarrassment, the Diamonts have agreed that Reginald will be your date."

"Mother, Reginald is a senior classman. He's much older than me. He will be embarrassed. It will look horrible. Mother!"

"Shanley, don't complain. It will be fine," her mother said, pinching her arm to point her toward the parlor. "I wish you were not so fat. You must stay out of the kitchens. It makes it so much harder to find appropriate clothes for you."

Shanley hated the clothes her mother insisted draping her in. She pulled away, feeling tears well up in her eyes. She felt so trapped in her life.

"Is Siobhan coming to the ball?"

"She is in The Mudlands visiting her mother's niece, that poor girl who married that awful Muddy man. Bagwell. Ugh," Mirror Rose made a face like she had bitten into something bitter. "Delilah Sage is not a good person, and I want you to stay away from her and your half-sister. They live a lifestyle that is inappropriate for a girl of your social standing."

Captain Delilah was a pirate as was her half-sister, Siobhan. Shanley vehemently disagreed with her mother. Ambriland would be nothing without its pirates.

Shanley adored Siobhan with immense envy. She wished her half-sister near to comfort her. Siobhan never blamed her for Xante. Shanley wished she could travel with her half-sister. Her mother would never allow it.

"But Siobhan…"

"Your father does as he should for his bastard girl. Everyone makes mistakes. Siobhan is your father's business. Not ours," her mother said. She softened which allowed Shanley to take a breath. "Shanley, I know you dislike my helping you, but it is for your own good so that you will have a good future."

Husk Grayvesone stepped out into the dark hall.

"Madame Rose, I am done. Xavier is well-advanced in his studies. He is without a doubt the cleverest boy I have ever met," he said. "He asked for some water."

"Thank you. I will see to him," Mirror Rose said, a smug look of half-approval and skepticism. "Shanley, I will meet you in the parlor."

Shanley watched her mother glide away into Xavier's room. She turned as Husk caught up to her. "Is my brother feeling poorly?" she asked.

"No. He's fine. Dry throat is all. And I wanted your mother to leave you alone," Husk said. "Shanley, you are not fat. You are fine. Please, don't take the things she says badly. She is bitter. With Xavier sick, and little Xante dead, it must be hard for your mother. And you need not worry about Reginald Diamont. He plays at being a jerk, but he's ok. He'll be kind to you. He understands how things are with your mother."

Shanley could not understand this sudden kindness. She stood watching Husk disappear around the corner on his way out. She made her way to the parlor feeling dazed, being fit for a dress that she would wear one time under protest only to have her mother complain about its cost. The stiff dress of itchy fabric did not fit. Shanley's mother thought commissioning smaller clothes would somehow make Shanley smaller.

Shanley found herself in the village of Marinplaz to get more material for the dress that would not fit her without a good bit of revision. One of her classmates passed her by, sniggering. Shanley thought she heard the words "porridge-face". The other girls did not like her at all. She ran her hand along her cheek, feeling the acne that came more often in the last months.

She looked up and saw a sign at a vacated shop. She read it, not thinking much of it at first.

The wicker woman has moved to the cottage in the jungle. Please visit there if you seek her aid. She has kittens available. If anyone wants one.

Shanley heard a villager say, "Oh, what a shame. I really hoped to get that tea today. We will go tomorrow."

For reasons Shanley would never understand, she found herself meandering up a broken path from the docks of Marinplaz, following it to the jungle and to the cottage mentioned on the sign. She had heard wicker women had clever cures for things like acne and other ailments that were particular to young girls.

The cottage seemed old, but the wicker woman new to it. Almost no furniture decorated the front room. The garden was overgrown, and the place felt unlived in.

Shanley tapped on the door and found a younger woman than she expected, shuffling crates around. The dark-haired wicker woman had one chair and one book out, a massive tome with a great black dragon engraved into the thick cover of leather, its binding exquisite, labeled in gold in a language Shanley did not know.

"Hello?" Shanley said.

"Yes, I am not open yet," the wicker woman said. "I am only moving in today."

"Oh, I am sorry," Shanley said. "I saw the sign in the village. It didn't say…"

"My, you don't look like any of my usual customers," the woman said, holding Shanley in a fixed gaze. "What brings you here, child?"

"Oh, it was an impulse. You see my mother wants me to be pretty and small and I am not either," Shanley said. "And my acne is awful. And I am fat. I don't know. I just thought, I had heard…"

"Oh dear, come on in. Let me see what I can do for you," the woman said. "I am Madame Darke. Who are you?"

"Shanley Rose. What is this book? It is beautiful and a bit scary."

"Well, it's a grimoire. However, it is not mine, and it doesn't do anything fun," Madame Darke said, throwing a kitchen rag over it. "Now, don't be afraid. Come in. I am sure I can help you."

"My mother wishes that I was small and pretty like Rebekah Diamont…"

"Forget your mother, child. What do you want?"

"I want people to stop looking at me the way they do," Shanley said. "You see my brother, Xante, died five years ago. I was seven. Yet, everyone blames me for his death. And I didn't do it."

"Why do they blame you?"

"They say he drowned, and I let him. I was seven. And I know he was alive in his bed that night. After our swim. I know it," Shanley said, feeling herself let go of five years of fury.

"That is terrible, child. You could not be responsible. Was no one watching you?"

"Our nanny quit that night. It was such a hot night, and the pool was fabulously cool," Shanley said. "Is there a way to prove I did not kill Xante?"

The wicker woman's violet eyes went wide. And then she smiled. "Yes. I am sure we can. I will need a few things from you, and I will make sure no one blames you for the death of this brother."

Shanley did not understand any of it. She was not even sure why she complied with the bizarre favors. Perhaps, because within three days, her acne was gone, she had grown an inch taller and a good couple of inches thinner. Her mother was thrilled. The dress she had ordered fit beautifully. It felt like magic.

Buoyed by the new-found confidence that came with her improved appearance, Shanley acquired the ingredients the wicker woman required. A lock of her mother's hair, a drop of blood from her father, and a vial of blood from her first mooning which came the week after she first visited the wicker woman.

The spell was to be cast after hours, once the wicker woman had seen to all her regular customers from the village. And naturally it rained. Shanley sat in the now well-appointed cottage on a little sofa with two cats glaring at her and making her sneeze.

She expected the spell to result in some kind of document that showed that Xante had not drowned. Or spark the memory of a maid or gardener who knew that Xante had been in his bed alive after the swim. Something similar to the detective books Shanley so loved. She imagined apologies from her mother, that they would bond and understand one another at last.

The wicker woman seemed to be reading a book with a dark, red cover of fine leather. Shanley started to inquire if there was something she should do when her mind drew a blank. She could not remember why she was there. She knew there was something wrong that the wicker woman was meant to fix but could not remember what.

"Madame Darke, pardon," Shanley said. "But are we done?"

"I think so, dear," The wicker woman said, pushing the book aside. "How do you feel? Are you well?"

"I think so," Shanley said. "My, it's dark tonight."

"Yes, it is. But the rain has stopped. You were waiting for it to stop."

"Oh, yes, that's right. The rain. Of course. Thank you. Do I owe you anything?"

"No, you paid. Oh dear, you must be very tired. Go home. Get some sleep. Let me know if you need anything else and do tell your friends about me, if they should require my services."

Shanley woke in the morning, sun shining hot, feeling she had dreamt. Her mother knocked on her door.

"Shanley, you've overslept your breakfast," she said. Her

mother never cared if she missed breakfast. "The pastries are delicious. I have saved you one."

Shanley pulled on a simple, white summer dress and greeted her mother. "Pastries? Has the new cook started then?"

"A baker from The Silver Swann Culinary Academy. She will make the ball spectacular with the desserts we will serve," her mother said. "Oh, Shanley, you look so lovely this morning. I am proud. You needed to take off that baby weight, and you have done so. Come, we will have those pastries with a tea to celebrate."

"Celebrate what?"

"You. We have received your marks for this term. You did so well. Your father and I are best pleased."

Shanley took a sip of the sweet, orange scented tea, and her mind went clear. She remembered Xante. She remembered the witch. And the magic had worked. She took a breath and took a chance.

"Mother, do you miss Xante terribly?"

"Pardon? Who is Xante?" her mother asked. "Oh, are you asking about my uncle that died last year? Dear, I barely knew him. I met him once when I was younger than you. How did you know about him?"

Shanley put her tea down. Had the wicker woman removed Xante entirely from existence? That was not possible.

"You said you wanted me to learn more of my family," Shanley said as an excuse. "That is all."

"Oh, well, that is good. I must take you to Jebellen when you are a bit older, to see where I grew up. Now, please, do be home by four hours past the noon. To get ready for the ball. It's going to be a wonderful night. And Xavier seems well today. He can go for a little while."

Shanley felt elated and fearful all at once. She did not want to lose Xante, for him not to exist. She found herself seeking the tombs beneath the Rose Manor, spiraling down the long, stone staircase into the depths. She stood before Xante's tomb, lantern in hand. Xante Rose had lived. He had died. And his tomb was still here.

Sidon Bagwell stood up to excuse himself, his teacup empty as it had started.

"Trick, want to go fishing?"

"Yes but no," Trick said, feeling a fog fill his head. "Dad, who is Xante Rose?"

"Oh, you mean Xavier," Aunt Delilah said. "He's Siobhan's half-brother. He's been sick lately, but my, such a clever little boy. He is near your age, Trick. You two would get along famously. Xavier loves ships as much as you do. Laynie, you must bring the family to Ambriland for an extended visit."

"No, Xante. Who is Xante?" Trick said, feeling a cold dread take him.

"I don't know that name," Delilah said.

"He died. Mom, you went to his funeral. Don't you remember?"

"Trick, you should go out and play," his mother said as if she had not heard him at all. "You don't want to be stuck inside on a day like this, do you?"

Trick sighed. He was too late, and he did not have the kind of magic to undo the terrible spell. He turned to go outside where his sister, Sid-Jynx, and his cousin, Siobhan, would have to face a future that would be hard. It would be too dark. He turned and spoke. No one was listening. He was only six.

"I am too young. My brain doesn't work right. I couldn't fix it. And this will hurt the world."

Piss Water Beer

The Rooke took a long sip of ale to find The Cross-Eyed Hag transformed into two pubs. One was full of citizens gambling, drinking, watching scantily clothed dancers, all oblivious to his presence. The once empty area, filled with Idylls & Grimoires tables, overflowed with people, a pair of musicians playing ancient tunes on acoustic guitars, voices silkily repeating the tune of *The Wreck of the Dair Muir*. His magic worked exactly as it should.

He turned to reassure Kentigern, finding his friend with a look of horror on his face. The old scrivener pointed toward the other part of the pub.

"You smell it, right?"

"The beer is awful over there," Zac Grimm said. "Smells like sweet piss. Glad this part opened up with the fancy stuff."

"Sweet piss…?" The Rooke missed a beat. He surveyed the crowd. Spytes would be there. The smell was unmistakable. They were on the hunt, unmasked and yet invisible.

"Can they attack us here?" Kentigern asked.

"No, but we can't stay here," The Rooke said. "Gather the others. We will have to make a run for it."

Aldo pulled Tavares and Aleron in front of The Rooke. "Careful of their poison. You want to take them out with one hit, one slice," Kentigern said. "And be fast or they will release their venom."

"How do you recognize them?" Zac Grimm said. "There's always some gimmick to find disguised things in a game."

"This isn't a game," Thiago said. "Not everything works that way."

"Yeah, it is a game, Thiago. It's an end game. So how do we recognize these Spyte assassins?"

"By their stench," Kentigern said. "Sweet piss mixed with dead, rotting meat. Nothing else. They can be anyone. While they are often children, that is not always the case. Still, they are always beautiful and they only stink when they are about to kill. It's their venom that permeates that vile odor."

"So, you'll need to take off your robes, my friend," Aldo said. "And then we will go up to our rooms, gather our things and take the next train to Dream Land."

"If I take off my robes, the magic that is protecting us right now will dissipate and these Spytes will become aware that powerful magic has just happened."

"We go straight for the train then. Blend in with the crowd," Aleron Ramses said. "Mika will go back and retrieve our things. She and Anwyn. That invisibility will be useful."

"How long do I have?" Mika Finn asked.

"An hour. Come, I will go with you," Aleron said.

"You are far too visible, my friend," Mika said. "Give me all your room keys. Ani and I can manage."

"I am coming," Cymbre said. "No one is looking for me. I can blend with the crowd. I can help."

"Get what is most essential only," Aldo said. "I'll have my contact here send anything else to Talon. To Kentigern's son, Paul. To keep for us."

Mika returned to the crowded train with as much of the party's gear as she could gather. Cymbre followed. She looked exacerbated.

"Scarlets tried to stop us."

"You are good a liar," Mika said.

"I lied with the truth. My sleeve vouched for me. Aldo, it is good work you did on this thing. I said I am a teacher on vacation. They believed me," Cymbre said. "I am going to Talon. I didn't know there'd be so much danger. What are you all doing that is so bad?"

"Telling stories…" Thiago said, trying to explain.

"About witches and magic?" Cymbre said. "No one will care. People my age love that stuff in the empires. And the imperials find it harmless because it is all pretend."

"Spytes are not pretend," Kostas said. "And neither are Nacharye, demons, nor sorceresses and dragons. It's all real, and the empires don't want you to know. They make sure you think it is all pretend and childish and silly."

"Rooke, something has gone very wrong," Mika said. "The empires know exactly where The Reliquary is now. And they are looking for you. They are offering an award for you that would make the one who stops you richer than the greediest man's dreams."

The train sped down a winding track around the mountain, going down and down toward the harbor town of Dream Land. When they stopped and got off at the station, it was crawling with Scarlets. They were checking everyone's sleeves.

"This is no good, Rooke," Aldo said. "We need to head inland. We'll have to cross the valley into Talon."

"I'll get us transport," Mika said. "Aldo, come help me. We have to distract the Scarlets so the others can get past."

Tavern VII:

The Last Resort

Darkness can be disrupted by the tiniest sliver of light. Never give up on a world. Nights are long, but dawn forever lies in wait to destroy even the foulest of evil.

The Idylls of Alleysiande, Vol XII, Pedariel's Rock
author unknown (translated by Hazel Kyran)

The Empyri Keeper

The old inn looked in shambles, decrepit. The Rooke's party chose it on his recommendation after their transport broke down, thinking no one else would purposely stay there. The wind blew cold, the clouds heavy promising a late winter storm. The Last Resort had once been a lively and eloquent inn at the far edge of civilization.

The Rooke felt a shiver pass through him as he looked at the corpse of his favorite haunt from before The Evanescence. It was off the busy thoroughfare the empire had built, and so few knew it still existed.

A young man who looked Empyri, slant-eyed and dark-skinned with sharp ears, greeted the party as they entered. He would have little standing among the imperials as indicated by his steel sleeve with white ribbon and symbol indicating that he was a service worker. He was young, mid-twenties perhaps, and looked frightened.

The Rooke had held the party back as Scarlets departed the inn. The Empyri young man appeared nervous, rattled as if he had been harshly questioned.

"Calm yourself," The Rooke said. "We are seeking shelter from the coming storm. Can you accommodate us? We will pay you a bit extra."

"I can. I can," the young man said. "I am Wataru Toura. My family purchased this inn in last month. We are in the middle of a renovation. That is why there were soldiers here. I fear we are not within regulation…"

"It is fine, lad. Give us rooms as you have, and we will pay," Aldo said. "The storm is getting bad. We simply need a place to wait it out…"

A young boy stepped out from behind the desk, making Wataru appear frantic.

"Taki, no. I told you to stay in the office," Wataru said. "Sorry. I have to look out for my younger brother, and he never listens."

Taki said something to Wataru in another language. The Rooke observed the child, perhaps of age with Kostas. This boy was more than Empyri. He was Gnolgia. Impossible. They were all gone, but here he was. Sharp ears, round, multi-colored eyes like a rainbow, smooth and perfect features, a rare jewel among the Empyri people.

"Speak Acarian," Wataru said. "It is forbidden to speak the ancient tongue…"

"Do not be afraid, brother," Taki said, smiling. "These are not imperials. Well, not all of them. This is a rooke. He will tell good stories. I am going to go with him. I have maps."

"'The Fifth Offers The Rooke The Last Gnolgia Cartographer'," Thiago said, reciting from The Rooke's list. "Well, that only leaves us The Fourth, The Sixth, and The Seventh's choices."

"He's a little kid," Anwyn said.

"So are you, and you're on the list," Kostas said.

"I am not a little kid. He looks younger than you."

"Taki, I am pleased to meet you, but listen to your brother. You should cover those eyes," The Rooke said to the small boy, bending over to look him in his wild, multi-colored eyes. "Those who would hurt you are following us."

"My brother doesn't understand danger," Wataru said. "He never has. Follow me, I will take you to your rooms. Taki, go to your room and stay there until you are willing to cover your eyes and ears so that you are not spotted. Real imperials will hurt you, and then I would miss you."

The rooms were sparse, but the beds were made and clean and warm. The Rooke could not complain. He welcomed Kentigern and Aldo into his room as Thiago and Kostas argued over beds in the adjoining room.

"I thought we'd go down to the pub for bite and drink before bed," Kentigern said. "This blizzard could be bad. Might trap us here."

"As soon as there's a break in the weather, we will go," The Rooke said. "But not tonight. I am exhausted."

"Then maybe no tales tonight," Aldo said. "We are the only guests."

"We should take time to perfect our disguises," The Rooke said, pulling at his artisan sleeve.

"Yes, about that," Kentigern said. "We think you should cut your hair..."

"What?"

"Lad, you look nothing like an imperial, not of the accepted class. They are priggish as old school Acarian nobles. Sartorially speaking."

"I am not cutting my hair..."

"You look like a rooke, something from old tales as you would, but the world has changed. Short hair, uniform dress is all the rage among the common citizens, artisans or not, as we are trying to make you seem."

"Surely, artisans still wear their hair..."

"Too obvious for a rooke. They'd check too closely. Only celebrated artisans are afforded sartorial freedom."

"But it's hair. Why would they care?"

"Your magic is not connected to your hair," Kentigern said. "Steven Fowler had short hair."

"I have never worn my hair short. Not even when I was a child..."

"You don't know that..."

"I do know that," The Rooke complained. "I don't want to cut my hair."

"And we don't want a Spyte to cut you," Aldo said. "Best to blend in. Play the part. Make it easier to move invisible among the masses. Even Zac Grimm is dressing his part to remain hidden, having to wear the gray, the spectacles, have his hair shortened and neatened."

"You are cutting Zac's hair?"

"He let Cymbre cut it. She made it nice," Aldo said. "It is not too short. He wears it tied back. You could do that."

"I will tie my hair back. You won't have to cut it."

"No. Yours is too long. While lovely, it must be done. Especially because you are aging now, Rooke. It won't look right," Aldo said. "Mika, you have the shears?"

"We should have had it done before we left," Kentigern said, letting Mika Finn into the room with her daughter and the puzzle box. "Mika says she knows how to style hair."

"We will make you unremarkable whatever sleeve we slap on you," Mika said. "Come. You will still be pretty. After, as reward, the drinks here are surprisingly good as is the food."

"You are keeping your eye on that box," The Rooke said as he let Mika take her shears to him. "That's good work, Ani."

"I am not guarding it. I am trying to figure it out," Anwyn said. "I don't know how it works. I don't understand. What riddle are we trying to solve?"

"It's the card you and Kostas created when you opened the box," The Rooke said. "The Last King of Ambriland. The answer is to do with the card."

"Maybe we should go to Ambriland then?" Anwyn said, her little eyes squished up in thought. "Makes no sense. And what will the magic do? What are the Archaics?"

"That box is supposed to change the world," Kentigern said. "There are Twelve Archaics, one for each of Alleysiande's Sentinels. If you can draw them out of that cube, it is written that Alleysiande will be restored to Aerda. Never been done before. You'd make history child."

"You cut your hair," Kostas said to the obvious as The Rooke made his way downstairs. "It's weird."

"I like it," Thiago said. "Makes you look imposing. Which is good, father. An imperial will believe you a frustrated artist."

"I am an artist, and frustrated," The Rooke said as they entered the pub at The Last Resort.

Apart from The Rooke's party and the Toura brothers, it was empty with a roaring fire. Little Taki Toura sat in the corner, working on a map. It appeared to be a rendering of The Mudlands from before The Evanescence with the location of all forty Urian clans marked with colorful icons.

He was on the point of asking the boy about his map when Taki pointed toward young Anwyn Finn who had given the puzzle box to Kostas. She was wearing The Rooke's red robes. She began to speak, casting everyone in the room into Hell on the day Chrysalis Rabican had her throat slit in Heath's Night.

The Gnolgia Cartographer

Taki Toura did not speak to ghosts. His grandmother taught him this was a great transgression for any of the Gnolgia. He did, of course, see the ghost. A dark-haired woman endlessly knitting something. She seemed very interested in his maps. He felt tempted to show her his current masterpiece, a colorful rendering of The Mudlands prior to The Evanescence.

He did not stay in his rooms. The new visitors interested him, and if that rooke told a tale, he wished to hear it. He put on the eye contacts to make him look ordinary, so ordinary. He did not think it fair he had to hide. He liked his multi-colored eyes and fine, sharp ears.

The cap that covered the tips of his ears itched and pinched. He sighed, giving the ghost a sidelong glance. She seemed to understand that he would not speak to her. Instead, she pointed to Anwyn Finn across the table.

She is alive. You can speak to her.

The ghost spoke in a faint whisper. Taki startled. This was not like him. Sometimes ghosts did speak to him but something about this felt wrong. He looked at the puzzle box. Voices from ages past told him to beware of it.

"You must release a curse, or you will die," he told Anwyn and Kostas.

"It was only a little curse. Made us sleep a bit and have night-mares," Kostas said. "And we can get a great treasure. We have until the Dragon Moon to solve a riddle."

"No, the curse has not yet happened. The curse is a price to trade for the treasure. Solving the riddle will get both the curse and the blessing. Do not solve the riddle, the box will explode and kill everyone for miles around. That is how Ambriel's box works. Even simple-minded people know this," Taki said and went back to his maps.

Now Anwyn was wearing The Rooke's robes. She slipped away from the table and to the front of the room. Taki sighed. The ghost was not going to shut up. She slipped inside the girl. This ghost insisted on being heard. He wondered what his grandmother would say to this. He decided to listen. That was not the same as talking. Listening was always better. Especially when trapped in Pandemonium.

The Tale of The Hierarchy

Phaedra battled a demon for the soul of little Chrysalis Rabican.

"Give it back. Ours. Ours," the demon said as Phaedra burned the damned beast with what little light she had shared with the child, freeing the soul of Chrysalis before Pandemonium could claim her.

"She belongs to no one. Not me. Not to your damned legion. You will never have her," Phaedra said.

The demon shrugged its ethereal form as it slithered away into nothingness. The damned and demonic surrounded Phaedra, celebrating her failure and their victory.

So many new souls for their endless appetite, a taste, a sliver of something lost, something they could never have. Phaedra could feel them in the absolute darkness, struggling for forms that they might use to destroy her.

It was all she could do to cling to her name. She repeated her name over and over to herself so that she could not be fooled when Pandemonium began its onslaught as the nothingness around her turned to horror.

Phaedra's vision focused as the newly captured souls of depraved child slavers twisted from rat into the grotesque. Shrieker demons she called them, souls that fell for The Hierarchy's lie that they could exchange their names for eternal peace.

Phaedra gave everything a name, to keep track of it, to remind herself of the lies she was told, the ones she repeated when necessary. Better to endure the pain than give up her name. Visions of shadow exposed the transformation of rat into the demonic.

Eternal peace took the shape of hairless humanoid creatures with sharp ears and mouths full of rotting, jagged teeth, running on all fours, clawed, and bloodied for all eternity like some wretched hound. The newly formed demons screeched in agony, ripping at their own forms with genitals, both male and female, protruding from their bellies.

The murderous demon that had taken Chrysalis from Phaedra slunk into the fray to steal the strongest of these soul-destroyed beasts, a foul tax, cackling all the while, wearing the corpse of the headless slaver it had claimed. The pack turned from Phaedra to follow their new master, leaving her ever surrounded by rats. Always with the rats. She could never clear those from her vision.

Well done. A good take, denizen. We could not have torn the barrier better ourselves.

"Who are you? Identify yourself, demon," Phaedra said to the darkness. She believed this one of the High Hierarchs or all thirteen of them speaking as one. They never showed themselves.

We are one. We are no one. We are legion.

"I am Phaedra," came her answer, defiant, full of venom.

You lie. You are us and we are you.

"I am Phaedra." Her voice rang silent against the void.

A creature materialized before her in black robes crafted from darkness, immersed in the stench of sulfur and burnt flesh. There were lots of these monstrosities in Hell. Phaedra dubbed them auditors.

They did not call themselves anything at all. These monsters had never known life, not like Phaedra. It did not suffer the knowledge that there was another way, one of light and infinite creation.

"We are most pleased, denizen," the auditor demon said. "We are well-fed because of its endeavors. The Hierarchy, dear denizen, is perfection achieved. No more pain, no more want, no more questions. Step forward and take your reward."

Phaedra saw as one did inside a dream, and she knew this lie well. Sweetness to make her forget. Nothing more than a trick.

The demon extended a clawed hand toward Phaedra, a sealed scroll extending the proffered prize. Phaedra examined the insignia, searching for a name among the symbols. A snake-wrapped woman, the mark of the wrathful queen of Pandemonium and its Hierarchy.

"Well?" said the waiting demon.

"Time means nothing here. What is your hurry?" Phaedra considered leaving the scroll sealed, but the rats climbed her, and she wished to flee them. It was more bearable if she were moving. She complied with the anxious auditor.

"Yes? Yes?" the demon prodded.

Phaedra read the scroll.

"Banking? Are you kidding me?"

"We do not understand. A banker of souls is powerful. Your hunger satiated. It will reside in the Boundless City with us. With all of us. Now, your name. Let go of it."

"No."

"It jokes. It is not funny. It will cross the bridge. Into the city it will go and its name it will leave behind. Reside with us in the Boundless City it will. Our every desire granted for all eternity. Any shape. Any form. Any desire. Nothing is denied."

"Your desires are not mine," Phaedra said and turned away from the demon.

These things could do little to her but chase her about and hiss at her. Worse horrors would follow her until she found her next opportunity to cross into a living world, one that had long eclipsed the world in which she had died. So many dimensions opened from Pandemonium, she had long despaired of ever finding her way home.

Phaedra tore the scroll to shreds, letting it scatter about her. The scroll was nothing but a lie set to illusion.

She floated away, passing shadows of a mock rendering of creation. She glided past broken buildings, barren gardens, muted conversations of lost spirits repeating a routine of their long-past lives. They did not realize their mortal bodies had long turned to dust. They never saw her or the demons. No matter what she did, she could not wake them, get them to see her.

A phalanx of demons, scaled creatures wearing human pelts that looked as if they had truly been burnt in hellfire, surrounded her. Phaedra shuddered. These echo horrors formed an impenetrable barrier of darkness. They pushed her toward a great bridge, one that crossed from this netherworld into the Boundless City where the demon lords ruled.

In that place, the damned existed free of the torment of their mortal lives and their names. Golden and gaudy, the city cast a shadow over the bridge like a painting by a floundering impressionist.

Step echo, step echo, like walking through a tunnel. The legion that followed Phaedra blocked her retreat, forcing her onto the bridge. Dread filled her.

She took in the symbols that flanked the bridge. There was the queen and her snake to the right. The symbol on the left upset Phaedra to her core. A monstrous being stretched so high that all were forced to acknowledge it. The echo horrors rang out a scream in worship to it.

The mouth of this great demon was a pit filled with razor teeth. Its many arms stuffed its foul maw full of screaming mortals. For a flickering moment, this being came to life and Phaedra heard the screams of the damned as the monstrous creature devoured them. She shivered.

"There will be no more suffering. Let go. Give over that insidious name," the echo horrors said, a flat note like the scratching of metal on metal.

Do as we command. Easy, denizen. Easy.

The invisible Hierarch spoke inside her, as if it were a foul insect that had festered its way into her being, trying so hard to calm her, to horrify her, to claim her, to convince her to relinquish her identity.

"I am Phaedra. I am not a denizen. I am not a demon. I am not legion. I am not a banker of souls. I am Phaedra."

She took a first hesitant step onto the bridge. Snakes slithered toward her, one wrapping itself about her and the others striking with poison-tipped fangs.

"I am already dead. I do not fear this torment. Stop trying it."

Her will dissolved the ugly delusion as she stepped further on the crumbling planking, heedless of the rats. The echo horrors laughed. Unimaginative.

The rats recalled to Phaedra her murder. She died unable to scream, paralyzed as rats ate her alive. How her murderer delighted in her torture up to the point when someone killed him all too late to save her. She would never know his name again. He surrendered it to the demons when she chased him into Hell.

Phaedra saw him now, waiting on the far side of the bridge to escort her the rest of the way into the Boundless City. Charming. This creature was nothing more than a mock representation of the one who had murdered her back when she was first a woman of flesh, perfect and broken all at once, a glorious being Phaedra refused to renounce.

It ought to be raining.

This new reflection shaped inside Phaedra. She felt the disapproval of the infernal legions that surrounded her. She shielded her vision, erasing the bridge and the looming phantom on the other side. She relished this memory of rain, the sound it made like the tiny dancing feet of life.

Oh life. Such a forbidden word to The Hierarchy. It resonated with possibility to those who spoke of it. Amid all her rage and despair, Phaedra recalled joy like a pinpoint of hot light. She remembered a crisp autumn breeze on her living skin, diving into a pile of newly fallen leaves, her father laughing.

"Father."

Phaedra said the word out loud, equal parts joy and agony as she remembered a moment of purest delight, a single breath over and done. Lost forever. Phaedra imagined her father with a pang of longing. A word eluded her, one of great power, a word The Hierarchy knew but twisted. Phaedra reached for it, but that word was lost to her.

Imagining the showers of new spring that would never come again, Phaedra teetered between hope and despair. She wanted misty wet on her face, a live heart beating in her chest, lungs filled with damp air, the warm towel wiping the rain from her hair, the hot soup made of herbs and vegetables from the garden as the tin roof sang.

Phaedra sank into herself and began to howl at all she had lost. These memories grated at her soul, pulled harder than the allure of The Hierarchy's promise of eternal forgetfulness.

Sterilization awaits to free you from this torment. Give over your name. We will give you another. It is only a name.

"Father, save me. I am lost. I want to come home," Phaedra said, pushing the penetrating voice aside as it tried to steal the last remnant of her soul, her being, and her voice. The momentary memory shattered, the fine autumn day and the stormy spring night, reduced to wisps of a dream.

Nothing will harm you again. No more pain, no more sorrow, all your wants and needs met by The Hierarchy. Stay, Phaedra, stay. You need not concern yourself with such harsh judgment. There is no sin here.

"I am Phaedra. It is my name, and you may not have it."

Phaedra gripped cold railings, staring down into pure

darkness. She could see nothing. She heard an illusion of water churning below, unlike the still rivers of Pandemonium. What was it?

Phaedra pulled on the railing, heedless of the spiders crawling on her wherever she grasped the hold. The bridge shook unsteadily, threatening to crumble under the weight of her crushing guilt.

The flesh-robed demons kept their vigil, following her slow step after slow step toward the phantom on the other side.

"I am Phaedra," she repeated as she climbed.

Don't resist. There is no need for such discomfort. This is a well-earned reward. Here, we rule. There, we pay.

"Give me your infernal name, Hierarch," Phaedra shouted, causing her escort of echo horrors to ripple, moving the wall a step back.

We are yours and you are ours. Join us. Submit, Phaedra. Submit and all will be well. There is nothing to fight for anymore. Nothing at all.

"Dream. Redemption. Freedom. Possibility. Creation." Phaedra spat forbidden words back at the unseen Hierarchy as fast as they came to her. She pulled herself to the bridge's pinnacle and turned toward the wall of horrors. "I will not squander my joy for impotent power. You are meaningless. All of you. I will never join you."

Eternity ticked away like seconds as her fate crashed down on her. The horrors exposed their grotesque faces and echoed their deceit at her.

"Banking souls is a good existence. It serves well and all will be forgiven and forgotten. Such rewards are earned. No more death. No more sorrow."

Lies. How could there be rewards if Phaedra no longer recalled her name? She would evaporate into The Hierarchy, a tool to be wielded like the horrors that now surrounded her.

"I will not give up my name. It is mine. I am Phaedra. I will always be Phaedra," she said, sending the flesh-robed demons toppling backwards into one another.

She turned her back on her tormenters and stood like a statue a few steps shy of the highest point of the bridge, her vision turning to the imagined river below that stretched out into unseen depths. Would it take her away from here? She could not, must not cross the bridge. That would be her end.

Phaedra crept forward to the place where the railing was low and crumbling. She ached for touch and feeling. She did not know where this odd yearning originated. Leaves in autumn, late spring showers flashed through her essence, the desire it aroused. She wanted pain, feeling, joy, grief, all of it.

She glanced up to see the specter in her murderer's shape charging after her, a sickle raised as if it could cleave her name from her. She felt the blade scrape against her essence, searing her soul, as she crossed the railing. The sound of water churning vibrated through her. A whisper of faith called her. She did not look down as she flung herself from the bridge into the darkness.

The Blizzard

The Rooke emerged from Hell to find rats running in circles around little Anwyn as Wataru Toura chased them away.

"No rats, no rats," he repeated, swinging a broom comically after the evaporating rodents. He turned to The Rooke and his party. "There were no rats. See. No rats. This is a clean place. No rats."

Taki Toura confronted young Anwyn who pushed the red robes toward The Rooke. "You are bad," Taki said, his pointed ears bursting from his falling cap. "Do not talk to ghosts. See what happen. Bad. You bad."

"I didn't…" Anwyn said. "Phaedra is not bad. It's like she told that Urian pappa. She's not a demon. I know it."

"She is dangerous, child. There will be nothing left of you. Do not let her take you again," Kentigern said.

"Give me my robes," The Rooke said, snatching them away, his tone sharper than he intended. Fear made him careless.

"I only borrowed the robes," Anwyn said. "I didn't steal them."

"Father, she can't have stolen them. I tried a million times to put them on when I was twelve and thirteen. They wouldn't go on. It had to be Phaedra, but it's impossible," Thiago said. "The robes don't work that way. Even for Phaedra. They belong to the one who gave up their name. You have to give permission for someone to use your robes. But that story, it felt real."

"It was weird," Kostas said. "Ani, you can't just put on a rooke's robes. That is not on."

"It wasn't me…"

"Ani, we've all seen you," Mika Finn said to her daughter. "What were you thinking?"

Somewhere a bell rang. Wataru bowed, giving his brother a glare. "Stay hidden," he said. "More guests have come. The storm must have brought them."

"Guys," Zac Grimm said. "That smell…"

"Spytes…"

"I have no other guests," Wataru said. "There are no assassins. The Spytes are all gone. King Killan drove them out of Acaria more than two centuries ago."

"Yes, the king drove them out. Right into Chazir," Taki said, removing his eye covers and surveying the room. "One has come, hiding, waiting to strike. It sees us. It has magic. Dark magic. It is forbidden."

"I will go and see," Wataru said. "I will make sure this monster does not find you." The young man scampered away, locking the double door into the tavern behind him as he went to greet the new guests.

"We have to get out of here," Kentigern said, testing the sword he wore in a scabbard at his side under his long coat.

"The blizzard…" Tavares said, pulling his scarf close around him. "We won't survive out there."

"We won't survive in here," Aleron said. "Tavares, help me guard these children. Let us leave."

"Come with me," Taki said. "I know a secret way. You die now or you follow me."

"I vote for following," Zac Grimm said. "Not in the mood to die. I don't want to go back to that Hell Ani just took us to."

"Tavares and I will cover your escape," Aleron said, pulling his sword from his side belt.

"Mind your weapons. If you brandish them, use them. Hesitate, you die," Wataru Toura said, reentering the room. "The Scarlets have come back. They are coming in now to escape the storm."

Taki stepped up to his older brother. He put his hands on each side of Wataru's face. He spoke softly in an ancient tongue that sounded like music to The Rooke.

"I understand, but you stay at the temple," Wataru said. "You'll be safe, and you won't be here to be found. I will distract the soldiers and this monster that hunts."

Taki guided the party through heavy wind, stinging ice, and blinding snow to an old-fashioned cellar in the ground, buried body deep in snow behind The Last Resort. It took Tavares, Zac, and Aleron digging a quarter hour with Taki yelling directions to find the door and force it open. They slid into the cellar which seemed nothing but a dark room full of old tools and equipment, empty barrels, and crates.

The Rooke, back in his red robes, produced a light from one his pockets. The group crowded together. The Rooke counted heads. "Taki, Anwyn, Kostas, Thiago?"

"All here, father," Thiago said.

"Zac, Aleron, Tavares, Kenny, Aldo, Cymbre, Mika?"

"Wait, where is Cymbre?" Zac asked. "She was supposed to have dinner with me."

"I didn't see her in the tavern," Thiago said.

"She must have stayed in her room, said she had a headache," Mika said.

"I will go get her," Zac said. "Grandmaster Mist told me to look after her until we got her to Talon. I messed up."

"We'll go get her together," Mika said. "We won't stand out as much as these will. Zac, say you're my kid brother if imperials ask."

"I'm coming too," The Rooke said.

"No, that's not happening," Kentigern said. "We can't risk you."

"They'll need my magic to get back here," The Rooke said. "Taki, if we're not back in twenty minutes, you take these people and get them away. We will meet you at the temple."

"I am coming. I'm your guardian," Aldo said. "Rooke, you can't go without a proper guardian."

"I'll guard myself. Robe Thiago if the worst happens," The Rooke whispered. "They'll be able to do it at The Temple of the Tail."

"All right…wait, where did Zac and Mika go?"

The two had not left The Rooke any choice. They had gone to retrieve the missing party member.

The Rooke and the others shivered in the cold cellar for what seemed an eternity before they heard scraping above. They pushed the door open to let the party members back into the cellar.

"What happened?" The Rooke asked. "Cymbre, why did you not come to the tavern?"

"I fell asleep," Cymbre said. "I could have gone the rest of the way to Talon on my own. After the storm. I feel terrible you've risked your lives for me. I'm not worth it."

"You have to stay with us, lass," Aldo said. "For security reasons. Until Talon."

"We go now," Taki said, opening a passage behind built in shelves. A mundane albeit cleverly hidden door. The passage was a clean tunnel, sloping down through a rounded, cemented opening. "Old dweller tunnels. The Empyri and Gnolgia had them throughout Aerda before The Evanescence. Some remain. They are much fun to explore."

It was neither a short nor warm journey. The party had to stop and rest twice before the tunnel hit a series of steep stairs going up and up. Snow began to blow inside as the passage opened into a natural cave close to the Temple of the Tail. They could see flickering lights below them in the night sky through blowing snow, and a frozen river and bridge at the end of a close-by frozen path.

"Not far. Not far. We go," Taki said, pointing at the path.

"Wow, this is a real adventure," Kostas said. "This is fun."

"People are trying to kill us," Thiago said. "How is that fun?"

"I don't know," Kostas said. "It just is."

"Adventure is good," Taki said. "It gives required purpose. If life not in danger, life not being lived."

"Interesting philosophy you got there, kid," Zac said, wrapping himself up. "Not sure I agree."

"You all go first. I will use my magic to warm you from behind," The Rooke said, letting each of the twelve party members pass before him into the slowing blizzard, believing they had reached safety.

Tavern VIII:

The Dragon's Tail

Ghosts are manifestations of regret, sorrow, horror, and love denied.

The Idylls of Alleysiande, Vol IV, Sandalphon's Symphony
author unknown (translated by Hazel Kyran)

In The Temple

*T*he Rooke followed the group through a high wall of melting snow. He heard a loud crack as Aldo and Kentigern disappeared down the steps that would take them to the temple. In front him, he saw the maw of a dragon as it screamed to him, and all went black. He could not move. His breath froze in his lungs, pain and then nothing.

He awoke to a failing sun against the remnants of a dying storm. His arms were stretched above him as someone dragged him over icy rocks through an embankment of snow. He tried to call out to his sons but could make no noise at all. His eyes could see little as darkness enveloped him, cold wet of snow turning to icy rain, hard rock under his back. Pain dulled with each meter he was dragged, fighting to stay conscious, to stay alive.

Someone stripped off his wet clothes, inaudible whispers filled with concern and urgency. He felt himself tucked into bed, a soft pillow under his head and covered with warm blankets. He drifted in and out of consciousness, shivering as cold seemed to prick him despite the shelter.

"Drink this. It will help," a gentle feminine voice said, bringing a hot tea to his lips. "It's all right. You are safe now."

The Rooke fell into a dreamless slumber and how many minutes, hours, or days had passed, he had no idea. He woke up to find himself in a comfortable bed, a solitary figure sitting cross-legged in a stuffed chair by the fire. He sat up.

"Who are you?"

The Rooke cleared his vision and saw a woman, young, strong with amber eyes, dark hair that shone the firelight. Rats scurried around her which seemed of no matter to the woman. Impossible. She could not be here and so unchanged. Still, it was her. No question.

"Hello…," the woman said. "It's been an age."

The sorceress, Phaedra, said his name, his true name. He heard it, felt all the guilt and pain, joy and despair that came with it flood back into his mind. The Rooke shook with a grief that threatened to destroy him.

"Phaedra?"

"Relax, your name will disappear with your unpleasant memories in a moment. My magic is not so strong as it once was," the sorceress said. "You are telling our story to The Hierarchy. You must be careful. This is a story they mark as a victory. But if we are clever, we can use it to undo them."

"It was my fault. I was deceived, Phaedra or I would have told you," The Rooke tried to explain why he had made the miserable choices he had all those years ago. "It made me want to die when I found out what I'd done. Even without my name, I carry the pain even if I can't remember why. I was young and stupid, and I believed…"

"You believed your eyes and not your soul," Phaedra said. "The heart can be so deceitful. I remember how broken you were. In the end, you jumped from that cliff, knowing you would never fly. I expect you did not realize you might survive, and now, here we are."

The Rooke wept. And slept until the memory of his name and the guilt of his awful choices left him. The pain went back into that distant corner of his essence, a part of a tale that he would tell as he ventured further away from the shelter of The Reliquary.

None would blame him. It had not been him that put the world on course for its current plight. He could not be held responsible.

"Stop that. Self-pity is not a good look, my dear friend," Phaedra said, startling The Rooke and causing his eyes to pop open. "You have redeemed yourself. More so than I did, would you not say?"

"I don't know. Please, do not say my name again, Phaedra,"

The Rooke said. "How are you here? How have you kept the Nacharye body?"

"I haven't. Nacharye girls are not ageless. That body died pushing Malcombe the Second into Hell. This is not my body that you see. Illusion for your comfort and my safety. I do not want The Hierarchy knowing that I still exist in this realm. Remember, I was a sorceress of some power."

"Yes, that I do remember," The Rooke said. "Do you have a new body, or do I speak with a ghost?"

"I am working on finding flesh I can keep. Little Anwyn is a useful conduit, having the blood of one I once used."

"Please, do not take her," The Rooke said. "Her mother would grieve. She is not in need as Chrysalis Rabican and Sile Pyn."

"If I was desperate, I would have her or her mother already," Phaedra said. "Anwyn begs for my power, offers me everything to make her stronger, to stop her distress. She is very dramatic."

"Not unusual for girls her age."

"Or boys. Only, not your sons. They are fine young men. You make a good father. Better than you probably realize. Or remember."

The Rooke smiled, knowing the sorceress well enough to know she was trying to distract him. He needed answers.

"I've seen your rats."

"They are not my rats. But they go wherever I am. A curse I've yet to break."

"They are souls you damned. Have you been around for a while? I have been seeing rats for ages now in The Reliquary?"

"When Ambriel's Unbreakable Cube was first put into Shank's vault, I found myself able to see through those cursed rats as they were fed to The Reliquary's menagerie. They all whispered to me, begging me for a mercy that I have no power to grant. I had Anwyn retrieve the box for me and when it opened, I found myself able to influence things as I did before Chrysalis Rabican gave me her flesh those few, exquisite hours."

"Did you return to The Hierarchy you showed us at The Last Resort when you got rid of Malcombe II?" The Rooke asked.

"A place between held me. I ended up in Ambriel's Unbreakable Cube. It felt like no time, a dreamless slumber," Phaedra said. "I could feel myself fading into nothing. I almost lost my name."

"Sounds better than the Pandemonium you escaped," The Rooke said.

"The place I ended up was not the light that I have rightly earned," Phaedra said. "I want to go home. Until this cube is fully solved, I will never be free."

"You might be glad to have slept through The Subjugation," The Rooke said. "The Evanescence was awful for those left behind. I had to begin again in a world that was full of dull-witted, frightened, spineless people who simply gave into a meaningless existence and never questioned what they had lost."

"The world before was hardly a paradise although far more fun. I miss wyverns, dragons, and all the pit beasts that roamed The Mudlands. I miss the Urians, how everyone called them Muddy meaning to insult them, and they wore it like a badge of pride. They were the kind of people that kept The Hierarchy in its place. I loved that everyone obsessed over them, and yet, never tried to understand them. Their ways made for such amazing times," Phaedra said, drifting over to the oval window to stare out into the darkness. "I love hearing your tales. It takes me back to moments of horror and joy that lift me beyond this cruel and dull world and keep me free of Hell."

The Rooke found himself in a fine room, paneled in crafted wood, shelves filled with properly bound books, a great stone hearth warming him. The blizzard cleared with a gentle snow mixing with cold rain as dawn battled the clouds outside the narrow-arched window. He raised himself from the bed and shuffled closer to the window to see trees stretching beyond his sight. In the distance he could make out twinkling lights of a village or settlement.

"Where are we?"

"The Temple of the Tail," Phaedra said. "Your companions are safe, and we have some time to speak."

"Can you help the children? Can you take the cube and help us solve it?"

"The cube is bound to the children, and they must solve it. Grandmaster Mist has trained them well. I believe they can do it," Phaedra said. "It is in my interest these two succeed. If they do not, I will be damned forever more. And I suspect you will share my fate, my dear friend."

The patter of feet echoed in the hall and Phaedra disappeared or The Rooke truly awoke. He could not tell which. The door opened and Thiago and Kostas, dressed in bright white long tunics and trousers, tumbled into the room followed by a man and woman The Rooke did not know.

"Father, you're awake," Kostas said, running to hug him.

"And you are well, my son?"

"So much better now that you are ok," Kostas said. "And so hungry. Will you come to supper?"

"We were so worried," Thiago said.

"The woman who was here…"

"Here she is. She is an alchemist and healer," Kostas said, turning. "This is Tejoy Broomes only she goes by Tee. She saved you. She was born in Heath's Night. Did you know it still exists even though it was once a cursed place? Only it is a very large city now with thousands of towers and millions of people."

"Hello, Rooke," Tee Broomes said.

The Rooke saw intelligence and belief. She was younger than he would have expected, no more than in her mid-thirties. Alchemy was a difficult art that took many decades to master. She was dark-skinned with short, curly hair that made her lovely face shine all the more, and eyes dark with care and consideration. She wore the customary black and aqua robes of the ancient alchemy guild. The Rooke wondered at that. Few knew of the guild since the time of Subjugation.

"And I am Joel, Tee's husband," the man with Tee said. "I am training as a guardian and exorcist, but I worked as a researcher and technologist back in Heath's Night. I can help with the newer technologies that have emerged since the last rooke journeyed into the empires."

He was tall, lanky, with a long neck, narrow face, and wide smile, a bit older than his wife, close shaved hair, with a well-managed goatee. The Rooke saw good humor in this man's eyes, a strong trait for one who wished to chase away demons.

"Hello, Joel and Tee. Thank you for saving me," The Rooke said.

"Your friend, Kentigern, wishes that I travel with you. He said he is recruiting for The Relic. I am pleased to go with you," Joel said.

"And I go where Joel goes. If you feel up to it, you may get out of bed," Tee said. "We are having supper at the The Dragon's Tail."

The Dragon's Tail Pub was a short walk in the cold rain from the Temple of the Tail. Thiago and Kostas held The Rooke's arms, guiding him through the wet streets as if in doubt of his ability to walk on his own. He did not object, grateful that his sons and the rest of the party survived. He felt grateful to hear that Cymbre Varian had gone on to Talon. He did not wish to put that girl in more danger for being in the wrong place at the wrong time.

Aleron and Tavares had become fast friends, huddling together in front of The Rooke, pointing at different shops and structures in the ancient city that operated much as it had a thousand years past.

"I always loved this place," Kentigern said. He stood behind The Rooke with Aldo. "Peaceful. A reminder. Such a simple way of being."

The Rooke loved the old pub, a memory of how things had once always been. A magnificent hearth filled with flickering flame that warmed the stone pub, tables surrounding a hand-carved bar on three sides, a band playing ancient music, the musicians dressed in pre-Evanescent garb. Massive cande-labras hung from the ceiling, filling the darkening tavern with soft, orange light. The smells of fresh baked bread and cooking meats and herbs filled the air.

Tourists remarked on the bread, and The Rooke had to agree that the small brown loaves were heavenly. He found himself at ease, laughing with his friends when a rumble rang through the pub. He turned around to see her, a bounty hunter of the Illegal Procreation Department.

"Don't panic," Kentigern said, standing up and making his way toward her. "My guess is this woman is on your list."

"Is that....?" The Rooke asked.

"Yes. Looks to be one of the twins. Never thought a woman like Raven would have daughters so compliant to the empires," Aldo said, giving Kentigern a knowing look. "Tell a tale, Rooke. Distract her. There are a number of families that will not want her eyes on them."

"Joel, Tee, can you get the children out that might be target-ed?" Kentigern asked. "That will include Thiago, Kostas, Anwyn, and Taki. Take them back to temple."

"We want to hear the tale," Thiago said.

"We'll hide them behind The Rooke and sneak them out back door after," Tee Broomes said, herding the four children into the shadows behind The Rooke as his tale transported them into a mansion in the tropics.

A Treasonous Bounty Hunter, IPD

Rintyre Grayvesone had visited many temples in her travels. This one was special. She and her twin sister, Carling, had been born at this temple's clinic twenty-seven years ago. This was the first time she had been back. She felt a shiver of doubt mixed with wonder. It was like stepping outside of the world, outside of time.

The Temple of the Tail, a castle-like structure surrounded by a walled village that looked something out of legend rose over the horizon, surrounded on all sides by the fork of raging white waters of the Isfe River where it met the breathtaking Stora Dragga Waterfall.

While Rintyre appreciated the beauty of this wild part of the world, she did not like leaving her home in Aroghotto City. She loved the noise, the bright lights, the endless tall buildings, the little cafes, all the buzz and things to do. Everything began in Aroghotto City. All the best music. All the best theater. All the best livelies. All the best restaurants. All the great world events happened there.

She saw the rot like everyone else, the vagrants on the streets, the dark alleys average citizens feared to go. The corruption weighed on her, but Aroghotto always corrected itself and remained Aerda's greatest city. Her mother had taught her that you don't destroy the whole of something because a part is broken. You try to mend the broken bits or carve it away.

Rintyre would miss the whole week of the Unity Conference where the Chaziri Emperor, the Megdonian Second, and The Fistian Seat would join all the world's leaders and elites in hopes of bringing peace to the entire world of Aerda. A big event where new systems would be created including hospitals, schools, resource distribution, and housing. It would be a glorious thing. A historical event.

She sighed, reminding herself that the city would lock down, and navigating the streets would be irritating. Her girlfriend was angry at her leaving, and missing the events, but work forced Rintyre here in this remote corner of the world, back to her childhood haunts.

The Dragon Tail village promised to be a trove of riches, more bounties that would fill her coffers for a year or more. Few bounty hunters came here, not knowing how to find anything. Rintyre knew.

There were so many hiding here, so many children taken illegally to avoid their IPE evaluations or the procreation fees their parents owed. She took a deep breath, pulled her long, black leather, fur-lined duster close about her as the freezing rain and snow blew around her.

She repeated the lie she needed to keep her going. Her new assignment was better than the old. It paid better, gave her more flexibility, allowed her to travel, to see her family and old friends. She had not meant to end up in the tax collecting end of the IPE. Rintyre Grayvesone wanted to rescue children that had been taken for foul use.

She wanted to investigate, to see if there was any truth to what Bittore Rose said on the SIN before the famed luminary disappeared. With all Rintyre was, she hoped it was all the conspiracy her peers claimed. But why? Why would such a famed luminary say those things when it would cost her every-thing? Rintyre had been such a big fan of Bittore Rose. She could not understand it.

Rintyre's supervisor told her to forget it, that such insane accusations were the product of a troubled mind. He recom-mended assignments that would not require heroic rescue, given the loss of her twin's child. The compliance side offered Rintyre more credit than she had ever dreamed making, and for the main, it was only rebels who ran afoul of the Illegal Procreation Department when it came to IPE avoidance and fee collection.

Rintyre's twin loved this part of the world. Carling begged her to come and live in Talon with her and Bryter. Primordial Boreal did not suit Rintyre with its antiquated ways. Although, the quiet part of her longed for the forest-filled, mountainous vistas, to fade into a tranquil background free from the obliga-tions of her silver, green-ribboned sleeve.

Rintyre gave her adoration to the river before her and its natural grandeur. She took a deep breath and trudged across the drawbridge over the river into The Dragon Tail village that surrounded the temple.

If Rintyre could collect half dozen bounties, she would have enough for her and Mia to get a place in Plentiful Borough on the west side of Aroghotto City near the Palace Grounds. While no amount of credit could cure her sister's grief at losing a child, she could pay for Carling and Bryter to try again. She had already procured the permission for her sister's next pregnancy.

She hid her sleeve under her coat. People were naturally suspicious of agents like her. The little symbol engraved in the silver of her sleeve proclaimed Rintyre a bounty hunter with full authority. People took it wrong. Only those who were defiant needed worry, and only if they refused to pay the penalty or present their children for missed IPEs.

She wound her way through the streets among throngs of tourists visiting a world long gone. They pointed at the architecture, ducked in and out of shops among the smoky air and the aromatic scent of fresh cooked bread and herbs. Many dressed in what they believed people had worn thousands of years ago when the temple was first built.

It was a magical atmosphere. Rintyre remembered her sister talking about it, how she and Bryter had visited on their marriage sojourn. This trip had convinced them to move from the southern part of New Chazir to Primordial Boreal, to make their home in the village of Talon.

Rintyre felt a bit winded as she climbed up and up a winding slope to the old Dragon Tail Pub where she was to meet her contact. She took a deep breath and entered. It was crowding with the fading day. She surveyed the room with her sleeve's screen, scanning it for targets. She found three, not a procreation fee paid for any one of them, huddled in a booth with their young parents. She ran the calculations and saw the amount she would collect.

She loaded the tranquilizer to calm the parents who already had looks of despair on their faces when she found herself in a pirate mansion on an island in the middle of the jungle. She growled.

A rooke appeared, familiar, a face from her childhood and a story about her ancestor, Husk Grayvesone. Her father never shut up about him, and Rintyre did not want to hear. She turned to leave, but it was a rooke's tale. She had to stay and hear about a sick child and the sister that loved him.

The Tale of The Ambrien Tutor

Haunted. That is how the Rose Garden Manor felt to Husk Grayvesone. No one was dead, not yet, but already the phantom of little Xavier Rose filled the once opulent manor with despair. A sudden storm trapped Husk at his employer's home through uncomfortable hours as his young pupil fought against his dying breath.

The old guest room on the second floor suffered the musty odor of long disuse and neglect. In the span of five years, the Roses had gone from hosting week-long soirees for the rich and notable of Aerda to deeper and deeper isolation as they spent what wealth they had to find a cure for their only son.

Husk crept down the stairs from the guest room at the dawn, hoping to sneak out before anyone noticed. He nodded his head to the exhausted physician he passed on the stairwell. The man's demeanor reverberated defeat as he retreated to the room the Roses kept for him.

At the bottom of the stairs, Husk met Daedalus Sams entering the manor, his priory robes splotched with rain. Husk was happy to see his friend and cottage mate. Daedalus worked as a scribe for the clerics of the priory, keeping all the records of Janusians who lived on the six islands of Ambriland.

"What are you doing here, Daedalus?"

"I was sent to check on the situation, as soon as the storm broke, to see if Glorious Thierry needs to be summoned for final passage. Is it really that bad?"

"I fear it is so," Husk said. "I hate this. Xavier is such a bright and clever kid. How unfair his body should give out to this vile wasting."

"Devastating. I am going to call our patron and make one last plea, even if the Janusians object. If The Silver Swann would send her physician, maybe there is something he could do."

"I thought Dr. Rege already tried to help."

"Mirror Rose did not like what he had to say about Xavier's condition. He said it seemed to be a disease that passed mother to son. She took it badly. And even if Dr. Rege was right, there was not much he could do to reverse it. However, he could treat it, give Xavier less pain and more time."

"Pity. I will see you home this evening?"

"I am staying with Reginald tonight," Daedalus said. "Give you a chance to grade all those final papers."

"Reginald should just move into our cottage," Husk said. "We could use another flat mate."

"You hate Reginald."

"Only because he tortured me those first years when we were at school together. I know he's important to you," Husk said. "And we've made our peace out of love for you."

"Ah, you'll make me cry, mate," Daedalus said. "We could use Reginald's considerable resources at the cottage. I will discuss it with him. At any rate, we'll give you some space."

"I doubt I can concentrate enough to finish grading first year papers," Husk said, his head pounding at the very thought of reading papers on Hazel Kyran's translations of the first volume of *The Idylls of Alleysiande* written by eleven-year-olds. "I want to get out of here before I am spotted. I hate the storm that trapped me here. It's not pleasant in these walls. This place feels rotten."

"The Rose Manor is haunted on the best of days. Add a dying child…"

A young medic appeared from a narrow hall which led to Xavier's sick room which was located below the house in the old dungeons. The illness that claimed the boy made the sun and light toxic to him.

"Dejan? How is Xavier?" Daedalus asked.

"In pain still. The doctor could do little for him. I am going to retrieve a stronger pain remedy from the apothecary," the medic said. "Grand Cleric Clarence wants to see you, Daedalus. I imagine he wants to send for Glorious Thierry."

"See you later," Daedalus said, nodding to Husk. "You might go out the front door. Between doctors and the clerics, everyone is coming and going through the kitchens like Dejan there. You are more likely to get out unseen by the main entrance."

Husk realized too late he should have taken the crowded route through the kitchens. Xavier's older sister, Shanley, stopped Husk short of the front door. He could see the girl was sleep-deprived and had been crying by her mussed long hair and puffy eyes. She took him by the arm.

"Go to the wicker woman," she said.

"Shanley, I can't. There is no time. Send a servant. I have so much to do."

"My brother adores you. He is more than your student, Husk. He is your friend. You have been his constant companion for more than five years now," Shanley said. "And I can't go. No one will miss you. Xavier is going to die. Your other students can wait another day for their damn marks."

"What would be the point, Shanley?" Husk asked, feeling his own despair taint the question. "Your family enlisted all the greatest physicians in the whole of the civilized world. What can an old wicker woman do that the Rose gold cannot?"

"The wicker woman cured my acne when I was twelve," Shanley said. "She has magic. Besides, what could it hurt? She can hardly make Xavier deader."

Husk could see the desperation in Shanley Rose's brown eyes. He hated watching Xavier waste away at such a young age. The boy would not see his eleventh birthday. Husk wanted to help. Shanley clung to his arms, her fingernails digging into his flesh, asking him for hope.

"Do you know where this wicker woman lives?" Husk asked, relenting.

"You don't know? I thought Ambriens always knew…"

"About wicker women? Shanley, this is not time for your romantic notions of us natives. Where did you find this wicker woman when you had your acne cured? Will she even be there? It's been over five years."

"Yes, she's still there. I am certain. Reginald Diamont went there just last year with your friend, Daedalus. They got what they needed. Go to the woods. I don't know what path I took. I needed to find her, and I did. That is how it works."

"Nothing works like that," Husk said. "I will go to the village. The locals go to her for their ailments. They can tell me how to get there."

"There's no time for you to go to Marinplaz and ask," Shanley Rose said. "Go to the woods. Find the wicker woman and ask her to help Xavier. Tell her my family will pay anything she likes if she will save my brother."

"I do not believe she can cure a wasting if no physician in all the world can," Husk said. "Wicker women are not magical, Shanley. Yes, they can brew a tonic that will help you concentrate, make a poultice to cure acne or hemorrhoids, and teas for the pain of childbirth. The best thing to do for Xavier is to be with him. Go hold your little brother's hand, read to him. There is so little time left."

"No, Husk. You must do this. I can't lose another brother. The physician says he will live another day at most."

"Another brother?"

"It doesn't matter. Xavier is going to die. Please help."

"I don't believe…"

Shanley stomped in frustration, grabbed Husk's glasses off his face and broke them. "Believe this, Husk Grayvesone. Your patron, The Silver Swann, will not pay for another pair of these fancy spectacles nor will my father in his grief at losing his only son. He will not need you as a tutor if Xavier dies, and you can say good-bye to living in that fancy cottage and making application to Dalmeade. The wicker woman can fix these stupid things. Only she will fix them. Go. Find her, you half-blind fool. Save my brother."

There was no arguing with Shanley Rose's temper so into the woods Husk ventured on that foggy morning, the smell of last night's storms still in the air, the humidity heavy, causing his thin tunic to stick to him. Although the stretch of jungle was narrow, Husk could not recall how he found his destination.

He felt too angry with Shanley threatening all his plans and dreams, sleep-deprived, stressed, and grieved to be fearful as he might have been, straying from the paved paths between the Rose Manor and Marinplaz or the Kingswell College.

He plunged through the tight trees, stepping on what looked like worn paths in the dirt until smoke rising from a chimney summoned him.

A Refused Token

"Stop." Rintyre Grayvesone glared at The Rooke, no longer the sweet, little girl he once knew. "What are you doing?"

Aldo Thierry and Kentigern Dagan Leesh stepped forward to silence the young woman.

"Rintyre, reach into The Rooke's pocket," Kentigern said. "You won't regret it."

"No. I will not."

"Rintyre, I knew your mother and father," The Rooke said. "I helped raise your father. We aren't going to hurt him."

"You and your lot are all a lie," Rintyre said. "I don't speak to my father. I can't help you find him, and even if I could, he wants fuck all to do with you fanatics. I am leaving. Do not contact me again or you'll be sorry. I have no time for schemes of the rebels and their allies."

"But your mother is in trouble," Kentigern said. "We want to help…"

"I know who my mother is," Rintyre said. "Close your robes, Rooke. I want none of your magic tokens."

"My, aren't you a jolly soul," Thiago said. "Your father was behind getting two rookes killed."

"Look, I can't stand my father for being such a weakling," Rintyre said. "But it wasn't him that betrayed the rookes. It was her. Baroness Teriss Amber. She destroys everything my father loves. Who are you?"

"This is my son, Thiago," The Rooke said.

"You have a son?" Rintyre asked.

"Two, actually," Kostas said, stepping forward. "And you are beautiful. Like you're not even real."

"Cute," Rintyre said, fiddling with her sleeve. "Two sons? You had a woman? I was under the impression that women were not of interest to you, Rooke."

"We're adopted," Thiago said. "And it's perfectly legal. Before the Illegal Procreation Department existed. Why would you work for such a corrupt organization?"

Rintyre Grayvesone growled and turned on her heel and stalked out of The Dragon's Tail. She disappeared into the darkness like smoke. The Rooke and Kentigern exchanged glances.

"That could have gone better," The Rooke said.

"She's on the list," Kentigern said. "And she disrupted the robe's magic."

"Not that surprising considering her parents," The Rooke said. "She has a magic she doesn't believe in. Lovely. And my sons will be in danger from her. There will be a large bounty on them regardless of when the IPD was formed."

"I could satisfy her bounty and pay her," Aldo said. "And Joel and Taki might be able to keep her safe from her employers."

"This is dangerous, Kenny," The Rooke said. "These people really need both revelation and revolution."

"The people do try, and people like our lovely Rintyre make sure they don't succeed."

"Well, there is one good thing," The Rooke said. "She is conflicted. I can feel it. We might win her over in the end."

"I don't know, Rooke," Aldo said. "She seems comfortable in her chains."

"Unfortunate, really," Kentigern said. "Your tale did not even move her. She'll be a hard nut to crack."

"She's already heard that particular tale told a thousand times by a father she despises," The Rooke said. "It's not surprising it has no hold on her even when I tell it."

"The Seventh Offers a Bounty Hunter, IPD," Aldo said, pushing through the crowd of people, hoping for tokens.

"Indeed," Kentigern said, patting The Rooke on the back. "We'll sort it."

"Have you contacted your son, Kenny?" The Rooke asked.

"I did. Paul and Laurel are expecting us in the morning," Kentigern said. "We can't all stay with his family. Some will have to go on into Talon."

"We should start traveling separately in any case," The Rooke said. "The tokens will tell each of our party where to go. After Talon. Once we reach Astarte."

"If we reach Astarte," Aldo said. "I have never known a rooke to be pursued before crossing the Boreallean Sea."

"Someone inside The Reliquary betrayed us," The Rooke said. "And it wasn't Bracken Grayvesone or that horrible woman that seduced him. He could not have let Scarlets in. It was not Ambriel's Cube either. Someone who was already in The Reliquary did that."

Tavern IX:

Tem's Tavern

The mortal body is little more than a fading illusion. Rotting flesh is a sign of transformation as true as that of the caterpillar that becomes a butterfly.

The Idylls of Alleysiande, Vol V, Haniel's Elixer
author unknown (translated by Hazel Kyran)

Shades of a Better World

Mika Finn looked annoyed at the ox-drawn cart that greeted them at the little rail station in the quaint village of Talon. The Rooke felt relief at sight of the tiled rooves that lined the cobbled lanes, smoke rising from the chimneys, the stacked stone cottages, carefully crafted in an age gone by, surrounding a town square with the large inn, just visible down the road.

Joel, Tee, Zac Grimm, Aleron, Tavares, and young Taki turned toward the inn that was within view of the station.

"Zac, you're welcome to join us," The Rooke offered as the young man helped Anwyn onto the cart.

"Thanks, no. I want to make sure Cymbre got here safely," Zac said.

"You have a girlfriend," Anwyn said to him, laughing.

"And you have a boyfriend," Zac shot back, smiling as Kostas took a seat next to her. The two children looked at each other and made sick faces.

"You're ridiculous," Anwyn said.

"We will meet you at Tem's Tavern tonight," Kentigern said. "I wish there was room for all of us at my son's place. Taki, you can come with us if you like."

"I wish to stay at the inn," Taki said. "I like inns. They feel like home."

"We'll make sure the lad is safe," Tavares said. "I could do with a nap."

"No modern vehicles are allowed in Talon," Paul Leesh explained as he loaded the last of the packs onto his large cart. "I am chuffed you are here. Worrying rumors and signs have come before you."

Kentigern embraced his son before pulling himself on the cart next to The Rooke and Aldo. "I have missed the valley," Kentigern said. "The last years The Relic kept me too busy to visit."

The evergreen trees made a tunnel as they ventured a short way into a forest that opened to a wondrous glade where Paul Leesh had built his home.

A pang of heavy sorrow and wonder in equal measure assaulted The Rooke as the little cart slogged along a cobbled lined path against the backdrop of coming spring as snow melted away and patches of yellow green appeared in the valley around them.

A large house stood on a bump of a hill with a well-thatched roof and stacked stone covered in vines with tall windows on every side. Animal noises echoed within a barn of weathered wood, and the smell of hay drifted on the breeze, bringing comfort to The Rooke. A small guest house sat between the barn and the main house.

"We have been busy making the guest house extra cozy," Paul Leesh said. "For you, da. I wish you and mum would consider living here. Anyhow, for tonight, Aldo and The Rooke can stay there. The rest can stay in the main house. Of course, Mika, you and your girl can stay tonight if you wish."

"Thank you, but we'll stay at the inn," Mika said. "It'll be late after The Rooke is done I feel sure, and it seems a bit crowded already."

"It's beautiful here," Anwyn said. "So many animals. I miss my dog. And my snake. We had to leave all my animals behind we had to leave so sudden."

"We have goats, cows, and chickens," Paul said. "And sheep and three dogs to manage them. And about four cats to keep the rats out of the barn."

"Heavenly," Anwyn said, as a little girl emerged from the house, long auburn hair, wild and tied with multiple ribbons.

"Pappy, pappy!" she called as she threw herself into Kentigern's arms. "I am so pleased you've come."

"Holly, I have brought you a friend," Paul Leesh said, smiling at his eldest daughter. "This is Anwyn Finn. She is the same age as you. She wanted to see the animals."

Holly Leesh wanted to come to the pub. She made quite the fuss about it, and The Rooke smiled as Paul looked to his unflinching father for support.

"Anwyn gets to go," Holly said, giving the girl a tight hug as if to claim the girl.

"Anwyn must go," Kentigern said. "She and her mother are staying at the inn tonight."

"I still want to go hear The Rooke's tale," Holly said.

"I don't know," Paul's wife said with an approving smile. "Rooke's tales can be a touch intense. I don't want you having nightmares."

"Fine. I am older than Kostas. If he gets to go, so shall I," Holly Leesh argued.

"You're not a puzzler," Kostas said.

"I can do puzzles without fancy classes in it," Holly said, giving Kostas a little shove and a large snarl.

"We'll look after her," Anwyn added. "Right, mother?"

"Sure," Mika said, suppressing a bit of a chuckle.

"And we won't give her more than a half pint beer," Aldo added.

"Not helpful, Aldo," Paul said.

"If Holly goes, I want to go," her eleven-year-old brother, Jace, said. "She is only ten months older than me."

"Yes, but you're a boy and very immature," Holly said. "You should stay and play with Embla."

"I am not immature," Jace said, sulking.

"If you go, Holly," Paul said. "Your brother is going too. If your mother says it is all right."

At this, the youngest Leesh child, Embla, began to cry, the four-year-old enraged that she might be left out. Her mother picked her up.

"Embla, I say we have a special girls' night, just you and

me," Laurel Leesh said. "Paul, take the children. It's only Tem's Tavern. We're not sending them on The Rooke's quest precisely. And what if they never have a chance to hear a rooke's Tale again? They are old enough to hear a story."

"And have a pint," Holly said, strengthening her stance, hands on hips, legs firmly planted in a fighting brace.

"Of cherry ginger," Paul said. "All right, but no shucking your chores in the morning, either of you. It'll be a late night."

A fading sun and a perfect breeze greeted the group as they parted Paul's house, putting their feet to a tree-lined cobbled path toward sparkling lights in the nearby village of Talon. The Rooke felt elation, a renewed hope at the promise given in the soft rustling limbs and the fresh smell of winter's surrender to the coming spring as they wound their way on the short hike to the village.

He thought of Phaedra and her moments of joy and understood what had allowed her to escape Pandemonium. That mad and wonderful sorceress. Terrifying in her power, unparalleled in her sacrifice to reclaim Alleysiande for a world that did not deserve it.

Smoke rising from chimneys from the quaint cottages that peppered the valley and wood around and in Talon greeted the chill in the air. An imperial sign served as a reminder that the empires had extended their reach although it was a tenuous one. Few who lived in the inner part of Primordial Boreal in towns like Talon wore implanted sleeves, and some none at all.

The Rooke heard the children laughing as they half-jogged in front of the adults, chasing each other, teasing Thiago with words and pinching him and running away before he could grab them. Thiago determinedly tried to walk in step with Aldo, Kentigern, and Paul, a man grown and not a boy to be teased into silly actions, until the serious young man broke, and took off at full sprint to catch his brother in a headlock and throw him laughing into a thick field of grass.

The two wrestled together, happy, young, forgetful of their troubles. As childhood ought to be. This could well be the last night in a long time that his boys could enjoy being children.

Tem's Tavern stood at the middle of the village square, a long low building with multiple chimneys, built of stacked stone and thick wood planks. Delicious scents of wondrous cooking emanated around the tavern as villagers and valley dwellers straggled in for the evening, greeting each other happily as if they were all family.

Tee and Joel Broomes, and Taki Toura met The Rooke's party outside the tavern which was connected to an inn by a low stone building that housed several shops, now closed for the evening. Taki spoke quickly to Thiago, pointing at Kostas who laughed in delight. His sons turned to introduce Jace and Holly to Taki and they all embraced as if they had known each other for years. It was the sort of social grace that often suffered under the steel grip of the empires beyond this Northern realm.

Paul Leesh greeted neighbors who recognized both Kentigern and Aldo. They all fell into talk as they entered Tem's Tavern under the painted sign of a silver, blue, and white dragon. The Rooke felt himself tugged forward as Paul pulled him to the fore.

"Do we have a treat for you tonight," Paul Leesh said, addressing his neighbors. "You are to have a rooke's tale."

The people who dwelt in The Valley of the Tail still nurtured a love of music and fireside tales. By the time The Rooke and the group were sipping on ale after a full supper, Tem's Tavern was full to bursting. People had come from neighboring villages to hear his tales, bringing their children with them, some younger than Anwyn, Taki, Kostas, Holly, and Jace.

Aldo loudly ordered another pint as Kentigern pulled out his tome and got to his feet to make the customary introductions. The Rooke pulled off his overcoat to expose the red robes and like a wave breaking, conversations silenced.

In a table, alongside the makeshift stage, sat Anwyn Finn and his sons while Zac Grimm and Cymbre Varian crept forward, making their way through the crowd, trying to get closer. Aleron stood up and offered Cymbre his chair. People were packed in, arm to arm, head-to-head, even with The Rooke's magic extending it beyond its natural borders.

The Rooke took a breath, a feeling, a recollection shuddering through him as he saw the inside of the Rose Manor. He had walked those planks once upon a time as a man or a boy in the flesh before his robes scrambled his memories. He had met little Xavier Rose and played music for the little lad. He let out the story, as if through his eyes, meeting Husk on the stairs, hearing him entrapped by the lovely Shanley Rose. He followed Husk down the path into the jungle.

The Hidden Spyte

*I*n The Reliquary, the people painted the women who ruled the Spytes as evil, monstrous witches whom they dubbed gutter baronesses. Cymbre Varian thought this most unfair when she first arrived in the mountain sanctuary, her wrists scarred and bloody. Quite convincing.

Spytes never wore implanted monitors. Cymbre faked the wounds typical of those who decided to quit SIN the moment Aleron found her. Pure luck that gave her a way into the secret Reliquary.

Baroness Teriss Amber sat across the table from her in the White Tower, a village within sight of The Dragon Tail Village, tapping her fingers, a vision of loveliness that Cymbre would never match. She related all she had learned about rookes, about The Reliquary, about the taverns they had visited, about the little Nacharye girl with the magical box.

"There is more to learn I am certain," Cymbre said. "The Rooke has a list of some kind. It seems this Nacharye girl, Anwyn, is on it. As is a Gnolgia boy called Taki. It'll be seven from what I can ascertain, one for each of those odd Aspects."

"Did these Aspects suspect anything?"

"Not at all. For a time, I struggled with the magic, could

not remember why I was there. I made up a number of stories, not my best work. But it was expected I suffered from trauma which drew sympathy. I played the grateful, broken girl. Kept humble and silly and weak. I grew flowers. I taught children their letters and their numbers. I even made biscuits, sweet ones with chocolate and caramel."

"Have you seen this list?" the baroness asked, a hint of impatience as ever.

"Oh no, not at all. I won't risk raising their mistrust," Cymbre said. "They think me a bit simple. I am even love struck if you want to know. A young man, Zac Grimm, travels with them. You know of him?"

"The gamer and crude luminary? Despicable and acceptable all at once? That Zac Grimm? He disappeared."

"Yes, the very one. I found him hiding in The Reliquary with that awful father of his," Cymbre said. "He's not much to look at truth be told, but he's gullible and sweet. He's not a terrible lover."

"Clever. You are doing well, girl," the baroness said. "Here is what I would like you to do. Snatch that magic box and get it to Nox Verre. I will grant you a castle if you can do that."

"Could be tricky. I secured a teaching job for the nursery in Talon. It would give us access to new recruits."

"Did you?"

"Of course. The difficulty is that in Primordial Boreal, my magic isn't working right. I tried to grab the box once I learned of it back in Sentinel Peake. I couldn't even get to the part of the bar where The Rooke was speaking. And tonight, I am missing another tale as I did at The Last Resort. Do you have a cure for this?"

"Use your lust for Zac Grimm to overcome the magic. Hear the tales but do not listen. Those stories are full of deceit and dirty magic. Rookes can be dangerous, Cymbre," Baroness Amber said. "I captured and married a rooke's apprentice, who was married, with children eight years younger than I pretend to be. I got him to abandon all his tired, old ways, to help 'save' me, and for pleasures his ex-wife could never hope to give him. I will supply you with arryl weed. It will help you keep this Zac in line in the same way I captured Bracken Grayvesone."

The grin on Baroness Teriss Amber's face was like a crocodile smiling at her, a beautiful, wicked, and insatiable reptile. Cymbre did agree with the people of The Reliquary in one regard. Gutter baronesses posed a danger to all around them. They were perilous women, and one day, Cymbre hoped to be one of them.

"I will bring Zac to our cause. What else can I do for you, Baroness?"

"If you can dispatch little Anwyn Finn and her mother, you will be promoted. We can't leave Nacharye wandering about the world unchecked," she said. "And Gnolgia should be eliminated anytime they are found. You will get a nice bounty for that child's head. And I am afraid, we would need his head as proof. Ears, eyes, you know, the usual checks."

"I have someone on it already," Cymbre said. "What of the bounty for the girl and her mother?"

"Any limb will do for Nacharye. Arms are easiest. Then you will have title and riches to go with your castle. You'll love Nox Verre. It is second only to Aroghotto City in luxury. I have a summer home there on the coast in the new IBT resort towers and suites."

The two looked out into the cold rain as a few people tracked away toward their homes as the sun began to set. Cymbre shifted, considering a question she desperately wanted to ask. She took a sip of her drink, mustered her nerve. She needed to know.

"What of the baby I stole for you four-years ago?" Cymbre asked. "Is he working out as you hoped?"

"Dear, that is none of your business." A scowl soiled Baroness Amber's perfect face. Cymbre pushed through a momentary fear. Baroness Teriss Amber was known for her temper, sometimes irrational and always cruel. A beat and then the scowl retreated.

"I'm sorry. Of course," Cymbre said, putting on her meek,

subservient persona to deal with the baroness. "I am anxious to learn how to turn children as I find them. It would be a good revenge for the terrible rebels of this place."

"You remind me of myself at your age. How I wanted to prove myself," Baroness Amber said, turning to leave and signaling Cymbre to follow. They walked arm and arm like sisters outside into the cold, early spring evening.

"I do want to prove myself," Cymbre said. "I would like to raise a house full of young Spytes, a veritable arsenal of weapons for our cause."

"I love the way you think. I can teach you, but it is best to start with an infant. We had to be so careful with you because of your age. Four is a late start. It was easier as your parents were both neglectful and abusive. They, unwittingly, did a good bit of the work for us," Baroness Amber said, putting on her sad face. "Truly, Cymbre, you are my greatest achievement in all the Spytes I have created over the years. The death of your family was pure artistry. No one even suggested you as suspect. I loved the horror lively they made about that case."

"It was not too accurate," Cymbre said. "The rebels they suspected were far too stupid to have done as they showed. I was not so messy. Although, it was useful that they conclud-ed that I died, that the rebels had taken me and eaten me. Lovely touch."

"It was for effect, dear," the baroness said. "Once you are fully promoted, I will share all with you, and we will make our dynasty. We will bring the Chaziri Emperor, The Megdo-nian Second, and The Fistian Seat all under our yolk. You will be the greatest baroness of all, and I will be queen of this forsaken world."

"Baroness, I have marked little Embla Leesh," Cymbre said, unable to contain herself. "It was her twin I took to substitute for the child I brought you."

"Extraordinary. What of her parents?"

"Pure rebels," Cymbre said. "This little girl could give us a way into Primordial Boreal. I would be her teacher in the autumn. However, her parents are not neglectful or abusive. It will take work."

"My. I am not sure I have ever been so impressed with one of my pupils," the baroness said. "I have some ideas that will help you pull the soul of that child from her."

"Thank you. It is nothing compared to your accomplishments."

"Perhaps," the baroness seemed caught in a delicious daydream. ""I have to go to Aroghotto City for the Unity Conference. I hope to get a nice supply of suitable newborns there. All three empires owe me tribute. I must also entice my husband to commit suicide, and that has not gone as well as I had hoped. The death of the famous Bracken Grayvesone will lift my celebrated status, the grieving widow. I will do a massive campaign on mental illness, drug abuse, and grief. I may even go to rehab, for recruitment. The SIN will love it. It will be a busy few months for us, my dear."

"Is it possible for me to birth an heir of sorts?" Cymbre asked, the question coming unbidden to her lips.

"With Zac Grimm as the father? Let me think on it," the baroness said as they arrived at the small train station. "Your train will be first. I have to go to Mal Leshen and take airship. I tried to birth a Spyte myself, you know, but never could manage it. Too much magic will wither the womb after all. Which is why I had you steal my husband's grandchild. My little Jude will be great in time. He has already soiled three nannies, and he is only four."

The train rumbled its way toward the small village of Talon where Cymbre had performed the mission that earned her first promotion some four years ago. Unsavory that. Find a dead infant, unmarked, to trade for a live one. The twins made a perfect opportunity. Strangle one, leave the other, cast a spell to make the parents forget they ever had twins. Give the dead twin to the mother of the infant Baroness Amber wanted.

As Cymbre disembarked the train in Talon, she felt that awful dark cloud descending, that voice that told her how fallen she had become. She felt like she might start screaming as unwanted feelings assaulted her regarding a memory.

The screams of the mother she had left the dead infant for haunted her. She found herself wishing she could tell the mother that the dead infant was not hers, that her child would live and be so rich. A good life, better than one in the provincial town of Talon could offer.

Transporting a live newborn across the Boreallean Sea had been awful. Strange. She recalled looking into the child's wanting eyes as her ovaries screamed for her to have a baby of her own. Unwanted visions of a pastoral life in a country cottage with a loving husband and three or four children running about a yard with dogs and chickens while she held an infant to her breast about drove her mad.

She felt broken from the day she handed the infant to Baroness Amber in the imperial hospital four years past. A wave of self-hatred passed through her like an illness from which she would never recover. Fury shook her.

She would be powerful. She would be wealthy. She would ride Zac Grimm like one of the broncos he talked about from his childhood in Southern New Chazir. She saw the young man outside the inn by Tem's Tavern. He smiled and ran to her.

"I missed you. I am so pleased you got here safely," Zac said. She spied a couple she did not know with young Taki. The other children were nowhere to be seen. Aleron and Tavares both smiled and waved, disappearing into the inn.

"You're here?" she said, feigning surprise. "Oh Zac, I got so scared. When you came back for me at The Last Resort, I knew I couldn't put you in further danger trying to look after me. All those soldiers so after our splendid night together in White Tower, I knew I could not go to the temple with you. And now I am here. I guess it'll be good-bye soon."

"Nonsense," Zac said. "You won't start a new teaching job until autumn, right?"

"Yes, but I have nowhere to live. I have so much to do, to

get my life together," Cymbre said. "It's so beautiful here but lonely. I do miss living in a city. Do you?"

"I never did live in a city. Fox Glove was an hour train ride away from The Broken Fingers, and even it wasn't so big as Heath's Night or Aroghotto City or Nox Verre," Zac said. "Let's have a meal. The Rooke will be here tonight to tell his tale. Oh, and you should meet Joel and Tee Broomes. They are going to come with us."

"My, our party is growing," Cymbre said. "Who are Joel and Tee?"

"Tee is an alchemist, a good one," Zac said. He looked so happy. "I was thinking, you know, with your headaches, Tee could brew you up something to make them stop. Joel is a scientist but has gone religious like and thinks he's a demon hunter even though he doesn't want to ever see a demon and has never confronted one. But he knows technology. He'll be useful."

"Demon hunter? That's so silly," Cymbre said, a little warning going off in the back of her mind. After all, Spytes made frequent use of demons.

"Tell me about it," Zac said. "All of this is silly. And terrifying."

"Hey, can we get to the tavern a bit early. So we can get a good seat?"

"Sure, anything you want my Cinderie Cymbre."

Zac and Cymbre lost track of time in their room in the inn. When they arrived at Tem's Tavern, it seemed the entire village had come to hear The Rooke's tale.

"Oh good, you won't have missed much," Zac whispered. "He's retelling the tale he told at the Dragon's Tail. It got interrupted like I told you. Hey, there's a seat with the kids up front."

Cymbre followed Zac but found herself creeping through a jungle, coming to a fairy tale cottage, caught up in a rooke's tale. She tried to turn it off, to escape the story, but she was trapped, and the tale carried her away into the far distant past.

The Tale of The Wicker Woman

The wicker woman's cottage appeared like something out of half-forgotten cautionary tale. Skins of slain animals were stretched out to dry in the sun. Wildflowers and herbs grew furiously along a fence groaning under the weight of clinging vines. An orchestra of scent both bitter and sweet greeted Husk Grayvesone as he pushed through the gate.

The woman was sweeping the cobble stones around a front garden, her back to him. "What brings you to my home, boy?" The wicker woman did not turn as Husk stood inside the gate.

In Ambriland, such women were common as dirt. She did not merit the shiver that ran up his spine. Exhaustion no doubt flamed Husk's imagination. His words came to him as desperate as the look in Shanley Rose's eyes.

"I need your help. A boy is dying," Husk said.

"Tragic. And who are you?" She turned to face him, a woman on the brink of her elder years, her youth fighting the hint of gray in her hair and the wrinkles around her dark, violet eyes.

"My name is Sebastyn Grayvesone, but everyone calls me Husk. I was born fat. Husky my dad called it, but then he died, and the nickname stuck."

"You have clearly outgrown the fat, but I like the name." The wicker woman stepped closer to him and looked him up and down. She smiled at him. "I did not need an explanation."

"I babble when I'm nervous."

"You've naught to fear from me, young man."

The wicker woman varied from other such women Husk had encountered. She was not an Ambrien like him nor Blesayre as most of Ambriland's wicker women tended to be. She was a hearty plump, sturdy and not quite tall. In her violet eyes, Husk saw wisdom or something darker.

"I am not afraid. I am tired. Xavier Rose is dying. His family will pay if you can help him."

"And they sent you? Why not send one of his family to bargain for the life of their kinsman?"

"Xavier's sister sent me. Shanley Rose. She has romantic notions of wicker women and native ways, one her family would not approve."

"I am not a native, and you are no islander, yourself. You've the Ambrien jeweled green eyes of Ambriel's own people. The dark skin is perhaps of the islands."

"I am a native. Ambriens are the most native to Ambriland."

"No, not so. They came after the Blesayre were already here. When they escaped the fall of Alleysiande. They gave the islands their name. No matter. What do you think, Husk Grayvesone?"

"I don't want Xavier to die. I have been his tutor for five years, all through my university years. He is a good kid and a better friend, but he is so ill. I fear there is little you can do. He may not last another day."

"What is there to lose then? You best come in and give me those broken spectacles of yours," the woman said.

Husk followed her into the stack-stoned cottage. His eyes squinted in the dimness of the smoky front room. She disappeared into another room behind a beaded curtain, taking his spectacles with her. Shadows of light obscured the details of the cottage he might have seen had his glasses not been broken.

In a massive stone hearth, a black cauldron bubbled without the benefit of flame or heat. Husk found himself unnerved by the room. From the tall, beamed ceiling, a fan spun cool air about although the humidity pressed its advantage. The stench of herbs and something unpleasant mixed with the wet heat. A movement in the shadows caught Husk's gaze. Cats. It was the stench of too many cats. They were everywhere.

A tortoise-shell feline startled Husk, jumping from the chair in which he attempted to sit. In all the niches, corners, and crannies of the room, tabby cats, imperial long-haired cats, black cats, gray cats, white cats, and a huge royal blue mountain cat lorded over their positions, taking little notice of Husk or each other.

"Be glad of my sweet cats," the woman said from the room where she prepared tea. "They keep the spirits of this place tame, you see."

"I don't know much about cats," Husk said. "My mother didn't like them. She said they were like to steal my soul and trade it off to some demon for a fish. After my mother left, I went to orphanage. When my patron, The Silver Swann, took over the place, she donated cats to keep the rats away. It did not go well."

"How's that?"

"The orphanage was in Tiponi Marsh. Swamp rats are monstrous, often bigger than the cats."

Husk reached out to stroke a purring cat's fur but drew back at a sudden movement, a snake he had failed to notice. The thin, blue-striped serpent curled up atop a stack of books leaning over the cat's resting place, its narrow jaws open to expose dripping fangs. Husk pushed himself back, blinking hard at the slithering movement before him.

The high bookcase ran the full length of the back wall, stuffed with both books and live snakes. He thought he must have screamed for the wicker woman appeared between him and the serpent. She deftly moved the angry, hissing snake to a higher shelf.

"Don't mind the snakes, dear. If you don't annoy them, they will leave you be."

"Damn thing nearly bit me. I don't like snakes," Husk said.

"That's fine, my dear. They don't much like you either," the wicker woman said as the tea kettle whistled from the back room. "And that's tea. Stay put. I will gather that and some little cakes I think you will enjoy."

She left Husk alone with both cats and snakes. The slithering serpents appraised Husk with their lidless, dead eyes rebuking him while enveloping the books they protected.

Both horrified and enraptured, Husk did not hear the wicker woman return with the tea and his mended glasses. He put his spectacles on, and the room became brighter, the snakes more fearsome, and the books, oh the books.

There were several rare, priceless tomes in the wicker woman's collection. Venomous serpents swirled around these volumes, one giving Husk a warning with a show of dripping fangs, sending his eyes searching another shelf.

Endless rows of brown leather volumes lined the shelves, hiding their titles in the uniform binding. Husk supposed this helped hide any banned or forbidden book. He and Daedalus employed the same technique for their little library of contraband. For reasons Husk could not fathom, King Charon had taken to marking several books as illegal for the common people to possess.

He spied a massive tome with a great black dragon etched on the thick cover of fine material that stood out from the others in both its ornate binding and the number of snakes curled and piled about it. He longed to touch the book but feared the serpents.

"Drink your tea," the wicker woman said, pushing the cup in front of him, offering him honey and lemon slices. Husk complied, dressing the steaming liquid. "Milk?"

"Yes, thank you," Husk said. She pulled a small pitcher from the tea tray and poured.

"This is one of my special teas. It will help you relax, Husk."

"Uh…what should I call you? I know you're the wicker woman they talk about at the college and in Marinplaz, but I have not heard your proper name."

"Don't have a proper name," the woman said. "It's dangerous for women like me to have a name, but you may call me Madame Darke."

"That's a dreadfully scary name," Husk said.

"I'm a dreadfully scary woman."

Husk swallowed hard. A wave of fear coursed through him. He dismissed it. Most women horrified him at one level or another. He opted for a change of subject.

"You have lots of books. Is that big one about dragons?"

"A bit," Madame Darke replied. "It's my late husband's grimoire."

"A spell-book?" Husk examined the book skeptically. "Are you a witch, Madame Darke?"

"Witch? I don't like that word at all, given all the silly tales written about such women dancing naked under the moonlight and eating children," Madame Darke said. "I never eat children."

"That's a relief," Husk said. He grinned to himself. "The dancing naked?"

"Hardly exclusive to witches I think."

"I do enjoy a good dance," Husk said, grinning to himself, feeling a smidge of tension release. "Please forgive my witch comment. I do not wish to offend."

"But you do hope I might be a witch with magic enough to help this dying boy."

"True. His sister believes in your magic, Madame Darke. She thinks it was something beyond a poultice that cured her acne when she was twelve. I remember. We were at school together. She was a few years behind me. Shanley was a horror, and her face matched her disposition. Once her acne went away, she softened, became less awkward, confident, and kind. I believe you also gave assistance to my friend, Daedalus Sams, and his boyfriend, Reginald Diamont, in recent months. Your work?"

"Your skepticism in this is merited. There is no magic in either of those cases. Teas, ointments, nature's course, a bit of hard study. Nothing supernatural. Husk, crude people might mark me as a witch, but I am only an old woman who enjoys helping people with forgotten arts."

"Xavier has seen near all the traditional healers in the whole of Aerda. None can help him."

"Then why come to me?"

"Shanley. She believes in magic and if you had some, she thought…"

"I do. I have the grimoires to prove it."

"How does that help? Can I have a look at your husband's grimoire?"

"You do not believe in these arts? Odd for one of Ambriel's own people. You are brimming with magic, young man. I feel it emanating off you."

"Me? Magical? No. I am musical although the two are similar. Please, I would like to have a look for myself."

"I will allow it, but I must warn you such tomes are perilous, more dangerous than your average book. Their bindings are infused with a captured soul."

"I will be careful. I love rare books and have never had the chance to read a true grimoire before. I did not believe in them. At least, not as they are in the Bone Master game of Idylls & Grimoires."

"They are not what that wretched game makes of them. Magic is not a common art. I doubt you will be able to read it."

"I graduated top of my class at Kings Hollow College two years ahead of schedule and am now a teacher. I do know more than a bit of Asciendien and the ancient runes. I learned when I was a child," Husk said. "My da's old ship captain taught me. Captain Jolly is a fine Muddy pirate, and most of his maps are scribed in Asciendien. It is the language of Alleysiande, right?"

"It's older than that," Madame Darke said as she pushed away a couple of black snakes, and one bright red and orange serpent to pull her late husband's grimoire out. She let Husk look at it. He felt a shiver run through him as he ran his fingers over the letters.

Husk turned the thick pages, translating a word here and there. He knew the language well-enough, but he had not mastered the full alphabet. A black cat hopped up onto his lap and pawed open a page.

"You like this page?" Husk asked the little feline. The cat mewed in response. "Madame Darke, are these exclusively spells? Or alchemical formulae as well?"

"My late husband was a dabbler. I doubt there is a full spell in there although you might find his recipe for spiced rum if you were clever enough. My grimoire is far more complete although it might not fascinate you as much as you might think.

It's also not so grand in its cover and binding. Would you be disappointed to know most of my spells are nothing more than recipes for favorite teas?"

"Coffee is the preferred beverage here in Ambriland," Husk said, absently.

"I am not from Ambriland and never acquired a taste for its coffee. Can you read my husband's grimoire at all?"

"A little. These glyphs are odd. Perhaps, it is merely the script?"

"That book is ancient. My husband was not its first holder, and I do not believe the original author meant to create a grimoire."

Husk cleaned his spectacles on his sleeve, and once more pondered the glyphs in front of him. He made out the glyph for calling or was it seeing? Calling what? Seeing what? Husk rearranged the tense and words in his mind. He recognized a series of glyphs, spoke the words in Asciendien they conveyed out loud, meaning to ask Madame Darke for a proper translation.

The world went blank. Husk felt himself falling and spinning into a great darkness. A dim light illuminated a silver-masked creature, robed and stinking of blood and rotten eggs. It hissed at him before taking him by the throat with black-nailed hands.

Husk tried to scream but made no sound. A second creature, foul in a feminine form, one that looked half-eaten, intestines dripping from her belly, grabbed hold of the masked demon holding Husk and tore him away.

"Wake up," she said to him. "Or you will be trapped here forever more like me. Come, we can both escape, but you must wake up."

"Wait. Who are you? What are you?"

"I am Phaedra."

The Winter Faerie

The people of the tavern stood up to applaud as The Rooke let go of his spell in order to give everyone a break. There were children here that needed to be in bed. It would not do for them to live inside a story. He assured them that all would be well.

"See, I knew reading was dangerous," Jace Leesh said to his father. "You shouldn't be making me do it."

"Learning is dangerous. It might lead to thinking," Paul Leesh replied to his son. "But life is not worth the living without the learning."

"That makes no sense," Jace said.

"I love to read," Holly Leesh said. "And I wouldn't mind letting a demon out at all if I got a good story out of it."

"Young lady, that is not comforting," The Rooke said. "Leave grimoires alone and you'll be fine. Your father has created quite the library for you and your siblings."

The Rooke watched Cymbre Varian as she blushed at Zac Grimm, trying to urge her forward. He wondered what that was all about. Aleron and Tavares joined them.

"Cymbre, would you like to meet some of your perspective students?" Aleron was saying.

"Rooke, Rintyre's twin is not here as I expected," Aldo said, pulling him into a dark corner by the back door behind the bar. "The barkeep informs me that Bryter Days is playing at The Dragon's Toenail across the bay from Warring tomorrow night. We should go there."

"Bryter Days?" The Rooke asked.

"That is a band, Rooke. Carling is married to Bryter Kenn. They have dubbed their band Bryter Days. Very popular in these parts. They play ancient music that has been updated to today's standard. According to some of the young folk here, they are extraordinary and well-loved."

"That's great. Why are you telling me this?" The Rooke asked.

"That is where we will find Rintyre. I had thought to skip The Toenail and go straight to Astarte but seems we will take the traditional path after all," Aldo said. "Let's get back to Paul's place. We might get a decent night's sleep."

Wild blueberries were in full blossom in the lands around Paul Leesh's cottage. In the pre-dawn hours, Jace and Holly picked a basket full for the final breakfast before The Rooke's quest began in earnest. The Rooke woke to the smells of bacon and eggs, the smokes from the stone stove and boiling kettles greeted and warmed him as he entered the kitchen.

Kentigern sat contently with little Embla in his lap, the little girl's head on his chest, her soft blanket in her chubby hand. "Coffee is up if you want," he said.

"You want to remain here, don't you?" The Rooke said.

"I do," Kentigern said. "But I have my own redemption to work on. I had thought this Bryter Kenn might make a good recruit from what Aldo has told me. Faster I finish recruiting, faster I can have this time with my family."

Holly skipped into the cottage kitchen through the back door, putting her basket of plump berries on the counter. Jace lifted his, smiling with lips and teeth blue from eating most of his take of berries.

"I picked more than Holly," he announced, chest puffed out.

"Doesn't count," Holly said. "You ate most of yours. Grandfather, I think I saw a garden faerie at the dawning."

"Did you?"

"She didn't," Jace said. "They all left with The Evanescence… whatever. They're all gone."

"Sometimes Tem wakes up to take a poo and then the faeries wake up for a bit," Holly said. "He can't sleep always, or he would be dead and not sleeping."

"Faeries are wicked creatures," The Rooke said. "Tricksters. Be grateful there are none here or they'd turn your berries sour the moment you picked them. Garden faeries think everything that grows belongs to them."

"As the old tales would have us believe," Kentigern said, smiling.

"The Fishers could tame them," Jace said. "The women, not the dragons."

"The Pella. The women Errapel made were only called

Fishers because of their dragons," Holly said, holding her head up. "Morrigan Doune had a sprite, not a faerie, didn't she?"

"You know the tale of the Last Fisher?" The Rooke said. "Paul, you and Laurel have educated your children well. Holly might make a fine apprentice in happier times."

"Faeries and sprites are the same thing," Jace said.

"They are not," Holly said, giving her brother a sisterly shove that earned a glare from her mother. "Sprites belong to the water."

"Not true. Morrigan's sprite was a water sprite, but there are garden sprites and ice sprites and dark sprites," Jace said. "Because they are the same as faeries."

"The Last Fisher did have a sprite, aye, or it had her. Difficult to say," Kentigern said. "She also had a Fisher dragon called Squishy."

"That's a stupid name for a dragon," Jace said, laughing.

"What would you call a dragon if you had one?" Laurel Leesh asked her son.

"Sir or Ma'am," Jace answered straight away.

"For we are crunchy and taste good with veggies," Holly said. "Dragons demand respect and songs."

"And tales and poetry," Aldo said, entering the kitchen and taking a mug of hot tea from Laurel Leesh. "Thank you, dear."

"Did Kostas join you, Holly?" The Rooke asked.

"No, he didn't want to get out of bed," Holly said. "I wish Ani was still here. She's my best friend now."

"Mum told us leave Kostas be. He has a long journey ahead," Jace said. "Pappy, why can't we go with you?"

Kentigern frowned, put little Embla on the floor. She ran over to her father who was washing his hands at the basin.

"I need you to look after things here, lad," Kentigern said. "Sing your songs, tell your tales, chase your faeries. Keep the ice dragon dreaming."

"What do faeries like?" Jace asked.

"Berries," The Rooke said, helping Laurel prepare the breakfast for the group.

"And flowers," little Embla said. "I would name my faerie, Flower, if I had one, and it would not be nasty. It would be sweet because I would share the mountain red berries with it."

"You don't like those berries," Holly said.

"That is why I would share them."

"Holly, if you do see a faerie," Paul Leesh said. "You need to tell me. If you really see one. And do not speak to it or go near it. Flee it. Children, faeries are as dangerous as venomous snakes, deadly spiders, and thrower scorpions."

"There are no venomous snakes here," Jace said, looking worried. "And pit beasts like thrower scorpions don't exist anymore."

"Da, I did see a faerie," Holly said. "I wasn't making it up."

The Rooke bristled. Faeries were not what children's tales made them to be, nature-loving, mischievous, and harmless. No, they were little tormentors of mortals, and they woke with the dragons. And the loss of Alleysiande had left them angry and spiteful.

Faeries of all kinds wanted the gardens of men and creation for their own and would delight at watching humans choose between slow starvation and quick poisoning before the dragons took flight and wiped Aerda from the universe.

Worse, only innocent children could see the creatures for what they were and could be easily enchanted by them. And changed by them. Adults and imperials would only see plagues of locusts ravishing their crops and stores of grain if legions of faeries began to awake with the dragons.

"Rooke," Aldo said, sliding next to The Rooke. "We have to hurry. Tem is not napping if Kenny's girl is seeing a garden faerie."

"What did this faerie look like, Holly?" The Rooke asked, as he poured himself a tea.

"It was blue and silver, had wings like ice cycles."

"That's not a common garden faerie. Those are green and pink. It is a winter faerie. It won't stay down this low," Aldo said. "Relax. It'll be too warm for it and winter faeries are solitary creatures. Probably the spring thaw drove it down this way. It'll go back to sleep. Tem will dream after last night's tale. It was a worthy one."

Tavern X:

The Dragon's Toenail

Time is everything and nothing to a demon.

A Walk in the Abyss by Sabarino Riley, translated by Hazel Kyran

Warring

*T*he breeze blew cold, and clouds grayed with promise of rain as The Rooke stood on the dock of the village of Warring, by the backside of the mountain. The journey by carriage had been rocky and unpleasant. They could use no technology, no trains nor trams, to avoid imperial tracking. It had been the only transport that Kentigern and his son could muster over the night that would take them from Talon to the coast.

The fishing boat looked old and dirty and far from comfortable. Taki Toura and Mika Finn inspected it and made some modifications here and there as the sun rose toward mid-day, talking to the captain who nodded, looking a fair bit scared. He was risking much to let The Rooke and his party sail with him.

Joel Broomes paced back and forth nervously as his wife shook her head. He looked at the boat then at his wife.

"We are going to drown. Or freeze."

"It is good boat," Taki said to the nervous man. "I make sure."

"You're a little kid."

"I know ships. You not be nervous."

"He gets seasick," Tee Broomes said. "I will give him something. He will calm down soon."

Zac Grimm and Cymbre Varian cuddled together, her head on his shoulder, both laughing. The Rooke did not mind. He sighed, wishing he could recall that high of being newly in love. Centuries blotted it out. A tickle in the back of his mind told him that was just as well, and he hoped the sorceress would not plague him with his truth again.

The Rooke took a seat on a rock by the cove peering across dark and choppy waters at the island of Dracik Taenagle across the bay by the Boreallean Sea. Dread of the future filled him.

This was the last bastion of the old world. He took a deep breath. He felt years falling on him, time running short.

"Zac and Cymbre do seem quite taken with one another," Kentigern said, patting him on the back and offering him a warm tea. "I hope Aldo is right about Rintyre Grayvesone. The list calls her treasonous. That worries me. Is she a traitor to us or the empire?"

"If she is treacherous to us that will be a problem. She will know we are hacking SIN to board our sleeves," Aldo said, fiddling with his craft to make new sleeves for Tee and Joel.

"Are we really recruiting that IPD agent?" Mika asked. "If so, I would like to have better guard around the children. Two of the kids will be in danger. Anwyn is Nacharye. Taki is Gnolgia. And what will Rintyre find if she looks into your boys, Rooke?"

"That they are legally adopted, and I am their father," The Rooke said. "Do not worry. The Relic put her on my list for a reason. Let us go."

Bryter Days

Carling Grayvesone smiled to hide all the darkness as the band played a roaring anthem in the small pub room. How her husband, Bryter, loved these small, intimate venues. She put her hand over her heart to feel its beat wondering how something so broken could keep functioning.

A SIN message vibrated on her wrist, lighting up the square screen. Her sister.

Where are you? Why are you not on stage?

Carling craned her neck to survey the crowd. Her sister, Rintyre, insisted on wearing black. Lots of black. Made it hard to find her in a dark crowd.

"By the bar. Voice is shot so no performing tonight."

She spoke into her wrist and watched the words type on her screen. Looking at her sister still felt something akin to staring in the mirror to see an angrier form of herself staring back at her. Carling watched Rintyre stalk across the room, fuming. It hadn't worked. She knew immediately.

"It was a trap," Rintyre said without Carling asking. "That ancient rooke is looking for father."

"Why is that a problem?" Carling asked, confused.

"I am no fan of our dad, Carly. But I don't want him dead," Rintyre said. "What do you imagine The Relic will do to a man they blame for betraying them and getting two rookes murdered?"

"Oh, well yes," Carling said. "Rin, I don't think they would…"

"Oh c'mon…"

"They would listen I think," Carling said. "The baroness is responsible for those deaths…"

"We can't prove that…"

"But I know it," Carling said, lowering her voice, giving her sister a look that said she was not going to argue. Not now. Baroness Teriss Amber was not what she seemed. A baroness was nothing. Just a titled sleeve, nothing more. But Teriss Amber was not that. She was something else. Carling never could get her head around it.

Carling still loved their father, even if Rintyre hated him. She had forgiven him. Men could be stupid when it came to women. She knew that because of her own husband. If she had the evil designs on Bryter as Teriss Amber had on her father, she felt certain she could manipulate him into doing about anything to keep her happy. Not that she would. She truly loved Bryter. They joined at the soul.

"Dad didn't have to fall for her crap."

"It wasn't his fault, Rin. It was her," Carling said. "It was Teriss who did the betraying."

"He didn't have to…"

"Mother forgave him," Carling said. "Why can't you?"

"Let's not talk about it," Rintyre said. "Bryter and the Days sound good, but they are not whole without you. What is wrong with your voice?"

"I've had a wretched cold," Carling said. "Look, Rin, our

new house is amazing. I love it in Talon. It feels right. You and Mia should come stay with us during the Unity Conference."

"I have asked Mia. She is so busy right now. She is furious with me for leaving at this time," Rintyre said. "She stands to make a great many credits during the conference. My guess is she will stay put, but I will come. I want to see your little cottage."

"Mother is coming next month," Carling said. "I talked to her this morning. I think I have her convinced to leave New Chazir at last. First, she is going to Jebellen. Really being mysterious about it."

"Jebellen would be better for her. She loves the wine," Rintyre said. "I'll talk to her. Carling, there are too many rebels in Primordial Boreal. They are dangerous. Maybe we could all move to Jebellen. It is a beautiful place."

"I don't know, Rin," Carling said. "Something feels wrong about the whole world right now. I don't like Chazir and Dagger being joined this way with The Fistian Seat, Gerrard Al 'Dhar, and Princess Lilith getting married. It's too much power in one place. And it's always the same people who have power. Rin, why can't you see it? Mother is not wrong about that."

"Yes, if you're a rebel and see it like that. Emperor Malcombe, Second Absalom, and Seat Al' Dhar are all figureheads. Nothing more. Besides, the people love the pomp and ceremony of a grand imperial wedding," Rintyre said. "They went all starry eyed when father married Baroness Amber, and that was a lesser royal wedding. It's just for show. It is the three senates who rule. And they are properly elected."

"Mother doesn't think so. She says it is all an illusion to make people think they have power. Only those with green ribbons on favored sleeves can be elected…"

"It's not perfect. But the world is mostly at peace because of it," Rintyre said. "Let's not argue."

"Let's not," Carling said, giving her sister that look only twins know. "I created a nursery in our cottage after you got us permission to try again. Bryter and I are having a lot of fun trying, but nothing is happening."

"Give it time, Carly. You will have a child," Rintyre smiled. There was no doubt of the love between the twins. "And then you will have to give up all this."

Rintyre clapped her hands as Bryter Days finished the tune, an old favorite of hers. The yellow-haired man bowed, an infectious smile. Bryter Kenn renewed Carling's hope. She turned to say something to her twin, seeing a look of absolute horror cross her sister's face.

"Wow, this is an honor," Bryter said from the stage. "We have a rooke here. Come, sir, play us a song. Tell us a tale. We welcome you."

The twins gasped as they found themselves in a tropical garden full of topiary animals after a great storm. They looked down a path decorated in bright flower peddles of yellow, pink, and blue.

The Tale of the Sorcerer's Snake

The great gale of 8646 left the grand topiary garden of the pirate estate, The Swamp, in chaos. Seashell Swann had evolved from the cruel Black Swann of her youth into the well-loved Silver Swann in her mature years.

She brandished large sheers against her damaged shrubbery as her Malachian monkey squeaked and fussed from the garden wall, hopping from post to post. The creature looked more squirrel than ape with its squat back legs and fat white tummy against piercing black fur.

Seashell repaired an eagle's beak as her white-haired valet prattled on and on about all manner of Swamp business from the mundane to pressing, raising his voice to be heard over the chattering simian.

Gerloch Nett kept a distance in respect for The Silver Swann's shears as she contemplated the footless flamingo and the pig with a bird's leg stuck in its snout. Pink flowers covered the cobbled garden path leaving a flayed apparition among a puddle of fuchsia blood.

This was Seashell Swann's private garden. Despite the wreckage of the latest storm, she found peace here. Her valet waited patiently for her to reply to his latest report. She had not been paying attention. She gave him a sly look and smiled.

"What was that?"

"I thought we might send Dr. Rege to Admiral Rose," he said. "Mirror can hardly object at this point. Xavier Rose is close to death. Your ward, Daedalus Sams, sent a message this morning. Glorious Thierry has been summoned for rite of Final Passage."

"No, no, no, no,no, nooooo, no-no, noooo," Seashell's monkey squealed. The creature's bark sounded like a negative on every question asked. Seashell knew the creature's tone. It was hungry, bored, and anxious. Three conditions that seemed perpetual with her pet familiar.

"Yes, Noe, I will get you food in a moment. Now hush, I can't hear myself think," Seashell said. "Sorry, Ger Nett. Yes, I will courier Bernard myself. Tell Dr. Rege to leave immediately. Was there anything else?"

Before her valet could answer, the bright garden disappeared and turned to ruin. Seashell could hear her valet calling for her as she found herself facing a horde of demons pursuing her other ward, Husk Grayvesone.

Help me, Seashell!

Seashell recognized the voice that pleaded to her, unwelcomed from the darkest bit of her past. Jezebel Darke, an unrepentant dark sorceress who Seashell had once called friend.

It's your ward. I can't free him. He's dying. Help me!

Husk wrestled between life and death, caught in the memory of when he first met Seashell Swann, when she first learned of the atrocities that were going on the other side of Tiponi Marsh at The Seaside Orphanage.

She saw Husk as a small boy, flanked by a plague of demon rats, legion to the parasite now attached to her ward, a foul thing in feminine form, intestines leaking from its belly and rectum, its eyes eaten out, fingers like claws. Seashell felt a mixture of horror and revulsion.

A spell spilled from Seashell's lips, memory calling it back up, and the deformed rats scurried away, back into Hell.

The Silver Swann had not seen her grimoire for a decade, during her last days as The Black Swann when her hair had been as pitch as a starless night, her face smooth and full, her youth maintained by her magic. She cursed at the awful hellions, but that parasite refused to unlatch itself from Husk Grayvesone. It pleaded mercy.

I am not a demon. I am Phaedra.

Straining for long unused magic, The Silver Swann pushed Husk out of his memories and back to Jezebel Darke's cottage in the jungle. Damn woman. She should have left Ambriland fifty years ago. What was that woman doing with Seashell's ward? A sudden shove sent Seashell tumbling backwards into the humid morning.

She swooned at the black memories the summoning recalled. She had broken the void's hold on Husk, but something else followed him through, a creature far worse than the odd parasite that Husk had bound. Dark magic came in waves, ancient, destructive, hunting, seeking her. In a flash of purple light, a silver-masked, black-robed specter appeared.

Don't interfere, old woman.

A loud pop sent a brightly colored serpent coiled and ready to strike. Not fast enough. Seashell sliced the venomous creature in two with her sheers and turned to cut down its hooded master. Gone.

Terminus, the grim specter returned. The Silver Swann knew this vile demonic creature all too well. Had he been at full power with a strong body at his command, the little sorcerer snake would still have its head and she would be cold and dead, lying in her great topiary garden.

What in the world had Husk Grayvesone gotten himself into? Had he somehow interrupted some vile spell of Terminus to bind that awful creature that gave herself a dragon's name?

Seashell steeled herself against the trembling that threatened to overcome her, weaken her, forcing herself to stand straight and tall. Noe scampered up a willow tree to survey the scene below, screaming in alarm. He would try to devour the snake. Seashell warned the creature.

"Not this one, Noe. It will make you sick. Your flaming poo will not hurt it. No good for Noe."

Seashell's valet pulled her back, letting out a scream of both fury and fear. Gerloch Nett despised snakes, but he feared losing his employer more. He stepped in front of her, watching the cloven snake writhe its last on the pavers before them under the shade of the crippled and balding flamingo topiary.

The scene amused Seashell, and she felt a hint of a smile cross her face, the horror erased by the courage of her valet. She gathered herself up and took control of the situation.

"Gerloch, we will need a groundskeeper, if you please."

He stood holding his tablet and quill before him like sword and shield, looking between her and the dead serpent, one or two strands of his white hair uncharacteristically mussed. "Ma'am?"

"A groundskeeper, one that will know how to deal with this situation. We can't leave the beast here. It will regenerate if we don't have it burned, and if I try to do it, well…"

The assassin snake would come back to life and finish her off if she so much as breathed on it. It was a clever little device used by only the best or worst warlocks, depending on where one stood on the subject of dark magic. It was not a spell she had ever mastered or would ever try to duplicate.

Noe whined above, his squeaks clearly speaking her familiar's fear.

"What is a sorcerer snake doing here?" Gerloch Nett asked.

"Wondering how it lost its head? I have no idea. Now, off with you, fetch."

"I can't leave you alone with the beast, madam…"

"It's not in any shape to get frisky with me. Go. We must have it burned."

"A groundskeeper then. Anything else?"

"Yes, I will need to visit Husk and Daedalus, and I will need my grimoire."

"Ma'am, you told me I was never to give you the vile book again. After what happened in the orphanage?"

"I am older. I am wiser. And this was a magical attack on my home which I cannot defend against without the aid of my grimoire. You may take it back once The Swamp is secured again."

"Yes, ma'am. I will make the arrangements and I will fetch a groundskeeper. The new one. He's not afraid of snakes."

Seashell plopped down on a bench next to an enormous gorilla topiary as a great weariness descended on her. This great bush needed a trim, and she started to pick up her sheers again but found no strength to lift them.

The leaf boogers protruding from the nostrils of the gorilla and the finger picking at them would have to wait until she regained her composure. Noe climbed to the top of the great ape, whining in concern. She felt the creature's keen awareness of her discomfort.

Madame Darke's summoning brought it all back, the horror of finding such evil so near The Swamp's front door. Seashell's little wards, Husk Grayvesone and Daedalus Sams, arrived at The Swamp fourteen years ago in such a pathetic state; both beaten and malnourished. She cursed the Mammon sisters, well paid by the crown to look after sea orphans.

How many skeletons had they found in the bogs? Too many, and Seashell could guess who those children had been. There should have been dozens of Ambriens at the orphanage, left by the tsunami that hit the islands of Gyo Gladden and Petit Kyo twenty years back.

When Seashell sent her people to investigate the claims of Husk and Daedalus about the events at the orphanage, not one other Ambrien child was found alive. Not one. Not even a half-blood.

Only Islander and Outlier orphans were given care, and she used that term loosely. Some had been sold to Fistian slavers whose operations were discovered on Ambriland's outlier islands. That had been a decade ago. Seashell had demanded the orphanage's proprietors, the Mammon sisters, executed for their crimes.

Both priory and Queen Sapphire refused. Not enough evidence to sentence the women for murder the royal court proclaimed. There had been no record that the Ambrien children in question had ever been sent to The Seaside Orphanage in Tiponi Harbor, and no way to determine to whom the remains in the bog belonged.

The Mammon sisters were imprisoned for malfeasance, a soft sentence and a short one. Seashell had taken to her grimoire for the last time. She only meant to punish the three Mammon sisters; Inez, Hester, and Nell, a powerful trio of witches with great, dark magic that required much blood.

The spell-summoned plague could not be controlled. Children died. Villagers died. They all met their end in agony, the guilty and the innocent. Hester Mammon escaped when taken from her cell to be put in hospital, killing four guards. The awful witch was never found.

Noe's chattering brought Seashell back to the present situation. That specter would seek out a body to mimic and who knew what that mean ghost plaguing her ward might do.

Seashell feared that this spirit, demon, or whatever it was, however weak, might possess Husk. She needed to act quickly. She wished to raise a shield around The Swamp and its grounds, and to set wards around Kingswell College to protect Husk and his students.

Seashell could not remember the spell. She stood watching the pieces of the serpent as it started to regenerate. Panic rose inside her and she held tight to her sheers. She considered making a run for it when she heard voices. Her pet familiar sat with its tail wrapped around a low branch, threatening to swing itself between her and the zombie snake should the need arise.

"Stay, Noe. You die, I die, my dear," she said in a whisper. At that, the little squirrel-like monkey went silent for a rare moment, its round ears perked up at the sound of approaching conversation.

The Twins

The Rooke pointed Kentigern toward the Grayvesone twins. "That is them, together? They look alike but not," The Rooke said.

"Identical yet distinctly different young women," Kentigern said. "Both a perfect mix of their mother and father. Both in good standing which may be good for us or maybe not. They are both angry with their father. Maybe, they will tell you more. Carling's husband already seems well-disposed toward you."

"I doubt Rintyre will trust us after the fiasco at The Dragon's Tail," The Rooke said.

"She might," Kentigern said. "I lied with the truth to bring her to the temple. She didn't know she was being set up. And I wouldn't have done if she had been anything but a bounty hunter."

"That is surprising," The Rooke said. "I never imagined a daughter of Raven and Bracken would do something so pro-empire. Although, with how Bracken sold his soul…"

"I feel there is more to the Bracken tale than we know. The Relic seems keen that he can be redeemed," Kentigern said.

"They might. I don't. Gareth's good wife is dead because of Bracken's poor choices," Aldo said, flanking the two men. "The twins have developed nicely."

"I always featured Rintyre as someone who kept bar, a chef, or an innkeeper if I'm being honest," Kentigern said. "Like her mother. I remember a little girl who loved restaurants and pubs and inns. She was so fascinated by them. Drove Raven about mad as she always wanted there to be a menu even when they ate at home. Back when they lived in Talon."

"I remember that. She always wanted greens with stinky, salted fishes and herb sauce," The Rooke said. "Carling was more like Kostas. Fish and chips suited her best. Their mother would make both and she and Bracken made the best of it. I remember a happy family."

Bryter Kenn coaxed the twins toward The Rooke. He smiled broadly, laughing at the scowl on Rintyre's face.

"Oh, come on, Rin," Bryter said. "I love horror stories. It was like we were there in that garden with that assassin snake. It was better than any book I ever read or lively I ever saw. I have to know what this Phaedra creature is or was."

"Spoiler. She was a sorceress and Husk Grayvesone survived. Obviously," Rintyre said, trying to squirm away from her sister and brother-in-law as The Rooke opened his robes. "Or your wife and I would not be here."

"I know that, but this is how she became so powerful…"

"Well, she's dead now so it doesn't matter. All those people disappeared despite this power she supposedly had, maybe because of that power. Her existence is just a sweet tale of quaint horror," Rintyre said. "I don't want to do this."

Little Anwyn Finn stepped forward, looking ready to hit Rintyre. The Rooke smiled as his sons pulled her back from the twin women. The girl took offense at Rintyre's assessment of Phaedra. The Rooke laughed.

"Phaedra is not dead," Anwyn said.

"She was never alive," Rintyre said. "You're a kid. You don't know the things Carly and I do."

"Rin, leave the kid alone. I'll get tokens for both of us," Carling said. "You'll thank me later."

"You're going to get me fired," Rintyre said. "I need my job. Mia and I barely get by."

"You hate your job," Bryter said. "And besides, it's not all roses with Mia, is it?"

"We can cover you, give you all the credits you'll ever need," Kentigern said, stepping forward. "Please, dear girl. We are all so fond of your mother. And there was a time we loved your father. We remember you as small children. Let us help you."

"How many credits?" Rintyre asked.

"How many do you need?" Aldo asked. "We need to find your father. He will get justice as he deserves. That much you must know of The Relic."

"We don't want him dead," Carling said. "He didn't do the horrible things you think. It was Baroness Teriss Amber. Our dad lost his mind for a while. Mom says Teriss poisoned his soul with some evil weed, a narcotic that scrambled his senses."

"That might well be, lass," Aldo said. "Get your sister to join us. We need her. Both of you if you like."

"Hey, Bryter Days could tour with you," Bryter said, his enthusiasm infectious. "I don't want a celebrated sleeve or anything. But your stories make for great songs. Yeah?"

"I would be honored," The Rooke said. "I enjoyed your music tonight."

"Rintyre will come around," Carling said, as her sister hesitated before The Rooke.

"She is on a list of people who are destined to assist me," The Rooke said. "To assist saving this world."

"Yeah, I am no one's savior," Rintyre said. "But ok, ok. Bryter Days needs a break anyhow. They can do sets between tales and become outlaws one and all. It'll be grand. I will love being directed to arrest my own sister and brother-in-law."

"It won't come to that," Carling said. "I know you. You'll become a rebel before you'd do that. Even if it cost you everything, and I won't let that happen."

Tavern XI:

The Dark End of The Rainbow

Only fools make deals with demons thinking any good can come of it. Such has been the rise of many of history's worst tyrants, bereft of their humanity, their triumphs horrific and their falls legendary.

About Specter Level Grimoire Spells
By Tarana Holic (translated by Hazel Kyran)

Pathos, Astarte

*T*he Rooke and his party took a sky-boat over the Boreal-lean Sea from Dracik Taenagle to Astarte, landing in the city of Pathos. The children loved flying in the hovering, ballooned ship.

The Rooke felt unsteady in the strange technology, especially with Taki explaining how it all worked in great detail. He preferred the magic he remembered of the Erelahian Ships from before The Evanescence. He took a deep breath, straightened his new imperial clothing. He disliked the stiffness of the white-collared shirt, the close fit of the dark vest and long suitcoat that matched his trousers.

New disguises and sleeves had been issued with Mika and Rintyre giving conflicting advice about how to navigate the inner working of the Sleeve Imperial Network. Aldo and Kentigern strongly recommended that The Rooke pose as an imperial librarian, a copper, green-ribboned sleeve that caused ordinary citizens to avert their eyes and move on for fear of being chastised for unapproved sleeve correspondance.

The Rooke wished to keep his rose gold, artisan sleeve. He found himself overruled considering Rintyre's considerable expertise in navigating the empires.

"It is customary for IPD agents to travel with librarians," Rintyre said. "Librarians can issue receipts for fees collected and reassign guardianship for children held illegally."

The new clothing made the children, including Taki, invisible among the throngs in the little village of Pathos, Astarte. They blended in their imperial improved grays and dark blue androgynous outfits.

Crowds flooded the market of little shops filled with glittering prizes of every imaginable kind. There was laughter and a general good feeling on this early spring day. This glimpse of life caused The Rooke to hope that these people might wake up and save themselves. If only they recognized their peril. Few did.

The empires kept the people comfortable while power consolidated behind closed doors, faces and names the people never heard. The little atrocities, the tiny slights, the unbearable hope that one day fortune might come ensnared the people into submission, fearing any objection might ruin their prospects.

Taki and Kostas signaled to The Rooke at the window of a shop filled with model ships and other sea-related trinkets.

"Dad, can I get one? Look, a perfect model of an Erelahian ship," Kostas said.

"I like ships," Taki said. "Old ships. Like before the people disappeared."

"We gathered," Mika said. "You helped fix two ships so far, one water and one air."

"They were not working correctly," Taki said. "I do not like drowning or crashing."

"I didn't think the imperials believed in the Erelahian Fleet or Alleysiande or Pre-Evanescent history or Ta-She-Serra or dragons or anything good," Thiago said.

"They don't," Kentigern said. "Regardless, the Erelahian fleet was comprised of real ships. And this one is a beauty at that. I wonder which one it is. Why can't I remember?"

"It's the Green Mist I think," Kostas said. "Funny they have such a perfect model of it."

"The empires simply do not believe that this was a real thing once," Aldo said. "They think it a dream of a fiction that could never truly be."

"Let's have a look around," Rintyre said. "I adore this shop. It always has fun knick-knacks. Candles and gifts and such. Mia and I came here for our anniversary last year."

The group entered the shop in twos and threes, Zac and Cymbre giggling together as they pointed to colorful trinkets, making their own private jokes.

"Father, Rintyre says The Canticle Fair is near," Thiago said. "I've heard good things. Could we maybe go there?"

"We could stay at The Rainbow, and you could tell one of your tales there," Rintyre said. "It's one of Bryter Days favorite venues. It's on the grounds of The Canticle Fair."

"It's really fun," Carling said. "And a glimpse of what Aerda can be at its best. It's a bit like The Dragon Tail Village."

"You might see the better part of the empires," Rintyre said. "And maybe I can help the empires calm down a bit about rookes. Prove to them that you are not subversive, and your tales are not dangerous."

"Rookes are subversive," Thiago said. "Art is supposed to be. Signs of a dying society is marked by the diminishing of its artists and its art."

"Did you read that in a book somewhere?" Rintyre asked. "Don't talk like that in places like this, kid. Imperial children don't talk like that."

"Dad, dad, look over here," Kostas said, pointing to a shelf full of dragon statues in miniature.

"Talk like your brother," Rintyre said. "Beg for shiny things. That's how imperial children talk."

"I am not a child. I am almost sixteen."

"My mistake," Rintyre said, giving him a smile.

Thiago shook his head and then his eyes went wide. The puzzle box was hanging out of Kostas' pack. Thiago pushed it back in, giving his brother a meaningful glare.

"I'll trade you for that puzzle box. I am authorized to spend a good many credits for such work."

A young woman appeared from behind the shop's counter and pointed at Ambriel's cube which Kostas had only managed to stop from falling to the ground. The Rooke had to work hard to control his expression of dismay.

"It fell out of my pack," Kostas said.

"He is forbidden to trade the box," The Rooke said. "It was an elder gift."

"Ah, I see," The girl said. "I love the wood. Do you know what it is made of?"

"I am afraid not," The Rooke said. "However, we would be pleased to purchase that ship in a bottle."

"Oh yes, fine work that," the woman said. "The artist died some years ago. During the insurrection."

"Insurrection?" Kostas said.

"Oh, I'm sorry. I did not mean to speak of it, librarian," the girl said. "Sir, forgive me, I realize the education of your son…"

"He knows of it," The Rooke said. "But does not fear it. Long reign Emperor Malcombe."

"Indeed. It's four-hundred credits, but I will give it to you for two hundred and sixty," the girl said.

The Rooke grasped his younger son's shoulder, willing Kostas silent. He knew the boy longing to ask questions. He looked to see Mika with her hand over Taki's mouth, to make sure he said nothing at all. Taki looked annoyed.

The Rooke made his purchases and handed the bottled ship to Kostas. Taki glared as Rintyre and Mika escorted him out of the shop.

"Silence is deadly," Taki said, stepping in front of Rintyre after leaving the shop. "Why are people not permitted to speak of things that are true?"

"Easy, Taki," Mika said. "She did not want you to say anything that might cause us to be noticed."

"Yeah, if you say Emperor Nicholai, people lose their minds," Anwyn said. "And you were going to start jabbering on and on. I could tell."

"Taki, I don't advocate silence," Rintyre said. "Only peace. We are a society that requires order to prevent war. We have only recovered from the terror of Nicholai Sacripant's decade-long coup."

"This is no peace," Taki said. "This is death. I do not like it."

"Weren't the Gnolgia pretty oppressive to your people?" Rintyre said, in hushed whisper. She did not know Taki's secret.

She saw a young Empyri boy. "They enslaved all the Empyri. They protected their technologies violently."

"For the protecting the world. See what has happened. The empires misused our technology. That was not from using silence," Taki said. "How do you think the Gnolgia had such advanced technology a thousand years ago?"

"You're twelve. How do you know?"

"I have the memories of all my ancestors. I remember the first breath of my first ancestor. I am not twelve. I am eons old. Only my body and mind are twelve."

"You are weird, kid," Rintyre said. "Don't make me arrest you. Keep your mouth quiet. Imperial citizens are a sensitive bunch. They don't want to hear about rebellions and disruptions in their lives. Nicholai almost destroyed everything. They'd like to forget."

The boy stormed off down the cobbled road between the brightly colored shops and residential buildings, the others having to up their pace to catch him at the monorail station.

The Rooke wanted to laugh and cry. The Gnolgia had been a menace in the Pre-Evanescent Era. They could disrupt the prosperity of entire cities with the slightest provocation. He thought, remembering his tales, that he might prefer having demonic Spytes after him than the super-logical assassins of the Gnolgia. He hoped Taki would truly be on their side.

The monorail glided silently by the coast and turned inland to flat, green lands peppered with concrete, steel, and glass blocks of Pathos, stopping at The Canticle Fair.

Mika and Rintyre secured rooms at the columned resort called The Dark End of the Rainbow within the boundaries of the famous fair. Zac Grimm and Cymbre Varian disappeared inside for hours, The Rooke suspecting he would see little of the couple. The children, even Thiago, were buzzing with excitement looking at all the entertainments on offer.

"I will inspect the rides to make sure they be safe," Taki said. "Then we ride."

The boy looked up at Aldo with pleading eyes.

"All right. It would look more suspicious if they didn't go. Children, I need you all to stay with the twins and Bryter and Tavares and Aleron," Aldo said. "Back at The Rainbow by sundown."

"Sure, we can do that," Carling said. "Come along, Rintyre. This will be fun."

"You remember fun, right?" Bryter said.

"Oh, so funny, my dear brother-in-law," Rintyre said. "Carling, how's your voice? Will you be able to perform tonight?"

"Yes, it is better. Why?"

"I may have to arrest your husband as an annoyance so you may have to lead Bryter Days."

Carling smiled. "I can do that."

The Lost Apprentice

*B*racken Grayvesone had to be careful. No one could overhear. He transferred the credits through a secure channel, one which his ex-wife, Raven Sage, set up for him. That had been awkward.

He felt a twinge of pain, thinking of how many things he had done wrong. A demon, an actual gutter baroness of the old tales, had taken him like his sister used to warn him about back in New Chazir.

Teriss Amber appeared to be flawless, a rare beauty, never letting a hair out of place. Until that night. She did not know he had seen. He recognized the brand on her neck, the thorny protrusions on her back, the snake like skin she shed to keep up her appearance of everlasting youth. The bath of blood she bathed in only confirmed it all.

It was all Bracken could do to pretend he did not know her secret. He feared the addiction to arryl weed would soon take his life. He craved the smoke and teas with such veracity, it was all he could do to stay sane. Yet, in the end, it was what had saved him. Strange that. Seeing the demon gave him immunity to the dangerous weed.

"You look half-past dead, mate," his contact said. This man with blindingly white teeth went by Bobby without a surname, off grid with full access. "I remember a prettier man."

"This place used to make me so happy. I took my girls here when they were little with my first wife. Thought it might help to be here for a moment. The Rainbow is the same, the smell, the shine, the understated luxury, so comfortable."

"Well, your new wife is a piece of work. Still, I get it. Back in my single days, I'd have fallen for that," Bobby said, sliding into a booth at the back of The Dark End of the Rainbow.

"And you'd be as damned as I am for doing it," Bracken said. "What did you find out?"

He did not expect the child he and Teriss Amber were raising to be his. She gave her favor generously despite their marriage. Not all were like his first wife. Raven had been all his. He shook his head, trembling with guilt and rage.

Regardless of to whom the child belonged; he would not allow the boy to be sacrificed to the wicked Spytes. Raven said he should kill the child, for mercy's sake. He could not. Would not. He was a small boy. Carrying a big demon. There had to be some other way to save the child and his soul.

"Well, it's perplexing," Bobby said. "Bracken, the boy isn't even the child of Teriss Amber. But he does have your blood, but you are not Jude's father. Bryter Kenn is his father."

"What? That's impossible."

"How bad is your marriage?" Bobby asked. "I've heard the rumors. How often she cheats. Expected for your lot so no one cares. Though I expect you might."

"What do you mean?"

"How did you not notice your wife faked a pregnancy?"

"Wait. What are you saying? She stole my grandchild," Bracken said, putting it all together, his worst fears, the sum of his transgressions laid at his feet. He thought his soul would collapse right there. Not his son. His grandson carried that demon. His grandson.

His daughters would never forgive him this. The poor child,

already well under the guile of some demon. What had he done? And how had she managed it?

"It would seem. I can offer my services once more," Bobby said. "A clean death…I don't normally take on royals, but we have an old score to settle. Have I told you what happened to my village back in Marlinea when I was a boy?"

"Lots of Marlineans suffered under the imperials…"

"Royals. To give them their titles and land and status, our land, our villages taken from us. Our people murdered with subtle arts -plague, famine, despair so some bloody baroness could have her estate. Three royals own almost ninety percent of Marlinea while the rest of my people live on the scraps while doing one hundred percent of the work. Rubs a man wrong that."

"It's like that everywhere, mate. Did Teriss murder a newborn to steal my grandson? Raven saw the dead body of Carling's child. And it was a girl."

"Murder is not a problem for your stunningly, lovely wife and her ilk. One at her level can affect any illusion she wishes. Royal privilege being what it is. Where is little Jude?"

"I have sent him to my old estate in Jebellen with a nanny I hired myself," Bracken said. "My ex-wife is retrieving him."

Raven offered little hope in saving the child. She would take him before The Relic, see if they would offer their help. Bracken composed a message to her in his mind, trying to think how to tell her. Do not kill him. Our grandson, Raven, our grandson.

Bracken pushed his fingernails deep into the skin of his hand, clenching his fist so tight.

"You trust your ex after what you did to her?" Bobby said. "I do not think the criers exaggerated your little addiction problem."

"My ex-wife is far less perilous to me than my present wife," Bracken said. "Teriss has been trying to kill me, trying to get me to take my own life before she does that. And I damned near did it. Thanks to you and Raven, maybe I will survive."

"Your daughter did not realize she was having a boy?"

"She and Bryter wanted it to be a surprise. They cared little what sex. They picked out the name for boy or girl. Gabriel or Gabrielle. Gabby. A good name."

"Well, here's your proof that Jude is the son of Carling Grayvesone and Bryter Kenn. It's clean. It'll hold up. But the royals won't let you get away with it. Best you take me up on my offer."

"Mate, I know you're tough, but you are no match for this baroness. Steer well clear of her. You understand? Raven, your wife, all those daughters of yours, will not thank you if you get yourself killed," Bracken said. "I think I'm going to be sick."

"You go to it," Bobby said, looking around as the light began to fade outside. "I'll be on my way. Contact me through Raven. Really, I'll do you a good price if you change your mind. The world will thank you."

"Go on. Get lost," Bracken said. "I will change my mind only if I decide I want you dead. Believe me, many have tried to kill the baroness over the centuries. She survives."

"Centuries? You're barking…"

"I wish I was. I wish to Ta-She-Serra that I was," Bracken said. "You best go. Before someone works out who I am."

"Good on you, mate. Good on you," Bobby said. "Ah, look at that, would you? Did you know your daughter and son-in-law's band were playing here tonight?"

"What? No. What?" Bracken stood up. He had to get away. He was not ready to confront his daughters. He had to work everything out first. He quit the pub and made his way to his room in the inn. And waited.

He would sneak down once the place was full, blend in with the crowd to listen. He missed being able to play music before a crowd. He missed his work as a thespian, on live stages and livelies that told such intriguing stories. And he was so proud of the band Carling had made with her husband. Their music was well-loved by both faithful imperials and the rebels that opposed them.

Three songs in and Bracken felt as well as he had in years. People having a good time, drinking and eating and dancing. The music was good. And then he gasped. Bryter stepped forward and introduced a full red-robed rooke. The Rooke. The ancient one who raised him until age ten.

The one who had trained his uncle, the first victim of Teriss Amber's wicked campaign to destroy the entire guild of The Rookery. If only those red robes had let him remember that it was his uncle. He shivered. No way The Relic would ever forgive him.

The Rooke told the story of Bracken's ancestor, Husk Grayvesone. Who found himself entangled in The Hierarchy of Hell's tangled web much as he had. He sat down in a dark corner and drifted to the floor of a wicker woman's jungle cottage.

The Tale of One More Damned Thing

Husk woke to rats, snakes, and cats in a chaos of hisses, squeaks, and snapping of fanged jaws. He sat up in a pool of wet goo to find Madame Darke swatting at rats with her broom, her dark hair wild and loosed about her face, her violet eyes wide with a mixture of fear and annoyance.

"What do you mean casting a spell like that?" she demanded. "Look at what you've done."

Husk felt as if he had crashed into the floor from a high height and found it difficult to speak. He took another breath, crabbing backwards from rats racing across his legs. One black rat narrowly escaped a ginger cat only to be coiled by a large constrictor.

Husk watched in horror as the fat snake squeezed the life from the rodent and unhinged its jaws to feast. Sick crept up Husk's throat. It was all he could do not to vomit amid the chaos of the wicker woman's cottage.

"I never meant to," Husk said, stuttering his words.

"I warned you," Madame Darke said. "I repeatedly warned you. Such a typical man, never listening to your elders. Did you think I was playing a game with you?"

"No, ma'am, I…" Husk gathered himself and found his feet, trying to find a place free of snakes, cats, and rats.

You escaped. That enchantress called The Silver Swann saved you. And me.

Phaedra's voice exploded with triumph in Husk's mind. She sounded as if she were in the room with him amid all the rats, cats, snakes, and one angry witch.

"Phaedra?" Husk said out loud before he could stop himself. Madame Darke turned, eyes like ice to face an unseen presence between bookcase and hearth.

"You!" Madame Darke said. "The Silver Swann told you to be gone, parasite. Get out and take your rats with you."

Would that I could be rid of them. The rats are my curse. No matter how often they are banished, they always return to me.

"Husk, get rid of that foul spirit. Unbind it now."

"I don't know how, and she's not hurting anything," Husk said.

He realized how lame that must sound amid the broken side table, books tumbled on the ground, pictures loosed from the wall, crockery shattered on the wood floor amid the turmoil of scurrying and dead rats, irritated snakes, and cats, and one much vexed wicker woman.

"Have you gone mad, boy? That is a demon. Can you not see her?"

"No. I can't. What does she look like?"

"She looks like a demon. Your hair would turn white with one glance at her. No harm. Did you hit your head? Why do you not see her? You're the one that bound her."

Why can she? I did not wish either of you to see my damned form. The Hierarchy keeps me in this manifestation of ruin. It is vile and it is not me. I do not wish to be their horror. I am Phaedra.

"You are not Phaedra," Madame Darke said, swatting her

broom toward Phaedra's invisible form or so Husk surmised. "You are no dragon. How dare you invoke that most noble name."

I never claimed your legend. Phaedra is a common name in my lifetime. I was a real woman. Husk, do not listen to this witch. She is as unclean as I and will be claimed by Pandemonium in time.

"I do not interfere with The Icari, the ones you call The Hierarchy. I will not earn their wrath and I will not have you here, Phaedra, whatever you be."

You're a fool, old woman. The Hierarchy will never let you be. You have used their power and they will have your name just as this creature you call Terminus took that warlock you loved so much.

Madame Darke looked as if she might faint. The broom went lax in her hands, her knees buckling, as she backed away from the bookcase into her big armchair. The cats and snakes, even the rats, gave her wide berth.

"What do you know of Terminus, parasite?"

He is a dog of Pandemonium's Hierarchy, a favorite pet. He means to turn his wrath on Husk as he escaped being his blood sacrifice. He claims your world in The Hierarchy's behalf. They have instructed him to be wary in dealing with me. To him, I am a threat. To your Icari, I am but one more damned thing.

"Terminus is defeated. I banished him after he possessed my husband and killed our child, our son. It cost my husband his life."

Terminus has escaped. Keeping demons in books is clever to be sure but always temporary as The Hierarchy always holds on to a bit of them.

An overwhelming nausea assaulted Husk, sending him close to a dead faint. He took hold of the corner of an upturned chair only to draw back as a slick black snake slithered over his arm.

"I hate this place. This is impossible. This Terminus possessed your husband?"

"Yes. My husband was trying to unseat a tyrant. The one that ordered the Pathian genocide. He failed. He died. My son died. The Pathians all died. I fled and The Black Swann and I managed to trap Terminus in that book before we fell out. You know, your patron, the precious Silver Swann, is of Pathian descent as well on her mother's side. Her father was pure Ambrien, the source of her magic no doubt."

Madame Darke pushed her hands against her head as if trying to force her thoughts to clear.

"Your husband was a Pathian?" Husk blinked in astonished incredulity. "The Pathians died seventy-five years ago at the hands of the Parthals. You don't look that old."

"I have used magic much as your patron once did, delaying aging, not forever forestalling it. I feel it more than I look it," Madame Darke said. She looked on the brink of tears. "Husk, I loved my husband and I have lost his name. I can't remember how I found out that Terminus had taken him…"

When Terminus uses a body, he damns their soul. Your husband gave away his name in exchange for some kind of pretty bauble or power. You will never know it again. I am sorry.

"No, it was no bauble he traded his soul for, Phaedra. It was for our son's soul. For Calibor. Phaedra, be gone. I will not have you tormenting me or this young man."

I do not wish to torment you. It was not my doing that your husband lost his name. The Hierarchy hungers for my name and yours and all mortals. They will never be satisfied, no matter how many souls they devour, no matter how powerful they become, no matter how many worlds they destroy. Their lust for power has no bounds and so they must be destroyed.

"And what is it you want?" Madame Darke asked. "Do you wish to replace them?"

"She wishes the light. She wants to go home," Husk said. "I felt it in her. Phaedra spent a lot of time in my memories. When she did her mind-reading trick, I could read her as if she were words in a book. In that probing, she could not lie or hide from me anymore than I could hide from her."

I will never be allowed the light.

"Husk, stop talking to the demon. We will sort out Xavier. Then we will figure out what to do with this parasite."

Husk felt a curious wave of heat, panic coming from Phaedra in a burst of darkness.

We have a problem. We should run.

The room spun around them. Rats ran and disappeared, the cats bristled, the snakes wrapped themselves about the books.

The apparition of a sparkling black figure in a silver mask appeared in the hearth. Madame Darke screamed, and a blast of fire erupted in the hearth as if summoned. The figure disappeared as fast as it appeared.

"What... who was that?"

Terminus. He senses you, Husk Grayvesone. He has been unable to find another blood sacrifice. He wants you. He will never abide my freedom nor yours. We must hide.

"I must ward this place. Husk, sit. This might take a while."

The wicker woman looked stunned, lost. She shuffled through books, pushing aside rats, ignoring the snakes, until she found the volume she sought, a red book with a leaf etched on the cover. Husk offered her the grimoire, but she sneered at it.

"Put that away, will you?" she said, her voice quivering. "It will call him. It was his after all. Away, I tell you."

Husk pushed his hands over a discarded book, shook his head and wished to leave this place. It was too much.

"Go," he said. With that, he felt Phaedra snap away with a sudden click as the remaining rats evaporated into dust balls.

Madame Darke waved burning incense and hung planters filled with herbs and crystals. The witch shook her head in approval and disappeared behind the beaded curtains. In a short time, she returned with a white robe. Husk saw deep shock in the woman and her voice commanded no emotion.

"Strip and put this on. I will clean your clothes. Don't argue."

Madame Darke held Husk in a dead-eyed gaze. Glaring back at her, he pulled the white robe around him before undoing his trousers. The wicker woman gathered up his wet clothes and disappeared once more. The snakes writhed and hissed, earning annoyance from the gathered cats.

"Shut up all of you," Husk said in irritation. All of this because Shanley Rose believed he might save her little brother.

"You shouldn't let idiots like me near your mistress's grimoire. I think I've cursed myself."

Husk pushed the grimoire further from his grasp and a tattered book fell from its pages. Whether in answer to his rebuke or because it was what they did, snakes began to slither around the grimoire, caressing it, hissing in serpentine pleasure leaving the other book unattended. Husk shook his head, repulsed.

He began setting the room right, cleaning where he could. He tossed the old volume that fell from the grimoire aside into a pile of rubbish. He put the chairs back in order and sat the little table upright. He piled up books in front of the reptile-filled bookcases, fearful the slumbering snakes might strike at him.

The wicker woman returned to the room with a tray laden with freshly baked bread and stew and garden greens tossed in herbs and vinegar.

"The cottage is well-warded. I have cleaned that goo out of your clothes. They will be some time in drying so I thought we might enjoy an early supper or late mid-day meal."

She pushed away a few cats as she pulled a folding tray in front of Husk's chair with one hand.

"I don't mean to appear ungrateful, but I it is getting so late," Husk said. "Xavier Rose…"

"I can't save that boy," Madame Darke said with a tinge of bitterness. "If the most excellent and generous Silver Swann is doing nothing for him, what makes you think a pretender like me can?"

"Pretender?"

"That is what she called me back when she was The Black Swann. Oh my, her magic was a thing to behold. If she wanted to, she could preserve the life of this child. I wonder why she does not. She has always been fond of the Roses. She even made that fool girl, Astrid Rose, a duchess in Acaria when her own daughter, Victory, refused the honor."

"My patron is no healer," Husk said. "I would never have thought of her as magical. Powerful, yes, but…I mean I dreamed of her when I got knocked out by that spell or whatever but that can't be…"

"Your patron is a witch, Husk Grayvesone. And it would be in her interest to save the Admiral's boy, but she hasn't…"

"She can't," Husk said.

"She won't," Madame Darke said. She pulled a decanter from the grasp of an alarmingly green snake, taking two crystal goblets from a shelf and filling them both with a dark red wine. "Years ago, she might have helped the boy. She gave up her magic, and she has let more than this child die in that stubborn endeavor."

"Maybe she was right to give it up. It seems magic can go badly wrong."

"And yet, here you stand."

"Yes, but I did not believe you had this sort of magic. I thought you knew some better herbs, some alchemy. I had hoped for a healing that traditional physicians overlooked. Like a Urian or Haniel healer, both which Xavier's mother will not allow anywhere near her son."

"Mirror Rose will let her only son die for prejudice. Beautiful and not the first time. Has your Silver Swann sent her personal physician? Dr. Sound Rege is brilliant. Or implore Seashell now that you know her little secret. She will refuse I am certain."

"Mirror Rose fired Dr. Rege when his cure did not work. If my patron let go magic, she had good reason. The Silver Swann has been more than generous to me and my brother of choice, Daedalus. She saved our lives, gave us both a future."

"You were both victims of the Mammon sisters, were you not?"

"We survived. Others were not so lucky."

"Seashell gave up her magic when it was all that would defeat those three."

"Two are dead. Plague. One escaped. Hester, the worst of them. She left me a number of scars."

"Those three are witches in all that word implies. I doubt a one of them is truly dead. They had long since lost their humanity when they settled in Tiponi Marsh," Madame Darke said, her eyes going far away. "Ghouls. I knew them before they took over that orphanage. Those three actually eat children. Foul blood ritual magic. Why do you think only bones were found in those ruins?"

"That's foul," Husk said. "Why?"

"For power. And when something that evil has that much power, something else must balance it out. Seashell was a fool to give up her magic. At the very least, even if she could not defeat the Mammons, she might have saved little Xavier."

Husk sipped his wine, not tasting it, and looked back to the books. Silence hung in the air.

Madame Darke pushed aside her tray, and began to rummage through her belongings, picking up a framed picture that had been thrown off the wall. She stretched to hang it above the hearth but could not reach. Husk set aside his own utensils and went to help her.

"I have a foot ladder. I will retrieve it," she said.

Husk turned the frame and stared with both horror and fascination at the picture he held. The woman depicted in the painting was nude, standing in full glory with long pitch-black hair and a massive diamond-headed serpent wrapped about her private bits. Husk looked away, and once more, snakes greeted his gaze.

"Lecretia"

"Pardon?" Husk turned as Madame Darke took the portrait from him. He watched a rat scurry across the floor behind a bookcase. Phaedra was back. He said nothing and waited for the wicker woman to explain.

"You were going to ask. This is Lecretia or 'creature of the night'. That is the full translation from the Asciendien. She is the damned queen of Pandemonium. Perhaps, your parasite is correct. I am too close to The Icari, The Hierarchy as they refer to themselves. I wonder if I will be able to hold onto my name when they come for me."

"What do you mean?"

They take your name. You become them and no one. You become legion and nothing at all. I am Phaedra. I keep my name and so they will hunt me. Help me and I will help you both.

"Help us how?"

"No, Husk. Do not heed this imp. You will not come out the better for that bargain. We will have to seek out a powerful magic, better than I know, to undo the binding without it requiring your death and damnation," Madame Darke said. She looked at the exquisite painting once more and pushed it between hearth and bookcase, hiding it away. "If we undo the binding, Terminus will have no reason to hunt you. Or me."

"What if this Phaedra can drive Terminus away? What if she can help save Xavier?" Husk asked.

"She can't. She fears this Terminus as much as I do. And if she were capable of such, she would be more to fear than this specter. Since the grand and glorious Silver Swann will not, let us attend to Xavier as best we can."

"The Silver Swann has been nothing but good to the people of Ambriland. I have no doubt she only meant to do right. Evil cannot be fought or cured with more evil."

"You best hope that's not true or I doubt I can help you," Madame Darke said. "Describe Xavier's illness. In detail."

Husk did his best between bites of bread and chicken.

"There is one thing I could try," she said, begrudgingly. "But no one will like it. It is highly illegal and perilous. That said, it will buy the young man a few years and relieve his pain. It might allow time for healers to properly diagnose him and treat him before it rots his soul."

"Rots his soul?"

"It's addictive and all addictions cause both body and soul to decay," Madame Darke said.

"Xavier is dying. It's worth a try," Husk said. "What is this illegal means you wish to try?"

"It is a tea made from arryl weed, a most potent and magical herb," Madame Darke said. "Due to the magical nature, it is expensive and extremely rare. I happen to have a small supply."

"The Roses will pay anything," Husk said. "I think they would even sell their home to save Xavier."

"I have no need of gold," Madame Darke said. "I would require three drops of your blood. And your seed."

"Blood and seed?"

I don't like this, Husk. It sounds a trick. Do not do it, Husk Grayvesone.

"It's not a trick, Phaedra. Be gone from us. These are mortal affairs."

Good witches don't ask for blood.

"No, they don't. Besides, what would a damned imp know of good?"

More than you might expect.

"I have never claimed to be good. I need three drops. It will not harm him, parasite," Madame Darke said. "Husk, you are a pure Ambrien. You have the multi-faceted eyes. Most Ambrien eyes are jewel green, but flat like any other human eye. I think you might be the last of your kind, thanks to the Mammons and King Charon. Your blood has magic of sorts. All blood does. I only wish to study it."

"I am not the last. Daedalus Sams is Ambrien."

"He has smooth eyes. His blood is of broken lines."

"You know Daedalus?"

"I like his music very much."

"And my seed?"

"That too. It is my price."

Husk thought this strange. He looked at the wicker woman and felt Phaedra's exasperation. What could it hurt? He would survive losing three drops of blood and the embarrassment of producing seed. He could save Xavier, or at least, give him a painless end.

"What is so dangerous about this arryl weed?"

"True addicts use it in smokes but that would kill Xavier. My tea, however, produces feelings of euphoria like nothing else in the healthy. For someone as ill as Xavier, it will simply relieve his pain and clear his mind."

"But it will not cure him?"

"No. It will mask a great many of the symptoms you have described. Do not look so defeated, Husk. Death is certain for all of us, but it's timing never is. I will keep the dose small so that he might have both clarity and relief. Pain hurries a death."

"Let's give it a try," Husk said, thinking of Shanley's words. This could not make Xavier any deader after all.

"We will proceed then," Madame Darke said, pulling vials from drawers, various herbs and teas from jars and bottles. "I will prepare tea and potion as soon as payment is supplied."

Are you sure this is a good idea, Husk?

"It is the only one I have. Xavier should not have to die in pain. He is only a little boy."

Husk would measure the cost later. None of this would matter if Xavier died this night. He offered his finger for the pricking of blood. The rest of the payment he wiped from his consciousness.

He repositioned himself in the front room, picking up a purring, black cat. He stroked it while he waited for Madame Darke to brew her potion and tea, turning his attention to her vast library. The tattered book which had fallen out of the grimoire was abandoned by snakes and cats. It called to Husk.

He felt a shiver of joy flash through him as he picked it up. He examined it and frowned. Blank pages of a fine parchment were concealed in a worn, leather cover with a binding that looked new, hand-sewn in gold thread.

Take that. It has a power.

This Phaedra whispered so only Husk would hear. He held up the battered old volume. "Madame Darke, what is this?"

"Junk, I expect. I believe it was an old journal that was never used. I have lots of those."

"Can I have it?"

"Whatever for? I could get you a proper journal if you wanted something to write in."

"This will do just fine. It seems unused if a bit old."

Husk settled back in his chair. The snakes seemed unhappy

with the herb wards, crawling into darker corners, and leaving the old volume titled *Paradymn Daraugha.* unguarded. Translated this was *The Dragon Paradym.* Husk pulled it off the shelf and began reading the pages.

Husk gaped at this rare and expensive volume of the original *Idylls of Alleysiande.* This was no Kyran translation but in the original Asciendien, written in the ancient glyphs. Phaedra whispered translations in his ear. He felt her elation as she read to him the story of the dragon with whom she shared a name.

Husk thought of Shanley Rose and how she adored the Kyran translation of this tale. The girl loved her romances, and this was a story for the ages; love and betrayal, loads of sexual tension and a dragon in the mix.

The afternoon faded toward evening when Madame Darke appeared with her promised items, the instructions for both written on scrolled parchment.

"Can I borrow this?" Husk asked, holding up the volume. "I know it is valuable…"

"Can you translate it?" Madame Darke asked, sounding impressed.

"Maybe. I would like to try. It will be good practice. I plan to apply to Dalmeade as a novice archivist. I have to know Asciendien."

"I agree. It would be good practice. Be wary of the Kyran translation," Madame Darke said. "She took many liberties and changed the tale, subtly but its meaning is not what people think."

Phaedra bristled as Husk began packing up his things. The little black cat scratched at his heels, playful and timid all at once.

I should have been more vigilant. This witch has you in her power. Your name and your blood. Take that cat. Those are magical things. We'll need some help, you and I.

"I don't think I need a cat," Husk said as he reached for the little black feline that now scratched up the side of his leg.

"I think you will have that cat whether you will or no."

Madame Darke said, looking down at the small black cat with disdain. "He has chosen you. Pity. He sprays everything."

"Ok, if you say so. I will take the cat. What is he called?"

"He's never mentioned a name to me."

Sariel

This came from the cat. Husk dismissed this as his own invention and growing madness, granting the name to the feline. He felt sure he had once read about a man called Sariel in some book or another. He carefully stowed the tattered journal neatly into a little bag along with the priceless volume, *Paradymn Daraugha.*

The cat seemed to understand that it would be going with Husk and scampered out of the cottage into the twilight. He watched the little creature pounce as an unfortunate rat squealed its last.

He will do nicely.

Husk felt Phaedra's delight. He said his good evenings and promised to return the book to Madame Darke as he turned away. The light of the cottage disappeared behind him. Before him, he glimpsed at the edge of his vision a slender woman outlined in shadow with long hair blowing in an unfelt breeze.

A Quiet Exit

A crack of lightening followed total blackness as the lights blinked to signal the end of his tale. The Rooke thought he saw a familiar face, toward the back, making for the door. He could not be sure. Kentigern took him by the sleeve, pulling him from the stage as they had arranged before.

The Rooke gave way to Bryter Days, slipping off to the back of the stage so he could remove his robes and become the librarian again. They would not give the imperials a chance to stop him.

"I gave no tokens," The Rooke said. "We'll get no traction from here."

"Too close to Aroghotto City here," Kentigern said. "We have to go quiet after the magic. Aldo has us booked on a train at dawn bound for Ellyn."

Kostas and Anwyn ducked behind the stage as Taki followed them chattering in his way, holding up his own pack to demonstrate an opening in his pack.

"I keep it safe. You two blow up world. Not careful," Taki said. "Cymbre see it, and she almost take it to teach you lesson. We should rotate. Tell no one who has it."

"Dad, make Taki stop," Kostas said. "It's not my fault my pack burst open in the shop, and Cymbre was teasing me is all."

"What are you three going on about?" The Rooke asked, securing his librarian sleeve.

"The puzzle box," Anwyn said. "Taki says he should hold it. Only the box is bound to me and Kostas. We have to keep it."

"Anwyn, you keep it tonight, and I will look after you," Mika Finn said. "It's late, and Bryter Days will play some hours yet. Let's get you kids to bed. We have an early train ride to Ellyn."

Tavern XII:

The Glittering Raptor

Often the making of a man will begin with the breaking of a boy.

The Idylls of Alleysiande, Vol II. Metatron's Triumph
author unknown (translated by Hazel Kyran)

The Maligned Beggar

The train from Astarte let out right at the corner by a massive building that dwarfed all the others in Ellyn's largest city of Tandell. The morning lingered in cloud and haze as The Rooke and his party mixed with the crowds in small groups.

The Glittering Raptor cast a golden shadow over the bay that separated Tandell, Ellyn from the province of Bradamate. The Rooke did not like it at all. The external building was of black marble, reaching high, some sixty plus stories, with gold leafing around the doors and windows.

"Extra fancy," Kostas said. "Looks a place that kings might stay."

"It looks an Icarian tower," The Rooke said, remembering an old nightmare. "Kenny, are you sure about this?"

"The Raptor? Aye, only place in all of Tandell a librarian and a gilder would stay," he said. "We have to keep our disguises. It's famous for all the musicians and luminaries that visit."

"Kentigern is right, but something feels off," Aldo said. "Stephen Fowler came here on his way to Aroghotto City before the renovation. It was like all the other buildings, white with blue glass. None of this shiny marble and gold leaf, and half as high."

"Are we going to Aroghotto City?" Cymbre Varian asked. "It's a wonderful place. Zac, we should go. It's an hour train ride from here. We could be back in time for the next tale."

"I don't think so," Zac Grimm said, a foolish grin on his face, one of a man deeply infatuated. "You know with the Unity Conference going on, it'll be a mess. But another time?"

"You could visit me and Mia if I manage not to lose my position or piss off Mia before then," Rintyre said. "Aroghotto City is the best. For everything."

"It really is, Zac," Cymbre said. "Still, this will be a grand place to stay. I've always wanted to stay in one of these hotels."

"One of these?" The Rooke asked.

"There are ten or more now, all newly done, all over the world. They all have different names and configurations," Cymbre said. "They are owned by the same organization. Best hotels in all the world. You have to have one of the elevated sleeves to stay here."

"Which organization is that, dear?" Aldo asked.

"You're playing at being a gilder. You should know," Cymbre said. "IBT is a great enterprise. The richest man in all of Aerda owns it. Diomede Shalchar."

"Aldo, I really do not wish to stay here," The Rooke said. He gave his friend a stern look, trying to convey his misgivings. Names could be moved and put on anyone. Giving a man the surname of the king of Hell did not make him that. Adding the "richest" man in all of Aerda, however, showed probable influence of the vile Icari, Shalchar.

"You're paying for it, right?" Rintyre said.

"We can't afford this place," Bryter said. "It's like a thousand credits a night."

"I have it covered," Aldo said. "I tried to book Bryter Days. They were rude about the whole thing. Said you were not elite enough, and only luminary elites could book acts here."

"Could have told you that, friend," Bryter said. "We don't want to play here. And I left the band back in Astarte. Have a wrong feeling. Told them to go back to Talon, to hide. You only have me and Carly for your entertainment."

"You guys are fantastic entertainment," Anwyn said. "I think it'll be fun staying here. We can see what all the fuss is about rich people."

"This place is high visibility," Rintyre said. "Like Cymbre said. Everyone wants to stay here. The Rooke should keep his robes hidden."

"Aldo, this is not a great idea," The Rooke said. "Are you sure?"

Joel Broomes took Aldo and Kentigern aside, eyes wide,

arm gestating wildly. "We should not stay here," he said. "I do not hunt demons. I sense them. Then I avoid them. We should avoid them. We can't stay here. Tee, tell them."

"He doesn't want to stay here," Tee said, a gentle smile on her lips. "Joel gets agitated in crowded places."

"Demons hide in crowds. I tell you, dear. This is no good place."

"I think we have to," Kentigern said. "I am going to have a word with Aleron and Tavares. Tell them to be extra vigilant."

The food enraptured the group. The Rooke pushed back from the table in the Glittering Raptor's steakhouse feeling satisfied. And a touch drunk from the whisky. He saw the twins playing with the children, Bryter Kenn putting a card on the table.

"We're playing Conquest," Bryter said. "Care to join us?"

"I think I'll pass," The Rooke said.

"Father is terrible at games," Thiago said.

"Truly terrible," Kostas agreed, standing up to take a card from the table and pointing at Rintyre in a victorious yelp. "But I'm not."

"You little brat. How did you win again?" Rintyre said. "Did you cheat?"

"That's how you win," Kostas said. "Isn't that the point? No one ever conquered anything by playing fair."

"We go again," Rintyre said, filled with determination.

The Rooke took a seat at an abandoned table alongside the gamers. He spotted a discarded Idylls & Grimoires card. He wondered if Thiago had left it there. He snatched it up in wonder. He started to show the card to the players at the table. Something deep inside warned him against this.

He shivered at the card's familiarity, trying to think back to the times before his red robes, back when almost everyone played the game.

A figure in bloody rags stared up at him, crumpled over as a knight-like figure made to strike him down while a winged figure bathed in the light of a full moon looked on. He translated the Asciendien name on the card.

'The Maligned Beggar'

He stuffed the card into one of his hidden pockets and quietly made for his rooms. He found himself in two minds, one that knew he should flee and a stronger part which felt foreign, begging him to stay a while and relax. After all, the next Dragon Moon was still months away.

The Glittering Raptor was beautiful and full of fantastic entertainments. His sons were having the time of their lives on this quest. He stared at the card. Another from his list and wondered what to make of this.

The Rooke dug into his pack, the one he kept with him at all times apart from this night's supper. He pulled out a thin book, *Xherdan Kyran's Guide to Idylls & Grimoires Unique Cards.*

Thiago was right. The Rooke was not a skilled player. He felt certain he had never collected the cards back when it was popular and could not remember this card's lore. He leafed through the book until he found the picture of the card he had just claimed. He read the passage.

This unique card reads 'If you are kind to the Maligned beggar, you will lose the war and win the game.' It earns a flat ten points when played. It eliminates all un-played military cards from the opponent's hand. If the player is able to play this card after the opponent plays their last card, they win the game.

His head hurt, pounding in fact. The Rooke opened the supply cabinet in his room and reached for a remedy for his headache. Something warned him against it. A knock on the door saved him from the temptation.

He let Aldo in with Tee and Joel. The young man was back to being wide-eyed and gesturing with his long arms and rubbing at his bald head. The Rooke wondered if Joel had at one time had long hair that he had simply rubbed away.

"We are in much danger," Joel blurted out. "I told you not to stay here. We are being drugged. Tell them, Tee."

"I have something. It helped us. I want to give it to everyone in the party," Tee said. "Joel is a touch paranoid, but my husband is right. Something is amiss in the food we ate."

"I think I know what it is," The Rooke said. "Do you know anything about Glittering Raptors? The thing that gives this hotel its name?"

"The carnivorous flower? Do those still exist?" Aldo asked.

"They do in the jungles at the bottom of the world, but that's not my point. They are very beautiful to behold," The Rooke said. "All red and green and blue, purple, and yellow. Lovely. And they smell wonderful. Of course, the spores that make that glorious stank are venomous. By the time you get close enough to absorb the smell and think of picking one of its little blossoms, you're already dead. This hotel is literally a Glittering Raptor. We need to get out of here. Now."

He swept out of the room and ran directly into Kentigern. "We have to find the others," The Rooke said. "We're leaving."

"Now?" Kentigern asked. "I thought we could stay a couple of days…"

"Kenny, now. We have to go now. This place is not safe for us," The Rooke said.

"Good, good," Joel said, his long limbs spinning along to rush after the others. "Listen to Rooke. Demons here. The air is bad. It is all bad. We leave."

"Here, Kentigern," Tee said, offering him a glass of clear liquid. "Drink this. It'll come clear to you. Where are the others?"

"At that night club for evening parties that the young go so wild about. There's music and dancing and…" Kentigern took a sip and blinked. "And they are all drugged. Damn. I knew the whisky didn't taste right. I simply don't expect imperials to know how to make whisky."

"My husband and Aldo will gather all our things," Tee said. "Aldo can check everyone's room. I will help you gather the others and clear their heads."

They swept down the stairs and across a glassed bridge toward the rolling beat of the hotel's night club. The Rooke froze. He could see the revelers, demon oppressed people giving into their darkest desires, easily influenced to do any decadent deed at all. He made the decision instantly.

"Kentigern, watch my back."

He forced himself onto the stage, pushing aside a confused musician as he exposed his red robes from the vapor. He played an old tune, taking the audience back in time.

He started his tale at the beginning, back on the last day of Alleysiande, looking out at people who were like the ones that witnessed the execution of the sorcerer, Janus, who cheered his torture and dismemberment. This would be dangerous.

Ghita Mist

The black tower glared down at Ghita Mist. She put down her bag, tested her magic one last time. Still there. She could do this. Glittering Raptor. How could Kentigern and Aldo allow The Rooke to enter this place? It had a sign and everything to say 'hey, I am a big evil place'.

The Sixth Offers A Broken Spyte

That sent shivers down her spine. This Spyte was not broken once she left The Reliquary. She wondered what The Sixth had hoped Cymbre to be. Ghita had meant to ask. She had chased down Gareth Gillespie to ask him for an audience. The old guardian gave her a look of profound sorrow.

"The Aspects are gone. The dragon is awake. They left to re-open the Forge while there is still a chance. They took Shanks with them. They told me to organize the relocation of all these refugees to the valley. The Reliquary is lost. They said once the ice dragon wakes, the magic of The Reliquary will wane."

"I will find them at the Forge," Ghita had said. She remembered the feeling of panic. "Where is it?"

"I don't know. No one seems to know. It disappeared at The Evanescence. I think they have to rebuild it," Gareth had said. "I am getting my family out along with Aldo's and Kentigern's wife. Can you look after your puzzlers? This is a massive operation. We will have to build new villages below to accommodate everyone. The paths down are perilous. Oh Ghita, what will become of us?"

"Gareth, you can do this," Ghita said. "You are a great guardian. You are as great of any knight that the Forge ever made."

"I wish The Rooke were here, and Kenny and Aldo. I don't like doing this alone."

"You are not alone. I will inform the puzzlers, the Learning Circle professors, and their families. They will help you organize. I must go," Ghita said. She had to find The Rooke and his party before the worst happened.

It had taken her days to get travel out of The Reliquary and through the temple, down to Talon, to Warring, and on across the Boreallean Sea. She did not look back nor grieve as she left The Reliquary and then Primordial Boreal behind. This was not the first time she had to start all over again. Although, deep in her gut, she felt it would be the last.

Cymbre Varian was not at all who she seemed. Ghita's research found a horror story. At the age of seven, Cymbre had slaughtered her parents and her little brother. The empires blamed rebels. True crime livelies featuring the case were popular, especially in Torr where the crime had happened. A fictionalized account had been turned to a horror lively, and even that did not mention the supernatural.

The Imperial Investigative Agency would not look for something so unholy. They would want to affix the blame and hatred to the enemies of the empires. The ritual to bind the child, Cymbre Varian, to some demon had been completed that bloody night. Ghita recognized the signs all too clearly.

When Bittore Rose reported that Zac Grimm was in love with the girl, Ghita thought she might scream. She adored that boy, and he was on The Rooke's list. She felt dread building in her trying to catch up to the party.

Ghita ignored the throngs of people coming and going under the hungry maw of the black and gold hotel. She pulled her old, red-covered grimoire from her pack, and prepared for battle under the shadow of The Glittering Raptor.

So engrossed in her grimoire was she that she did not notice the beleaguered and familiar man come upon her.

"Grandmaster?" he said. She blinked. It took a minute to place him. For a moment, she saw a ruined Husk Grayvesone. She knew that could not be. She stepped back, in fear.

"Bracken Grayvesone? What are you doing here?"

"Trying to save my daughters," he said. "What are you doing here?"

"Trying to save my friends from this bloody black tower. How are you here? The Relic is looking for you."

"The Rooke is a damned fool," Bracken said. "What has happened to the whole of The Rookery these last decades? He's traveling with a Spyte. His magic must be failing if he can't see it."

"Yes, I know," Ghita said. "I would have guessed you were the one who sent her."

"Me? What? No. Damn," Bracken said, his face puffy in panic. "It's not what you think. Not at all. I was poisoned, deceived. My wife. She is a gutter baroness like in old Rooke's tales."

He spoke on, rambling between past and present, talking about a stolen child, about how his wife was turning his grandchild into a Spyte. Ghita put a stern hand on the man's shoulder, looking into his blue-green eyes. She had never been convinced he was blood-kin to Husk Grayvesone until this very moment.

"Slow down, Bracken. Tell me everything."

He did. And things were worse than Ghita surmised. She gave Bracken a tonic to keep him calm, silent, and out of the way. She threw him into an alley corner, leaving him there. She would come back for him after she freed her friends from the awful Spyte. Bracken knew all about Cymbre, had watched Teriss train her to appear sweet under that merciless interior.

Ghita ghosted through the hotel, finding the room she was looking for. She tapped on the door, hoping Zac would open it, safe and sound. She tapped again and the door opened. It was not locked. Inside, she gasped at what she found.

Zac lay on the bed, half-naked, pale with purple, puffy eyes. The stink was unmistakable. Spyte venom.

"Ta-She be damned," she cursed under her breath, rushing to the young man's side. She took his wrist. Still alive. Barely. She was prepared and administered the remedy with a needle.

Zac snapped awake as the antidote hit his system.

"Grandmaster, what are you doing here?"

"Trying to save your life," Ghita said. "Where are the others?"

"Others? I am not sure. I have to get sick."

He dressed after expelling his dinner loudly in the toilet, wiping his face. He looked bewildered. Then he sat down heavily. He picked up his sword, looking it over as if it might be damaged. He sighed. Ghita knew the young man to be clever. She did not need to summarize what had happened.

"Cymbre seduced me and drugged me," he said. "And now she has that puzzle box. And she's gone. She hated this sword. Good thing. I'd have really missed it."

Ghita took his sword, looking at the engraved initials. She smiled. What a rare thing. A Pharoah Sol sword. Cymbre would not be able to touch it if the blade still possessed the magic that forged it.

"You have survived. We need to get that box back or it will bring devastation which will irritate the awakened dragons," Ghita said, trying her best to comfort the young man. "How long ago do you suppose Cymbre left?"

He looked at his sleeve screen in the copper band. "Yeah, not very long. Maybe half hour," he said. "We were…well, anyhow, I was telling her how happy I was about stuff and then everything was black."

"Not a fatal dose. You must have charmed her, or she would have done a better job murdering you," Ghita said. "I am going to go after your young paramour."

"I'm so stupid, Grandmaster," Zac said, gripping his sword as if he were going to swing it to stop his grief and discomfort. "I thought I loved Cymbre. Thought she was loving me. I should have known. Girls never really like me."

"You are not the first man or woman to fall prey to the blindness of a hopeful heart and a pretty face," Ghita said. "You can feel sorry for yourself once we get you out of this black tower. I will meet you at the side exit. There's a fellow there that will sympathize with you. Keep watch on him until I return. Keep that sword handy. It'll protect you."

Ghita cast her spell. Cymbre had not gone far. She spied her amid a legion of degenerates. She was giving them instructions. Ghita was no match for a Spyte who could command demonically possessed men.

"I will pay you well, and you will not hate this task," Cymbre said. "Indulge yourselves. Enjoy the greatest pleasures of these pretty children. I am afraid, however, when you are done with them, you must kill the two Nacharye, Anwyn and Mika, and of course, you can't allow a Gnolgia among you. He will hurt you if allowed to live so you must take him out first."

"We have everything in place," a tall, shirtless man dressed in leather that left nothing to the imagination, exposing his buttocks. Ghita could see nothing of human decency behind his flat, black eyes.

"Bring your prizes to Nox Verre to collect rest of the awards," Cymbre said. "Do remove the bodies from the club when you are done. Hide them."

"This is not our first mission, Varian," the exposed, leather-clad man said. "Although, this is proving to be interesting. We are so very bored."

"Once I am elevated, I will see you are never bored," Cymbre said. "My tithes will bring you pleasure. I assure you I will not take your services for granted as Baroness Amber has done these many years."

Ghita wasted no time. When she entered the club inside The Glittering Raptor, it was dark, filled with so many innocent people who did not know their good fortune. The Rooke's magic paralyzed the revelers that might do them harm. The moment he finished, they would strike. And there were too many people. Zac found Ghita.

"Too dark, too loud, too crowded. I can't find any of them," he said. "I came because that Bracken fellow was freaking out about his daughters. And I really like Rintyre and Carling. They're good girls. But I can't find them."

"Stay with me," Ghita said. "When The Rooke stops, there will be a battle. Can you use that sword you carry?"

"I could if it worked. It's ceremonial. Won't even cut through paper," Zac said. "I thought I'd accidentally cut my best bud, and it didn't even tickle him."

"That's because your friend was not trying to murder you," Ghita said. "If you have to fight, that sword will only harm those who mean to do harm."

"That sounds impossible."

"You thought that about Ambriel's Unbreakable Cube too."

"Good point. Be ready. The Rooke is getting into some new stuff now. He's going to be finished soon. What do we do?"

Ghita made to answer but found herself in Seashell Swann's topiary garden where a dead snake tried to revive itself. She saw faces from her past and for a time, she felt paralyzed.

The Tale of Saltwater Frain

Gerloch Nett pushed a young groundskeeper in front of him.

"Be wary," the valet said to the young man. "There might be other snakes, other dangerous beasts."

Seashell Swann felt she should know this young gardener's name. She tried to know all her staff. This young man hauled a heavy sack over his shoulder filled with equipment. A look of jubilance passed his face when he took in the zombie snake as it writhed trying to rejoin its head to its tubular body.

"Ah, mistress you got it, surely you did. Nice, nice," he said, his head bobbing up and down in approval. "My pa told me about how fierce you was. He not exaggerate, not one bit. And a true sorcerer snake. Never seen one before. My family being all pious and whatnot, but don't you worry none. I know just what to do. Burn it with holy oils and herbs. It not bother us again."

Seashell regarded the young man, not able to place him. His sun-brightened brown hair and gentle swamp-green eyes suggested a touch of Ambrien blood mixed with Blesayre descent. Not a touch of Chaziri in him. That chin and the crease of his forehead reminded her of someone she knew long before this man had ever been born.

"Slow down, young man. Might I know your name?"

"Sorry, sorry, mistress," the young man took a deep breath, put down all that he was carrying and bowed low. "Saltwater Frain of Gyo Gladden. My da was a fisherman, my mother had a little shop in the village before the tsunami. Me, I loved plants. Did me an internship with the famous botanist, old Mistress Janet Shipwash. Grew up hereabouts, after the flood and all, so I'll know about snakes. You can call me Salty. Most folks do."

Seashell stared opened mouth as the young man spilled out his breathless, unending answer. She waited for him to pause a beat, to let him catch his breath. The name struck her, common enough, true, but with his look. A memory flickered. Before he could start rambling again, she spoke.

"Frain? Are you one of Spray Frain's boys?"

"Nah. Spray was my grand da. My father was his bastard by my grandma, a rich Blesayre woman she was and then she wasn't. Disowned. Fraternizing with a pirate like that. Grand sailed with your late husband when he was a little lad. Grand gave my da a fishing boat, my grandmother a cottage and garden by the sea, and that settled that. Made us honest folk, not pirates. Never that, meaning no disrespect. Being all pious and all."

The groundskeeper set to slicing the serpent into pieces with a cleaver, using a pole with a hook to put bits of snake into a clay jar, pouring oil and herbs on top of the carcass.

Seashell wondered what kind of pious this young man was

claiming to be, and why in all of Aerda, would he get the idea she would object to pirates. Did he not understand who she was?

"You have Spray's look, that fine chin and thick hair. Your grandfather was notorious for getting my husband in all sorts of trouble. I do not know what you were told, but old Spray sailed with my husband until the very end. They died in battle together. You should never be ashamed of Spray as rough as he was. He saved Ambriland from Fistian raiders, Daggera assassins, Chaziri fleets, and Megdonian Spider vessels more times than you have years of life. He was a hero of the second Coffee War."

The young man gave Seashell a stubborn look, standing upright. "I am no killer, ma'am. I am not like him. I'm not a pirate. I do a respectable trade," Salty said. "I mean no disrespect, but I was raised Penitent. We eat no meat that is not from the sea. We spill no blood. We do no magic. I'll burn this in the moonlight next to the waterfall."

"You need not do all that. Burn it now." Seashell smiled at the man proclaiming to do no magic while describing a ritual spell he would do to get rid of the assassin snake.

Noe scampered down from his perch and began chattering at Salty. This young man scooped the creature up and patted him like he was a puppy, something Noe showed immense approval of by burrowing his head against Salty's chest and murmuring a stream of "no's in a low rumble that mimicked a cat's purr.

"Ma'am, you said you knew my grandfather. He played too much with magic, Almighty Ta-She-Serra rest his soul. This be a sorcerer snake, one summoned by magic to curse you. It is a dangerous thing, and it will come back to exact its price if this isn't done proper."

"No, no, no, no-no, nooo," Noe chirped.

"See, Noe agrees with me," Salty said. "Where did you get a Malachian monkey? I never seen his like. They are supposed to be mythical creatures."

"Not mythical. Merely rare," Seashell said. She grinned to herself. Noe was a creature of her magic, a familiar like the one called Jabber who accompanied Janus, the famous sorcerer of legend featured in the famous *Idylls of Alleysiande*. Noe had been summoned at the moment of her husband's death in the last Coffee War.

Seashell had never been fond of traditional familiar creatures like wolves, cats, snakes, falcons, or owls. She had spent years concocting the spell to summon Noe, the only way to get a Malachian monkey to show itself.

She had worried that her spell with the immense energy required caused the freak bolt of lightning that struck her husband dead in the height of battle. After all, Marsh Swann had given a bit of his soul for her grimoire.

It would not have mattered that he was a thousand miles away when she cast the spell. The possibility that gaining such a powerful familiar cost her husband his life continued to haunt her. Once upon a time, power seduced Seashell Swann to the edge of damnation.

Noe squiggled his way loose of Salty's arms and scampered onto Seashell's shoulder to reassure her of his protection.

"I will burn the snake at the waterfall tonight," Salty said. "This jar with its holy oils and herbs will prevent its regeneration beforehand."

Seashell started to object. He could burn the thing and cast it into the marsh. A purification spell was wasted on such serpents. She was opening her mouth to find a polite way of expressing herself to this peculiar young man and thought better of it. Salty spoke true about those herbs and oils. The serpent would remain in pieces in that jar.

"Do as you think best. I do not wish to pay a price for that."

Seashell watched Salty trot off, the young man looking far too happy to be carrying the remains of a deadly sorcerer snake. Gerloch Nett glanced at her and took a deep breath "Perhaps, some calming tea?" he suggested.

"Yes, I think so," Seashell said. "And then we've much to do, Ger Nett. I need you to summon Goolsby Lamb and Phineas Tunvel with the utmost urgency. Oh, and that funny man with the mismatched eyes. We met him once a long while back. I can't remember why he was here. His wife is Delilah Sage's niece. They came for some event. Was it Siobhan's ninth birthday maybe?"

"Sidon Bagwell. I will try, but I don't know how likely they are to come," Ger Nett said. "It is Gathering season in The Mudlands, and the season of storms. They will not want to sail."

"They will come. Captain Jolly will bring them on Lorelei," Seashell said. "Tell them Terminus has returned, the same demonic specter that caused the destruction of Irialfar and was at the heart of the Pathian genocide. And tell Goolsby Lamb that Phaedra, the one he confronted at Heath's Night, might be back. On hearing that, they will scramble across the ocean to aid us."

The Swamp bursar complained bitterly about the expense for the clay, crystals, and rare flowers when Seashell ordered dozens beyond the ones she sent to The Rose Manor. Her valet and the little bursar were still yelling at each other after she requested another twenty pounds of Ambrien clay which must come from the base of Mount Ambri.

She did not allow Salty see her fashion the urns from magic nor the magic which caused the marigolds to grow from seed overnight, or the magic she did so that the marigolds and daisies blended to create the hybrid blossoms.

Salty did not object to pulling barrels full of water from the glittering falls on the north end of her property. He spoke in great detail about how he and his girl had conceived their child in the waters of the falls to ensure a hearty infant. He professed a deep love of that waterfall, finding it an 'enchanted' place. Which was true. Those falls had been the bathing place of Ambriel herself before the fall of Alleysiande according to legend. A story Seashell believed as that was where she had come into her magic decades ago.

Seashell had wearied of having colorful assassin serpents

appear every few hours. The last one had nearly struck true and left her little rat monkey frantic and refusing to come down from the massive candelabra in the great dining hall. Noe had cast down a couple of small fire balls crafted from his poo to dispel two of the zombie snakes.

"Noe, stop that," Seashell had reprimanded the little monkey. "Monkeys do not do magic. And I do not wish to have my home burned down. Control yourself. I will deal with these creatures."

Give me Husk Grayvesone and I will cease my attacks on you and yours.

Another fire ball turned the specter's illusion to dust. Noe had spit and sputtered in complaint, put his little round ears back, and climbed higher into the vaulted ceiling of the great dining hall.

"That's enough, Noe. Please, I will have a full barrier up presently and we will be left in peace," Seashell had said, trying to hold her composure. "If it is discovered you do magic, Noe, it will not go well for either of us. Please, behave yourself."

Noe complained at length, making a terrible racket when Seashell exited the massive room to finish her protective wards. She could still hear the creature, squealing and whining.

"Indoors, one plant in every room, and then one per six yards in each vestibule and corridor," Seashell said, checking her calculations once more as Saltwater Frain stood by. "Outdoors, you have the diagrams. One gross of the planters in all. Salty, you and I must inspect each of them once they are done to ensure they are effective. I expect this done by sundown."

"Ma'am, yes ma'am," Salty said. "You'll have no slackers here. It'll be done exactly. I hear any grumbling, I'll set your valet on them."

He stumbled after her into the front entrance of the Culinary Academy. None of the drat snakes had appeared here, but Seashell was taking no chances.

"The kitchens will pose a challenge as these herbs must be kept separate from all food."

"Why? None of these herbs are poisonous to the best of my knowledge."

"It is not that. They are fragrant and will cause all food to taste like pasty mint, and I will not sacrifice my beloved Culinary Academy to a dark sorcerer."

"All the kitchens? That is quite the task."

"Hire extra workers if you need. I will pay for it."

"Should we not warn…"

"No, that would alert the sorcerer that keeps sending those dreadful snakes. I will give him no more opportunity to strike," Seashell said. "Salty, you know how cruel magic can be. Stick to our story. Red pin snakes. They are common enough in these parts. If people knew a warlock specter was mucking about, we'd have a panic."

"Yes, I be a bit alarmed myself. Most times I am cool as a new breeze," Salty said.

"You are a brave lad," Seashell commended the strange young man. "Now, I must see an old friend. I am trusting you to handle the distribution of these planters."

Silence was easier than words. The Silver Swann sat across from Jezebel Darke, sipping tea, watching two kittens dance about the room in a playful fight. The snakes could not be seen. The herb wards had sent them away. A thousand questions filled Seashell's head. They all sounded like accusations when she went to form them, and that would get her nowhere. She took a spoon to the honey, making a show of sweetening her bitter drink.

"I could not destroy his grimoire without freeing him," Madame Darke said after a long pause. "We knew we had not banished Terminus forever."

"Then why did you give the book to Husk?" Seashell asked.

"He should not have been able to cast that spell or even open it to that page," Madame Darke said. "You can't think I would release Terminus on purpose. I had no idea Husk had magic nor did you so don't give me any of your shit, Seashell Abrecan. Husk should only have seen recipes for teas and tonics, perhaps a repellent for biting insects. The book is well-guarded. You can see for yourself."

"Even with Ambrien magic, I would not think his Asciendien advanced enough to read it," Seashell said, placing the grimoire aside, bristling from the use of her maiden name. Jezebel Darke did not approve of her marriage to Marsh Swann. "Had you cast any spells recently?"

"No. I never use his grimoire but for a bit of show. The book is meant to reveal beauty teas, poultices, that kind of thing. The expected wicker woman protocols," Jezebel said. "Why would I free that awful specter? We both know what he intends to make of Aerda if he ever gets his wicked hands on it. And to do that, you and I will be on the top of his kill and destroy list."

"Yes, I had noticed. He had sorcerer snakes raining down on The Swamp like ash from an exploding volcano. He also tried to make a deal with me, to hand over Husk as blood sacrifice. His lust for Erelahian blood is not sated in the time spent trapped in that book."

"You have a plan?"

"For Terminus? Certainly," Seashell said. "However, I would know more of the parasite that has attached to Husk. It seems she and Terminus have a history."

"I sense that as well. However, it is one of animosity. Phaedra protects your ward. This does not mean she is not dangerous."

"More than we can imagine, I suspect. Jez, she's the demon of Heath's Night," Seashell said. She handed Jezebel a scroll, the recorded events of that horrific place. "That creature also called itself Phaedra and slaughtered almost one hundred Fistian slavers and their mercenaries and clients."

"I could almost admire her for this," Madame Darke said. "She saved dozens of children in doing it. Don't look shocked. You feel the same, Seashell. Look at what you attempted to do to the Mammon sisters. If this is the same Phaedra, she could be useful in combatting Terminus, but it is a measured risk."

"I did think the same. Only, I feel Phaedra will not be controlled," Seashell said. "But my ward, Husk, might be able to exercise some measure of influence. As long as Terminus remains weak. And does not kill Husk to undo the binding. I could train him although if Dalmeade discovers this, they will never admit him to the Archives for training. He would not consent to that."

"Dalmeade can burn. It is a cursed place."

"It is a blessed place and Husk would be the first Ambrien admitted there in a thousand years. It is why I sent him to Kingswell College."

"Forget Dalmeade, Seashell. It will never yield its secrets to the likes of you and I."

"I cannot forget the Archives of Dalmeade. Still, I will train both Husk and Daedalus in secret. I won't even tell them," Seashell said. "They need not know why I am instructing them beyond allowing them to guard against the specter that hunts Husk."

"Maybe we should ward Husk's name. We can't let Terminus take another soul."

"Your husband is the only soul he has taken since the fall of Irialfar. Right?"

"Yes, my son was Calibor Pelles. I still have his name. Terminus still needs two more souls to return to full power," Madame Darke said.

"One more," Seashell said.

"Two."

"He took a soul in Irialfar to destroy the Fishers. We have no idea of the name of the man he took to accomplish that slaughter. Then he took your husband before we banished him. He only needs one more and he will be at full power," Seashell said. "It is our coven's job to prevent that."

"And as we are all that is left of our coven of thirteen…"

"Exactly," Seashell said, trying to carefully form her next words. "Jez, we can't go the way of the Mammon sisters. We can't. You have to be stronger than your magic. I suspect what you intend, but Calibor is dead. You can't bring him back any more than I can bring back my son, Joshua. Let his soul rest and let us save Ambriland together."

Revelers

The Rooke paused to find Aldo and Kentigern gesturing wildly. He sauntered over to the edge of the stage.

"We found Tavares and Aleron, none of the others."

"All right," The Rooke said. "Can Joel calm down long enough to get the lights on? Then we can run."

"A good plan," Aldo agreed, scurrying off toward the alchemist and her husband. He could make out Joel nodding his agreement.

Unthinking, The Rooke removed his red robes. He did not realize what awaited in the shadows.

The revelers attacked, not with weapons, but with malice. The lights came up and The Rooke saw a large man, holding Anwyn Finn by the hair with one hand and trying to rip at her clothes with the other, laughing wildly.

Several women were being assaulted. Aleron saw and leapt into the crowd, pulling the would-be rapists away. The Rooke dove down into the fray, grabbing the man assaulting Anwyn by the throat. He pushed her toward Tavares who gathered Taki, Thiago, and Kostas.

"Run," The Rooke said to Anwyn. "Follow Tavi out of here. Go, children."

"Where's my mom?" Anwyn asked. "She's being hurt. Help her."

The Rooke turned to find Mika on the ground, screaming as two men held her down and a third pulled at her trousers. He roared and with the help of Aleron pulled Mika's attackers away. Mika stood up, furious and pulled a knife from her coat. She drove the blade into one of her attacker's throats.

"You fucking asshole," she screamed. Her rage unbridled. "Ani, run. Get out of here."

"Them's the Nacharye," someone growled. "Kill them."

The Rooke reacted too slowly. A man wearing spiked gloves punched Mika in the chest as she drove her knife into his eye. She toppled over. Aleron and Tavares managed to pull Anwyn away.

"Mom! Mom!" Anwyn screamed.

The Rooke picked up Mika and ran. "We're leaving," he said as Rintyre disentangled herself from a reveler trying to molest her, leaving him crumpled over holding his crotch. "Let's get out of here. Rintyre, where's your sister?"

"They didn't come down here," Rintyre said. "She and Bryter stayed in their room."

"We will go back for them," The Rooke said, pushing her forward. Mika weighed almost nothing. However, she was not moving. Anwyn continued to shriek as blue lights signaled the arrival of imperial law enforcement.

Out in the night, there was no clear way to go without being sighted. This would not have been a problem but for the dead body The Rooke carried. There were people everywhere.

"We need to get to Bradamate," Aldo said. "It's not far. We can cross the bridge."

"Bridge is too far and too many Scarlets. Let's cross the park," Joel said, his hands full of wires and little black boxes that looked as if they had been forcibly dislodged from their proper place. "We can make the last ferry across the bay if we hurry. I have disabled SIN in this area."

"Let's go," The Rooke said. He knew Mika was dead. He could not carry her onto the ferry. He gave Kentigern a look. The old man nodded, pushing the others ahead.

The Rooke tucked Mika's body down an alley, hiding her behind a large block of bins. He put his librarian coat over her. He ran to join the others, feeling empty inside, ignoring the rats that ran toward the darkness of the alley.

Joel pushed the others onto the ferry as The Rooke joined

them. He took Aleron and Tavares aside. "I need you two to go back," he said. "Find Carling and Bryter, Zac and Cymbre."

"None were in their rooms when I checked," Aldo said. "Thought they'd gone with the others."

"They are probably in their rooms by now," Tavares said. "They won't be distracted by the police that high up. It's that sort of place. They will cover this night of carnage up. It's not the first I have witnessed. There are protected people who do horrible things that no one wants to talk about."

"Mika is dead," The Rooke said, pulling Tavares and Aleron aside. "I hid her body on a side alley between the park and the hotel. Can you dispose of her body in a respectful way?"

"Poor little Anwyn," Tavares said. "That scavenger was so good to me and my wife. I will see she is treated with honor."

"Me as well," Aleron said. "What was wrong with those people? Right in public where anyone could see?"

"It is normal for revelers. They are demon oppressed. It reveals the darkest of human desires. They enjoy their carnage," The Rooke said. "I never thought there could be so many. I thought them defeated long ago."

"More demons coming this way," Joel said. "Let us go. We must run. They are fast. Very fast."

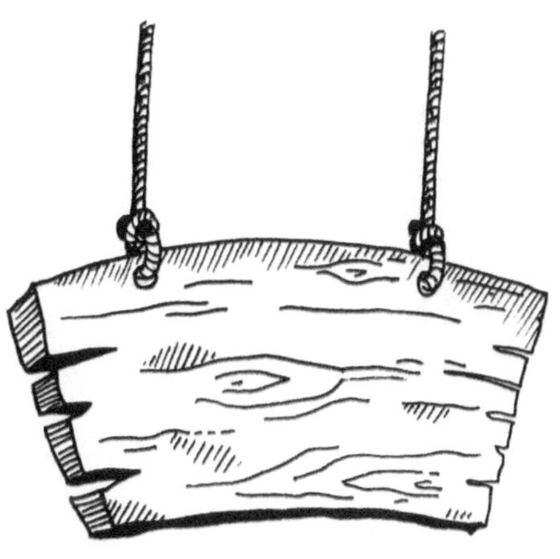

Tavern XIII:

Millie's Sad Dunk

The stories of knights slaying dragons are poorly conceived fairy tales. A true dragon is pure elemental magic. It cannot be destroyed or controlled. Not by mortals. Not by demons. Nor by angels.

Mordecai's Grimoire by Felix Wren of 'Those' Wrens
Preface by Hazel Kyran

The Peon Dunk

The city of Tandell glared across the bay at The Rooke. He pushed the party through the night, finding little pockets in parks and alleys where they could hide. They all needed to sleep. The Rooke and his party had been dodging Scarlets from the moment the ferry took them across the channel from Ellyn into Bradamate.

Thiago and Kostas tried to keep Anwyn walking. Her cries had become sobs and now a whimpering. Taki seemed unphased by the trauma of the last hours. He moved through the dirty streets between the tall gray, bricked buildings with their dark windows ahead of the group. Once and a while, he would turn and tell them to follow.

"What are you doing, Taki?" Rintyre said.

"Mapping. This be a village of Iscillian before people disappear," Taki said. "Now it very ugly city."

"People commute from Tandell to Aroghotto City to work. People who can't afford to live in the capital city," Rintyre said. "They make more there than they would here. It's common."

"Aroghotto City is in Chazir. This is far from there," Thiago said.

"They have train," Taki said. "Two hour there. Two hour back."

"What a miserable way to live," The Rooke said, absently. "It's getting late. We need to find a place to sleep and wait for the others."

Kostas stopped. "Father, Zac had both the ship and box. We've lost it. We need to go back and find Zac."

"Zac will still have it when Aleron and Tavares find him, won't he?" Anwyn asked, her red eyes looking up at The Rooke in such pain.

"Hush, child," Joel Broomes said. "It will be all right. They be strong men. They get everyone back."

"How can it ever be all right?" Anwyn said. "My mother is dead."

Tee Broomes looked down a dark alleyway. "I used to live here," Tee said. "For a short time. I was poor. I think I know a safe place for us to gather away from inquiring eyes and SIN."

She turned down an alley, filled with bins teeming with garbage, rats and pigeons scurrying about, looking for scraps. In the dark, it looked something out of Phaedra's Hell to The Rooke.

"No, too dangerous," Rintyre said. Her sleeve buzzed again. "I have to stay in touch with my employers and with Mia."

"Rin, this is not the time," The Rooke said. "Turn off your sleeve. Put it in sleep mode."

Rintyre looked at her wrist, tears welling up in her soft eyes, a sharp contrast to the hard expression on her face.

"I have to go to Aroghotto. Mia needs me," Rintyre said. "This can't be real. Everything is going wrong. I should never have agreed to go with you. Where is my sister? What is happening?"

The Rooke stopped and put his hand on her shoulder. "I am sorry. I wish there was time for me to help you. We will find your sister and there will be comfort later. We need to move now, and this is not a good time for you to leave us. Rintyre, be strong."

"Well, going into a slum is no way for us to be safe. Despicables live here and they are dangerous," Rintyre said. "They hate people like me."

"Stop it," Anwyn said, turning on the woman. "My mother is dead. She wouldn't want us to die. Forget your stupid girlfriend, your stupid sleeve, your child-hating employer, and let's get out of here. I am so scared. I am so scared."

"It's ok, it's ok," Kostas said, taking Anwyn's hand. "I have you. Nothing will harm you. I will take care of you. We have magic, Ani. We will win in the end."

"I don't know how to do anything without my mom," Anwyn said, her tears starting again. "She's my whole world since my dad died. She's all I have, and now she's gone and it's all my fault."

"Not true," Kostas said. "You have me. And your mom saved you because she knew you are the most brilliant girl in the whole world. Do not give up, Ani."

"Anwyn, easy, child," Tee said. "I am going to give you something. Just to help you through these next few hours."

"We can't have her high with Scarlets after us," Rintyre said. "She has to be able to move."

"She will be able to move, and the Scarlets won't follow us, Rin," Tee said. "Millie's Sad Dunk is down here. No one with any status will even look for us, but all of you must turn off your sleeves. Joel, dear, disable their sleeves, even the false ones. Follow me."

The Rooke hesitated at the uneven doorway, standing on the cracks in the pavement, and listened. The peon dunk lived up to the sad reputation of such places. There was nowhere else to run. Tee Broomes pushed him through the door into the badly lit dive.

Angry conversations competed among disregarded people deep in their cups, sometimes laughing, others jeering, saying nothing at all in amplified voices accustomed to being ignored.

Ambient music served no other purpose than the fill the emptiness and mask the despair of men boasting their plans when they got rich. Others remained silent, having long since given up their dreams. Those came to drink away their lives. Unwittingly, these men and women who nobody wanted, disturbed the dreams of sleeping dragons.

"No assassins wait for rookes here," Tee said, her breath sweet in The Rooke's ear. "These people are so beaten down, you could not even call them rebels. Each and every one hates the empires, but the imperials no longer see them as threats. Those that once prospered have been stripped of their wealth.

Those who ever spoke out, no matter how meekly, have been quietly denied their prospects. Notice their sleeves."

"These people have all said no to demons," Joel said, surveying the room. "And they have paid. In the end, it is better to have black bands and nothing than wealth in service to a demon, although I would not know how to convince them of that."

"Joel, demons are not responsible for everything," Rintyre said. "These people fell on hard times as people do."

Every one of these people wore sleeves that were old, unpolished with threadbare ribbons, evidence of a time before Emperor Malcombe IV, in those ten years when the last true Sacripant emperor had given the people a glimmer of hope for a better life.

Most imperial citizens, like young Rintyre, were trained to despise Nicholai Sacripant for the freedom he brought, for the independence he sought for all the nations of Aerda. Here, in this dirty room, were the ones who suffered most after his fall.

The Rooke recognized sleeves of engineers, money changers, bakers, soldiers, sleeves from every class, guild, and background. The Rooke saw none who were allowed to work or trade under the steel grip of Emperor Malcombe IV.

The only new ribbon seen on old sleeves of these people was thin and black, enough to get them a public assistance coin to keep hold their tongues in their cages, enough so they could drink in these peon dunks, the only places those sporting black bands were allowed.

These despicables were kept alive to give favored imperial citizens someone to hate, someone to put their pain on that was not The Hierarchy or the emperor and his allies in their gilded castles.

The stink of bitter ale, half-burnt food, urine, and the sweat of people under unbearable duress greeted The Rooke and his party as they moved into the smoky, artificially lit room. The food looked paltry and not the kind that would do much more than sate hunger while earning those consuming it angry bellies and weak hearts. Slow poison. How The Icari loved enticing humanity into torturing themselves.

"We have an advantage, dear Tee," The Rooke said. "The Icari never change. They never learn. They are always cruel. They are always arrogant. And only the very mean and stupid follow them willingly. We can use that to find our victory."

"Or we could just let these dragons of yours wake up," the alchemist said. "Look at them. Would it not be a kindness to take this world from The Icari and free these broken souls?"

"You are spending way too much time with Kentigern, my dear," Ghita Mist said in whisper, running a hand over The Rooke's shoulder and slipping between him and Joel. "He and you are of the same mind. Defeatist the both of you."

"Lovely to see you too, Ghita," Kentigern said, stepping in and embracing the master puzzler.

"Kentigern, I am so glad you have managed to keep The Rooke alive," Ghita said, turning back to The Rooke and fixing him in her violet gaze. "Unfortunately, Rooke, both dragons are awake. You will have to tell your tales to soothe them, or this will be a very short quest."

The Rooke startled to see the old woman, wearing a tattered artisan sleeve with the newly black public ward band that made her blend in with the patrons of Millie's Sad Dunk.

"Ghita, where did you come from?"

The Rooke looked up and was pleased to see Zac Grimm, Aleron, Tavares along with Carling and Bryter Kenn. He watched as Rintyre embraced her sister, showing her wrist and sharing her pain.

He startled to see Bracken Grayvesone, holding back, looking broken and weak. Rintyre listened to something her tearful sister was telling her.

Rintyre turned toward her estranged father, and without preamble, punched Bracken Grayvesone in the face.

"You fucking bastard!" she said, silencing the Peon Dunk. "How could you?"

Kentigern and Aldo stepped forward. Bracken made no

answer, no protest, holding his head down, wiping the blood oozing from his nose, and putting the other hand up in capitulation.

"I surrender," he said. "Kill me now if you want. It is better than I deserve."

"I really am tiring of these self-pitying men," Ghita said. "Please do not kill Bracken. He has done badly, but he was not prepared for the power wielded against him. I will explain in time."

The Rooke noticed the newly arrived party members had all well-prepared and wore the black ribbons alongside their old common sleeves. He wondered how Ghita managed it.

"Where is Cymbre Varian? Did she go back to Talon?" The Rooke asked.

"Oh no, Rooke. She was your Spyte. She poisoned young Zac there, commissioned revelers to kill Ani and her mother. And stole that blasted puzzle box and that priceless ship in a bottle you managed to procure," Ghita Mist said, making The Rooke feel like he might vomit. How often he was fooled by people. He always expected them to be good. No matter how often they betrayed him.

"They murdered Mika…"

"So Aleron told me. We could not retrieve her body. Scarlets and imperial police were everywhere," Ghita said as Anwyn and Kostas embraced the old woman. "Hello, children."

"Grandmaster, we messed up," Kostas said. "Zac told us. We should have puzzled out that Cymbre was on the list. Only, she wasn't so broken, was she?"

"My mom is dead," Anwyn said, voice even and full of despair.

"I am so sorry, my dear," Ghita Mist said, as she put her fingers under the girl's chin. "It is awful to lose someone like this. But your mother always told me how strong you are, and she is right. You are strong. You will endure, my girl. And you are going to help save the world."

"Cymbre is a Spyte?" The Rooke said, his mind reeling. It

explained why she had never taken a token and missed the majority of his tales. And the smell at both The Cross-Eyed Hag and The Last Resort. The girl had meant to kill, and then thought to do worse. He sighed.

"Cymbre was a high-ranking Spyte, known by the gutter baroness that seduced Bracken. There is much to say, no doubt," Ghita Mist said. "Now don't fuss. Remove your sleeves, all of you. Only two kinds of people are allowed here. Black ribboned, disregarded people and those with no sleeves at all. You are making a spectacle of yourself."

The Rooke looked up to see a woman burst into tears and put her head down on the bar in shaking horror. He realized too late. The patrons saw in him and the others danger with their acceptable sleeves, and they were all afraid they had come for them. Or worse, to shut down their last refuge from the world outside.

The Rooke moved to expose his red robes but stopped short.

Bryter Kenn shook The Rooke's hand, giving him a wink.

"Let me calm this crowd. Then, we'll see about a tale."

Bryter moved like a force of nature, unmoved by the hiss of the gathered patrons or the gasp of fear from the others. He looked ragged, dressed in an ivory tunic, blood-stained as if he had been fighting. He took a stool from the bar and took it to the center of the room. He played a forbidden tune, filled with defiance and determination, put to a driving beat and minor notes. Hope disguised in song.

The Rooke took a deep breath, steeled himself as Bryter finished his tune and silence rose from the crowd, a few trying with all their might not to clap and cheer. The Rooke summoned forth the blood red robes, displacing his fancy imperial garb.

He cleared his throat as Tee offered him a flagon of clear, cool water with a hint of some alchemical substance that tasted of fresh lemon. Whatever it was, magical or merely organic, it loosened his stuck tongue. He accessed the magic from the robes, letting it explode outward.

It might have been imagination but in that moment, the food

in the peon dunk became more wholesome, the spirits purer, the water, fresh as from the waterfalls produced by the untouched glaciers of Boreal. The odors of decay were replaced by burning herbal candles, the smell of fresh baking bread and properly cooked food.

The Rooke did not question it as he lost himself in memories of ghosts and told his tale. The audible gasp from the crowd as The Rooke's magic produced light from nowhere and transported the crowd to a pirate dock in Marinplaz, Ambriland.

Mikhaela Chrysalis Finn

Mika Finn floated through the house in pre-dawn searching for her crying child. Confusion rattled her, trying to remember what was happening. She had never lived in such a large house, yet here she was.

The baby kept crying. She called out for her child, opening door after door to the same, bland bedrooms. Identical, one after the other. Gray carpet, single window, with dirty, translucent curtains, a single bed, dingy white sheets, a duvet cover that gathered dust, the same square, dark wood frame. Heavy dresser. Heavy end table.

Panic welled up in her. She had to save Ani. She stopped, realizing the rooms mimicked the awful guest room in her grandmother's house, a memory at the beginning of a dark journey.

She stopped at the top of the stairs, a straight way down to a landing that had stairs to the right leading to the parlor, and to the left leading to the kitchens.

Mika could hear the ghost of a forgotten conversation from her early childhood. Her mother and grandmother hissing at each other, raised whispers she was not meant to hear. She sat down, the baby still crying across time and space. The sibling that she never had, that her mother aborted so their family could survive. She looked at her hands, a memory of young hands, a child's hands.

"I told you not to have children with that man," her grand-mother was saying. "And now you want another? Mikhaela is ..."

"She is a child. As any other," her mother said. "Can you not be happy, mother?"

"No, I am not," her grandmother said. "Maybe, you'll get lucky. Maybe this one will be a boy. But if it's not, you risk our entire family. Get rid of it. And tell Mikhaela what she is so she can learn to hide her abomination."

"There's still time..."

"No, there is not. There never was," Mika's grandmother said. "Chrysalis, I have had to hide my entire life because your blasted father did not tell me of his origins. There has never been and never will be tolerance for women like you. I don't want a life lived in the shadows for my grandchild. I didn't want it for you. Hiding one is hard. Hiding two is impossible."

The baby wailed as the house faded away and pain exploded in Mika's chest. She screamed without making a sound. She felt herself paralyzed, unable to move, unable to close her eyes. She could hear little Anwyn's anguish. The nightclub of the Glittering Raptor consumed her. She heard the pounding of the beat, the flashing of the neon lights, all of it.

Run, Ani. Damned it all. Run!

She willed as she could not speak. She watched The Rooke cut down their assailants, monsters all wearing human pelts. Mika tried to move.

"Mom, mom. No! No!" Anwyn cried as Tavares Flaco pulled her away toward safety. Demons danced around them, foul, degenerate creations filled with contagious rage and lust and hubris, infecting the humans around them.

Anwyn struggled as Tavares did his best to calm her. Mika felt The Rooke scoop her from the floor, carrying her away from the raging demons. She felt her breath failing as her lungs fought to move air through her body, her heart struggled to beat. She was going to die.

The Rooke put her down in a clean alcove behind empty bins. He covered her with his long, black, and gold coat that accentuated his librarian disguise.

"I will have someone retrieve you," The Rooke said, a voice full of sorrow. "We will make sure Ani is safe. Sleep now, Mika. You've done well."

Mika did not know how many hours passed as she lay unable to move, unable to scream, under that coat. The cold stung at her. The wound in her chest throbbed. She wished to sleep, to escape the horror of her paralyzed body.

The first sign of life was a rat. Had anyone been there to see, they would observe tears running down her cheeks. The terror horrible as the rat sniffed at her.

Mika could not see what removed the coat from over her face. She heard no steps at all. She struggled with all her might to move as more rats found her, starting to nibble. The voice seemed to come from inside her as well as from without.

This is a most terrible poison. One of the favorites of The Icari and their adherents. It once was used to murder the body that made me as I am. Be still. My rats will not harm you.

"Who are you?" Mika asked without making a sound, thinking she must be going mad. No answer came in words spoken. Only in exasperation. Mika already knew.

I am Phaedra. Do not fear. I cannot save your life. But I can free you from this pain. While my rats will not feast, your lungs, your heart will cease functioning. You must let me in as the one who granted you your middle name did all those centuries ago.

Mika did not hesitate. She agreed. It felt so strange. She saw herself rise from the ground, disregarding the long coat. Phaedra took all Mika's pain, fear, and distress away.

Mika watched as if outside her body, with vision that was sharper than human eyes as Phaedra used the latent magic of Mika's blood to transform herself into the powerful sorceress of legend. Her skin turned a whiter shade of pale, her hair thick, hanging about her shoulders, and dark as true night, her eyes like burning embers of black flame in the body that rose from the alley.

Mika felt herself willing Phaedra to take revenge on the monsters that had attacked that night. Phaedra complied.

They drifted through the streets into the club in The Glittering Raptor. The monsters there did not see their peril. Mika delighted at the power pulsing through her veins even as she was revolted at the carnage in the nightclub.

Phaedra ripped revelers away from the drunken guests. Rats filled the club until there was nowhere to step that wouldn't find one of the vermin scurrying under one's feet.

Mika saw nothing human in the creatures that surrounded Phaedra, all exposed and grotesque. Mika felt fear. They intended to have their way with the magnificent sorceress.

"The rats are the least of my curses," Phaedra said to Mika. The revelers thought Phaedra spoke to them. They were too stupid, too drunk on their own lust to notice all the vermin. "Nothing can touch me without reaping a heavy price."

"We do not pay for our sins," a big reveler, fulling erect, his mouth dripping with the blood of some poor victim. "We play. Only you will pay."

"I am Phaedra, you fucking idiot," Phaedra said, folding her arms in front of her.

The reveler grabbed her and burst into flame. His screams delighted both Phaedra and Mika alike. The fireball that erupted from Phaedra lit the entire place, burning revelers to ash and letting their victims escape, all screaming out about a fire.

"Enjoy your time in Hell," Phaedra said to the burning monsters, walking through the fire which soothed her instead of burning her. Mika rejoined her body, feeling wind and breath. "They'll be back. We have much to do, you and I, Mika Finn. At last, I will have my army, and nothing will stop me."

Mika tried to hold on. Her body felt to her a wild carnival ride, and she wanted to keep going. A song and a gentle breeze on a sun-filled autumn day beckoned her away.

A meadow appeared before her, both memory and eternity shined before her as joyful people sauntered toward musicians playing lovely acoustic tunes in celebration of life, love, and all things good and right. She found herself holding hands with someone she loved who loved her in return.

A voice called out to her and reassured her. Great love will call Anwyn and all souls home in the end. And that was the only truth that mattered.

Phaedra stood behind, and Mika could feel the despair solid in the sorceress who was unable to follow her into the light. She wished she could tell Phaedra that she was not being rejected. Only delayed.

Mika was gone. The light receiving her with a blinding exultation that left Phaedra feeling cold and frightened. She must journey, once more, across the landscape of Hell.

Phaedra stood alone among the chaos. She needed her grimoire, and that would be a perilous journey. She had hidden it in Castle Mal Tombs where she had lost the body of Sile Pyn some centuries ago.

She once kept a cottage in the Dusk Forest near the castle. She hoped it still existed. This world's foundation shook as she felt the dragons stir in fury. Somewhere, not too far away, that ancient rooke told her story, one he could not finish. Phaedra prayed her story would end better than it began.

The Tale of The Birth of Phaedra Pyn

*P*ink and golden light of the dying day illuminated the Marinplaz docks as Husk Grayvesone went looking for a drink. He could not think how he would get this tea to little Xavier. He needed to sort out his head. What had he been thinking?

A good many ships filled the docks needing repairs and restocking at the Marinplaz shipyard. Workers flooded out onto the planks as the evening bell sang away the sun. Sailors looked for drink and company. This was a seedy bit of Ambriland avoided by most of the country's notable citizens. Husk loved it. All the bustle and the noise, the variety and song.

He felt Phaedra like a dull ache in his brain as she bristled in disgust at a blue-skinned woman held at the end of a chain by a man in ornate clothing.

There are young girls in slavery here.

"There are not, Phaedra. Slavery is illegal in Ambriland," Husk said to Phaedra's hissing. He saw what the ghost objected to. He did not approve, but not for the same reasons. "Sile Pyn is putting on a show. For money."

I see through your eyes. There is a girl being forced to do things no child, no one at all, should be forced to do.

"That foul man is not of Ambriland. He is a Fistian aula called Dax Kappa. King Charon allows him here as it increases tax income from the docks and Ambriland is in deep debt to The Fist."

Why is that girl blue? Are many girls like that in your world? I have known another girl like this.

"Quite rare. That is Sile Pyn. She is a Nacharye girl. While young, Nacharye can change their appearance which is useful to the man that holds her chain."

Husk felt himself go sick as he explained the phenomenon of Nacharye women to Phaedra, realizing that Sile Pyn had been a child when she began selling herself. She was seventeen now, but he remembered three years ago.

He begged her to stop, but Sile told him she would be rich and free before she was twenty if she continued. Sile said in The Fistian Empire, she would be enslaved until her death and made to do far worse. In Ambriland, she said, she had a chance to live for herself.

Why does she allow this aula to hold her like that? She is powerful if she has magic as you claim.

"You are not wrong to despise the aula. Fistians have always ill-used Nacharye girls for centuries, ever since the fall of Irialfar," Husk said. "There's nothing we can do about it without starting a war with The Fist. And Ambriland can't find an army big enough to beat them. We are short of the pirates that once gave these islands real strength."

Can this girl change anything about her appearance?

"Not everything. Skin color, eye color, height to a limit, weight to a limit, but she can't change into a man or a monkey or anything. She can appear younger or older, and she can be invisible for short bursts," Husk said. "Quite a few Nacharye were born in Irialfar before it fell. Some escaped to The Fist only to be enslaved. Occasionally, they show up among the Muddy People, but only Fistian aulas use them in this foul way."

I can do something for this Sile Pyn. She is a child, and she is afraid. She does want to service this merchant who Dax Kappa wants to sell her to. Look, look. She's being hurt.

"We'll be hurt if we interfere..." Husk said although he wanted to interfere.

He liked Sile. She worked at The Shark's Mouth when not working for this foul aula. Sile told him that Dax paid her well, and that in three short years, she would never have to work again.

Sile had her eye on a cottage near the one Husk shared with Daedalus. And Captain Delilah Sage had once threatened Dax Kappa with a mysterious death at the hand of her crew of pirates if he continued to abuse his charges. He had a lot of women and pretty men in his employ. Unfortunately, much of Captain Sage's crew made use of Kappa's services.

Husk wished for Sile's freedom. He had appealed to the priory to no avail. The Ambriland Codex said people could trade their bodies as long as they paid their tax, and that was that. Sile had claimed she acted willingly when interrogated by the priory. In front of Dax Kappa.

A child being traded for…no, no. This is not happening. Read from that book we took from the witch when I tell you to.

"The Dragon Paradym or the blank journal?"

The journal. I am going to find it some power.

"There is nothing to read in the journal."

There will be when I tell you to read. Do it.

Husk had no actual control over Phaedra. He could not stop her from doing whatever it was she thought to do. And for a long spell she did nothing. The night seemed to press on without further disturbance as Husk made his way toward The Shark's Mouth in search of refreshment.

He saw Captain Delilah Sage and her daughter, Siobhan Rose, Shanley's half-sister, sauntering down the docks toward him.

He momentarily forgot about Phaedra, The Fistian aula, and Sile Pyn. This was a blessed answer. Captain Sage could get the tea to Xavier, and no one would object.

"Hello Husk," Siobhan said with a lovely smile. They were of the same age and had known each other long. "What word of my little brother?"

"It's not good," Husk said. "In fact, I have medicine for him. His mother won't approve but it will bring him relief. If he still lives."

"Still lives?" Captain Sage said, pushing a crate she was carrying into the arms of a sailor accompanying them. "What are you saying?"

"Three days ago, Xavier's health failed entirely. They were sending for Glorious Thierry this morning to give him final passage. Shanley sent me for medicines. I have acquired them."

Husk pushed the tea with the scrolled instructions into Captain Sage's hands.

"What is this medicine?" Siobhan asked.

"Arryl weed and some other herbs to be seeped as a tea with honey and citrus. No milk," Husk said. "The wicker woman who lives in the jungle gave it to me. All other cures have failed."

"We will take this to him straight away," Captain Sage said. "In tea form, I can get it past Mirror. Come, Siobhan, your half-siblings are in need. I will tell them we brought this back from Acaria. Xavier's mother will like that."

Husk watched the two pirate women hurry away, causing him a smile of relief. He took a heavy breath and began toward the bar for that long-anticipated drink.

Your imp has gotten away.

This information came from the cat or seemed to, as Sariel weaved in and out of Husk's legs. He picked up the small feline and stood back as a commotion drew the attention of the early evening traffic of the docks.

"He's tried to murder her," someone called out.

"She's drowned," someone else said. "That dirty aula. Help her!"

"Where did he go? And that fat, degenerate, Pick?" someone asked. "Sile has a right to refuse that old aula's customers, especially a prick like Pick."

Husk ran to where the people were gathered at the edge of a dock, surrounding a young woman. Not blue from her skin but blue from not breathing. The collar Dax Kappa held her by had shattered, and her appearance had changed.

She was raven-haired, gleaming black eyes, thin, deathly pale, and looking the young girl she truly was, the edge of seventeen. Two sailors were trying to revive her.

"What's happened?" Husk asked.

Read the book. Now or Sile dies.

"She did not want to go with that merchant, Ford Pick, real knob that scoundrel. He stole money from me I needed for my girl and my kid," one sailor said. "And that aula slapped her, and the girl fought back."

"That doesn't sound like Sile," Husk said, fumbling with his pack to pull the ramshackle journal loose. He opened it and was surprised to see letters appearing one after the other on the page. He read words he had never heard before.

On the dock, Sile coughed up sea water as her skinned pinked up although she was a paler shade than any living being had a right to be. A wound on the front of her head seeped blood that the girl wiped away.

"Sile, are you all right, girl?" One sailor asked.

"Sile is good. Sile is gone," the girl said. "She has claimed the light. That slaver murdered her body. Her head hit the dock and she drowned. She no longer lives here."

Husk sprang forward to help the girl to her feet, slight feeling of panic that turned into resignation. He scarcely reacted when the newly revived Sile Pyn grabbed the tattered journal which was now plumb full of words. She read from it. Husk felt a hot flash of air and his vision fogged. The gathered crowd wandered away, carrying on with their lives as if nothing had happened.

"Sile?"

"Were you not listening, scholar boy? I am Phaedra."

"What did you do?" Husk asked.

"I made them forget," Phaedra said, all in flesh. Had she always been there? Husk's mind reeled.

"What happened to Sile? Are you possessing her?"

"She died and her soul fled into the light apart from the bit she gave this book. She has no need of this body. I, on the other hand, am in particular dire need of flesh. I can hide here, you see."

Husk gaped in horror and could not make a sound. He had, after all, unleashed this creature.

"Oh, stop that. It was not me who took Sile's life. She was drowned by those foul men," she said. "I am Phaedra. This is my body now."

"What happened to Dax Kappa and Ford Pick? Did you kill them?"

"No. I merely gave them the gentlest of shoves into the water. The sharks did the rest."

The Disregarded

The patrons of the peon dunk rumbled in anticipation as The Rooke finished his tale. They took no notice of the rats that scurried across the back of the bar and behind Bryter and Carling and their guitars.

"Is that all?" one patron asked. "Could we hear a bit more?"

"Did Xavier Rose live?"

"What of The Silver Swann? Was she able to defeat the specter?"

The Rooke wanted to continue but for the exhaustion that came over him like a crashing wave. Anwyn Finn took him by the robe, her gaze intense.

"Sile Pyn died? What does that mean? If her body is still alive, then she's not dead," Anwyn said. "Did she have to be dead for Phaedra to take her. Chrysalis was not dead, and when she died, Phaedra went away."

"Ani, your mother is gone. I am sorry, even if Phaedra were still about," Ghita Mist said. "Sile did die and so Phaedra had total control. Sile did not even look as she had before. Phaedra always takes the same form, this dark-haired, painfully pale creature of the night. She does not possess bodies so much as replace them."

The Rooke did not know what to say. How to react. Phaedra might bring down The Hierarchy of Hell had she not stood in full defiance of the Almighty God, Creator of All, to do it. He shook his head and made to say something when a commotion interrupted him. He looked up to see Bracken Grayvesone standing before him, with great fear in his eyes.

"We have to get out of here," Bracken said. "I went out for a breath of air. They are coming for you."

There was no time to question the broken man. He watched as Bracken went to rescue his daughters, both still glaring at him with such fury. He wondered what he had done as this was something more than the abandonment of their mother.

The firebomb hit the front of the peon dunk, sending people into the air and engulfing half of them in flame. A man grabbed The Rooke by the arm.

"This way, out the back," he said as another explosion echoed.

The Rooke tried to turn but Kentigern and Aleron had him,

pushing him out. Bracken had his daughters and the children. They ran out into a narrow alley. A dead-end until the man who was leading them, knelt and opened a sewer grate.

"This won't be fun, but it's the way most of us go home every evening."

It was difficult to understand the muscular man with the close-cropped hair, bright eyes that sparkled in the fire, almost as if he found it humorous. He spoke with a thick accent that sounded as if he had cheeks filled with nuts.

"All those people," Thiago said.

"Already forgotten, lad," the strange man said. "It was a matter of time. They never leave us our dunks for long. A rooke gave us hope, and that is never permitted. Them that died are in a far better place than this."

Tavern XIV:

The Tin Green

The Daughter of the Night never deals. Whatever Lecretia asks for will benefit her more than whatever she gives the idiot who thinks to trade with the Queen of Hell.

The Spells and Curses of Lecretia, by Elfrydah Nix
Translated by Hazel Kyran

The Tin-Sleeved Thieves

The sewers exited above ground into a walled-in square. A battered metal sign in faded red paint called the dark and dingy buildings 'The Tin Green'.

Not a plant, scarce a weed grew anywhere in sight. It was all black rock and tall, box-like buildings in gray with tin roofs, filled with broken windows and broken people that The Rooke followed the man from the dunk into. Smoke filled the air, and the orange and black flames of the burning peon dunk exploded behind them. Another of the patrons, an older gentleman, confronted The Rooke.

"This is your fault. That was last place we could go to get away from all this filth," the man said. "Why would you come to a peon dunk?"

"Leave him," another woman said. "That was the most hope I have felt in years. They'd have found a reason to burn down Millie's eventually. No rooke needed."

"We're all expendable," the man leading them said, wearing a tin sleeve, something The Rooke suspected did not belong to SIN. "I am Jamey Milner. Folks call me Millie. That was my dunk. And there are people here that will help you and yours. The Tin-Sleeved Guild operates here. Most would call us thieves."

"Thanks, Millie," The Rooke said. "We need sleep. If you can steal us a bed, I will take it."

Around them, he saw people much as the ones he had encountered at Millie's Sad Dunk, milling about around barrels of flame. He saw amid the black-ribboned people, multiple sleeves of tin attached to rounded instead of square screens at the wrist. He wondered if the empires could distinguish the tin from the disregarded. He suspected not by the ruinous surroundings.

Millie led the party into another ugly tunnel out into a clean, well-tiled floor among sturdy, white-washed walls with well-installed and brightly painted doors to each side. They followed Millie down the hall and then down several sturdy staircases that were illuminated with gem lights, similar to those in The Reliquary.

"I'm afraid you'll have to stay in the bunk rooms. The flats are all full," Millie said. "There are only three open tonight with six beds each. The common area is shared by the entire community. Includes two water closets and a bath. Mostly stays quiet so should be able to sleep."

A dozen of these bunk rooms all opened onto a large common area with artisan-crafted, colorful rugs, round and square pub tables and chairs, a bar with running water, and worn, cushioned armchairs in little conversation circles. It was lovely, clean, and quiet despite the smattering of people gathered around, talking quietly, enjoying drinks and small snacks.

Taki, Anwyn, Kostas, Thiago, Tee, and Joel took the first bunkroom without any discussion. The children were asleep before they hit the bed. Tee and Joel checked each of them, shooing The Rooke out, assuring him they would be safe this night. Tee offered a sleep remedy which Ghita inspected with approval.

"We all ought to take it," Ghita said. "It will allow a small amount of sleep to revive us."

Aldo, Aleron, Kentigern, Taveras, The Rooke, and Bracken Grayvesone took the next, giving their thanks. Rintyre, Zac, Ghita, Carling, and Bryter shared the last bunk room. The Rooke observed as Zac seemed to gently care for the elder grandmaster, getting her a bed closest to the door and sectioning it off from the other five beds.

The Rooke sighed at the sight of the small bed, only just big enough for him. He was surprised at how comfortable it felt, how clean the linens were, and how warm the blankets felt as he drifted off into a dreamless slumber.

Morning found The Rooke rising sometime after the others who were enjoying a lively breakfast with other members of the community. Aldo hailed The Rooke.

"Rooke, we have a problem," Aldo said as Aleron stood before him.

"I think some of us should go home," Aleron said. "This Cymbre Varian. Ghita and Bracken have explained it all. The Reliquary has fallen. My children could be in danger. Cymbre was alone with both my girl and my infant son on multiple occasions. They say infants are most vulnerable to such creatures."

"Easy, there mate," Bracken said. "Cymbre Varian was not a baroness. She can't turn those children, although she would mark them. If what Ghita says is true, The Relic is not around to unmark them. Or judge me."

"You know Cymbre?" The Rooke asked.

"One of my wife's favorite pets. I thought The Reliquary guarded against such beasts."

"Father, why are you here? You can't think you could make this right," Rintyre asked. "What you told Carling and Bryter? Is it true?"

"I didn't know. I never would have guessed," Bracken said. "Until I reached Astarte where Bryter Days were playing at The Canticle Fair. I suspected Jude was not my child. I did not realize Teriss faked a pregnancy…"

"He can be saved?" Carling said. "My son can be saved?"

"What is going on?" The Rooke asked. "Your son?"

Bracken told the tale and told it well. The Rooke understood why The Relic insisted on collecting him. He felt revulsion.

"Can our child be saved?" Bracken asked.

"He can."

The answer came from Joel Broomes who stepped forward, with his arms articulating as they did when he was excited.

"It is rare to turn a Spyte back to a person," The Rooke said. "Although it has happened. But all instances I know involved the use of purifying wyrms, the graffing wyrms used by the Urians. And those are all gone."

"No, not so," Joel said. "I was a Spyte once. I killed my brother. I stopped being one."

"How?" Bracken Grayvesone said.

"I do not know," Joel said. "It is all, how do you say, foggy. I was twelve when I became Joel Broomes. When I was small, I made my family rich, and they were happy for me to be this Spyte. I was meant to spy on my classmates. I was sent to a special school for the wealthy, for children of important families. I was walking home after school one day. And there was a sleeveless man, dirty, with a wild beard, bright eyes, and he didn't stink as most vagrants do. I went to kick him, being malicious and a truly vile Spyte. He laughed even as he bled, and he called me Joel Broomes."

"He just said this name to you?" The Rooke asked. "What did you do?"

"I froze," Joel said. "I changed. That was not my name. Not the one my parents called me by. The people I believed to be my parents willingly gave me to the demon, you see. I never made it home that day. I ran away, filled with horror at all I had done, knowing I had done wrong. I tried to die, but that vagrant wanted me to live."

"Oh, dear," Ghita Mist exclaimed. "You are the broken Spyte. Not Cymbre. The Relic made a mistake."

"I do not know about this Relic," Joel said. "I wanted to help. I know it is Spytes murdering the rookes. I sense when they are about. I knew one was following us when we traveled with Cymbre. I simply had not worked out that it was her. Very few are girls. I thought it might be Taki until I found out he was Gnolgia. Demons use the girls in other ways."

The Rooke felt revived after a couple of days in The Tin Green. He shared his tales, and let the others work through their grief and confusion.

Carling and Bryter had determined that they would join Bracken to retrieve their son once he was rejoined with their mother and arrived in Talon. They waited to hear from their mother, using the same devices Aldo had brought from The Reliquary.

Bracken woke everyone early one morning with news. Raven informed him that the nanny transporting Jude Amber Grayvesone to Jebellen had been found dead. There was no sign of the boy.

"Is my son alive?" Carling asked, a wild look of fear in her eyes, Bryter holding her steady.

"I wouldn't worry," Ghita Mist said. "It is likely the boy, a Spyte, murdered this nanny."

"Don't say that," Rintyre said. "You don't have to be so cold about it."

"It's the truth, and we have to deal with it," Ghita said. "We need to find this boy. And Bracken's gutter baroness."

"Our priority must be pursuing Cymbre and Ambriel's Cube," Aldo said. "The dragons are awake. If we don't find that cube, I don't think any rooke's tale will sate them."

"I know where Cymbre is going," Zac Grimm said. "Nox Verre. She was trying to talk me into moving there with her. She got really angry when I said I was going to finish this quest first. She said I wasn't really part of it and would be in the way. She really fooled me."

"Spytes do that," Bracken said. "Don't worry about it, kid. One got me too. You're lucky she only poisoned your body. Seems you kept your soul. Not an easy thing to do with one so advanced as Cymbre Varian."

"We will decide how to proceed in the morning," The Rooke said. "I don't like the idea of splitting us into two groups. But not sure we have a choice. We must find little Jude if there is any hope in saving him from the demon that controls him."

"Jude is not his name," Carling said. "We would have named a boy Gabriel Ryan after my great uncle and Bry's best friend. Gabby. His name is Gabby."

"That might be a way to save your son, free him from the demon that controls him," Joel said. "We give him the name of love. I think that this is a way to remove a demon. Once I was Joel, the demon could not touch me anymore."

"Dad, I saw the dead body of a baby that was supposed to be mine," Carling said. "Who was she?"

"This was four years ago in Talon?" Kentigern asked. "You saw the dead body of my granddaughter."

"I remember our child was born the same day as little Embla. Laurel and Paul sent us flowers. They were so good to us," Bryter said. "Embla was healthy."

"Paul and Laurel were sure they were having twins when Embla was born," Kentigern said. "The midwife claimed there had only been one. Embla was so hearty and beautiful, they thought little of it. My wife worked as a mid-wife for decades. She felt sure it would be twins. A storm prevented us from attending the birth. We received word of a healthy granddaughter and that was that."

"If Cymbre was the one who performed the switch," Bracken said. "Your living granddaughter, the living twin, will be marked. That one wanted to be elevated to a gutter baroness, and my vile wife was considering it. I overheard her fighting with her sisters about it."

"We have much to think on," The Rooke said. "Kentigern, send a message to your son, to Gareth. Bracken, you have much to do to earn our trust..."

"I understand," Bracken said. "I know I deserve no mercy. I have done wrong. My mind is clear now. I knew something was amiss, but my drug habit paired with the problems Raven and I had...it's not an excuse."

"You're right about that," Rintyre said. "Still, admitting you did wrong. That's a start."

"Father," Thiago stood in the archway between the common area and the bunkroom where talks were going on. "Are you done with all the secrets?"

"Just about," The Rooke said. "Why?"

"Well, there's supper. It's delicious. Old Marlinean food, Tavares said, like he used to have with his granddad. So good. I think Kostas likes it better than chicken and chips," Thiago said. "And people are wanting a tale. Could you?"

The Decoy

Fake smiles and put-on enthusiasm greeted the announcement of The Fistian Seat's engagement to a girl half his age. Gerrard Frederic Al 'Dhar looked at the teenage Chaziri princess with something of loathing in his heart, looking at the spider he was meant to marry. Not for the benefit of his country of Dagger and Fist.

Gerrard understood the politics. It was Chazir's endgame to pull the Third Empire under the grip of the First Empire. Megdon had surrendered decades ago to the point that their Prime was now called Second. All the great elites saw The Fistian Seat as weak, malleable.

He wore the jewel around his neck in defiance. The blue gem glowed against the fading light of the first day of the Unity Conference. A strange couple, a woman in a black-scaled dress and a man in a silver-scaled suit gave him a look as if they knew him as they passed by on the white, marble floor below. He turned to inquire who they were.

"Who is that?" he asked. He had thought he knew all that attended this conference. He was far cleverer than this group guessed.

"Who is who?" Princess Lilith asked.

He pointed to find the couple gone, replaced by a group

of royals, surrounding Baroness Teriss Amber. He wondered faintly where her famous husband might be.

"Baroness Amber and her sisters," Princess Lilith said. "She is divorcing her husband. Have you heard? She is leaving today with her sisters. They have both recently had children. The Baroness wishes to be with them at their Nox Verre estate."

"No. I did not know any of that. I don't follow gossip."

"Is that meant to be an uncut sapphire?" Princess Lilith asked him in her quiet voice that was meant to sound meek. She was not. Gerrard knew as the gem around his neck informed him that he was engaged to a viper.

"Not really. Just a common, blue crystal," Gerrard said. Lilith Absyrtus was a spoiled child. She would demand he hand it over to her if she believed it valuable. "It is but for show, to make my eyes look pretty. Do they look pretty to you?"

"Not so much," Princess Lilith said, shrugging. She was bored. She did not want this marriage any more than he did. Her father, Emperor Malcombe IV, insisted. What could the poor girl do? "I wish you would not be so fat."

"You think I'm fat?"

"You are fat," she said, venom dripping in her soft words. "Emperors are meant to handsome and powerful. Once we have a son, he will be emperor. Not my useless brother. We will remove him at the first opportunity. I will make sure our son is not fat."

"You would have been happy with my brother," Gerrard said. "He was skinny. And handsome. And funny. Of course, he's dead now."

"He was too old," Lilith said. "How many years were there between you two?"

"Eighteen," Gerrard said. "I surprised my parents. I can tell you that. They were much relieved to have a spare at the time. But then Konstantin married and had a son. He also adopted the son of his wife, a wickedly clever woman, a force of nature she was. Even as a small boy, I saw that. I loved her, such a good woman and mother."

"She was a nobody. The boy he adopted would never be emperor," Lilith said, sounding angry.

"Whoa, princess. He's dead. My brother. His wife. Their two children." It was Gerrard's turn to sound angry. He wanted to see if the princess would react, if she was truly the viper the voice in his gemstone warned him about. "Konstantin's son was newborn, less than six weeks old. His adopted child, a fine boy, was only four. All murdered. Their bodies were never recovered. Only my sister-in-law, and she was cut into pieces. Sloppy as far as assassins go. It seemed personal."

Lilith glared at him. "Yes. This is known. What is your point?"

"I think your father had them killed, princess," Gerrard said. Nothing. She looked away. Then her gaze turned to fire.

"He was not emperor then…"

"He was. It was before Nicolai's coup. It turned the world against him, all but Chazir who convinced their people that the Arisea of The Fist were …oh, what were the words, infidels and barbarians, religious fanatics," Gerrard said. He rose. "I need to relieve myself. Smile while I am gone. We have to sell our charade. This is, after all, the Unity Conference."

Gerrard made his way through the throngs of people, heading far from the customary elite toilets. He had no intention of going any further into the viper's den. His brother would understand. He had made the showing. He had evaluated the situation. And the little gem around his neck advised him to leave Aroghotto City in all haste. The gem said its mother was coming, and she would bring her wrath down on the city.

He did not worry about how a gem might have a mother. Rocks did not have parents. However, dragons did. And the mother of the dragon hibernating in his necklace was the most famous of all dragons. Phaedra, the fire dragon. He smiled a little. Konstantin would have a good laugh at this.

He threw off his sleeve, screen, and monitor, pulling off his fancy tunic and undoing his fat suit to expose a gaunt and thin man. He pulled off the layer of makeup that puffed up his face, disguising a less disgusting figure. He threw the trappings of The Fistian Seat in a trash bin. He put on a tin sleeve that mimicked common steel, and dressed in dull, imperial grays. He made his way to the underground. It would take him several hours to arrive in Bradamate.

He wondered if his brother was still at the Tin Green or had moved on. Konstantin was meant to be dead so he could not stay in one place too long. He had one of those faces one did not forget. Gerrard could not wait to be anonymous again. He hoped Phaedra and her fire would accommodate him.

Gerrard Frederic Al 'Dhar felt a pang of unquenchable guilt as the train sped toward the border of the city. Children ran and played in the gardens among the dull, brick buildings. Common-sleeved people worked, doing the most uncomfortable jobs that paid for the least amount of comfort. And Phaedra, the fire dragon, would not spare any of them. Gerrard, like so many of his ancestors, understood dragons well enough. They were not the enemies of humanity. Nor were they allies.

He closed his eyes and spoke to the dragon within his gem. She fluttered. She assured him that these children would not suffer. They would awake to Eternity. And again, she told him that dragon fire cleanses. No corruption would ever touch Aroghotto City again.

Freddie, for that is how Gerrard Al' Dhar thought of himself when not being the seat of power for his home, scooted off the train among a small group of people returning to Bradamate from their work in Aroghotto City. He made sure no one looked at him as he descended into the sewers toward his goal. Millie met him outside the sewer grate.

"Hello, Freddie," his old friend said. Jamey Milner had been his manservant since he was a boy, and the only of the tin-sleeved thieves who knew his true identity.

"What's news, Millie?" Freddie asked. "My brother still lurking about?"

"We ran out of vodka. He went searching for greener pastures.

And supplies for our brothers in the East," Millie said. "But we do have a rooke. He's managed to stay alive. I expect The Unity Conference has kept the empires careless and focused on Aroghotto City. Still, he's something else. You'll enjoy his tales."

The Tale of The Rose Tombs

Hope evaporated with each passing minute. Shanley Rose stood outside her father's study. She started to knock for a third time, changed her mind, knowing there would be no comfort to find within. As she turned away, a call beckoned her.

"Shanley?"

She opened the door and entered to find her father in his white and gold admiral coat behind his great desk surrounded by all his metals and awards, shades drawn, lamps dim, face in his hands, trying to muster himself for the storm to come.

"Yes, father?"

"The Silver Swann is sending Dr. Rege to us. He should arrive in the next hour or so. Will you let him in and bring him to me?"

"Of course. Where is mother?"

"Nurse Katja has given her an elixir to let her sleep a little. Nothing too strong so when the time comes…"

"Mother can say good-bye."

"You best do the same. I am sorry, my girl. I know you love your little brother very much."

"Father…he might," Shanley stumbled for her words. She could not tell her father she had sent Husk Grayvesone to the wicker woman, so she gave up as she always did. And left him alone with his grief.

Shanley gripped her book to her chest. She wanted to retreat to her room with its bright windows where she could look out on her garden in its splendid colors. It was the only garden left to the Roses, the one she kept herself. She resisted the urge to hide away there in her own quiet world.

Her brother wasted away, slumbering on the razor edge of death. She crept deeper into the manor, into the tombs beneath where there were no windows at all. The stairs turned in a spiral down and down, so deep underground, her footsteps absorbed by solid stone in her descent.

Ancient sconces lit the way down a narrow hall filled with small chambers where the bones of people long dead slept. Shanley hummed an old tune under her breath to comfort herself as she descended into the ruins beneath her family home.

She hated the musty smell of the dead. Rose Manor had been restored from the remnants of an ancient castle, and its tombs remained unchanged but for the enhancement of an underground infirmary for her small brother.

Xavier lived and yet here he slept, in a crypt outfitted for some forgotten noble in a place the sun could never find. How convenient his burial would be, right next to the tomb where their other brother had been laid to rest.

Shanley shuttered at the memory of Xante. She stood by his tomb and read his name as she had so many times before. How was it no one saw his tomb? She wished she could undo that curse.

She passed by the brightly lit antechamber where the nurse, a medic, and a novice cleric played a game involving cards and dice to pass the time. They were far too enthralled by their game to notice Shanley.

Idylls & Grimoires was a favorite the world over, a game of strategy, luck, and wit. The three sounded delight and fury at each roll of the bones and turning of cards, all oblivious to the dying boy in the next room.

Shanley wondered if this trio cared about Xavier at all. Mugs of cool water left rings on an old game table as the medic, Dejan Carra, argued with the nurse, Katja Mare, about a card she played. Shanley scowled at them as she passed, annoyed that they did not even notice her open her brother's door and creep into his room.

An Ambrien clock adorned the wall of Xavier's death room. Its face had been crafted of glowing crystal, burning soft yellow, enough to see but not so as to worry her brother's extreme light sensitivity. Every tick of the clock sounded like a gong in Shanley's head as the minutes lapsed and her little brother's breath grew quieter and quieter.

Xavier looked monstrous. His head bald and scarred; his body skeletal with skin so pale as to be translucent. One brother dead and gone, and now Xavier. Boys did not do well in the Rose family.

Shanley took Xavier's little, cold hand and pressed her head to his chest to make sure he still lived. She could smell the sick on him, bitter rot rising from his little body. At his side, the smooth wood of his treasured model ship stuck out of the sheets. Swan Song. She had brought this favorite possession to him last night, hoping it would bring him comfort.

Shanley longed to move Xavier from this tomb. Surely, there were other ways to protect him from the sun's light. Nothing here said that a living boy breathed and dreamed in this chamber. Apart from the toy ship, none of Xavier's maps and books, swords and bows decorated this room. All the possessions that spoke to the promise of the man Xavier might become if not for this cursed illness had been packed away.

"Xavier?" she whispered. He stirred in a movement imperceptible. "Xavier? Hold on. Husk is coming with help. Shall I read to you?"

Xavier moaned, faint and weakening. He took a ragged breath and lapsed back into deep sleep. Shanley settled herself in the chair in the corner, turning on the lamp which glowed incandescent, strong enough so she could read the words on the page, weak enough that its light did not irritate Xavier.

Shanley opened her book, thumbing through its worn pages. She knew this was not a story Xavier would request. He would want to hear about pirates and sea ships and battles. This book seemed like a good compromise.

Shanley selected *The Pirate's Girl*, one of many romance books she kept secret. This story told of the blackest of Ambriland pirates, Feral Storm, and his love for an innkeeper's daughter. A hundred years ago during the First Coffee War, there had been lots of these pirates. This fiction was based on a real man.

In this tale, the town guards of Gyo Gladden exploited and abused the people they were meant to protect. Feral Storm, an Ambrien with those gleaming emerald-green eyes and skin in splendid sun bronze, played champion to the poor people of the harbor town.

Shanley read to her brother one of the action scenes where Feral aided the rescue of the innkeeper's daughter, Shanti, from the unwanted attentions of the harbor guard. Both could fight.

How Shanley wished she could be so tough as Shanti, both strong and desirable. Shanley had tried to get the girls at school to call her Shanti after she first read the tale, lying, and saying it was the short nickname her family called her. No one complied. She was Shanley Rose, the most unimportant of Admiral Bernard Rose's children.

Xavier loved a good sword fight. Shanley felt certain he would enjoy the story if he were conscious enough to hear. Before he fell ill six years ago, Xavier had played at swords and bows, back when music, balls, and brilliant light graced the Rose Manor above.

Like the tragic end of this glorious book, the Rose Manor had fallen into despair, its gardens overgrown, the ballrooms boarded up, the pools stagnant, and the entire guest wing closed but for a couple of musty rooms kept for visiting physicians.

Shanley prayed Xavier could manage a better ending to his story rather than the one written for Feral Storm and Shanti. She shivered as she recalled her feelings when she read how Feral Storm and Shanti died within calling distance of each other, their blood pooling together at the end of a cobblestone lane, mixing with the blood of their fallen enemies.

"Is this one of your silly love stories?" Xavier's voice came out in a raspy whisper.

"I suppose, but this one is about pirates. You like pirates."

"Husk is not a pirate. That was his father," Xavier said, a

tinge of regret flavoring his words. He turned away and fell back to sleep.

Shanley smiled. She shared such intimate secrets with her tiny brother, not realizing he listened even when he seemed to sleep. She had the worst crush on her brother's tutor, one she could tell no one about.

Her mother would be so awful about the whole thing, and her father. She could not risk him knowing. She so wanted to make her father proud, to be glad to have her as his daughter. Shanley closed the book, swallowed hard, wanting to escape these walls.

"Where could Husk be?"

She looked at the clock as it turned to afternoon, the crystal turning from morning yellow light to waning blue.

Shanley hated how much she thought about Husk. When she pictured the pirate, Feral Storm, she saw Husk with long-hair, dangling earrings of gold and diamond, scars on his arms, wearing tight leather pants and his chest exposed in an open, flowing tunic. Only Husk would be quicker than the ill-fated pirate, more cunning. She pushed the vision aside.

"He's been gone for hours."

"Shanley?" Xavier again, his voice straining to be heard. "It hurts so much. It hurts." He whimpered his pain.

"I will see if you can have some verlanium," Shanley said.

"That doesn't help anymore. I am tired of this life. Please, let me die. Tell mother and father to let me go."

"No, Xavier, don't say that. Husk is going to bring relief. I know he will."

"Make it stop. Everything hurts."

Shanley felt wretched and helpless. A fit took Xavier and he began to shake. She fled the room, calling for the nurse. The laughter over the card game stopped as the nurse charged in, and Dejan took the stairs two at a time to call for the doctor and the high cleric. Shanley wondered if they would have noticed Xavier's pain if she had not been there as a surge of fury shook her.

"Please, Husk, hurry," she said to the wall as the nurse skirted past her carrying a medical kit.

Shanley ascended the stairs to get out of the way, clutching her fists as her father breezed past her, the tail of his white admiral coat swooping behind him, his face red and contorted with grief. He did not see her there.

Shanley stood alone in the dark listening to her brother's weak cries of pain. Hopeless. Her childish fancies could not save Xavier, and who knew what that old wicker woman would ask of Husk?

The front bell rang and the rapping repeated, frantic, and insistent. Shanley ran towards it, praying Husk had finally come, nearly toppling the old steward, Greg Skerry.

The mother of her father's first child, Captain Delilah Sage, and Shanley's half-sister, Siobhan, stood there at the front door. Shanley burst into tears.

"Xavier is done for. The clerics are administering his final passing now. Mother has taken to her bed. Father is mess and Husk did not come back."

The two women eased into the house, both in loose fitting trousers and tunics, flaunting their reputation as pirates. Siobhan took Shanley into an easy hug.

"We ran into Husk at the harbor," Siobhan said. "You sent him to a wicker woman?"

"I...I had to," Shanley said. "He didn't go, did he?"

"He did, my dear," Captain Delilah said. "However, your father would not take the remedy your wicker woman offered by one such as your young Professor Grayvesone, so I have brought it."

"You have? That's, please, let's get it to my brother. He is almost gone."

Delilah Sage, a tall woman with the harshest of expressions, fixed Shanley in a stone gaze. No one would refer to this woman as "lady" or "ma'am". She was Captain Sage to most, but due to her relationship with Shanley's father, she was Captain Delilah.

"Stop this, Shanley Fleur. This is not the time for grief."

"Captain Delilah, Xavier will not see tomorrow if the wicker woman's remedy does not work. The doctors say…"

"No, you will not despair. The tea will work. For a time. Long enough for me to finally talk some sense into your father. Where is your mother?"

"In her bed. They may have awakened her to say good-bye to Xavier," Shanley said.

"Let us hope she stays abed long enough for me to administer this tea," Captain Delilah said. "Siobhan, I may need you to distract Mirror should she awake. Best she believes Xavier's recovery more a miracle than magic."

"Thank you, both," Shanley said. She regretted for a moment that Husk did not accompany them. She understood the thinking, however. Neither of her parents would trust her or Husk to bring a remedy for Xavier.

"Siobhan, have the staff remove the drapes and light all the lamps. Open up the guest and old servant's wing. Bring in additional servants from Marinplaz if necessary," Captain Delilah said, handing a stack of papers to the startled and mute steward. "Bring light back into this house. This dreariness is the last thing Bernard's family needs."

"Steward Skerry, do as she asks," Shanley said. "It will be good for us to have a breath of fresh air in the place."

"Ma'am" was all the steward said, taking the papers from Captain Delilah's hand. He glanced over them, nodded that he understood what was required.

He gave Shanley an encouraging look, bowed slightly to her, not her sister or her father's ex-lover. Greg Skerry had always been so kind to Shanley. She should remember that, she chided herself. She could be such a beast to him, to everyone. If Xavier recovered, she would be a better person she told herself.

Delilah Sage swept through the manor like a great wind, dispelling the grief and renewing hope. The same regal bearing graced Shanley's half-sister as well. Siobhan Indigo Sage Rose looked a queen waiting to happen, even in her loose sailor's trousers and peasant tunic.

Awkward, trying to play the host expected of her, Shanley escorted her sister into a tiny tea-room right above the kitchens. "Would you like tea or coffee?"

"Tea, please," Siobhan said. "Acarian Royal black tea if you have it, with milk and honey."

"Siobhan," Shanley said, trying to carefully phrase her question as the two sat together over their tea. "Did Husk seem all right when you and your mother met him at the harbor? What was he doing there? Did he seem vexed with me?"

"He was chasing a black cat," Siobhan said. "Why would he be angry with you? He seemed relieved to have found us to deliver the tea."

"I got angry and broke his spectacles and…"

"You broke his spectacles? Shanley, whatever for?"

"He didn't want to go, and I sort of snapped. I thought if he needed to have the glasses repaired. They are expensive, made special for Ambrien eyes and all. He did not believe the wicker woman could help, but he knows she can fix his spectacles." Shanley sighed. "He is probably at the tavern in Marinplaz with that girl, Gull, he likes so much, telling her about how crazy I am."

"Husk is not spiteful. He likes you, Shanley. You've been friends since you were children," Siobhan said. "I am glad you pressed him into visiting the wicker woman."

"You don't disapprove?"

"Why would I? I don't share your mother's distrust of Erelahians or magic."

"She says it would be better for Xavier to die than to sacrifice his soul to heretics."

"That is the Chaziri in her. They fear all that they cannot control."

"They fear ancient prophecies from Serra's Doctrine which claims Erelahians will destroy them."

The sisters sat chatting as the afternoon gave way to evening. They found cheese and bread for a light supper while the clock ticked ever forward.

As night deepened, Daedalus Sams, the handsome scribe that worked with the high cleric, Glorious Thierry, appeared, pulling off his robes. His sleeveless under-tunic was soaked through with sweat. His eyes did not have the jeweled façade of Husk's eyes. They were, however, the startling, bright emerald color that marked him as having Ambrien lineage. Daedalus sat between the sisters and took a long breath.

"Daedalus?"

"Shan, Siobhan. The crisis has passed. Your brother will live," Daedalus said with a grin. "I don't know what Captain Sage gave him, but it has restored his breathing, stopped his pain, strengthened his heart. Dr. Rege is astounded and proclaimed a miracle. Wait until I tell Glorious Thierry. His sermons will be unbearable for months."

Shanley let out a sob, and Siobhan took her arm. "Oh, that's amazing," Siobhan said. "See, Shanley, you have saved your little brother."

Seaworthy Junk

*E*veryone needed sleep. The Rooke took a breath, a small sigh of relief in the dark basement of one of the dilapidated buildings of The Tin Green. A young man, near thirty, late twenties, thick auburn hair, good size, wide shoulders, wearing a battered leather necklace with a rough, blue, uncut crystal at its end, assisted people looking for a place to sleep, and a quick meal.

Several people were wrapped in blankets, in makeshift beds. Each and every person in attendance had taken a token to combat the fear in the air, to bring some hope that a better world might be born of the darkness.

Bracken Grayvesone stood in line with people wanting tokens, head down, blending in with the disregarded who found shelter in these hidden buildings. The Rooke blinked in surprise. He understood. A well-claimed token would bridge the gulf of distrust that followed his lost apprentice. If Bracken were false, no token would be granted. In fact, for past rookes, it had only been those looking to kill them who were denied tokens.

Bracken claimed a glowing crystal token, exceedingly rare, one that would allow him to hear the tales far and wide while borrowing The Rooke's magic. A token that, customarily, only those apprenticed to a rooke would find.

"Dad, that's like mine," Thiago said, pulling his token from his coat.

"Of course. I was supposed your father's apprentice an age ago," Bracken said. "Mine is long overdue."

"What will you do?" The Rooke asked.

"I will go after my grandson, and I will tell your tales as I go," Bracken said. "Raven wanted me to be a rooke. To give up my name. I couldn't face that. I thought she was trying to steal my daughters from me, my ambitions..."

"And the baroness exploited your insecurities," The Rooke said. "I know what it is to be preyed upon in this way. I suspect I became a rooke to escape my own guilt. It doesn't work. You won't forget who you are, Bracken. It still sits there, informing you of your weakness, your failings, your pain. It allows a bit of sympathy for the devils in our tales."

"I know the tales you tell now," Bracken said. "For to me, they are family history. I expect I might even know them better than you."

"Where will you look for the boy?" Kentigern asked.

"I will start at the place where he murdered my nanny. Then to Jebellen to see if Teriss took him there. I feel her hand in this. He was not up to murder yet, only ugly mischief. He's only four. I am praying that it was Teriss who did the killing."

"Wasn't she meant to be at the Unity Conference?" Rintyre asked.

"She was. But only for the first day."

"My son did not murder anyone," Carling said, "Dad, it's the demon, right?"

"Yes. Jude...er, Gabby calls him Mr. Piss. That's how I know he's a Spyte because of Mr. Piss," Bracken said. "We will start in Jebellen. If we find the trail dead, we will meet your mother in Talon and start from there. We will get The Relic to help us once they emerge from hiding."

"I will go with you," Aleron said. "I can help protect the people back home, the ones that might have been harmed in some way by Cymbre. She had access to so many children."

A rainy morning saw Bracken, Bryter, Carling, and Aleron to the train, all back in proper sleeves. Bracken's dark and gray hair had been dyed yellow and his sleeve downgraded to escape anyone recognizing him. They would go back to Astarte, going from there to Jebellen and onward.

Rintyre decided to stay with The Rooke and his party.

"We should also look for my nephew," Rintyre said. "If Cymbre is involved, then the baroness is involved. Best I go with you. I am skilled at finding lost children."

"It's a good idea," Carling said. "We can use those devices Aldo brought from The Reliquary to talk in secret. They aren't on SIN. I will have my son back soon, and all will be well."

Rintyre said good-bye to her sister and brother-in-law. She did not show any sign of affection for her father, but she gave him a faint wave goodbye. The Rooke thought it a good sign until the young woman confronted him.

"I know a thing or two about Spytes," Rintyre said. "Carling knows too, but she'll never do what has to be done. If he's already murdered someone, that boy is no longer my nephew. And the only way to neutralize a true Spyte is to kill it. Is that not so?"

"Joel is still alive," Tee Broomes said. "And he was a Spyte."

"He's a kid who accidentally killed his brother," Rintyre said. "I do not believe, Joel, that you were a Spyte. I think you escaped a bad situation. In all the stories, Spytes are taken from their families and raised by older Spytes or the gutter baronesses that made them."

"You speak true. My mother was the gutter baroness, and I was raised with other Spytes," Joel said. "My parents were evil. Wealth and status are all that mattered to them. You would not be able to convince them that they were wrong. Having a Spyte child, for these people, is considered a high honor. I was a Spyte, Rintyre. I remember the demon."

"But they don't get to keep the child, the parents who do that," Tavares Flaco said. "Do they?"

"No. Joel's mother was likely not his birth mother. Teriss Amber is not the first to claim to be a Spyte's birth mother," Ghita Mist said. "Regardless, I think splitting up is a good idea. We need to recover Ambriel's Cube. And we should find this small Spyte. He is young enough that he might be redeemed. Joel's tale does give me hope."

"It is worth trying, Rintyre. We will do all that can be done to save your nephew," The Rooke said. "Although, aside from Joel here, I have only heard of one Spyte being truly redeemed. That Spyte held the damned soul of Tiernan Vasilis, responsible for the destruction of Alleysiande. And that involved the graffing wyrms of the Urians, the white purifying ones. And those disappeared at The Evanescence."

"We're not killing a kid," Kostas said, hoisting his pack over his shoulder. "If we're not taking a train, and we don't have proper sleeves, how are we going to get the box back?"

"We're going to steal you a ship," Millie said. "Oh, and Freddie and I have decided to come with you. None of you seem up to this quest of yours, a soft bunch you seem, no offense."

Taki was animated by the idea of stealing a ship. He wanted to take a very large ship. He explained how it might be done. In the end, it was a modest yet luxurious sailboat that took the party across the sea to what was left of the Blessed Kingdom of Acaria.

"My mother loved Acaria," Rintyre said. "She used to say the strangest things. Things that could not be true."

"Like what?" Ghita Mist asked.

"Like she remembered its kings. But Acaria has been without

a true king for centuries now. I do love my mother, but she is a bit crazy I am afraid."

"Do you know how Acaria got its name?" Thiago asked. "I am surprised the empires did not change it. Maybe they could not."

"Acari means angel's canon, so Acaria was a place of angels," Rintyre said, a bit of scowl on her face. The Rooke knew that Raven and Bracken would have taught their daughters of the old world. "Just as Icari means demon's canon. It's all mythology created by the Acarians."

"No, those words are Asciendien and the Acarians did not create that," Thiago said. "It's all true anyway. I don't see how a descendent of Husk Grayvesone, a woman who has the blood of Ambriel in her veins does not believe."

"Faith will get you killed," Rintyre said. "There are no solutions there at all."

"Darling, there are no solutions. Not ever," the tin-sleeved Freddie said. "Only compromises."

"You are both wrong. Faith will allow you to endure Hell," Tavares said.

"Tavi speaks the truth. Faith is everything," Joel said. "You don't realize how much you need it until you see true darkness, child."

"I am not a child," Rintyre said.

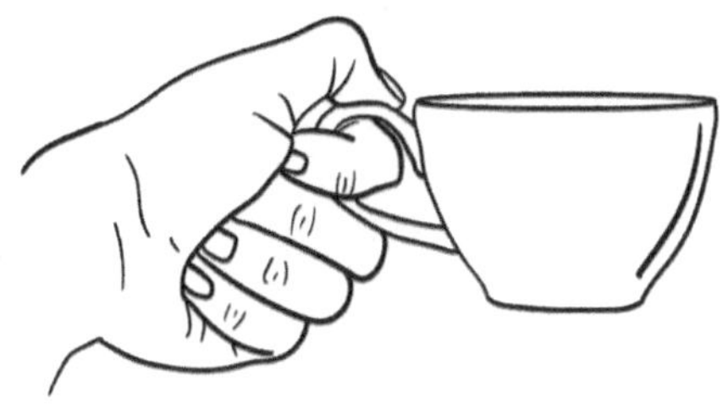

Tavern XV:

The Burnt Hand Coffee Shop

Hope is faith's lesser cousin. Where hope will set a tremulous foot on a perilous journey, it is faith that will withstand Hell itself and come out on the other end.

The Idylls of Alleysiande, Vol IV. Sandalphon's Symphony
author unknown (translated by Hazel Kyran)

The Hidden University

The sailboat got the party as far as Lesser Faroe, a rocky island well off the coast of Acaria. A sudden storm forced them ashore. Freddie and Millie wanted to press on to Acaria, but Ghita Mist objected.

"We will be safe on Lesser Faroe," Ghita said. "The empires always forget about this island. I do not think they know people still live here."

"We will have better options in Acaria," Freddie said. "Lesser Faroe is off course if we are trying to get to Nox Verre."

"I don't think this storm agrees," Ghita Mist said. "Please, do an old woman a favor, and listen to me. We don't want to storm the beaches of Nox Verre. Better we come from the land anyhow."

"You know, Freddie," Millie said. "Old bat is right. We could go to…you know…It's not as far as Acaria. We could take the train once there."

"Not a bad plan," Freddie said, although The Rooke could not understand of which plan he spoke. "Maybe my brother will be there."

"What are you talking about?" The Rooke asked.

"We are agreeing with the old woman," Millie said. "Going to make for that island. Going to skip Acaria after."

The coffee house did not look entirely stable. The stone looked ancient, and it leaned at a precarious angle over the rusty sign that read "The Burnt Hand".

Rain fell in sheets muddying the cobbled road from the docks. In the distance, faint lights glimmered from ancient stone buildings, heaped one after the other, leaning into each other, lining a road inland where a ruin of a once mighty castle stood.

The Rooke and his party were, by this time, entirely soggy. It was the first shelter they found as they left the boat moored to a rocky shore.

The Rooke glanced back at the sailboat which looked wrong, too modern, too out of place on this old island that had once been connected to the bottom bit of Dalmeade where the famous Unapproachable Library stood. All gone.

Most believed that bit of Dalmeade fell under the rising tides that followed a series of cataclysmic storms and earthquakes between The Evanescence and Subjugation. The Rooke suspected that part of Dalmeade as gone as Alleysiande, not to be found under the rising oceans. He shivered, wrapping his common, imperial gray cloak around him.

"Looks no drier than that sailboat," Zac said.

"It has a roof," Rintyre said, shaking her head in the unending drizzle.

Music erupted as The Rooke followed behind Tee and Joel into the Burnt Hand. The atmosphere surprised him. The patrons looked to be students, young, hopeful. His face must have spoken his questions.

"There is still a university here," Ghita Mist said. "Lesser Faroe used to be the pointy end of Dalmeade which Acaria claimed as theirs in the last days. You remember, Rooke? It is not so changed. I believe some of its magic still holds. The imperials do not have control here the way they do in their other institutions."

"My mother wanted my sister and I to go university here. To Lesser Faroe," Rintyre said, inspecting the coffee house, a look of wonder on her face. "It wasn't on any list that showed any kind of prestige. Neither of us listened. How different...."

She did not finish the thought. She wrapped her arms around herself, stepping closer to the roaring fire, as Aldo presented her with a cup of hot coffee, as he distributed a tea kettle, and series of mugs on a long table.

"More is coming. Here, dear. You look in need," Aldo said to Rintyre, coming back from speaking to one of the baristas. "There's a boarding house down the road. Let's get some food. Maybe tell a tale to these students, and then I will get us all some beds for the night."

"This feels wrong," Zac said. "There's no transports. This light is all like back at The Reliquary and candles and fire. Like they've forgotten technology. No visible way on and off the island. It's like a world that doesn't exist anymore. And yet, some of these people have sleeves. And ours work."

He pulled up the copper band around his left wrist with the small screen that was dark with a glowing green light around it to tell him it had power and connection to the outside world. The Rooke pulled out his tablet from The Reliquary to see a message from Gareth Gillespie. He showed Kentigern.

The Reliquary is abandoned. When you return home, go to Talon. Avoid Mal Leshen.

"Yes, I got the same message," Kentigern said. "Aleron and the Grayvesones have not found the boy in Jebellen. They met up with Raven, and she is guiding them back to Talon. They fear little Jude and his Spyte handlers will go after those that Cymbre marked."

The Rooke felt a bit unsure as he approached the trio playing ancient tunes on acoustic instruments. He felt some power inspiring this place. An older man approached him.

"Are you our new professor?" he asked.

"What? Oh no, I'm afraid not," The Rooke said. "I had wondered if I might offer a song to this group. And a tale."

"It is an open set. I am Professor Ljinder," he said. "I will introduce you after these are done. Might I have your name?"

"I am afraid I no longer possess one of those," The Rooke said, exposing his red robes. An excited murmur rippled through the Burnt Hand Coffee Shop.

"Oh my," Professor Ljinder said. He lowered his voice to a whisper. "I teach a class on your kind. If the empires ever discovered it, they would close our university down and with violence. Of course, we keep the university secret so they wouldn't know. Please, tell your tales. Tell us there is hope."

The Fire Dragon

The fire dragon appeared in the empty courtyard of Aroghotto Palace. If the people could have seen or understood, they would know the raging feel of draconian disgust. This palace did not look a castle at all. No story lived here as it once had.

There had been a beautiful castle here once upon a time. The ice dragon mourned its destruction. The fire dragon would have her consort soothed. Tem's magic melted away as the divine artistry of mankind was spoiled by the machinations of the demonic Hierarchy. Phaedra would wipe the slate clean so Tem could take to the skies once more.

Nothing of the new palace of Aroghotto City spoke to the magical and mystical creativity that people once possessed in mass. This gargantuan structure was cold and black stone with faux gold outlining the windows and doors. One of the thirteen Icarian black towers glowered from its center. Phaedra hissed at it, all square and dull.

This structure had no spires, no curves, no artistry. Great architecture spoke of great love of the people who made it. The palace of Aroghotto City shouted its contempt of the people that were ruled from this oppressive and rotten center. Machines had spit out the pieces to construct it. Bland rectangles, heaped on top of one another, formed with expensive materials.

The courtyard and gardens seemed as if marble had been vomited from some geometric machine that copied each square exactly. The gardens had no wildness at all, every blade of grass, bush, flowering plant, and tree put in perfect order and given no chance to fall out of that order by an army of gardeners with no skill at all. They lived on orders.

Guards garbed in imperial blue vestments, held long guns at their shoulders, standing and not seeing, placed at every entrance. Lights at the end of square, metal posts glared orange light as the day failed. The citizens that lived around the palace did not show themselves this day. They were ordered to stay confined, for security, plans that failed to account for a dragon.

Everyone else was inside the colossal structure. Planning to make themselves ever so richer while making the vast majority of people forever poor, forever dependent, ensnared in chains of gold.

The dragon felt their hubris, well-pleased with themselves, believing they were making a better world. How she despised them even as she felt the displeasure of the Creator at her fury. Greater love came at a cost to those who must suffer this fallen world.

A couple wandered out into the flowering enclosure. They did not see a dragon. They saw the illusion of a woman. The dragon, using its considerable powers, knew the couple at once.

The Princess Lilith Absyrtus, young and empty, made a small noise as Phaedra turned her back, pretending not to notice the girl and the flesh-robed demon that accompanied her.

"That dress! See the dress she is wearing. I must have it," the girl said. "I've never seen anything so beautiful. Find out the designer and get me that dress. And make sure that woman never wears it again."

"Of course, princess," the demonic man said. "Anything you want. I suspect your fiancé has left the city. That is unexpected. Everyone knows The Dagger and Fist are financially desperate. The wars in their borders destroy every province. This was the last chance The Dagger and Fist had for survival."

"I did not want to marry that fat Daggera man. Gerrard Al' Dhar is a disgusting pig, and I will never forgive my father for wanting to pawn me off on him. There are so many better men. And I shall have them all."

"I expect your father will simply conquer The Dagger and Fist now. Imagine, The Fistian Seat leaving the conference without telling a soul."

"Maybe he had an accident like his brother before him,"

the princess said, all too happily. "Oh, it would be lovely if he were dead."

"Come, princess, we should, at least, be present for the ratification of the treaty. You will sign for The Fist. They will submit. Especially if our puppet is dead."

Phaedra cocked her head and surveyed the demon, a big one. While this monster was not one of the fearsome thirteen Icari, it was a mighty legion. She searched her memory. She had expelled most of these immortal betrayers from the Eternal Kingdom herself.

Imodial. That's what he called himself to the Ancients. When he had a name and a conjoined soul. As all demons, he was shattered into a legion of fallen, forever damned. Let him enjoy this world in its damnation. It was all that creature would ever have. No light. No higher self. No purpose at all. He gave all that up for vacuous power over this small, mundane world.

She decided she could give him another quarter of an hour, her tribute to Ambriel, The Time-Weaver. Watch this princess put name in ink to a meaningless document.

Phaedra looked forward to sending Imodial back to Hell. And Malfus who inhabited the flesh of Emperor Malcombe IV, the smallest and most insignificant of The Thirteen Icari. Always, she was sending Malfus back to Pandemonium. Why that infernal Icari would not stay there, she could not fathom. Always, he would rise again, wearing a new Malcombe.

This time there would be nothing for that miserable horror to return to. When the new world was made, The Icari would have no part of it. The Creator had promised. Ta-She-Serra had made a pact with her, with all the Erelahians that a new world would be granted. One where the dragons could live again, take to the skies, and feast at a magical world of endless creation. The great dragon made by the Sentinel Mordecai, Phaedra of Purifying Fire, was tired of waiting.

Phaedra, the fire dragon, drew in a single breath, rose from the ground, casting a black shadow over those below, blocking out sun and moon with the full immensity of her body, and expelled her cleansing fire. And that was the end of the blasphemous city.

Nothing remained of Aroghotto City but a blackened and flattened landscape in thick black ashes. Not a hint that a single living thing had ever set foot on this ground. No one had a glimpse of a dragon. Only a woman dressed in a scaled, black frock that raised the envy of Princess Lilith.

The immense fire dragon circled to take out Astarte, drawing in her breath. She felt the ice dragon's resignation. Tem had long despaired that this world was salvageable. He did enjoy the tales, the memories. He could touch them, always insisting that the rookes be allowed to try, one after the other, each dying to these soulless people.

Phaedra, the fire dragon, could no longer feel the magic of those tales. They only stoked her resentment of all the lost possibilities. She recalled a moment, lost to the centuries, people gathered as a music played, dancing, sending The Icari into an apoplectic rage. Uriel's blessed people were all gone. Their songs never to be heard again.

"Stop, mighty dragon. Not all is lost. The Muddy might return to us and us to them."

The sorceress stood alone on a burning road among burning houses. An incomplete breath at the edge of Astarte, a village pretty to the eye, filthy in the interior. Phaedra withdrew her destruction as she encountered the old sorceress. She was looking upward, her magic mighty, almost full again. The two shared a name and little else.

"It is enough," the fire dragon said, letting her fire cool for the moment.

"Phaedra, the dragon that gave my name such power," the sorceress said. "Do not do this. If you do this, The Icari have their victory. They will have me, and any world you make will be vulnerable to them. Listen to me. I beg you."

The fire dragon stopped, formed the illusion of a woman,

and stood beside the pale sorceress. The flames smelled of wind and the embers of first creation.

"You have a point," the dragon conceded. "But the ice dragon. He suffers. I can't stand it. Always, he suffers. And I can't feel The Rooke's tales anymore."

"More time. That is all I need, and you and the ice dragon you love will be restored."

"You have asked this before…"

"This time I will be specific," Phaedra, the sorceress said. "Give me until your moon rises a second time. Twelve years and some months. For one such as you, this is no time at all. If Ambriel's Puzzle box remains unsolved, you can finish off whatever is left of the world when it exacts its price."

"They lost the box to Icari, to one of their human hosts…"

"They will get it back," the sorceress said. "Be calm, dragon. Beautiful dragon. Great love calls them. As it calls you."

The first dragon said nothing. She let her wings spread and took off. As the dragon flew, she looked down to see the lights of the world flicker. Some came back on. Others remained dark for some time. Her wings folded time and space, taking a great distance in a matter of moments. She wrapped herself around the volcano in the decimated, pirate islands and it blew out hot lava to greet her. In a distance, The Rooke told his tale. One that angered her in its memory. She let the volcano speak while the tale went on.

The Tale of Muddy Treasure

Eleven-year-old Trick Bagwell shuddered as he stood atop the deck of The Rabbit Run Pub looking down on the Igamie River.

He dreamed of crocodiles eating all the people around him. The nightmare repeated. He told his brother, Jesper, who told him there were no crocodiles in the river. Those were native in the Lion Clan territory clear on the other side of Pandemonium Peaks right alongside The Desolate Waste.

"There might be alligators, although those tend to be around the Muddy River," Jesper said. "You've nothing to worry about, Trick."

"It was only a nightmare," Trick said. Jesper shrugged and wandered off to see if anyone else wanted to worship his mighty, big brain.

"Trick, you don't like the food?" his mother asked, pointing to the long, table Trick had abandoned and his dinner. "You didn't touch a thing on your plate."

"It's a feast. We've been doing nothing but eating for days," Trick said. "And I am tired of it. Do you think it'll rain, mom?"

"I hope not," his mother said. "The celebrations don't really get going until the sun goes down and the Igamie sing."

Trick nodded. He watched his sister, Sid-Jynx, crouched below the deck with Emlyn Tunvel. They were kissing. Again. He wished they would stop. They had their whole lives ahead. They were engaged after all.

That's what kept Trick, his family, and practically the entire Fox Clan at the Rabbit Clan for a full week after the Annual Clan Gathering. He sighed. He supposed Sid and Emlyn had to get started somewhere. It would take a long time to have ten kids.

He told Sid-Jynx four years back that she would have an arsenal of children. She said she did not want any. She also said she wouldn't marry Emlyn Tunvel if the world was covered in dung, and he was the last man in Aerda living on a dung-free island. She loved Emlyn a lot. Even then. People never said what they meant. Especially Trick's sister, Sid-Jynx.

Jesper was talking to Evangeline Hickey, one of the daughters of the Rabbit Clan Mother. She was smiling and doing her best to make Jesper look at her and her new frock. He only saw the herbs she brought him and was going into a long explanation of all the potions he could make from those particular herbs. Trick did not have to worry about Jesper going off and getting married. He would not see a girl in that way, pretty frock or not. He only cared about his potions and remedies.

"Trick, do you want to go down to the river and catch frogs?"

Lucie Tunvel asked. They were the same age and would soon be brother and sister as their siblings wed. "Keile and I thought it might be fun."

"You'll get eaten if you do that. That water is full of monsters today," Trick said. "Let's throw stones in the river from here. See if we can get one of those alligators to show itself."

"We don't have many gators around the Rabbit Clan, Trick," Lucie said. "It's not warm enough. Not like in The Parish. You know, at the *Gator* Clan lands."

Everything kept changing. Trick had been certain one day he would marry Keile Maule-Finn, only she was going to die. In less than an hour. And Lucie would blame him. Then she would move away to Ambriland where she would be apprenticed to her grandmother to be an innkeeper.

He would lose his closest friends. He tried to stick his head into the present, to observe, to remember the future so he could change it. He looked down at his spawning graff and read the characters to make sure they still said the same as they ought.

Maz un nam halla

'Great love calls us'

Even if Trick could manage to see all the threads that made things change, he could not bind them, not stop them. Living backwards did no good at all. Seeing the future had no wisdom to it.

He sighed, trying to brace himself. He knew just where to hide. Only if he did that both Keile Maule-Finn and his brother, Jesper, would die along with his mother and Saylor Maule-Finn, the Fox Clan Mother. He considered a different action. His spawning graff burned, turning red.

What would happen if he did something different? He watched a dirt man take a seat between his mother and Saylor Maule-Finn, across from Jesper and Evangeline Hickey.

Keile's older brother, Nate, approached them holding his new sword. Everyone called Nate, Ox, on account of his Initiation graff which was a rampaging ox missing a horn. He had thick arms and looked strong for a young man of sixteen.

"Did you run out of people to show your new sword to?" Keile asked.

"Not yet, little sis," Ox said. "Trick wants to see my sword. Forged at the Scorpion Clan by old Pharaoh Sol himself."

"Are you sure that sword is meant for you?" Keile asked. "I can't think why the best weaponsmith in all the world would give you a magical sword. You're not even good at fighting with them."

"I am a pirate, and he gave swords to all the crew of Lorelei," Ox said. "His youngest son, Salah, is to join us in the autumn. You'll get one too, Trick, if you join the crew."

"You've no clue how to use a sword," Keile said. "You'll poke your eye out."

"Don't have to with this one," Ox said. "It only hurts enemies. See."

He stabbed his sister, and she laughed. It did nothing, not even a scratch. Trick snatched it away and tested the point. He remembered such magic from the far-distant past, a magic he never thought to see in this muddled future he had been hurled into.

"It's very sharp," Trick said. He was a bit distracted and not much interested in swords. He watched the Dirt man, trying to decide what to do.

"That is how long houses work," Saylor Maule-Finn was explaining to the Dirt man. Such people were always so curious about the Urian Clans, even as they disrespected their ways and called them Muddy. "No one is ever homeless in a Urian Clan. It is not like we are without hardship. However, if one person is hungry, then we are all hungry. If one person is homeless, then we are all homeless."

"That is impossible," the Dirt man said. "Why would you all work if you have no penalty for being useless?"

"Work is the way of Ta-She-Serra," Saylor said. "Work brings purpose. Work binds us to one another. We don't spend our time on useless tasks. We have no banks. We have no prisons. We have no castles. Nor kings nor emperors nor presidents."

"How do you rule?" The Dirt man was becoming exasperated. He did not want to understand. He wanted the Muddy riches. He believed they had large stores of gems and wealth.

"We don't rule. We serve our Creator by expanding creation. We serve one another by making our lives full and beautiful," Saylor said. "I am a Clan Mother, and as the title might imply, I take care of my clan. The Fox Clan. I appoint each chief for needed organization. Every eight years, a single clan is anointed to pick one of their chiefs to serve as Clan Master. Each clan gets a turn so only every three centuries will a clan have a Clan Master. It keeps the power from becoming noxious."

"What do you do when someone breaks the law? I don't imagine all of you are without vice?"

"Our spawning graffs keep us honest," Sidon Bagwell said, showing his graff which had some specs of gray, signaling to Trick that his father was getting angry. "We live by a higher power. That is the only treasure we have. It is not something you can put in a bag and take with you."

"Wealth is not always measured in gold," Phineas Tunvel said. "It is the wrong measurement, and often causes the most harm among people. And do not say we are immune to it, Si. We are always striving for more, to achieve more, to find more, and that can be corrupted. Our graffs will tell us we are going wrong. We do not always heed those warnings."

"People in my village are starving," The Dirt man said. "And we live in land adjacent to yours. Did you allow us this land because it was dead?"

"You do not work it properly and you do not share with your fellows," Saylor Maule-Finn said, her voice becoming more agitated. "We can give you food to help those who hunger in your village. We can send you workers to show you how to irrigate your land, how to build stronger homes against the elements. All of this, you only need ask. We can teach you how to live with this land."

Trick sighed. "Ox, can I hold onto your sword for a moment longer?"

"Sure, get a feel for it," Ox said. "Your pops says you are strong and good with weapons. You're going to be a great pirate, Trick. You sure have the name for it."

"Maybe," Trick said. "I don't know anymore."

"Trick, your graff," Keile said, pointing. "Why is it red? Spawning graffs are never red."

Trick did not answer. He walked over to the dirt man and stood there waiting. The man stopped talking. Below, on the river, flat boats filled with Dirt mercenaries motored toward them, coming to murder.

Trick stuck Ox's sword right through the Dirt man's throat. He knew as blood spirt from the man's throat that this one was intent on the murder of Urians. The third eye in the center of Trick's forehead opened up and the oracle inside him spoke.

"We are under attack," he said. "Arm yourselves. They do not believe what we have told them. They think we have treasure they can steal."

"Trick, what have you done?" his mother asked.

Trick said nothing. He closed his third eye and turned away. He handed Ox back his bloodied sword. "Here, you'll need this. It's a good sword against those who want to harm us. Very sharp."

Saylor Maule-Finn produced a long, three-pronged spear, one that might be used for fishing and called the Muddy to battle.

"Layne, go to the tunnels. Set up an infirmary. Jesper, help your mother. Phineas, stop gawking. We knew this man was not what he seemed," she said. "Trick, did you see those boats coming?"

"Yes, and last time I hid. Now, I don't know what is going to happen anymore."

"Come with me, son," Sidon said.

"I am not your son. You just don't remember. You were only a baby," Trick said, feeling true terror for only second time in his existence.

"Sid-Jynx, put down that sword and get the children to safety," Saylor said. Ox and Keile took their mother by each arm as their bearded father, Scanlon, leapt from the deck aside white-haired Phineas Tunvel to the ground to join the throngs to fight the invaders.

"Mother, you have no heir until Brie or Keile have a daughter," Ox said. "You will not be fighting. You will be hiding with Clan Mother Hickey and her daughter, Evangeline here."

The Dirts came like locusts, so many of them. Trick sat watching as Ox pushed his sister and mother toward the tunnels. He engaged as Emlyn Tunvel pushed him from a deadly blow. The exploding shot from a crude hand cannon ripped open Ox's arm. He dropped the sword. Trick picked it up and put it through the pistol-wielding Dirt's throat. Emlyn carried Ox toward the infirmary and Trick ran behind.

"Here, Trick, get Ox to the tunnels," Emlyn said. "I'll cover you."

Trick stood frozen in the tunnels that ran between each of the Rabbit Clan burrows, unsure of which way to turn, listening to the screaming and the anguish as the names of the dead came with each hour. He watched as Mother Maule-Finn sat with her one-armed son. Trick's mother could not save the arm. He supposed Ox could still be a pirate. They were infamous for missing limbs.

He considered telling Ox as much, as he pushed himself to move toward the battle as Phineas Tunvel arrived, limping and bleeding with his grandson, Emlyn. Sid-Jynx sprung to her feet and embraced Emlyn.

"They're dead. My parents. They're both dead. They were walking by the river when those invaders showed up. They never even had a chance," Emlyn said.

Trick looked up to make sure his friends, Keile Maule-Finn and Lucie Tunvel still lived. He had saved them. Maybe. He wondered what came next. The night deepened as the screams faded away. Phineas Tunvel gathered up a small band of men that included Trick's father.

"I have to go," Sidon said to his wife. "Jesper, look after your mother and siblings."

"Father, I can fight…." Jesper said.

"Not this time," Sidon said. "There are too many injuries, too few healers and alchemists. Help your mother."

"Dad," Trick said. "I…dad, use your magic. You have magic. Just call it. Here, a bit of stick."

Trick handed his father the rare, red oak branch he had been carving. This, at least, remained the same. Even if the way his father acquired it was different.

"This stick will break the first time I hit someone with it," his father, the grown son of the sorcerer, Janus, and Imogen Vasilis, said.

"No, dad. Don't be stupid," Trick said. "It's a staff. You have magic. A good fire ball will stop these evil men from killing more of us."

"He's in shock," Jesper said, putting a hand on Trick's shoulder. "Go, dad. Use a sword. Or a pistol. I'll give Trick something to calm him, poor kid. He saved everyone in the pub tonight."

"I don't know how to use a staff," Sidon said, lowering his head to look Trick in the eye. "Keep it for me. I'll be back."

Trick's father returned with Phineas Tunvel and Goolsby Lamb. For the first time Trick could remember, The Goat Clan pappa was not smiling. He rubbed his head. "What were these blasted Dirts thinking?" Goolsby asked.

"They thought they could get rich," Saylor Maule-Finn said. "Why are you here, Goolsby? I thought you had business in the Eagle Clan lands?"

"I was headed that way when I was intercepted by a message," he said. "Si, Phineas, we are called to Ambriland. Terminus is back. As is Phaedra."

In Darkness

*E*verything went black and silent. The Rooke drew the blood red light from his robes. He could not say what had happened. His head exploded in pain as the fire dragon's voice thundered in his mind.

Retrieve the stolen box. Protect my children. Restore the lost parts of your tales, Rooke. If I must sacrifice my children, I won't hesitate to sacrifice yours. This is your last warning.

"The fire dragon is awake," The Rooke said. "And she's let loose her fire. Somewhere. That is why we stand in the dark."

"SIN is down," one of the students said. "I can't raise it. My sleeve is all dark."

"Is yours implanted?" another student asked. "Mine is hurting me. It hurts so much, like it is on fire. What do I do? What do I do?"

Taki ran to the side of the young woman and took her arm. "I can make it stop. Hold still," he said. "This will only hurt a bit. Then no pain."

"What's happened?" Zac Grimm asked, looking at his square, blank sleeve screen. "I have never known SIN to go dark. Not once."

"Our tablets are working just fine. Gary sent me an urgent message," Aldo said. "SIN is down in Talon as well. The power blinked. Talon is now running on gemstone energy. He says it is like Talon has been fully thrown backward in time."

"Gemstone energy is banned," Rintyre said. "It's…"

"Unable to be controlled by your empires, and free and inexhaustible," Kentigern said. "That is why it is banned."

"But it can explode and it's bad for the natural world…"

"Yes, it can. And no, it is not. Gemstone energy is naturally occurring if a bit magical. Gnolgia always use. Always make better. Energy is always volatile. For there to be energy, there must be friction," Taki said. "The sun is not a peaceful nor safe thing. Harnessing its power is not meant to be safe. Good does not equal safe."

"This is bad," Zac said. "The entire network must have been attacked for SIN to go down. I can't get a tie. What is going on with the backup hubs? Gamers know this shit. We hate interruptions and this is more than that. This makes no sense. Joel, my man, what do you think?"

"If one of the major hubs was destroyed," Joel said, fiddling with his external monitor. He had been a technology worker in his days in Heath's Night. "It would bring down all the others. For a time. They should kick in quickly. Something is disrupting them all. Must have been a sunspot? I have heard that sometimes the sun can send off powerful waves and ..."

"It was the fire dragon," The Rooke said.

"Did she speak to you, father?" Thiago asked. "The ice dragon is going mad. He says he is sick, his magic fading. He says two of his children are in the box, and he needs them to heal, or he must allow Phaedra to finish her destruction. The dragons will kill me and Kostas if you don't save the dragon offspring. All of them."

"I do not want to die by dragon," Kostas said. "How do we protect the dragon children if the fire dragon is the one blowing up the world? Dad, why isn't she calming down? Your tales are great."

"We have to get the puzzle box back," Anwyn said. "I guess we'll be pulling some dragons out of that box if we keep solving its riddles."

"The dragons will not be summoned with the solving of the first riddle," Ghita Mist said. "The first archaic will be Ambriel's because all the others require time and space to exist. And Ambriel is the time-weaver."

The lights in the Coffee Shop flickered back on, a colored glow to them, different than before.

"They have gem energy here," Kentigern said. "I have switched them to that. This place is truly ancient, Rooke."

"It is familiar. Like a place where I used to meet Husk

Grayvesone in his elder years. Before The Evanescence, right after I got my robes. I think I might have met Hazel and Xherdan Kyran here," The Rooke said, sliding his hand along the hand-carved wooden bar that ran in front of a tall wood-burning stove.

"Aye, this place is ancient," Professor Ljinder said. "We have done all we can to preserve it. We are the last true Acarians of Dalmeade, the ones who were meant to protect that mythical place of learning. Rookes have always come to The Burnt Hand. It is said the very first rooke began here."

"We have to find out what is going on out there," Kentigern said. "We won't appease an angry dragon hanging about here."

"How much damage can this dragon fire do?" Rintyre asked.

"Dragon fire is cleansing," Ghita said. "It will wipe out everything – leaving nothing but a silver field of ash. Every brick, every blade of grass will be leveled. There will be no sign that anything existed before the dragon fire, and a new land will grow from the ashes. One that the dragon will control entirely."

"It'll be overrun with faeries and magic within the month," The Rooke said.

"You are all mad," Rintyre said. "There are no dragons. Or sorceresses. My parents were both crazy. I mean, that can't be…"

"A lot of stuff that can't have been has turned out to be," Zac said. "Rintyre, magic is real. I think you know it. I think you have magic. I feel it in you. I think you're just mad at your pops for leaving you and your twin. I get it. But that doesn't mean all the things he told you were lies."

"Aldo, do you know anyone in Aroghotto that has one of your tablets?" Rintyre asked. "I need to find Mia and so many. I have so many friends there. They can't all be gone?"

"No, girl. We send no one to Aroghotto since Steven Fowler's name returned to him," Aldo said. "Lads, Gary reckons it was Aroghotto City that the fire dragon destroyed. And the faeries are awake and raging. He believes they will be monkeying around with these other hubs. Transportation has been disrupted. Aleron says they are having to hike to the coast. Once there, they will have to find a boat. The old-style trains are still working so they can get to Talon. All the other things, the airships, the imperial tubes, all down."

"Good thing we have a boat," Freddie said, rubbing his face. He had gone pale.

"Good riddance to Aroghotto City," Millie said. "It was full of vipers and hateful people."

"It was not," Rintyre said. "It was the center of art and culture in Chazir. Sure, some of it was rotten. I lived there for years. It was filled with beauty, great architecture, literature. Everything good in this world started there."

"And was corrupted there," Joel said. "I am sorry. If this be true, Tee and I also lost many dear friends, good people who wanted to make the world better just as you do, Rintyre."

"All the emperors will be dead," Tee Broomes said. "Emperor Malcombe IV, The Fistian Seat, The Megdonian Second, and most of the powerful of Aerda. All dead."

Tavern XVI:

Smuggler's Cove

Without children, mortals are nothing but dust. A baby's first cry echoes to the heavens for the redemption of a cursed world.

The Idylls of Alleysiande, Vol III. Jeremiel's Refuge
author unknown (translated by Hazel Kyran)

A Ruined Land

Sea cliffs glared down on the lone sailboat as it glided over dark, choppy waters toward the rocky coast with no obvious place to dock. Kostas stood by The Rooke. He squinted as the sun broke through dark clouds in the faint light of the dawning.

"Father, are we to climb?" Kostas asked.

The ocean covered far more of the world than it had two centuries ago. The Rooke shivered as he observed a sharp rock rising from the sea, the remnants of the Dragon Clan Tower.

The pointed coast of Pallantia, the peninsula that jutted out from the Eastern rim of The Mudlands had disappeared entirely under the raging waters. Instead, Millie and Freddie, the two tin-sleeved boat thieves, who served as the sailing crew, guided the boat toward an opening in the cliff that reminded The Rooke of The Mouth Gate into The Reliquary.

A larger ship would not have made it through the crag as they glided into a world underneath the rock, a familiar feeling for those who lived long in The Reliquary. They might have traveled half the distance across New Chazir toward their target of Nox Verre when a cavernous opening found underground docks and a store of rebels.

"We're here, gov," Millie said.

"Where is here?" The Rooke asked.

"This be the Smuggler's Cove," Millie said. "I grew up hereabouts when my family had to flee The Veiled Pride."

"The Veiled Pride? Yes, that explains the accent," The Rooke said. "I don't catch any New Chazir in you."

"My family kept to themselves and the rebels," Millie said. "This will be a good place."

"How far are we from Nox Verre?"

"There's a train," Freddie said. "Runs about every three days between the cove and the coast. Then we'll need another ship."

"What if the train is not running like all the rest of imperial transport?" Rintyre asked. The girl had dark circles under her eyes.

Millie cracked a smile as Freddie laughed, stuffing that gem back under his shirt.

"This train is special," Millie said. "It belongs to the rebels you love hunting."

"I don't hunt rebels," Rintyre said. "I look after kids. Make sure they are safe."

"No, you hunt children," Freddie said. "Don't get offended. I've used your sort to locate missing kids. Some of you are competent at your jobs. Most don't even know what it is they are doing."

"What do you mean by that?" Rintyre asked. "We rescue children. We make sure they are taken care of, their fees paid, their parents adequate."

"Is that what your bosses tell you?" Freddie asked. "Like in all those livelies you watched as girl. Hero saves the child from abusive parent or nonce. It is a good recruitment tool."

"Leave her be, Freddie," Millie said. "Come, let's see if your brother is here."

The Rooke led the party ashore, no sun or wind or rain. All rock. Kentigern smiled as they followed through a well-supported tunnel lit by gems.

"The Reliquary can't have been the only hiding place, Rooke," Kentigern said. "And this isn't in the cold so high up you can't breathe. They won't need the magic of The Relic to support them here. My, a whole city state could fit here."

"These be old Dweller tunnels like behind my brother's inn," Taki said. "We make them. Gnolgia make them. And there was a whole civilization here once. This be part of the Old Kingdom. There are roads here that can go anywhere in Aerda. Anywhere at all."

"Taki is telling the truth," The Rooke said. "Kenny, we are

likely at the high end of Pallantia. They had Dweller tunnels that opened up there. Supplies from the Empyri came that way in the Pre-Evanescent Era."

"This is amazing," Aldo said, looking at the cavernous opening as the clink and clang of life erupted around them. People mulling about in this central hub, buying goods, working on crafts and such. All sorts of people, from every part of Aerda.

"Man, I lived maybe a hundred miles west of here in The Broken Fingers," Zac said. "Never knew there was a whole world underground or I'd have brought my pops here. But look, some of them have sleeves."

"Sleeves don't work here. Like back at Lesser Faroe," Millie said. "SIN can't get through the Empyri defenses."

"Gnolgia defenses. We make it so the new technology not hurt ours," Taki said.

"You're not Gnolgia," Millie said. The Rooke wanted to put his hand over Taki's mouth, to stop him.

"I am," Taki said, looking down and fiddling with his eyes. He removed the covers. "See."

"Pit's ass," Millie said.

"Rooke, are you mad?" Freddie asked. "Traveling with one of them. That lad will stab you in your sleep. They are lethal."

"I want Rooke to succeed. If dragon destroy world, then Gnolgia are meaningless. We must not be stopped in our progress. We need Rooke. We even need dragon."

"Taki, you would make a terrible spy," Kostas said, helping him put his eye covers back on. "And all the stories say Gnolgia are so good at keeping secrets."

"Is this place well-supplied?" The Rooke asked Millie and Freddie. "I have a rather selfish request?"

"What you need?" Millie asked.

"It is this young man's twelfth birthday," The Rooke said, pointing at Kostas. "Tomorrow."

"It is your birthday?" Freddie asked, pushing that gem back under his shirt once more. "And you are twelve?"

"Yes," Kostas said. "And I don't want presents, father. I want everyone to have a quiet night where we are safe."

"You'll have it, lad," Millie said. "Taki, cover your eyes. Our friends do not trust Gnolgia. And they might hurt you."

A painted, wooden sign hung over an opening before an arched blue door that read 'The Smuggler's Cove'. On a post by it, a menu was hand-written. Kostas pointed to it. "Chicken and chips," he said. "There, father. A pub with chicken and chips. Let us go there."

"Go on, Rooke. I will see about accommodations," Aldo said. "Joel is a bit under the weather. The sea didn't agree with him. Going to find him and Tee a bed."

"Can you find me a bed too?" Anwyn asked. "I want to be on my own."

"You need to eat, Ani," Ghita Mist said, putting a hand to the girl's forehead. "I know it is hard. Grief is terrible, but your mother would want you to eat."

"I would throw up. Even chicken and chips," Anwyn said. "Please. I just want to sleep."

"I will look after the girl," Tee said.

The pub was dark with hanging chandeliers that sparked firelight. It was warm and a bit stuffy until The Rooke exposed his red robes and transported the place to Ambriland as a small Muddy pirate ship pulled into Marinplaz by the Shark's Mouth Pub.

An Army of Rats

The rat stood up in a body that felt both alien and familiar. The pain transformed from the eternal to the mortal. A name attached that the rat found abhorrent though that name had called him out of Hell.

Luc deserved to be a rodent. Forever. He was nothing. He was nobody. He was a murderer. Shame shook the teenage boy that the rat now inhabited. The cage had opened. Another boy stood there, gaping at him.

"Please, SIN is down, we can escape," the boy said, his eyes filled with desperation.

The dark-haired kid looked about fourteen. Maybe fifteen. The rat nodded. He did not know what SIN might be. He did not know why he was in this cage. His skin stuck to his ribs, not a bit of fat to warm him, and cold struck him to the core as he discarded the ragged blanket that had covered him, leaving him in dull gray, thin trousers with matching tunic. The same as the boy in front of him.

The boy before him was starving. The rat could see it. Once this boy had been handsome and full of life. Now, full of fight that can come at the end. When all hope is gone, some found faith. A thing the rat knew little about but for Phaedra, that wicked and wondrous sorceress. Why had she let him go?

He sniffed and smelled death. Always, rats could find death and its spoils. The dark, metal tunnel was filled with cages illuminated with a harsh, orange incandescent light that blinked on an off. Hundreds of barred rooms with metal, locking doors, stretching towards a dead-end. The boy pulled at the bars of each one. Some opened. Some did not. The boy would curse when one would stay closed.

"I am Dominick," the boy said. "Who are you?"

"I am a rat."

"Shit. Of course, you're crazy. They cut you already?"

"Cut me?"

"It doesn't matter. Come with me. We'll fix the crazy or use it. We might have to fight. We might get killed though. But man, I am going to die before those bastards cut off my junk. I will not be a drone."

"I am already dead. I am a rat."

"Rat, help me. You've nothing to lose. Everything to gain."

"Nothing to lose," Rat repeated.

That sounded good. He liked this boy called Dominick. He would not kill him. He would be good. He would protect. Luc meant to protect before he murdered Chrysalis. He did not know why he did that. He had not wanted to. Then he had been a rat.

They scurried down the long corridor until they came to a massive metal door. Dominick sat down and put his head in his hands when the door would not open. Rat tried to force it. Nothing.

"What a horrible death this will be," Dominik said. "Nothing to eat, nothing to drink. Most won't get out of their cages if SIN stays down. The overseers are probably stuck too."

"How did you get out?" Rat asked.

"I stole some putty. I lodged it in my lock so the cage wouldn't catch when they closed it. Been doing it since I got here. They never notice. Too many to check, and the free workers are lazy."

The door clicked before them. Standing there was the fattest man Rat had ever seen. The face was pale, a bit red from exertion. His hair was a long, dull brown and curly. His eyes radiated a beautiful and broken soul.

Rat saw light there. He did not want to kill this man, even if that would give him food for ages. Rat had feasted on the flesh of so many people. His stomach ached for the taste of blood, bile, and meat.

"Come," the fat man said. "I can get you out of here. But we have to go fast. When SIN comes back up, they'll know."

"Thank you," Dominik said to the stranger. "Can you open the locks? With SIN down, some are stuck closed. I couldn't open most of the cages. And I couldn't get others to follow me."

"I have put in the code to open the locks, for when SIN is down. All the cages should open now with simple keys. Here. It's three-hundred and eight-six here. Get as many as you can to follow," the fat man said, handing both Rat and Dominick bulky, metal keys. "This is a small warehouse. So not so many workers needed."

"Workers? We are not workers. We're slaves."

"I do realize. I am trying to do the right thing. Only, I am not supposed to know you exist."

"Who are you?" Dominik asked. "And why help us?"

"I am called Jonathan. My father is the foreman here. He drinks a bit too much. Once told me about you all. He said if I didn't improve, start earning credits for myself, he'd see me here to make me lose weight, to hide me."

"You don't want that. They cut your junk off," Dominik said. "Most don't survive it. Not for long anyhow. I been lucky. They keep forgetting they didn't cut me yet."

"They did not forget," Jonathan said. "You are a handsome kid, worth something if they keep you intact. They had other ideas for you. We have very little time. Let's move."

Rat glanced inside his tattered trousers. He sighed. He reckoned being a eunuch was a touch better than being a rat. "They cut me," Rat said.

"Sorry," Dominik said, leading the thin young man down a corridor of cages.

He opened a cell at the very end of the row. Inside a girl stood up, holding her arms across her chest, looking in pain.

"She is rat," Rat said. "I know my kind."

"She is no rat," Dominick said. "Drone. They cut the girls too, only it is way worse for them. Come with us. We're getting out of here. Maybe we can get you some medicine."

"The pain is horrible," the girl said, weakly. "I am not a girl anymore. I am nothing."

"You're still you," Dominik said. "I know it seems awful now, but you don't have to live as a drone. Come with us."

"You are not a rat anymore. The pain is worth being free. Come with us," Rat said. "It is better than what you will suffer here. Dominick is our friend."

The girl hesitated and then stepped out into the hall as Jonathan joined them.

"I could only get about a dozen to follow, all kids. Not too many drones. A lot of them are too hurt or too afraid to move," he said. "We'll leave everything unlocked. There's food and well, a bit of everything. This is a warehouse after all. This is where the packages come from for all of Heath's Night."

"She will come with us," Dominik said. "What is your name?"

"I don't remember," the girl said. She moved her arms. There was blood seeping onto her gray tunic across her chest.

"We'll get you some medicines and bandages. I think I know how to find them in the warehouse. We'll get some food too. And water," Jonathan said. "Then we will go underground. There's a train I know."

"Can we call you Petra?" Dominik asked the girl.

"Why?"

"You need a name. Names are important," Rat said. "I am Rat."

"Petra was my mother's name," Dominik said.

"I had a mother. She had a name. I don't remember it. Why can't I remember anything?"

"You are rat too," Rat said. "Your name is in your nightmares and so you disregard it. And this body needs no name. It is mostly dead."

The warehouse they stepped into was vast, filled with boxes going to the ceiling. There was a refrigerated room to the left and an unending maze of shelves and offices running through the place. Rat found it disorienting.

"A rat? I was a girl. I wasn't a rat. I am a girl. I am neither rodent nor drone," she said, and began weeping as Jonathan went shelf to shelf picking up items that the group would need.

The fat man looked at the girl with such compassion. Rat felt something spark in him. He said nothing. He knew what to do. They would need to find Phaedra. She wanted an army. He would help her have one. The rat still stirred inside him, and rats could always find Phaedra. Whether she be in Hell or in the world of mortals. The sorceress would cure them. Only she could.

"This will be a touch tricky," Jonathan said. "But we need to clean your surgical wound and rebandage it. Or it will become infected. Here, I have medicines to stop infection and to stop pain. But you'll need to take off...."

"It's fine. I don't care. Do what you must," Petra said.

Rat blinked as they exited the warehouse by an alleyway. The sun hurt his eyes, and he realized he had not seen it in ages. Jonathan checked their new clothes to be sure they fit well and secured cheap iron worker sleeves over each of their wrists.

"We must try to stay unseen," Jonathan said. "When SIN went down, the authorities demanded everyone go to the residences and wait. I came here instead."

"Lucky us," Dominik said. "We'll stand out in empty streets."

"We go by sewer," Rat said. "I am rat. I know these sewers. This is Heath's Night. I have always been here."

"Yes, underground to the train at the edge of the city, above the dam. That is where we will go."

"How do you know about this train?" Dominik asked.

"A sleeveless man told me about it after some of my class-mates beat me within an inch of my life. I have felt such pity and guilt since I found out what imperials do with unwanted children and the ones that fail their IPE."

"How did the SIN go down?"

"We don't know," Jonathan said, waddling behind.

It took some hiding and running about to find a way into the sewer that Jonathan would fit. Rat understood they could not leave him behind. He was their rescuer.

The party, through many twists and turns, found their way to Jonathan's train. The station looked abandoned on the edge of Heath's Night, at the bottom of the hill, next to a massive dam. The Damnable Dam, Rat recalled. The Muddy were all gone. When those good people disappeared, this place became but another level of The Hierarchy of Hell.

The train rambled through valleys and hills, through barren lands, and long, forgotten forests, on and on until it sped into a tunnel through a mountain and down and down underground. Hours later, the train came to a stop at a station, filled with cobwebs. Long unused. The people rambled out, and as insects might do, traveled toward light and sound.

Food, water, and beds were provided by the rebels in this hidden place. Petra received care for her wounds. Rat accepted some pills, for his physical pain. Dominik wanted to go to his home. The people there said it would not be safe. The children were given care, Jonathan agreeing to look after them. Some claimed to be like Rat and insisted on staying with him.

They enjoyed the pub called 'Smuggler's Cove' night after night. Dominik, Jonathan, and Petra soon found friends and healing. Rat observed and stayed to himself. Rodents did not have friends. He did not deserve them.

One night, as they enjoyed pints of ale, plates of food, a rooke appeared and transported them into the world Rat seemed to remember as if it had been there but yesterday. He loved each tale and when The Rooke transported him to the popular island nation of Ambriland, filled with famous pirate ships and pirate lords with proper titles, Rat thought he might have liked the tropics. Rats in that part of the world ate well.

The Tale of Fell Feather

Sidon Bagwell did not care for Ambriland. Not the first time he had visited years ago. And not this time either. It was hot. It was humid. The smell of fish, both fresh and rotting pervaded the stuffy air of The Shark's Mouth pub.

A shared feeling of shock, grief, and dismay accompanied his voyage across the sea alongside his sons, Trick and Jesper. Goolsby Lamb had traveled with him along with Phineas Tunvel and his granddaughter, Lucie.

Sidon felt a lump of pain in his throat every time he thought of Edge Tunvel being gone, murdered along with his wife.

Scarce a word was spoken on the journey across the sea, and considering Goolsby traveled with them, that caused a feeling of dread and doom. Helping an old ally out with an ancient foe seemed less important as the Muddy Clans recovered from the slaughter conducted by the treasure seeking Dirts.

Where the Rabbit Clan survived, thanks to Trick and his

third eye, down the river, the Viper Clan had been obliterated to the last child, the clan villages razed to the ground. The considerable resources that the Viper Clan supplied to the rest of the Muddy taken, stores of useful metals in copper, silver, iron, and soft gold.

Sidon turned over the sword that Ox Maule-Finn had awarded to Trick for his help in saving The Rabbit Clan from the same fate as the Viper Clan. The peculiar blade vibrated to his touch as if enchanted. And for reasons Sidon could not fathom, he understood the magic, could see its glow in the same way he could see beyond the mortal coil.

"I am calling it the Fell Feather," Trick said. "It tickles the innocent but is fatal to the guilty. I think it is a good name and will suit its bearer when he gets it."

"Isn't that you?" Jesper asked. "Ox did give it to you, after all."

"No, I will need a sword that will cut whoever I want it to cut, guilty or innocent. A much bigger and frightening sword than that rapier," Trick said. "This will go to someone quite famous one day. I am only holding it until I meet him. If I meet him. I don't know how things will go any more now that I've changed everything."

"Fell Feather is not a rapier. You should learn more about swords," Jesper said. "This is a very nice short sword."

"It's not broad enough for a short sword," Trick said. "And it pokes like a rapier."

Sidon took a sip of ale, surprisingly good coming from such a low place. He held it up, offering acknowledgement to his young son.

"We will have a memorial service before the wedding for all the clans," Goolsby said to Sidon and Phineas, uncharacteristically morose. "Sid and Emlyn can wait until next summer for their nuptials. Once we get done here, we will make the arrangements. Sidon, you and I, as Urian pappas, must travel to gather our people that live outside The Mudlands. The other pappas will be busy administering to the clans in our time of mourning."

Goolsby had repeated these same thoughts a number of times, trying to fill up the silence and pain. Lucie Tunvel sighed. She and Trick looked out of place at The Shark's Mouth. It was not the kind of pub that children frequented. At the moment, it was filled with sea-faring men, scantily clad women offering comfort to those same men, as locals drank and sang and ate and complained. It was a good tavern. Sidon liked it.

"Can I come home for my brother's wedding?" Lucie Tunvel asked her grandfather in a small voice.

"You will come for both memorial and wedding. I hope your grandmother will come as well," Phineas Tunvel said. "Speaking of which? Captain Sage claimed that she and Suan would be here an hour ago. This feels strange, all of it."

"Pa Tunvel, why did you and Lucie's grandmother never get married?" Trick asked.

Sidon perked up. He wondered that too for his entire life. He had often asked Edge about his mother. His friend would only say she was in Ambriland, he liked visiting her, and she was a good mother. She looked after his estranged brother, Razor. Edge had not liked his twin at all.

"That is a very long story…"

"And he doesn't tell it to anyone," Goolsby Lamb said. "Although it is one of truly great love. The kind our graffs call out to, filled with sacrifice and longing."

"How romantic," Captain Delilah Sage said as she slinked into the tavern, flanked by two young men, and a ghostly, pale young, raven-haired young woman. "Suan is retrieving your other son, Phineas. He has been to sea and was still on Petit Gyo where his ship makes dock. He sails with old Robert Bracken, a good captain, a great Muddy pirate."

"I know Bobby well. I am glad he took on my boy. Razor doesn't want to see me," Phineas said. "He never forgave me or his mother…"

"Razor is stubborn. Reminds me of you back in the day when you used to visit more often," Captain Sage said. "Sidon, I am happy you made the trip. Why did Laynie not accompany you?"

"The Clans were attacked. The Viper Clan is no more. We left a lot of injured and sick behind. Every healer in The Mudlands was needed," Sidon said. "I brought Jesper. He's a decent alchemist. He can look after that boy, Xavier Rose. Who...."

"The Eye of the Storm by the name of Sidon Gale Bagwell," the pale woman said, interrupting and confronting Sidon. "I remember you. You tried to help me once."

"Phaedra. It's been a while, and you have haunted my dreams for over a decade," Sidon said, standing up, clutching Trick's sword. "Pardon me. I have to check something which has bothered me since Heath's Night."

He stabbed at the woman with the Fell Feather. It tickled her. Phaedra snatched it a way and gave it a look. She smiled, her deep black eyes filled with amusement.

"You've the magic of a Reckoner. That is very dark. I wouldn't have thought it from you," Phaedra said. She turned and drove the blade at one of the young men accompanying her, one with spectacles over peculiar, bejeweled, emerald-green eyes.

"Phaedra! Don't stab me," he said. "Oh, what has happened? That tickles. Is that a trick sword?"

"It's magical," Phaedra said.

"It only kills those who wish to murder," Sidon said. "Which I think makes you not a demon, Phaedra. What are you?"

"A woman. You are familiar, yes?" she said.

"Phaedra. Is it really you? I am Jesper. You once possessed my sister, Chrysalis. I always hoped you were real. You sometimes appeared in my dreams. Sid said she also dreamed of you."

"You were not dreaming. I was checking on you. For Chrysalis. She was beautiful. I am sorry she was murdered," Phaedra said. "She went into the light, and I turned her murderer into a rat."

"And I see rats still follow you about," Sidon said. "When we burned Heath's Night to the ground, the rats were all gone. Heath's Night was filled with demons. Did you release them?"

"No. I trap them when I can," Phaedra said. "Those monsters

that remained when I returned to Pandemonium were already there when the children were brought by those vile men."

"I wouldn't be absolutely sure that Phaedra is not a demon. After all, the priory teaches that demons are naught but fallen angels," the other young man said, also with emerald-green eyes, but flat and ordinary. Sidon suspected an Erelahian as this man was striking, extraordinarily beautiful, golden-haired, high-cheekbones, handsome, and radiating curiosity.

"I am not a demon."

"You're not an ordinary woman either," Captain Sage said. "Introductions. Sidon, this is Husk Grayvesone and Daedalus Sams. Phaedra lives with them. It was Husk who took her in although the story is unclear to me."

"He read a book," Phaedra said. "It called out a specter that was hunting me. I saved him."

"I rather think I saved you," Husk said.

"I did not need saving. It was not me who had the claws of a specter wrapped around my soul. You were going to be dead and damned."

"Suan and The Silver Swann thought Phaedra would be the best help with this monster," Captain Sage said. "It has attacked The Swamp and has tried to infiltrate Rose Manor. The Silver Swann has put up wards to keep it away."

"Terminus will not stay away," Phaedra said. "It wants this world for its own. Lots of demons do."

"Terminus. Is that its name?" Goolsby Lamb asked.

"Oh, goat boy. You're still alive," Phaedra said, frowning. "You're not thinking of trying to put this specter into some beast of burden, are you? That's worse than keeping a bit of it locked in a book."

"If we have its name...."

"Terminus is a moniker. Not its true name. If I knew that, I could destroy it," Phaedra said. "This creature is not a singular being. Remember demons never are. They grow their legions by stealing souls of mortals, corrupting them, stealing their names, damning them."

"This is the same specter that incited the genocide of the Pathians, the same that was instrumental in the destruction of Irialfar?" Phineas Tunvel asked.

"That is what Madame Darke said," Husk answered. "When I ended up with Phaedra here. This wicker woman is a Pathian."

"What is the difference between a specter and a demon? Are they not the same thing?" Jesper asked.

"There are all sorts of monsters in Hell. A specter is a peculiar kind of demon," Phaedra said. "Instead of possessing a person outrightly, it mimics a person that it steals and puts the body into a kind of coma. It needs the blood to do this. Terminus will be looking for a blood sacrifice to walk in this world unseen. It tried to take Husk. He would have appeared alive, murdered the old witch, and done a great deal of damage had he succeeded in taking Husk."

"Well, if the specter did not take anyone?" Sidon asked.

"It doesn't need to now that it is free...."

"Phaedra, you have to tell them. They are here to help," Husk said. "This Terminus is hunting her. And me. If it gets her, it will go away to return her to Hell. If not, it stays here and can be quite deadly."

"Chrysalis would not want Phaedra returned to Hell," Jesper said.

"I agree. We have to fight it. Terminus sent a sorcerer snake after my patron. And The Silver Swann knows this creature," Husk said. "This thing is a destroyer of nations. Ambriland is small but vital. I would not have my home fall to this monster."

"All of Hell despises these Erelahians that are left in Aerda," Phaedra said. "Husk and Daedalus here are Ambriens. At least, Daedalus is half an Ambrien. But he is also, I believe, part Sandy. That is to say he is one of Sandalphon's creatures, one of song and poetry and inspiration. Husk is pure Ambrien and likely the last."

"Can you tell the future? Ambriens can spin time and space," Jesper asked. "Like my brother?"

"I'm an oracle. I live backwards. Only world-spinners could

spin time and space," Trick said. "Most Ambriens could see through time and space and see that there were other worlds. Ambriel made my kind too. Only I am broken now."

"Broken how?" Phaedra asked.

"I changed things so no idea what will happen next. But I am glad to find you at last, Phaedra. We can't sacrifice her, father," Trick said. "She is the sorceress of Malachi. She will have all twelve magics. Janus said you would come, Phaedra."

"Whoa, what?" Husk Grayvesone said. "What is happening?"

Goolsby Lamb stood up, clapped his hands together, and then embraced a startled Phaedra.

"I will tell you what is happening," Goolsby said. "Alleysiande is coming back."

"Or The Hierarchy of Hell is about to have their victory at last," Phaedra said. "It could go either way. We must defeat Terminus, send him back. He is capable of tearing the veil between here and Hell, and letting demons wander freely. Black towers could rise again if we don't rid this world of him."

The Forgotten Ones

The Rooke finished for the night, pushing himself to his feet. A disturbance caught his eye. A teenage girl, or was it a boy, screamed and pointed at Rintyre. She glared with clenched fist at Rintyre and shouted.

"It was her. She took me from my mother….she did it."

"No, I don't do that," Rintyre said. "I have no authority to take a child. I collect fees and take kids to their IPE."

"You destroyed my life. You made me take that test and they came and took me from my mum when I didn't do well. She was screaming. I didn't deserve this," the girl said. The Rooke recoiled in horror as the girl exposed her blood-soaked tunic. "I didn't deserve this. I didn't do anything wrong. Failing your bloody IPE is not a crime."

Zac stood up and stood between Rintyre and the poor, mutilated girl. He started to speak and then his eyes focused on a young, olive-skinned teenager with dark, thick hair, and a face that would have been handsome with a few more meals.

"Dominik?" Zac said. "Are you Dominik Bursmith? My dad was your teacher. He said you were his smartest student. You were at one of my gaming conventions. My dad said you were dead."

"I was worse than dead," Dominik said. "I was locked in cage, made to work sixteen hours a day in a factory, packing boxes for your imperials enjoyment. They turn us into drones. Like Petra here. And Rat. We have no desires but to eat, to sleep, to work. Petra doesn't even remember her given name. And it's the IPD who sells us to our torturers."

"I never did that. I worked in compliance," Rintyre said. "Mia was so proud when I…we thought we were rescuing kids from bad situations. Parents too poor to feed their children. All those livelies. I mean, some people should never have children."

"Rescuing us from parents who don't want to live the way the imperials decide?" Petra said, covering up her tunic. "I can never have a family. It wasn't just my chest they cut. They sterilized me like I was a common alley cat. Because of a test. The foul doctors told me it was for my own good. They claimed I could have a happy life in that cage."

"They told these children that the cages were their very own flats," a fat man said. "To fool them so they wouldn't know that the bars, and the metal doors they could not open to leave except when they were required to work, were cages. Tell me, how do you not know who it is you work for?"

"They cut our balls off to keep us obedient," Dominik said. "And the ones who fight too much. They kill. Even if they are just little kids. Some come to the cages as young as eight. Too young to have taken an exam. Can't think what they've done to be put in those cages."

"They do worse. I was a rat. I saw everything. I am called Rat," a young man said, head shaved, teeth yellow with decay. He was so skinny that he made Zac look heavy. "For those that are pretty and compliant, they use as toys. I should kill you for what you've done, agent of The Hierarchy."

"Back off," Zac Grimm said, drawing his sword. "Rin is good. She's a good woman..."

Tavares and Joel rose and pulled the three youngsters away from Rintyre.

"I didn't know," Rintyre said, the distress on her face a mask of pain. "I didn't fucking know. I was doing my job. It was my bloody job. I didn't see a single child hurt. I saw tons of them fed when they were hungry. I saw tons of them given a proper home when they were homeless. I never saw a single child harmed. Not one. Not by me or the IPD. Now, I did see parents that did horrific things to their children. You all are lying."

"I know," Zac said, turning to her. "Rin, my father told me what they were doing, and I didn't believe him. It's how the empire gets away with all they do. They do good things to convince people that they are good. They are skilled at hiding the horrible."

"I really didn't know," Rintyre repeated. She ripped her sleeve away and began crushing it under her boot. "I didn't fucking know. They lied. They said this was something the rebels said to make people hate each other. I didn't believe. I didn't know. I really didn't. My life was good. The people I know are good. They only wanted to do good. We just want a better world."

"That's what we all want," Dominick said. "Rebels or imperial citizens. They all want a better world. We just have very different ideas of what that world looks like. And your kind thinks oppressing and vilifying millions of people is a fine way to get what you want."

"That's not true," Rintyre said. "You are a kid. You don't know anything."

"They lie to turn good evil," Joel Broomes said. "That's how demons start. They lie. They make you angry. They make you feel righteous in your indignation. Like this girl here. And Rintyre. And Dominick. Then they make you do horrible things while telling you that it is good, and that you are brave. Then you wake up after the demon has taken you and find your hands covered in the blood of some innocent."

"Or find that you are a rat," Rat said. "Who has killed your savior, one who might have saved us all. Welcome to The Hierarchy of Hell. Let us try to escape, shall we?"

"Rintyre, no one blames you," Tee Broomes said.

The girl called Petra laughed. "That's not true," she said. "I totally blame her, and all like her. They are so certain they are on the right side. Nothing will convince her that she's a fucking bitch."

"Stop it," Zac Grimm said, putting a hand on Petra's shoulder. "You don't know Rin like I do. She really is good. As good as anyone can be in this messed up world. She's a fighter, and she's lost everything to help us. Leave her alone. I am sorry what happened to you, but your anger is in the wrong place."

Ghita Mist put her arms around Rintyre and lead her past The Rooke who said nothing.

"You are a Grayvesone, Rintyre. I have known your father, your grandfather, going back so long. Come, child," Ghita said. "I will get you potion. You will need some rest. Our train has come, and we must leave. Things will not get easier."

The Rooke watched Ghita, Zac and Tee escort a sobbing Rintyre away as the three youngsters glared at her. A fat man approached The Rooke. He looked awkward.

"I apologize for the outburst. We are all deeply disturbed. However, sir, I feel I must trouble you," he said. "I wish to reach into your pocket. That is the custom?"

"Yes, do," The Rooke said. "Will you be following me?"

"No. I believe I will stay here and wait for your tales to find their way back here, unless I am otherwise compelled," the fat man said. "My friends might follow you."

The one who called himself Rat approached. "I will reach into your pocket and follow you," he said. "I need to find Phaedra. There is hope in these stories you tell."

"I cannot allow you to hurt Rintyre," The Rooke said. "She is one of mine."

"We won't hurt her as long as she doesn't hurt us," Petra said, also reaching into The Rooke's pocket. "We won't hesitate to protect ourselves from her kind. Even if they do what they do in ignorance. She is not the only one who has been deceived into doing horrible things."

"I'm going to stay here with Jonathan," Dominik said. "He saved us. And I like the idea of being a pirate in a Smuggler's Cove. And maybe, one day, I can go home again."

Tavern XVII:

Cabal Marrok's Folly

Eternity can be glimpsed in passing moments of pure joy.

The Idylls of Alleysiande, Vol IV. Sandalphon's Symphony
author unknown (translated by Hazel Kyran)

Nox Verre

*T*he train stopped outside of Heath's Night. The city on the hill was not the barren settlement from three centuries ago. It was a glass and black rock metropolis, and in the pre-dawn light, in the fog, looked full of gloom and despair. The power had gone out, a side effect of SIN being down and the city not being on a sub-hub. The streets were abandoned, leaving a feeling of utter desolation.

"Stealing another ship will be no problem," Millie said, rubbing his hands together with a smile that said he enjoyed this foray into pirating a bit too much.

"Can we hurry?" Joel Broomes asked. "I don't like being here."

"Nor I," Rat said. "I would not wish to be recaptured."

"We don't have any more time to waste," Ghita Mist said. "The puzzle box must be our aim. Take Taki with you. He will find you a good ship."

"No need. Let the kid stay here," Freddie said. "I know just the ship."

"Like you did last time?" Thiago asked.

"I know my ships," Freddie said with a bow. "And more importantly, I know which ones Millie and I know how to sail."

"Where could we possibly get a ship?" Kostas asked. "We are miles inland."

"The Malcombe River flows from here to the sea," Freddie said. "It's the largest and deepest river in Aerda."

"It is the Muddy River or was," The Rooke said. "People have always used the river to travel to the inner lands from the sea, even before The Evanescence."

"This is where Phaedra came into the world?" Anwyn asked. "It's not how I saw it in the tales."

"It is much changed. It was a mining town on the edge of The

Mudlands, right at the end of the Desolate Waste," The Rooke said. "It was dirty, always falling down. Now, it is as you see, but it feels the same. Damned."

"Literally," Thiago said, gazing down to the river as water spilled from the high wall where the party stood. "Still has a dam."

"The Damnable Dam," Rat said. "I remember."

The Rooke nodded, watching the pair of tin-sleeved men disappear down a stone stairway, toward the docks.

"He'll get us a good ship," The Rooke said. "That sailboat was better than it looked, got us where we needed to go."

"That sailboat was expensive. Like they would be pursued by Imperial Sea Patrols to ends of Aerda," Thiago said. "They are not…"

"You don't like Millie and Freddie?" Zac asked. "They have weird accents. If I didn't know better, I'd say Millie is from Pig's Spit in Acaria or maybe that Veiled Pride like he says, but that Freddie. He sounds Daggera to me."

"Father, I've seen Freddie before," Thiago said. "I know I have. Before we started our quest."

"He does look familiar," Tee said.

"He's not who he says he is," Ghita Mist said. "But who of us is?"

"That's the point of the tin-sleeved thieves," Anwyn said. "So that SIN doesn't see them properly."

"Probably running from something," Zac said. "Might have been famous before. Like Tavares here."

"I can't place him," Tavares said. "You know I think he's one of those people who resembles a lot of other people."

"He's attractive," Tee said.

"He is not," Joel said. "Why would you say that, dear?"

"He is. Objectively, Freddie is attractive. That's why we all think we've seen him before. The Rooke has that kind of look as well."

"Only Freddie has his lovely long hair," The Rooke said. "And he doesn't even tie it back."

"He's not needing to hide as much as you are," Aldo said. "Let's find a place out of sight while Freddie and Millie fetch us a boat."

Freddie and Millie stole a yacht. A luxurious one. The party could hardly object to the transport. Rintyre glowered at the thieves.

"As if we didn't have enough trouble already…"

"We'd have more if we tried to dock in Nox Verre in an old skiff," Millie said. He always sounded like he had a mouth full of boulders.

"I will give you that," Rintyre said. "We will garner less attention if we seem elite. However, we don't have the sleeves to pull this off unless we'll be cleaning dishes in some tavern or other and be laborers on this ship with no captain."

"Your bounty hunter sleeve would work if you hadn't destroyed it," Freddie said.

"It can be replaced. I still have plenty of metal and my kit," Aldo said. "I will get her another."

"Millie and I have sleeves for rest of us," Freddie said.

Taki for once kept quiet but his gaze spoke loudly of curious distrust. He shook his head, worried.

When Freddie and Millie came below deck, they picked out Rat, Anwyn, and Rintyre.

"Ok, Rintyre, you are going to play the role of yourself," Freddie said. "With Rat and Anwyn as your bounties, rescues, whatever. Only you'll be the hero. Anwyn is an orphan. Rat is being removed from an abusive situation. He has that look. Old Aldo and Kentigern, we have some gilder sleeves for you. The rest will be platinum with anonymous bands. We have some so they can't question us. We might want to keep these faux sleeves going forward."

"Did these sleeves come with the yacht?" Aldo asked. "We don't have those available to us. We can't access SIN security to create such sleeves although with SIN down…"

"Nox Verre will be back on SIN. The have their own hub. However, these sleeves will work. Yachts keep them so their rich customers can travel without being hounded by criers. We can join the sleeves you do have with them. We just don't have enough which is why some of you will act as our servants and Rintyre's esteemed young guests."

"This is true," Tavares said. "Bittore and I used to have anonymous sleeves for our trips together, when we were celebrated."

"I was a big fan of your wife's," Rintyre said. "Why would you give up so much to join rebels? I've been meaning to ask."

"Those celebrated sleeves come at a cost, dear," Tavares said. "You have no idea. Your sister and brother-in-law have been wise to reject them. You saw what happened at the Glittering Raptor."

"It can't be what Bittore said to the criers right before you disappeared," Rintyre said. "Everyone knows she had a drug problem…."

"My wife never did drugs. No one knows anything at all. She spoke the truth in a moment of grief," Tavares said. "Her handlers thought the drug story combined with a miscarriage sufficient to make people ignore what she said. Rin, the people who rule, they are like the Mammon sisters in The Rooke's tale. Maybe worse. And they make sure those granted great wealth and power do awful things so they can be exposed if they fall out of line. Both Bittore and I did horrible things and then witnessed worse things to gain our sleeves, to gain our wealth, and to keep our shame hidden."

"You will need to disguise yourself better than you did when you were properly famous," Freddie said. "I recognized you right away, Tavares Flaco. And whatever transgressions you committed; this company will not condemn you. Demons are what they are, and men are helpless to resist them without greater love to protect them."

"You need a better disguise too, Zac Grimm. My girls both knew who you were straight away back in The Tin Green," Millie said. "Kids love him for being a slob and the gaming bit."

"I never did nothing bad to get my status," Zac Grimm said, an inquisitive and worried look across his brow. "I was plain lazy and loved playing games. I worked at the tax authority for about two minutes once when I was done with school. Back when New Chazir allowed people to choose where they worked. I hated it so I left. Lived with my mom until she died. Lived off the games until I got popular. People just sent me credits to watch me play. Wasn't nothing shady. No dead babies. No women at all. Until Cymbre…"

"That went well," Rintyre said. "Most people don't do horrible things. I know a lot of famous people, knew celebrated people back in Aroghotto City. They were good. Some were not. But they weren't…not what Bittore Rose said. They didn't sacrifice babies."

"It wouldn't have been a conversation point," Tavares said. "A lot of luminaries clear their conscience by helping those like you. You know the acceptable, the workers, people who have less so they can feel ok about what they've done. What I did. What Bitty did. Let's go. This world won't right itself. We need that box back."

Zac had discarded his earlier disguise, the glasses, the neatly tailored clothes, and let his thin, long hair fall loosely around his shoulders against a disheveled white shirt with days of food and dirt stains on it. He took that off as Freddie gave him a new persona.

"Gamers were coming around to what the imperials were doing. Only no one cared what we said or thought. We were just lazy gamers," Zac said as he put on a gray imperial tunic with a copper sleeve and silver ribbon that marked him as someone of import. "Lots of us suspected something was off. With the kids. With each other. I should have believed my dad straight away. I could have hidden those smart kids away on my game hub. Something."

Nox Verre appeared clean and pristine with white sand

beaches at the end of glittering black sand beaches that ran into a gulch in the distance. Black glass buildings towered above the meticulously curated shores. Everything ran in a sort of perfect order. The divide between the elite and the serving class was evident.

The steel-sleeved workers did not look up, did not speak to those sporting gold, platinum, silver, and copper sleeves. They went about their work without complaint. Rintyre blanched as they passed a station opening where a horde of people, all dressed in gray, all with the same haircut, moving in concert to begin their days work.

"Drones," Rintyre said. "I never approved of the term. I joined a lot of people wanting to improve working conditions, to get rid of the term. I thought I was helping. I had no idea they had been mutilated. I thought they were doing work like I did when I first finished university. I didn't…"

"Dear, you didn't know in the way that your father didn't know," The Rooke said. "That is how The Hierarchy has always gotten us. By slow deceit, a gentle nudge toward their vile absolutism. Once upon a time, they got me too."

"You fall for the wrong girl like I did?" Zac asked.

"Something like that," The Rooke said. "But unlike you, Zac, I kept allowing myself to believe the lie even after I knew the truth. And I hurt people I really loved. Hurt them bad."

"What did you do?" Zac asked. "Since we are all in confessing sort of mood."

"I don't remember," The Rooke said. "But I know I did wrong. And not a little wrong. The robes took my name, scrambled my memories, but my soul knows exactly who I am, what I did, and the price I paid."

"I snapped out of it pretty quick," Zac said. "Cymbre poisoned me. You got to know a relationship is not right when that happens. Otherwise, I might have run off with her. She really had me going. I was crazy, man. Never been like that. Not over a girl. Not over a game. Nothing ever got me like that. I was obsessed. I would have done anything to please that girl."

"The box is somewhere close," Anwyn said, pointing down a side street that ran away from the shore. "I sense it. I feel it."

"Me too," Kostas said, his body becoming rigid like a pointing hound. "Follow us. We must retrieve it, or it will blow up. It's calling to us."

The party followed the children down the white-stone polished beach side streets until they came to a pub that was opening for the day. The Rooke saw the sign, knowing the place at once. He put a hand on his son's shoulder to slow him down as Ghita Mist took hold of Anwyn.

"Careful. I know this place," The Rooke said. "We need to be cautious entering. Seem like regular tourists coming for a bite."

The wooden, rickety sign with a spider depicted on it hung between two palm trees, reading 'Cabal Marrok's Folly'. It marked four wide steps that led up wooden planks to a large deck fitted with umbrellaed tables that faced the ocean surrounding a tavern with wide-open doors that let the sea-breeze fill the room that had been made to look the inside of an ancient war galleon.

"Cabal Marrok? Why do I know that name?" Kentigern asked.

"A Megdonian spider, son of a horrible warlord. Nox Verre was once a holding of Megdon, and this was the Marrok territory," The Rooke said. "His father paid the mercenaries that were behind the slaughter of the Rabbit Clan in my tale. When Cabal grew up, he married a Urian woman and betrayed her. The Folly was his ship. He caused great horror on the open seas for many decades. This place was made in his honor."

"Or dishonor depending on where you stood," Freddie said. "I know the tale. This place is no good for us. Why are you following children that have never been here?"

"It's fine. We come here all the time," Millie said. "To drink to old Cabal Marrok's severed head."

Freddie looked distressed as the party spread out into the beachside tavern.

"Rooke, if you expose yourself here, we will not have an

easy time escaping," he said. "We should go to the resort. I have rooms arranged."

"We may need to flee this place suddenly," The Rooke said. "Best that we keep our things with us. And this place is for families on holiday. It will seem natural that we have kids with us."

"The box is here. Someone has it here," Kostas said. "It is screaming at us."

Joel's Demon

Joel Broomes saw the demon as they left the train at the edge of Heath's Night. He wanted to scream. Tee noticed his distress. He could not tell her the full tale of his time spent as a Spyte. He remembered being in utter awe of the 'gutter' baroness that made him. Even as a small child. She promised him so much, telling him and the others that one day the Spytes and these women would all rule this world within the stretch of their lifetimes. His stomach turned as he recalled the child he wished to forget.

He worried he would not be able to rid himself of the entity a second time. He could not remember how he had done it the first time. He only knew that the empires all knew what he had done, and that they did not care. They rewarded him, a murderous six-year-old boy.

He attended an elite school with other children like him. His mind was sharp, inhumanly intelligent. Only it was not him. It was the demon. He knew even then. His soul had been trapped, used, and was slowly being devoured. He still recalled the darkness and pain of his childhood.

His parents gained wealth and status over his foul actions. And he had been trapped in his own body, screaming, unable to control his deeds, his words. The entity continuously tried to quiet his soul, to give over his true name to it.

"I didn't know my name," Joel whispered, not knowing he had spoken out loud.

"What's that, dear?" his wife asked.

"Nothing. Let us be gone."

He did not want to fight that battle again. He was not a demon hunter. He did not know how to get rid of them. He knew how to avoid them. He had done so at the Glittering Raptor. For a moment, he thought he had managed to save some from a fate far worse than death.

The yacht had been comfortable and beautiful. Joel saw demons through their disguises, an after effect of his long possession. He could do the same with men, although it came slowly when he finally recognized Freddie. He told Tee.

"Thiago was right about our tin-sleeve friends. That Freddie is The Fistian Seat," Joel said. "That is Gerrard Frederic Al' Dhar."

"No, it's not. Joel, The Seat was at The Unity Conference. We all saw on the livelies. He was sitting with Princess Lilith. Gerrard Al' Dhar is dead. Everyone is saying Aroghotto City was razed to the ground. No survivors at all," Tee said. "I mean, I see the resemblance. He's tall, the hair, the eyes, all common to the Daggera. He hides his accent well but not enough. But he's not, is he? The Fistian Seat is a much heavier man."

"Tee, this is his yacht. He didn't need to steal it. It's his," Joel said. "As was the sailboat. He had scraped the Daggera seal from its side, but it was his. And I expect if sea authorities stopped him, he would be able to produce a sleeve that verified that this yacht belonged to him."

"That makes no sense. Why would he be hiding with rebels and helping us? The Fistian Seat is one of the three most vile men in all the world of Aerda."

"That I do not know," Joel said. "But listen to all the whispers. The people are blaming The Fist for what happened in Aroghotto City. What if it were not The Rooke's dragon? What if it was The Dagger and Fist that blew up the city? He could have set the explosives himself. Chazir has always said The Fist possessed world-destroying weapons which they used to justify the last war."

"He would not have blown up himself," Tee said. "He was meant to marry Princess Lilith."

"That would have taken power from The Third Empire. He could have left before the dragon or whatever happened," Joel said. "We should be cautious, Tee. I don't think Millie and Freddie are really on our side."

He said nothing of the demon to Tee. Not even when he saw it enter Cabal Marrok's Folly. He felt cold dread. The demon saw him, and quickly merged with a small, striking green-eyed boy, traveling with a young couple.

Joel needed help. That Ghita Mist seemed to know a thing or two, and The Rooke had magic. He would go to them. He watched in horror as Anwyn and Kostas walked toward the couple that accompanied the demon-infested child, the little Spyte. Ghita Mist took them aside, and Joel sighed relief.

He tried to tell Tee. He could not say a word. He tried again to warn The Rooke when they were seated at a long table in the tavern. A band played lazy music as the aroma of cooking fish and chicken permeated the little beach place. The sun shone brightly as families and people on holiday trickled in, all looking dazed as the screens at the bar showed scenes of chaos near Aroghotto City.

Joel tried to speak to Zac, to get use of his peculiar sword. Again, his tongue would not speak. He rambled to the bar for a drink, to calm him. When he turned, frozen beverage in hand, he found himself staring at the demon child. It looked up at him and smiled.

"I am you and you are us," it said. "Come back to us, Phillipe. We miss you."

"That is not my name," Joel said. "Go away."

The child turned, squealing with laughter and ran away. Rintyre's eyes went wide as she spotted the boy.

"That's my half-brother. I have seen his likeness since he was born, all over SIN. That is him," Rintyre whispered. "Oh, no. He's my nephew. And something is very wrong with him."

Joel grabbed her arm before she could pursue. "No. No, Rin. You are not up to that fight. Leave him be."

Kentigern Dagan Leesh accosted him as he reached the table which he was sitting with much of the party. "Joel, you look sick."

"There is…I…" Joel could not find the words.

"Nod your head yes or no. Are we in danger?" The Rooke asked.

Joel nodded furiously. He pointed.

"We have to get our box back," Kostas said, trying to wriggle away from Ghita. "It's calling us."

"I must get it. That couple probably thinks it is a child's toy for the little boy they are with," Anwyn said, as Ghita Mist held her back.

"Rooke, tell a tale. It will distract this family. We will get Ambriel's Cube back."

The Tale of Shanley's Garden

The tea Husk had brought Xavier worked as magically as Shanley had dreamed. In a month's time, fine dark golden hair peppered Xavier's scalp, his skin pinked up, and he was lucid. He could even eat soup with Gyo noodles and was no longer bothered by moonlight or lamplight.

Trick Bagwell made fast friends with her brother, the two boys creating model ships inspired by the Erelahian Fleet from the stories of *The Idylls of Alleysiande*. Shanley's father admired their craftsmanship. The boys spoke conspiratorially, laughing and enjoying themselves over the last week.

Xavier had a friend. A life. He would attend Kingswell College in the following autumn where Husk would continue to be his teacher provided Xavier's health continued to improve.

The workers Delilah Sage brought in had finished restoring the luxurious house baths that morning, and they were going to test the ships as soon as the sun was fully gone. The Bagwells had arrived that week, and some potion that Jesper gave her brother made him even stronger.

"What time do you think Trick will get here?" Xavier asked, as the two painted the last of the twelve ships. "Shanley, the Agony is not red. It's black."

"Oh, sorry. I will fix it," Shanley said. "Trick will be back after supper. He had to see The Silver Swann about some business. Jesper said his little brother is a special case. Like you."

"Do you like Jesper Bagwell?" Xavier asked. "He is very strange. Like you are…"

"What?"

"It's a good thing, Shanley," Xavier said. "Who wants to be all normal and act like everyone else. How boring would that be? I like that you're strange. And so does Jesper. And Husk."

"Husk is coming for the maiden journey of your little fleet," Shanley said. "That's nice…"

"Yes. It is. Shanley, don't be uncomfortable around Husk. He likes you fine," Xavier said. "He likes people in general. He is good."

"And in love with Phaedra, the new girl that works in our kitchen now."

"Why do you say that?" Xavier asked.

Shanley did not get to answer as her brother began coughing and holding his chest. He doubled over, holding his stomach, letting out a little cry of pain.

"Xavier, what is the matter?"

"I need more tea," he said. "Can you make some more? Jester will bring me more potion tonight but until then. I need the tea. I really need it."

"Of course," Shanley said. "Get in your bed. I won't be a moment. And you should get a nap before tonight."

The moment became longer. The new scullery girl, Phaedra, who had moved in with Husk, was in the kitchen with Selkie Nett, the baker that had been serving the Roses since Shanley had been twelve. A pang of jealousy needled Shanley. She took a deep breath.

"I need to get some tea for Xavier," she said. "The special tea."

"Oh, that," Selkie said. "Was that the tea in the upper pantry?"

"Yes, what of it?"

"Glorious Thierry threw it out," Selkie said. "He said it was noxious."

"Oh no. It wasn't noxious. It was medicine," Shanley said.

"Is this the tea from the wicker woman?" Phaedra asked.

"It is and Xavier needs it. He is in terrible pain," Shanley said.

"I will courier Dr. Rege," Selkie said. "Phaedra, there are other medicinal teas in my stores. That Jesper Bagwell fellow recommended them, and Dr. Rege approved them."

"Yes, and I have other ways to ease the child's pain," Phaedra said. "I do not like small children to suffer."

"Thank you," Shanley said, not knowing what to make of Phaedra. "Phaedra, do you think Husk could get more of the tea?"

"I do not know. He is at the cottage. You might courier and ask," Phaedra said. "But he is busy and grouchy. Packing his things and busy learning new skills for this position at the college. They will not allow him his cat. He is vexed and now I must have a cat."

"Don't you like cats?" Shanley asked.

"They are useful creatures at times, but I wish a more substantive familiar. And this cat does not care for me," Phaedra said.

"The cat probably wants to stay with Husk," Shanley said. "I really need this tea, Phaedra. The medicines that Dr. Rege and Jesper provide do not give him adequate relief, and they make him sleep."

"Call Husk if you want," Phaedra said. "I do not wish to speak with him. He was rude to me this morning, and I accidentally set him on fire."

"Oh no. You did not," Shanley said, much alarmed.

"He is fine. He did not burn. Much."

Sun burst through the window of Shanley's bed chamber from her well-kept garden. Summer roses bloomed pink and yellow as bees buzzed about them. She cried in despair.

She could not call Husk, and no one seemed to understand that Xavier needed the tea, that it was not Dr. Rege or Jesper Bagwell's remedies that were making him well. For weeks now, Xavier played and chattered away like someone with a future. Being denied the sun seemed a little thing compared to that.

Shanley took out her garden tools. This glorious patch of flowering plants bloomed due to her labor. Until recent events, her garden had been the only one kept up on the property. Pulling the weeds out of her garden helped her think. There must be something she could do.

Selkie's tea had helped a little. And Phaedra had done something, but it had made Xavier sleep. She said he would not have any pain. Selkie said it was the tea. Either way, it was no good for Xavier to have to sleep to be free of pain. That was no kind of life.

Shanley watched her dog and smiled at his exuberance as he leapt after a pink and blue butterfly flitting about her bog daisies. She adored those yellow flowers even though her mother claimed them weeds, much the way her mother seemed to think of her. Pretty but common, her mother said of the daisies with that hint of disdain in her voice.

Shanley picked up the courier line to call Husk with the intention of asking him to go back to the wicker woman. Then she thought about Phaedra. Clearly, there was something between the two for Husk to take her in. And Phaedra said they were joined at the soul.

Jealousy filled her with despair. Husk was in love with Phaedra. How could he not be? Phaedra was brilliant and enchanting with her pale skin, dark eyes and dark, thick hair, and perfect body. Shanley was strange in the most uncomfortable way. Even Xavier saw it.

She reconsidered and put the earpiece back in place. Shanley never felt comfortable calling him. Most of the time it was all pretense. She wanted to hear his voice, to see him so she could dream about him. Foolish girl. She wished she could make it all stop. She wanted to cry as Husk was no longer Xavier's tutor. He had been promoted and would no longer be visiting regularly.

She dug out proper outdoor clothing from her chest, a long, sleeveless tunic and tight leggings, summer weight. She tied her hair back and opened her safe. She took out all the coin she had, a great deal by the measure of any of the citizens of Marinplaz. Certainly, it would be enough to buy tea to keep Xavier comfortable for another week.

In the bright sun, the thin stretch of jungle seemed less ominous than Shanley recalled from her earlier tracks to the wicker woman's cottage. She hummed to herself, hopeful to obtain the tea yet dreading what the wicker woman might charge her. In spite all the fear and doubt, it felt good to be taking charge of the situation herself.

It took her a good while to find the place. It seemed further from the manor than it had in the past. That was before Xavier was sick, back when she blamed herself for Xante's death. Now, she blamed herself for something worse, and it was too late to make things right for Xante's memory.

The wicker woman opened her door, letting two cats sleek out on either side of her, one tabby and one gray and white. Shanley could not find her voice. The woman looked wretched, as if she had been crying. She tried to find the right words.

"What is it, girl? Why are you here?"

Shanley stuttered and swallowed. The words would not come. The wicker woman's tone cut at her like a switch.

"If your brother's dead, it's not my fault. I told that Husk Grayvesone that I could not save him. I could only waylay his pain."

"Yes," Shanley said, her voice coming out as a whisper. She cleared her throat. "You did. I mean Xavier's pain went away. Only we are out of the tea. I thought maybe I could purchase some more tea. The pain has come back, and Glorious Thierry threw the rest of that tea out. He believed it had gone bad."

The wicker woman gave Shanley a weary look and opened the door further, escorting the girl inside. Shanley hesitated. Husk said there had been snakes, hundreds of them, and Shanley feared serpents. She took a tentative step.

"Arryl weed is rare. Very expensive. I am not sure you can afford it."

"I know, but I only need enough for a day or two, maybe a week?"

"I can do that," the wicker woman fixed Shanley in her gaze, directing her to sit in a thick, red armchair.

"You can? Oh, that's wonderful. What will it cost? I brought gold."

"Your gold is worthless to me, child," the wicker woman said. "You have paid me for other favors. Did I want gold then?"

Shanley looked about the room. Bookshelves reached to the ceiling, but she saw no snakes. And no cats apart from the ones that had escaped when the wicker woman answered the door. Had Husk exaggerated his experience? Cats had always been about the wicker woman, but Shanley had never seen a single snake in her previous visits.

Instead of snakes and cats, there were dozens of herb bowls giving off a pleasant minty odor. The Silver Swann had sent similar herb bowls to the Rose Manor, as a gift. Dr. Rege had placed four of them in Xavier's room. It halted death by cleansing the air, he said. He claimed it to be science although Shanley suspected magic.

"No, you did not," Shanley said, feeling a twinge of fear. "What then?"

"I wish for you to have tea with me," the wicker woman said.

"Is that all?"

"You did not let me finish. Tea every full moon for a year. I will supply you the arryl weed for as long as Xavier requires it as long as you swear you will attend these teas without fail and never touch a drop of the arryl weed I give you no matter what pains you."

"I wouldn't," Shanley said. "Phaedra, Husk's friend, says that it can be horribly addictive."

"It can, but your brother will die without it so what does it matter if he becomes an addict?" the wicker woman said. "It is more than arryl weed I am giving Xavier. It may slow his death, but it will not forever prevent it."

"I know, but he was able to play, to smile with the tea. I think if the effects keep up, he might attend school with other children of his age. He might live a little before he dies."

"Losing a child is horrible. It is hard to watch," Madame Darke said as she busied about, pulling herbs from pots, straightening books in shelves. "I had a son once, you know. He died."

"Oh? I am so sorry," Shanley said, startled by the revelation. "I never knew. Were you married then?"

"I was. Very much in love. My husband's body was taken by a dangerous specter who killed both him and my son. Which is why I wish you to have tea with me. You are an interesting girl, and I am a lonely, old woman. I would welcome talk. I will give you books to read, and we can discuss them."

"That is more than a fair bargain," Shanley said, helping Madame Darke set down a tray of tea and little cakes. "I happily agree. I am so sorry about your son. What was his name?"

"Calibor. He was everything to me. Such a handsome, bright young man. And kind. Would you believe, Shanley Rose? That a son of a witch could be kind?"

"I always thought you a generous person," Shanley said, and she meant it. "No one else could have helped me with my acne like you did. And whatever else you did to calm my awkwardness."

The tea had a taste of citrus and bitter, not unpleasant, but odd. The warmth of the afternoon prickled about Shanley amid smells of lavender and wildflowers, filling her head with such lovely visions. She nodded off. It felt like a moment, but when she blinked her eyes awake, her tea was cold, the cakes long eaten.

"Are you all right, dear?" Madame Darke asked.

The woman sat in a black cushioned-armchair that accentuated her milk-like skin and dark and gray speckled hair. Two cats flanked her, the gray and white from earlier, and a tremendous royal blue mountain cat in shades of gray, brown, and tan gazing at her with green and yellow-eyed stares.

"I…what were we discussing?"

"*The Pirate's Girl*, your favorite book? And Husk Grayvesone," Madame Darke said.

That sounded right. Shanley was always talking about Husk and books and stories and Husk and food and Husk and plants and Husk. She could not hide how taken she was with that beautiful, young man. His emerald-green eyes, that dark skin and the stubble on his chin, the broadness of his chest, the wink of a smile when he was pleased. Shanley loved Husk Grayvesone.

"I was so glad Husk agreed to visit you," Shanley said, feeling certain she was repeating herself. She did that a lot. People never listened to her, and that had caused her to repeat things and to sometimes speak too loudly. She was trying to do better, but it was a hopeless thing she suspected.

"He was brave to come here. However, I am glad you sent him," the wicker woman laughed. "I was happy to make his acquaintance."

"Good. Do you think he would ever…?"

"I am afraid my magic is limited. I can't change a man's heart. No conjured magic can do that. You will have to rely on nature and your own talents to turn his heart and head."

"It's impossible. He loves that girl, Phaedra Pyn," Shanley said.

"I doubt that," Madame Darke said. "He would never touch that girl though they may seem to be friends. That is a peculiar situation and nothing for you to fear."

"Is it?" Shanley asked, feeling hope explode inside her. She would save her brother and there was still a chance that one day somehow. Stop. Why could she not stop?

"Now, let me get you that arryl weed," The wicker woman said. "You can give it to Xavier as soon as you get home. I will also give you potion that will help you relax. That might help with your confidence."

"Thank you so much. You can't know how much I appreciate this."

"I will mark you on calendar for three weeks from today. That will be the next full moon. Right before your mother's famous summer ball. Three hours past the mid of day shall we say?"

"I will put it on my calendar as well, Madame Darke," Shanley said, rising to her feet, feeling light in the head. She took the bundle of tea, feeling uncertain. "Is that really your name?"

"No, but it is what I wish to be called," Madame Darke said. "Shanley, please eat well the next few weeks. You need to keep up your strength. I will not do for Xavier what I did before if he passes on."

"Before?"

"Never you mind. You best get going if you want to be home by dark."

Shanley left the cottage. Something had told her to pretend to have forgotten about Xante. She did not know why, but she suspected the spell had not quite worked for her late brother. If it had, she would not remember Xante either. She felt certain it was best that Madame Darke not realize that Shanley remembered.

A Puzzler's Last Stand

The Rooke looked out to see the beachside tavern filled to the corners, expanded four times the size it had been when he entered. Several patrons shuffled forward in want of tokens. He had been speaking all day and the sun was fading over the horizon.

Ghita Mist had her arms around little Anwyn Finn, using her body to shield the girl whose skin had gone a bright blue as the girl gobbled up a little cake to pink up her skin. Ghita pulled her big carpet bag open to show The Rooke she had managed to recover Ambriel's Unbreakable Cube.

"Ani got the box back using her invisibility," Ghita said in a whisper. "We won't have much time."

The Rooke nodded. The tricky part would be leaving. He could see the exasperation in Freddie and Millie's faces.

"We should go back to the yacht," Freddie said. "And someone needs to do something about Joel Broomes. He looks unwell."

The Rooke turned to see what was wrong with the Joel only to find Rintyre leaping forward after a young family.

"That's my nephew," she said. She pulled out her IPD badge and a strange tool, taking the small boy by the arm.

"No," Joel said, his breath catching, a look of absolute terror on his face. "He's a Spyte."

"You've made a mistake," the woman said. "This is our son."

"Is that you, Teriss? How?" Rintyre said. "You bitch. This is Carling's child. You stole him, Teriss Amber, you freak, you fraud."

"Hey, Jude. Protect your mother," the man posing as the child's father said.

The child's eyes went black, his face monstrous as a black smoke formed around him, and he let out a growl. Rintyre did not back down. She knelt over to eye-level with the fair child. He looked so like a young Husk Grayvesone, dark-hair, green eyes, a perfect oval face, handsome eroded by the evil force that held him.

"You are not Jude. You are Gabriel. You are my nephew. You are loved," Rintyre said. The Rooke understood. She was trying to call him away from the demon with a name of love. It was not working. The boy was too disconnected from his past, and too young to understand.

He went to attack. Zac Grimm leapt forward with his sword to protect Rintyre. She stepped between her nephew and Zac, taking the full point of the sword. It did nothing. The Rooke gasped.

"Rin!" Zac cried out, as Ghita Mist came forward throwing

out some kind of powder that exploded and caused the room to go very dark.

"I'm fine," Rintyre said, anger turning on Zac. "He's a baby, Zac. I don't want him dead. He is my nephew."

"He was going to murder you," Zac said.

"Run," Ghita Mist said. The Rooke pulled a light from his pocket to illuminate the door. The party sprinted out the opening.

The Rooke and party stepped outside into the twilight to take the short distance back to the yacht on the dark waters of the Acarian Ocean. They had forgotten their peril for those small moments and did not see the assassins in the shadows, waiting for them. They could not fathom how the child and the baroness had gotten ahead of them. The smell of sweet piss and death came with a small child with lifeless eyes. He laughed wildly as he leapt on high, black knife in hand.

Ghita Mist stepped in front of The Rooke, taking the full brunt of the knife meant for him. Tavares, Joel, Aldo, and Kentigern responded as a single unit. They lifted Ghita Mist from the ground as the Spyte scurried off into the shadows. She dug into her carpet bag and took a sip of something.

"I am alright," she said. "Run. We must escape. Run."

"To the docks, to the yacht," Millie said, gathering them, moving them out into the starless night.

Ghita stumbled, and The Rooke stepped back and put an arm around her, dragging her forward. Kentigern and Tavares brought up the back as Cabal Marrok's Folly and the Spyte and his handlers disappeared behind them.

Ghita Mist collapsed on the deck of the luxury yacht. Tee Broomes fell beside her, trying to help her.

The puzzle master held her hand over her open and bleeding belly, the pain on her face unbearable. She reached out to nothing. "Please, Phaedra. Help me. I helped you."

"Phaedra is not here," The Rooke said.

"We need a doctor. Tee is not a surgeon," Rintyre said. "We should take her to hospital. They can help her."

"Phaedra is back. I know she is," Ghita said. "I am… I was Madame Darke. I helped Phaedra into the world. That's worth something, isn't it, Rooke?"

"What are you saying?"

"Phaedra has the name you are missing," Ghita said, trying hard to keep breathing. Her time ran to its last. "You can't finish your tales without her."

"I don't understand," The Rooke said. "Tee, can you brew a potion to help the bleeding, to give us time to get her to a hospital."

"There is no time, Rooke. Listen to me. Phaedra kept my name for years until I made it to The Reliquary, to protect me," Ghita said. "Please, forgive me. The stories you will tell in the coming years will not paint me in a good light. The dragons warned me…"

"Ghita, you are my oldest friend," The Rooke said. "Whatever you did, Ta-She-Serra will forgive you. I believe that. I do believe the light will have you."

"I only wanted my son back. I wanted the life I made. I was a simple, Pathian peasant fighting an impossible war. Everything I did was for Calibor."

"We all do awful things for good reasons," The Rooke said.

"And end up murdering our saviors," Kentigern said.

"I never meant to cause any harm. I tried to help, to take on the demons on my own. All my people were murdered because of Terminus. I only wanted my Calibor back…" she said, and then her eyes opened wide. "Oh? He's just there."

With that, Ghita Mist who had hidden her name in the wicker woman, Jezebel Darke, for centuries, took one last breath of life and joined her son at long last.

Tavern XVIII:

The Minstrel Inn

A powerful magicker willing to deal with demons and unwilling to repent is a catastrophe to the fabric of creation. A dragon, unable to change, is a check on such beings seeking stagnant godhood.

The Idylls of Alleysiande, Vol IX. The Dragon Paradym
author unknown (translated by Hazel Kyran)

The Old Fruit Orchards

The Rooke agreed that Ghita Mist should receive a burial at sea. It would not do to have a dead body on the yacht. Zac Grimm shed tears with Kostas and Anwyn over the loss of the Grandmaster.

"She was a real nice old lady," Zac said.

"And we really needed her to help solve this puzzle," Kostas said. "What do we do now?"

"We hide," Freddie said as the yacht glided across the choppy waters of the Acarian Ocean. "We can't go further west. There are patrols out everywhere, and this yacht will not get us the right kind of attention from military vessels. We are going toward The Myrrh Isles. From there, I don't know."

"The Myrrh Isles? That will do nicely," The Rooke said. "They were once The Acarian Fruit Orchards. We might be safe there for a time."

"I know what you're thinking," Aldo said. "The Minstrel Inn. Yes, that will be a good place. The children can work on that puzzle together. Zac, lad, you'll have to help them. You are the puzzle master now that Ghita is gone."

"I will do all I can. I owe the Grandmaster that," Zac said.

In truth, the Myrrh Isles were the far-edge of the tropics and nowhere near Acaria. Rain came down in sheets as the group made their way toward the mythical inn. The Rooke remembered the great performers of the Pre-Evanescent Era, all coming to make their mark at The Minstrel Inn. He suspected he had done the same before the robes clouded his memory.

He caught up to Rintyre. "Has your sister and brother-in-law played here?" he asked her.

The inn spread out in whitewashed, many columned and flowered railings in two wings flanked by neatly tilled gardens of colorful flowers. The sea was bluer here where the Acarian Ocean gave way to the Ambrien Sea somewhere to the South.

"Yes. I remember it well. They were so excited when Bryter Days was invited to play," Rintyre said.

"Can you sing like your sister?" Zac Grimm asked. "I mean you are twins and all."

"It's not really my thing," Rintyre said. "I used to paint. I don't know why I gave it up. I guess it seemed useless once technology learned how to do it."

"Soulless. That's not painting," Zac said. "You should take it up again. It's good to do something that has nothing to with SIN, yeah?"

"Yeah. I wonder how many rookes have performed here," Rintyre said.

"After tonight, it will be all of them," The Rooke said. "Every rooke that ever came to the world performed here. The inn was formed right after the fall of Alleysiande. Or so legend tells us."

"Will you have more stories of the Grandmaster?" Zac asked. "She said they would not be flattering?"

"We have all done things we regret. Her tale is a long one. But I don't know yet if it is a tragedy or a hero's end."

Gaming

Rintyre pushed her misery and tears deep inside her so no one would see. Her despair felt impossible to forestall. She knew so many who died in Aroghotto, people who had been dear friends. Nobody seemed concerned that the innocent died with the powerful.

The rain gave way to a breezy and clear morning after. She headed outside where the world seemed at peace, oblivious to the disaster of Aroghotto City. She found Zac Grimm gazing out over the water. She started to turn away, reconsidered. After all, misery loves company.

"I am sorry about Cymbre Varian. She fooled me too," Rintyre said, plopping down on the dock, putting her feet in the water. The sun was pushing the clouds aside and a lovely sea breeze kept them cool and comfortable. The others were sleeping after a night full of tales and music.

"I am always a fool," Zac said, taking a seat next to her. "Was she there with Baroness Amber? Did you see? I wouldn't know the baroness or your father by sight."

"I think Cymbre was disguised as a man," Rintyre said. "Didn't really look male, the person playing at Gabriel's father. It's the kind of thing Spytes and their masters do. They mimic good and make it evil. A sweet, murderous family."

"Damn. Spytes. Regular assassins are bad enough. Add demons…" Zac shook his head, looking out over the ocean.

"I used to love the sea when I was a kid," Rintyre said. "I had forgotten about it. My parents used to bring us to this very inn every summer. Carling and I loved it here. My father used to play his music here. He had a gift for all kinds of theatrics; music, acting, even art. Not a Sandy, never that, more a luminary or thespian. His music was wonderful. People loved him. I loved him so much back then. When he betrayed us like…I can't forgive him. I just can't."

"He was fooled too, Rin. That woman, Teriss Amber, if she is what they say. Magic like that, even if she was just a normal hot woman, you women have a crazy magic over men like me. Like your dad. It's crazy."

"Gutter baroness. They are not even supposed to exist. Only we knew they did, even before I was born. There cannot be Spytes without their baronesses. I can't believe I ever did…"

"None of this was your fault. You could not have known. You made a good living within the rules you were taught. We both did that, and neither of us need to apologize. Not everything in New Chazir or Aroghotto City is bad," Zac said. "Cymbre. That's different. That was all my fault. I should have known something was off. If I had not been such an ass, the Grandmaster would still be alive."

"Ghita Mist was like a thousand years old. That's a damn good run," Rintyre said. "And she got us that box back. That's something. Don't be taking that on yourself."

"Thanks. That's real nice of you. And here I thought you just a merciless bounty hunter," Zac said, full grin on his face.

"You are right about one thing," Rintyre said, pushing herself to her feet. "You are a complete jackass. Come on, you're supposed to help those kids solve that riddle. And I have an idea about that."

"What's that?"

"The riddle is an Idylls & Grimoire card, right?"

"Yeah?"

"Let's go play some Idylls & Grimoires."

"Might get us in trouble. Game is supposed to be for rebels and people that are trying to bring down the empires."

"Well, that is the mission of The Minstrel Inn so let's have at it. It's a magical game," Rintyre said. "Let's tear down the fucking empires where everyone can see. We'll play in the tavern where the music plays. Where it used to be played in tournaments for champions."

The two old men, Aldo and Kentigern, joined the Idylls & Grimoire game with Rintyre, Zac, Kostas, Anwyn, Taki, and Thiago. They first played a game of dice to determine who would have the 'Last King of Ambriland' card in their hand.

Zac won. He looked over the card. He sighed. "But I don't know how to play this card," Zac said.

"It's a spy card sort of," Thiago said. "If you play it, the opponent gets the card, and you have to take a card that you already played and put it back in your hand. The opponent is awarded twenty points, and you lose the points of whatever card you pull back in your hand until you play that card again."

"Why would you do that?" Zac asked. "That sounds like a loser move. No wonder this guy was the last king."

"How do you ever win any game?" Thiago asked. "Think about it for a minute."

"Thinking is way hard for old Zac," Anwyn said. "Don't be mean to him, Thiago. Kostas and I have been trying to teach him this game for ages. Without SIN to help him, he's not too bright."

"Yeah, pretend I'm an idiot. Explain to me how using this card would ever do any good."

Thiago sighed. Rintyre said nothing so as not to reveal how confused she was by the concept. She had played a ton of Idylls & Grimoires as a child. Carling usually won. However, they had standard decks. No unique cards.

Thiago produced a book called '*The Idyll & Grimoire Masters*' by Xherdan Kyran.

"This book recounts every championship tournament held in Aerda going back three hundred years. Thompson Sacripant won a tourney in Ambriland in 8646."

Thiago stopped. His mouth open.

"Go on, brother," Kostas said. "That is the same year that Phaedra showed up."

"Exactly the same year. I wonder…"

"I thought the card belonged to River Swann," Aldo Thierry said, joining the children.

"It did. He lost it to Thompson Sacripant a night or two after he got it," Thiago said. "You see, Thompson had a unique card too."

"The Maligned Beggar," The Rooke said, joining them at the table. "Thiago, go on. Tell us about the tournament. That must be the answer we are looking for."

"Wouldn't it be better if we just played?" Thiago asked.

"It would be better if you practiced at being my apprentice," The Rooke said. "Take the stage and my robes will be yours for the next hour."

The Tale of The Gaming Tournament

The Silver Swann retreated into the breakfast room where she found her older grandson, River, heir-apparent to the Ambriland throne, wearing a morning robe, his arms around a girl with dyed blood-red hair. Damn. Tempest Redd had her claws deep in River, and the fool boy was to be formally betrothed to Emperor Alexan Sacripant's third daughter, Seraphina, at Admiral and Mirror Rose's annual Summer Ball.

"Stop trying to buy me a fairy tale, mother," her daughter, Victory, had once said to her when she had attempted to marry the girl to Duke Frederic Aenialle.

Bernard Rose's sister, Astrid, ended up with the duke. Victory ran off with a common pirate, one who had done well and ended up with a fine estate in Astrad in central Acaria. She wondered if River resented this marriage arrangement to the emperor's daughter as Victory had disdained the one with the duke.

Tempest had River in her sights for years, but the boy had been sensible and kept the minstrel at a distance. Seashell could see that sense had been abandoned. She was looking at a pregnant girl, perhaps a few weeks along. She wondered if Tempest knew. Seashell whispered a small spell. It was her grandson's child, a boy, sleeping under the girl's lustful heart.

For a moment, Seashell admonished herself. She was using magic all the time though she had promised Gerloch Nett she would only use it to protect her loved ones.

Seashell understood ambition and deceit by experience. This girl soaked in both, and her whispers might erupt a powder keg and put River's head in a noose. She did not have any patience with the situation.

"Out," she said, curtly, pointing to Tempest and the exit.

"Grandmother," River said. "What…"

"This is a dangerous place right now. You well know it," she said. "She needs to go, now for her own protection. And so do you. Go to the Emerald Eye, now. Get a room. It's the best place to be for the tournament."

The young man, looked down at his feet, trying to find that answer that would not further stoke her wrath. She knew. River differed so much from his younger brother, Lake Joshua Swann, a pirate's boy through and through.

River Jorge Swann was all Emerald Harrow's son with his slight frame, his golden mane of curly hair, and those blue eyes. Shell had tried to have him dubbed The Golden Swann, but the criers could not make it happen.

"Tempest is here at my invitation," River said. "A Master of Bones appeared at the boardwalk during the Idylls & Grimoires World Championship opening festivities."

"What did this Master of Bones do to you? Did you try to bargain with him?"

"It wasn't like that. The Master of Bones has given River one of those trick cards," Tempest Redd said. "He tried to give it back, but the creature disappeared in a flash."

"Blood or a roll of the dice?" Seashell asked.

"Neither. He gave me the card; told me I would be the last king of Ambriland. Then I felt sick, passed out, and…"

"I was there, with Husk and Daedalus, playing our music. I couldn't find Lake, and Husk and Daedalus had to be back in Marinplaz. I took care of him," Tempest said.

"I tried to ring Lake, grandmother…"

"He is on Petit Gyo. He is joining Robert Bracken's crew for a voyage to Marlinea."

"I know you wish I were the pirate like my brother," River said. "Grandmother, I don't want to get engaged to Serafina Sacripant. We don't care for one another, and this island kingdom does not need any more Chaziri influence. And Serafina told me in confidence, she is in love with a soldier, an officer. And as the Chaziri throne is secure…"

"Not now," Seashell said, in a growl. She felt all measure of control slipping from her. "River, you must marry, and it can't be to this minstrel. Greater love demands you sacrifice for your people."

"We are not…" Tempest started to object.

"Do not think me cruel, dear," Seashell said. "Ambriland is not a big kingdom. River will have to make compromises to keep it standing after the damage done by King Charon. And there is no one else for the throne. He will be a better king than he thinks."

No one would accept Tempest Redd as a queen after having been promised one of Alexan Sacripant's daughters.

"River and I have an understanding," Tempest said. "I will not do anything to risk my adopted homeland. I know I am not a queen, but I'm not what you think either."

"The last king of Ambriland?" Seashell said, changing the subject. She did not wish to argue with the girl. She would have to earn her confidence to deal with this pregnancy. "Show me this card."

"It would be dead useful in the tournament," River said, as he handed her the colorful card. "At least it better be."

"It's dangerous," Seashell said, not meaning to speak out loud. Her monkey snatched it from her and handed it back to River.

"We both know that, Lady Swann," Tempest Redd said. "You must think better of River. He's a better man than you know."

A dim shadow of man appeared on the card against stormy skies, a volcano erupting in its background, and the man overpowered by a large golden crown.

"I tried to burn it. Ripped it into pieces. I threw the pieces into Lake Ambri. It reappeared in my pocket. I put it in a lantern to burn it, floated it over the lake, watched it float over Mount Ambri. It kept coming back."

"It's a quaint, little magic. And only a card," Seashell said. "Master of Bones have no ability to predict the future. They only suggest it. Put it in your deck, hand it down to your children. It's not a card you can lose. Now, please, Ambriland can't have its heir in danger. Take shelter at the Emerald Eye."

"I won't be heir for long if Charon has his way," River said. "And now it seems he is trying to kill us. Just the way he did with mother and father, with Uncle Edward and his family."

"Regardless of who wishes us harm, I like this card. It seems killing you will not be successful. Last king is still a king," Seashell said. "And these attacks do not come from your uncle. Charon is not able to command the dark magic required to summon a sorcerer snake. He is a petty man, as most kings and such become, not an evil one. Your Uncle Edward took the woman he desired. Charon reacted in jealousy."

River retreated to The Emerald Inn for the tournament. Although, the first round was held at the boardwalk by Lake Ambri to accommodate the hundreds of players who came to play. There, he met an old friend. Thompson Sacripant, the fourth son of Emperor Alexan Sacripant of Chazir.

"My sister tells me we are not to be brothers after all," Thompson said without preamble. "Is it so?"

"We have not convinced my grandmother or your father as of yet. Serafina loves another," River said. "My heart is broken, and my grandmother is furious."

"It is better this way, my friend. My sister would not allow you to keep up gaming. She hates it about me. And she despises pirates. Ambriland would not suit her," Thompson said. "Now tell me. What deck will I face when we play?"

"I still play with the Icarian deck although my grandmother has tried to remove it from me a number of times. I am stuck with it such is the nature of Idylls & Grimoire decks," River said. "Are you still using your Erelahian deck? Or have you enough unique cards to use a standard deck?"

"I have two unique cards so I must stick to my Erelahian deck. A common deck with fewer than ten unique cards is useless for tournaments. I tend to win Idylls & Grimoires but lose cards to the bones all the time."

"I happen to have a dozen unique cards," River said. "And I

have only gotten the latest last night. I'll roll the bones against you for the card if you'll put up your Imodial card. I know you have it."

"I will take that bet," Thompson said. "As everyone knows about my Imodial card which makes it fairly useless in competition."

Thompson won The Last King of Ambriland. He frowned. The symbols marked it a common exchange card with a high point cost.

No one saw this dice game so going into the tournament, no one knew about the new card in Thompson Sacripant's deck although he was the defending Idylls & Grimoires champion.

Jesper Bagwell loved Idylls & Grimoires despite being horrible at the game. He asked his younger brother, Trick, to help him.

"Surely, you know what will happen," Jesper said. "Being an oracle. What you did in The Mudlands would not have changed things here."

"You lose," Trick said as they meandered through the throngs of people at the Boardwalk along the lake that separated The Swamp from Mt. Ambri, an inactive volcano.

"Help me not do that," Jesper said. "If I knew which cards were to be played against me…"

"It's not the oracle in me that knows you will lose," Trick said. "It's that you are a terrible player."

"Are you terrible?" the girl, Phaedra asked. "I was under the impression you were clever."

"Are you playing?"

"Yes, I have a deck. Erelahian. It belonged Sile Pyn."

"Who is Sile Pyn?"

"This body belonged to her. She gave it to me when she died. Your sister was giving me her body despite not being dead."

"Why did you not take Chrysalis Rabican's body when she was murdered?" Trick asked. "You could do that, right? It would have been a good match."

"I did not want a body with a slit throat. The demon almost cut her head off," Phaedra said.

"What?" Husk Grayvesone asked. "What are you two talking about?"

"Phaedra possessed my older sister once," Jesper Bagwell explained. "You know the story of Heath's Night."

"I was hoping that bit wasn't true about Phaedra," Husk said. "Glad your dad made sure she was not a demon."

"Little oracle, who will win this tournament?" Phaedra asked Trick. "I am anxious for victory."

"I don't know," Trick said. "I am not living backwards anymore. I changed everything. I have no idea what will happen. And it's the first time that I went forward without knowing what would happen when I woke up."

"We could wait until you're living backwards again," Jesper said. "It won't be like any time has passed for us, right?"

"I am not doing that," Trick said. "I don't want to live backwards again. I want to live and die and be done. Do you know what happens when I have to start over again?"

"You become a baby?" Jesper said. "And end up in an abandoned Icarian temple?"

"No. I grow old, very old most of the time. And I fail at what I am meant to do. And Aerda dies along with all creation. It gets sucked into a void, galaxies implode, stars explode into blackness, and only a single spark of energy remains, held by the Creator leaving Ta She Serra utterly alone, and all that was made is unmade. And then I wake up the day before my death and get cast backwards to try and stop whatever it is that causes Aerda to spark the destruction of all of Creation."

Phaedra bowed her head and laughed. "No pressure then," Phaedra said. "In the times you lived before, did you encounter me?"

"Yes. You were always the cause of destruction although you are meant to save Creation. Only I can't work out how. Something goes very wrong, but I have never worked out what it was," Trick said, the boy sounding angry and frustrated. "Not sure playing Idylls & Grimoires will help."

"I like games," Phaedra said. "And I will win. I like winning. Do not worry, little Trick. If Creation ends so will The Hierarchy of Hell. And this Creator, all alone, will simply start again."

Dejan Carra, Xavier Rose's personal medic, beat Jesper Bagwell in the first round of the tournament. Trick shook his head as his father put his arm around Jesper.

"Son, you are truly awful at that game," Sidon Bagwell said, laughing. "But it's a very pretty deck you have."

"I was sure I could win one match," Jesper said. "Husk, how did you fare?"

"I won against some Jarl from Boreal. Daedalus lost. You two are equally matched," Husk said. "Daedalus is terrible, and Phaedra is inhumanely intelligent and beat him easily."

"Husk Grayvesone, is it? I work for your patron, that Silver Swann, tough lady her. I am told we will meet in the next round," Saltwater Frain said. "Hello, Jesper Bagwell is it? That fine Shanley Rose tells me you know lots about plants. Wondered if I might pick your brain as one might say. I am trying to grow some herbs that are not typical for Ambriland. I am told you could help. After the tourney."

"Sure," Jesper said. "Plants I know. If only there was an herbal or an alchemy deck, I would have a chance."

The tournament went on for three days. The semi-finals and final match were held at The Emerald Eye. Phaedra made it all the way to the semi-finals after defeating Saltwater Frain only to be narrowly defeated by Thompson Sacripant.

"That was kind of amazing. You almost made it to the final, Phaedra," Daedalus Sams said to his cottage mate. "Your first tournament and everything."

"It was not," Phaedra said. "Sile Pyn played all the time. I have her skills and memory. Thompson Sacripant is talented.

We should be careful. He would be tempting for the specter, being a royal of sorts. Terminus is attracted to power."

"Thompson won't be of interest," Husk said. "He's a spare, the fourth son, the seventh child. Like his younger brother Jordan and his cousin, Malcombe Absyrtus. Both are coming to Kingswell College in the autumn, not a place where those who will inherit real power attend. Even River Swann did not go to Kingswell College. Thompson has been disowned by Emperor Alexan because of his gambling. And Jordan is like twentieth in line with seven older siblings and a bunch of nieces and nephews, and little Malcombe is not properly in line as he is cousin by marriage and not blood. His mother is the sister of Empress Anastasia."

"Terminus will simply murder his way to power if he thinks it worthwhile. It is what specters do. And he would settle for influence. It is safer. No one thinks to dethrone the influencer," Phaedra said. "Who won the other semi-final?"

"Dejan Carra beat Elder Cleric Clarence Gillespie," Husk said. "I can't believe the old cleric is that good. Glorious Thierry will be so jealous."

"Thierry did not show up," Daedalus Sams said. "He felt ill. Something is wrong with the old man."

"He is getting pretty old, Daedalus," Husk said. "You might get Dr. Rege to look in on him. He won't think to have a doctor help him. Let's get a good view of the final."

The medic, Dejan Carra, had an exceptional draconic deck. Quickly, he was up by twenty points. Everyone thought that Thompson Sacripant had finally met his match as his cards fell flat against the deck of dragons.

Thompson played his other unique card, The Maligned Beggar, causing Dejan to sacrifice all his military cards. He only had two.

As the cards appeared and the points tallied, Dejan found himself up by more than fifty points, an almost impossible gap for Thompson to overcome. With only one card left in each hand, Thompson played the Last King of Ambriland, allowing him to replay any one of his cards on the board. He took up The Maligned Beggar. Dejan Carra understood as he put down his ice dragon card which eliminated all points that Thompson had on the board, a sigh of regret at a game well-played that he would not win.

The Maligned Beggar lost the war and won the game. The Emerald Eye burst out in applause as they had never seen this strategy work before. Dejan shook his head.

"Well, so much for that house for me and the missus," he said. "Good game, mate."

"Ah, you deserve a house," Thompson said, in good spirits. "It was a well-played match. I'll split the winnings."

When he thought no one was looking, Thompson Sacripant handed River Swann back the Last King of Ambriland.

"Card not to your liking?" River asked.

"No, I like it a lot," Thompson said. "But I will never be king of Ambriland or anywhere else, my friend. Good night to you."

Those might have been Thompson Sacripant's last words. He stepped out of the Emerald Eye into the night, unobserved on the docks of Tiponi Harbor by anyone. And was never seen alive again.

A Last Peace

*T*he Rooke gave Thiago a hug as the Minstrel Inn gave him a round of applause, followed by a series of questions. They all suspected Terminus. They all wondered how the world had not come to an end as to them, the danger had passed. The Rooke wondered. Trick Bagwell had disappeared with the rest of the Urians in the end. Had the oracle managed to save the universe. Was it more than Aerda in danger?

Thiago gave him over his robes, and The Rooke gave out his tokens. He felt a bit of relief. His son was well-trained, and he knew exactly where they must go.

He wondered if the light Phaedra sought had been offered to Ghita Mist. Had she been redeemed? She saw her son in those last moments. Surely, that meant the light had been granted her at last.

He walked past the crowds without seeing, making for his room. He did not care that Freddie and Millie would not allow the use of their yacht to go to Ambriland.

When The Silver Swann refused the bargain for Husk with Terminus, slowly but surely, Ambriland had been given to Hell. And still, that is where The Rooke must go with his children.

"Rooke, should we not be leaving soon?" Aldo asked, following him.

"Yes, we are running out of time. We've maybe a week. Find a way to get us to Ambriland. We leave in the morning."

Tavern XIX:

The Barnacle Rose

All books contain a subtle magical. They change a reader for better or worse. Bland books full of nonsense can dissuade a person from reading anything at all, narrowing their world forever. A compelling tale powerfully told can inspire a reader to change the world. Irrevocably.

The Idylls of Alleysiande, Vol VIII. Malachi's Sorcerer
author unknown (translated by Hazel Kyran)

Ship of Fools

*J*oel pulled The Rooke back from the dock. The Rooke had never seen such an enormous ship as the Barnacle Rose, a floating city in lights. He understood that the myriad of colorful sails were decorative, not functional. The effect was one of wonder.

"I see demons. They are everywhere," Joel Broomes said. "There and there. Oh? Almost all the passengers are revelers."

"I'm not surprised," Aldo said, looking a proper elite with his golden gilder's sleeve and expensive white and gold outfit. "They are the only ones who can afford to sail in such luxury. We should take another ship, something more modest. Revelers won't sail with lower sleeves."

"Taki and I checked. There are no other ships or airships going to Ambriland right now," Rintyre said. "This is it. And Ambriland is filled with elites. It is not the islands of pirates anymore."

"We must go there," Tee said, pulling Taki's sailor hat down securely over his ears. His round-shaded glasses were well in fashion with the elite as was his garishly colored shirt. He would fit in as long as he kept quiet. "We will keep to ourselves and enjoy the entertainments so as to not raise suspicion."

"Steps have been taken," Kentigern said, securing his thick, golden sleeve. "We will have cabins together, all suites, all secure. And our own tavern. Freddie and Millie have made it so. They claim connections to the ship line that owns this behemoth."

The dark waters of the Acarian Ocean gave way to the bright azure of the Ambrien Sea within a few hours of setting sail. Thiago, Kostas, Taki, and Anwyn had found cushions and long chairs and were lounging after a day playing in the sun and the mammoth pools and slides on the many decks of the massive ship. They found it easy to stay away from most of the passengers on the gigantic ship.

Things seemed to be going well until Zac Grimm showed up, pale as a ghost and looking scared. "Inside, kids. That little kid is on the ship, the one that murdered the Grandmaster. I think he saw me."

The Young Puzzler

Kostas sat between Rintyre and Zac Grimm. He did not like leaving Zac alone with Rintyre. Whatever she said, she seemed every bit as dangerous as Cymbre. The Rooke's whole group was holed up in this little tavern that was smack in the middle of the ship with decks above it and below it.

The two tin-sleeved thieves, Millie and Freddie, sauntered in and sat across from him, both looking a bit bleary-eyed. Freddie wore a rare platinum sleeve with a blue gem glittering at the wrist. Kostas wondered how Freddie managed to pull off such an elite sleeve, and why Millie agreed to act as his manservant. They were an odd pair, and Freddie kept staring at him. Kostas did not like it.

"Why are you looking at me like that?" Kostas asked. Blunt was sometimes the best way to get information. A lesson the Grandmaster had taught him.

"You are a fascinating boy."

"Don't get any funny ideas. Phaedra is not the only one that will tear someone apart that messes with kids."

"Sorry. No. I would never. It's just you are in such danger traveling with your father," Freddie said. "Spending your twelfth birthday like you did."

"I had a fine time, thanks. We were safe for about two seconds. It was nice."

"You are generous soul, Kostas."

"What is that thing you wear around your neck? It messes with your disguise, looks a common rock."

"Crystal, rare type from my country. Would you like to see it?"

"Ok," Kostas said. Freddie pulled the thing from his neck and handed it across the table. Rintyre took it and checked it like it was a bomb or something.

"Just a rock," Rintyre said. "I like uncut crystals. They are comforting. My mom collects such rocks."

"I like common," Freddie said, as Kostas took the necklace.

He ran his hand over the sharp stone and felt it warm up. Then it cast a bright blue light across the table. "Wait. What was that?" Kostas said.

Freddie almost leapt from his seat to take the necklace back. He tucked it back under his shirt. "Quiet. It is only a trick," he said. "Did you like it?"

"I don't get it," Kostas said. "And I am hungry."

The door to the tavern opened a crack, and Thiago's eyes went wide.

"Oh no, Zac, that girl," Thiago said. "She just peeked in here, like she is looking for someone. Looked a bit like Cymbre."

"Get your dad. Have him tell a tale. She'll have to leave. She can't bear hearing a rooke's tale."

The Tale of Ambriel's Library

The disappearance of Thompson Sacripant caused a good deal of trouble in Ambriland. The engagement of River Swann to the emperor's daughter was revoked. Husk knew that his patron's grandson relieved. And Tempest Redd thrilled to no end.

She had not changed her mind about the baby the day the news broke. Husk felt a twinge of jealousy. He still felt a deep attraction to the singer and thought fondly of their couple of nights together a year ago. How carefree those days seemed now.

"River will never marry you," Husk said as he and Daedalus accompanied her to the wicker woman's cottage. "I am sorry,

Tempest. My patron won't allow it. She believes that River must be king, that the Swanns should rule Ambriland once more as they did in the glory days of pirates."

"Well, I am more of a pirate than some foreign princess," Tempest said. "River loves me."

"Then have the baby," Daedalus said. "Force the issue. Give him an heir. Besides, you could tell our patron who you really are."

"And risk my vile father finding me. No," Tempest said. "And I don't want a baby. Not now. Not when our little band is doing so well. Husk, I wish you would abandon this silly notion of being an archivist and commit to the music."

"I will kill your father," Phaedra said. "For what he did to you. Then you may tell The Silver Swann that you have royal blood."

"Husk, did you tell her?" Tempest stopped on the jungle path outside the wicker woman's cottage. "That was meant to be secret between us three. Not shared with every girl you take to your bed."

"He told no secrets. I read your fears, your shame. It was not your fault. What was done to you by your father is unforgivable. I will give you justice," Phaedra said. "And I do not share a bed with Husk. It would cause him to catch fire."

"I don't care that you are sleeping with Husk. We're not together. I am with River. You are really crazy," Tempest said, turning on Phaedra, shaking a finger at her, and then storming off, away from the wicker woman's cottage. "She's crazy, Husk. Make her go away. She'll stab you all in your sleep."

"Tempest, we're here. Madame Darke is expecting you," Husk said, glaring at Phaedra. "Where are you going?"

"Daedalus is right. I am keeping the baby."

Husk turned on Phaedra. "You can't say everything out loud the moment you think it, Phaedra," Husk said. "We need Tempest. She won't understand about your magic."

"Of course, she understands magic," Phaedra said, looking non-plussed. "She came to this witch for magic, did she not?"

"It's not magic she came for," Husk said. "She came to abort her pregnancy. The clinic in Marinplaz won't do it."

The door to the wicker woman's cottage opened as Shanley Rose emerged. She startled and stumbled over her greetings. "Husk, I would not expect to see you here," she said.

Shanley appeared different to Husk, dressed in a white, summer frock that suited her well, bare-footed, and an arm full of books.

"Hi Shanley," Daedalus said. "What brought you here?"

"I was having tea with Madame Darke," Shanley said. "We do each month. She's lonely, you know. Everyone always comes to her because they want something. That was me too. No one at all comes to visit her as a friend. No one. I know what that's like."

"You are a good person," Phaedra said. "We are not. We want something."

"Tempest doesn't want anything anymore," Husk said.

"We want to ask about your nightmares. No one is getting any sleep at the cottage," Phaedra said. "And the priory probably thinks our cottage is haunted. I am certain they can hear your screams."

"You're having nightmares?" Shanley asked, her eyes soft and concerned.

"It's stress," Husk said. "Is Xavier well?"

"Oh yes, the Bagwells have him well-sorted," Shanley said. "And the tea you acquired. Of course, Glorious Thierry keeps throwing it out. I can't think why. The first time is an accident. This last time he was just being nosy and mean. It's none of his business. I have to hide it in my trunk in my room."

"Did you get a dress for that ball of yours?" Phaedra asked. She worked at the Rose kitchens two days a week.

"Yes, Selkie found something perfect," Shanley said. "My mother won't like it. She'll be too busy to do anything about it. Are you coming to the ball, Phaedra?"

"I would but Husk will not join me," Phaedra said. "He does not like balls."

"I really don't. My patron made Daedalus and I attend so many when we were growing up," Husk said. "It was agony."

"If only your mother would let our band play," Daedalus said. "I hear you and Reginald have a special arrangement?"

"What? Oh, no," Shanley said. "My mother is vexed with me. She introduced me to some heir to some vineyard in the Flowery Kingdom. I hated him. He was awful. So now she thinks no one will ever love me, and I will never marry and have no way to take care of myself. She got it into her head to form an heir-bond with Reginald so she can get hold of the Diamont money. It's gross. It is not like what my father did with Siobhan. She was conceived the usual way, not on purpose. Not that Reginald is gross, Daedalus. I don't mean it..."

"No, I know what you mean," Daedalus said. "I told him it was unnatural and cruel. We had a row. We are going to adopt sea orphans. He doesn't need to sire a child. Although, his family is threatening to marry him off to a Turien princess."

"Reginald has a brother. A married one," Shanley said. "I don't understand parts of society at all."

"That's adorable," Husk said. "You are a rich man's daughter that doesn't understand why people hate the aristocracy so much. We should probably leave the wicker woman be. I kind of feel bad now."

Your nightmares are a danger. Come, human.

The black cat, Sariel, weaved between Husk's legs and pawed at the cottage door. It swung open and the cat leapt inside. Shanley took her leave. Husk and Daedalus followed the cat inside.

Ever since his first visit to the wicker woman, Husk woke up screaming every night as the silver-masked specter chased him through his nightmares. On the cliff where the priory stood, he saw a black tower rise as people he knew were torn to bits and fed to the citizens of Marinplaz.

He and Daedalus, in these awful dreams, would escape the

priory as it transformed into this horrific tower much as they escaped the orphanage in the swamp. They would run from the specter, only to be trapped at the cliffside.

Daedalus would jump, and Husk would stand, feeling the approaching specter, as he gazed down and saw his friend, dead below, his head split open by the rocks, the sea taking him away. He would feel the specter's clawed hand grasp him as he awoke and screamed.

The nightmare left a mark on his shoulder, blackened and sore. Madame Darke examined it as Phaedra went on and on about the black tower.

"I would love if Husk would stop dreaming about my death," Daedalus said. "Although, it is touching that he mourns me so in the dream."

"It's terrifying. It feels real," Husk said. "Not like the usual nightmares where I am lost and opening doors to nowhere. That is me worrying about the future. This is something else."

"It seems an omen," Madame Darke said. "And Terminus is after you, Husk. He needs one more soul to reach full power. He wants you."

"Because of his blood. He is not fully human. Neither of these are," Phaedra said. "They are Ambriens, yes? Partially at least."

"Exactly. But I think you and I can protect Husk, Phaedra," Madame Darke said, as she pulled a boiling pot from the hearth. "Which is why I am in such a state. I wish we could find Thompson Sacripant. The child of an emperor is just the sort Terminus would mimic, and keep."

"But we remember Thompson's name. He's not been taken, right?" Husk asked.

"Not yet. It takes Terminus a long time to absorb a soul. He's not collecting like other demons do. He is taking over to claim mortal power," Madame Darke said, pouring some liquid into a teacup and offering it to Husk. "Drink this. It will guard you against Terminus entering your dreams. It will not stop him physically pursuing you. Keep up your wards. And take them to Shankly Hall when you move there."

"I will. I don't understand about this specter. What is he trying to do?"

"He must fully absorb a soul to gain power. Like he did in Irialfar. Like he did in Parthal. This creature is responsible for two genocides. The women of Errapel, and the Pathians," Madame Darke said. "If he gets a third soul, I fear you will see thirteen black towers in Aerda, and the Hell of The Hierarchy will claim this world as they have claimed and destroyed so many before. We must stop him."

"I do realize, woman," Phaedra said. "And I am trying. But I am still weak. He also murdered me in another world, in another time. Only he never got my name. It seems the thing Hell wants most of all. I can't think why. I have seen the souls of mortal keep their names and escape into the light I am denied over and over and over again. Why? Why will the light not accept me? I was only a young girl when I was murdered?"

"I did not mean to imply it was your responsibility, Phaedra," Madame Darke said. "The Silver Swann and I stopped him before. We only need more magic as our coven is too few now. I understand you better now, Phaedra. I fear I will be rejected by the light as well."

"What do we do if we run across Thompson Sacripant?" Daedalus asked.

"Flee him and come to me," Madame Darke said. "And Daedalus, if you find yourself pinned to that cliff, don't jump."

"I have seen people make that jump before," Daedalus said. "But I have a better idea. Husk, let's get those nightmares fully undone."

The sea billowed its song in the breeze, beating the rocks below Husk in an unceasing melody. His breath stilled as he took in the height of the cliff by the priory. His nightmares, recurring with greater frequency, showed him trapped between the specter, Terminus, and this cliff. He would never jump. It was suicide.

Daedalus Sams plopped down on the rock, swinging his legs out over the deadly depths, heedless of Husk's warnings, all the while smiling up at him. Reginald Diamont chattered on about the ball at Rose Manor.

"How can there be a ball? Mirror Rose acts like nothing has changed since Xavier almost died," Reginald said.

"The ball will be fine apart from your parents insisting on this heir bond," Daedalus said. "I can't believe you'd even consider it."

"It is a good thing," Reginald said. "If I produce a child, my family will stop trying to marry me off to every rich girl in the islands. And we'll have a child. I like Shanley. The three of us will make a great family."

"I don't want to talk about it," Daedalus said. "You know how I feel, Reginald. It's cruel to Shanley. And to the child."

"Yeah, really stop," Husk said. "So unnatural."

"None of this matters. We must focus on the specter that is hunting Husk," Phaedra said. She grew impatient with the mundane. However, there had been no sign of a specter for some time. They all worried about Thompson Sacripant. His disappearance after such a notable victory had been odd. "And, Husk, I would like to attend this ball. Shanley said I could come if I brought you."

"I don't want to attend a ball, Phaedra," Husk said. "They are dull as mud. And Mirror Rose can't stand me and Daedalus. Erelahians make her uncomfortable."

"I have to go on account of this heir bond none of you want me to do. But my father wants it. What can I do?" Reginald said, as he peered out into the azure Ambrien Sea beyond the white foam as the water assaulted the rocks below.

"If we are ever cornered by a dark sorcerer," Daedalus said, interrupting Reginald's latest excuses. "This is not the place to run too. I have an idea…"

"You're not thinking of jumping, are you?" Reginald said. "Husk sees you die in those wretched nightmares."

The black cat, Sariel, chased a butterfly, and stopped to

observe the three young men as they pulled away from the cliff's edge.

I wish a fat fish.

"You're a cat. You are perfectly capable of getting yourself a fish on an island brimming with water filled with food for you," Husk said. Sariel's murmurings came out as audible meows that others could hear even if they could not interpret.

"I have heard that fish is not good for cats," Reginald said. "We never give it to Sophie. The little bones could choke her. She likes chicken best."

Phaedra gave Husk a sly smile as if he had read her mind. "I can barely keep my eyes open. It will be a blessing for this summer to be over," Husk told Phaedra.

"Maybe you should jump. Might wake you up," Phaedra said. *You have thumbs. Catch me a fish. The cat is famished.*

Sariel jumped on a rock to put himself near face level with Husk, extending his claws threateningly at his face. Husk ducked away and shooed the cat off the rock.

"I have fed you already, you mad cat. And you have claws. Make use of them. You could finish clearing the rats out of the cottage."

Why should I? I do not like the taste of rats. They stink.

"You don't have to eat them. Simply get rid of them," Husk said. "I will get you fish if you chase off the rats."

"Why will they not let you keep a cat at this place you must stay in the autumn?" Phaedra asked for the hundredth time. "He won't stay at the cottage, and he is always lurking about your dorm."

"I've told you," Husk said, trying not to look down as they climbed down a sharp hill that ran into another cliff.

"He's a real talkative cat. He doesn't approve of cuddles at all like Sophie," Daedalus said. He and Reginald adored their tortoise shell kitten, Sophie. The two cats did not get along. "Ok, watch your step here. This part is a bit tricky as the guard rail rotted away eons ago."

Further up the cliff, there was a break in the volcanic slate that looked to be a sheer drop down to the rocks below. The sea burst white against the cliff's bottom.

Husk would never have guessed the steps were there had Daedalus not shown him. The first step down gave Husk a rather unpleasant sensation, a fear of imminent falling, as it curved into a little platform with the remains of a wood railing.

Husk decided he would have it replaced with metal railing, high and narrow so no one could slip through. Below this enclave was nothing but rock. No one would survive such a fall. The crack in the cliff wall hid the entrance into a dark cave running deep into the rock. Daedalus slipped through, followed by Sariel who had come upon them unheard.

Husk let Reginald in before him. Phaedra seemed happy to take the rear. Sariel waited for Husk, his black fur blending into the shadows, his eyes glowing yellow.

There is evil here.

"What would a cat know about evil?" He said this so that only the cat would hear.

Everything.

"Cats do know a bit about evil. They are forever wandering in and out of Pandemonium. I once escaped in a cat. Fool thing took me right back," Phaedra said, whispering in his ear.

"Fantastic." Husk squeezed through the crack as Daedalus lit a torch line that illuminated a path sloping downward in hazy, red light. "Yeah, looks like a legitimate place. Daedalus, how did you find this?"

"I followed Glorious Thierry here one night. Last winter," Daedalus said. "There is a hidden passageway down to the shore, close to the Shark's Mouth. He was helping some poor girl escape Dax Kappa's clutches."

"Sile was the one helping them escape," Phaedra said. "She would not go herself. She saw no better future for her, but she would not let other girls give in so easily."

"Who is Sile?" Daedalus asked.

"I was," Phaedra said. "What did your cleric say about you following him?"

"Nothing," Daedalus said. "He didn't know I had followed. Anyhow, we can get away this way if we are ever pursued by a specter trying to kill us. Or we can flee Tempest if we make her any angrier."

"I bet this is a pirate's smuggling tunnel," Reginald said. "You think Aldridge Thierry was a pirate?"

"No, but his brothers all are," Husk said. "They sail with Captain Robert Bracken on The Raving Parrot. He is well-ashamed of that as he thinks the pirates and their quest for freedom is immoral and delusional."

"He is rather offensive, isn't he? Especially considering who Husk's father was," Daedalus said.

"We ought to go the ball, Daedalus. We could dance. It'll be scandalous," Reginald said.

"The Bagwells are going. Jesper said he might ask Shanley. Mirror Rose did not like that idea at all," Phaedra said. "The little oracle says Jesper will be a renowned alchemist one day."

"Jesper is going to ask Shanley to accompany him?" Husk asked. "He did not seem the sort."

"He is being polite. He feels bad for Shanley," Phaedra said. "He does not like the way Mirror Rose speaks to her daughter. And she was hurt that you would not go with her, Husk."

"Mirror Rose would hate that more than her going with a Urian that will leave in a few days," Husk said. "The Urian pappas and Phineas Tunvel have done all they can for us."

"Watch your step, Husk. The rocks are loose here," Daedalus said.

Husk had to lean over a touch to keep his head from dragging the rock ceiling for the first part of the incline. "This is creepy, Daedalus."

"We know the route now. Let us go back," Reginald said. "This seems almost as dangerous as the cliff."

All of Ambriland's main island rested on the remains of some forgotten world. Husk found that he could dig below any house or clearing and find ruins, this even more so as one came closer to the center of the island at the foot of Mt. Ambri, the great dormant volcano that hovered over it.

"Husk, are you alright?" Daedalus asked.

"I felt a bit dizzy," Husk said. "I suppose I don't like being in enclosed spaces."

"The dark sorcerer will catch you in here," Reginald said, after struggling his way into the new passage, now lit by glowing crystals in a long, straight hall. "You can't move fast enough and there are no places to hide. He'd trap you, skin you alive as all the best dark sorcerers do and bury you in that cave before you ever got this far. No one will ever be the wiser."

"There is a way to block the entrance behind us," Daedalus said. "It will slow him enough for us to get down to the harbor."

"At least his fire balls won't hit us," Husk said. They came to an intersection of hallways, the narrow one they walked and a sealed door. "What's behind this door, Daedalus?"

"What door?" Daedalus asked.

"What door indeed?" Phaedra said. She fixed herself against the entry of stone that blended with the cave apart from the metal that outlined it. "Let us explore."

"I want a drink," Reginald said. "Let's go to the Shark's Mouth. I have to get ready for the ball soon."

"Maybe if you miss the ball, Mirror Rose will tire of this heir bond idea," Daedalus said. "Can we even open that door? There is no handle."

Husk pushed against it. "And it's locked," he said. "I really want to know what's behind this door. Probably storage for the pirates. Might be wine, coffee, treasure. We have to get past it."

"Stop worrying, scholar boy," Phaedra said. "I can open any door."

"And often does without knocking," Daedalus said. "Let's see what there is to see."

Behind the door was an impossibly immense chamber. An army could have fit there. A dragon could have slept comfortably there amid the endless stacks of books and treasures illuminated under the light of glittering crystals that hung from the high ceiling that felt as if it extended far beyond the boundaries of the land under which this chamber stood.

"I will be accepted to Dalmeade," Husk said, smiling as he slipped past the others into the gigantic room. "Daedalus, this is Ambriel's library. It has to be. Remember, it disappeared when the original priory fell into the sea a thousand years back. This would be where it was. The volcano didn't hurt it. It simply enclosed it underground."

"This time weaver you go on about is of interest to me," Phaedra said. "All your stories say she is a myth. Or she disappeared millennia ago."

"Both things can be true," Daedalus said, opening a trunk full of fine linens. "We should get some things for the cottage. I think pirates did use this place. Ambriel would have approved."

"What is that awful smell?" Reginald asked, as he picked up a chalice in tarnished gold with jewels surrounding the cup.

"Fish. Dead animals," Husk said.

Death is here. We should leave.

"Death is everywhere. Stop being alarmist, Sariel," Husk said as he pulled a volume from a low shelf.

"Careful with that," Daedalus said. "Old books are delicate."

"It's perfectly preserved as if some archivist takes care of it even now," Husk said. "You don't suppose Glorious Thierry found this place. Only, if he found Ambriel's Library, he would tell."

Phaedra picked up a cube of wood, carved, looking an unopenable chest or a puzzle box. She stared at it with such intensity. She cocked her head, looking at something in the shadows under a tall shelf filled with old volumes.

"I have found Thompson Sacripant," she announced, stuffing the box into her shoulder pack. "Well, his head at any rate."

"What?" Reginald Diamont said, the alarm in his voice causing it to go up several octaves.

Husk and Daedalus rushed over to find the dismembered

head of the Idylls & Grimoires tournament winner mounted on a silk pillow of blue, like some prize.

"This is not good," Husk said.

"I'm going to be sick," Reginald announced as he began to heave.

"This is extraordinary," Phaedra said, no emotion or alarm in the pale woman's voice. "He resisted the specter. Terminus could not get his soul. He got his life but nothing else. That is unprecedented."

"He's dead. He didn't win anything," Husk said. "What are you talking about?"

"He is not being mimicked. He cannot be used by Terminus once he is dead. And we still know this is Thompson Sacripant. But who is he really? Only a powerful being could resist a specter once captured."

"I resisted him," Husk said.

"You had me, scholar boy," Phaedra said. "And I am a powerful being. Tell me, who is Thompson Sacripant?"

"He's one of Emperor Alexan's children," Husk said. "He's dead. This is not the time for a history lesson."

"No, Husk, everyone assumed he was dead," Daedalus said. "We thought a gambling score to settle. Thompson played with dangerous people. He sometimes cheated. But if he resisted this creature that pursues us. Phaedra, the Sacripants have been ruling Chazir for thousands of years. It is said they were the first emperors after Alleysiande fell. They defeated a fellow called Malcombe who had been intent on conquering the world."

"Were they Erelahians?"

"No. I wouldn't think so. They were not from Alleysiande," Daedalus said. "There is a castle, still exists where they rule from, deep in the Dusk Forest called Castle Mal Tomb. The story is that a Lord Tombs built the castle. He had two daughters. One married Dmitri Sacripant who stopped Malcombe and founded the Empire of Chazir."

"Who was Lord Tombs?" Phaedra asked.

"No idea. His named line died with him. It was thousands of

years ago," Daedalus said. "We could find a rooke who could tell us more."

"What is a rooke?"

"A magical storyteller," Husk said. "One came to Ambriland when Daedalus and I were kids. He told about the founding of the Muddy Clans. It's like you are there when you hear the tales. You learn things no book could tell you. We have tokens so if a rooke is about, Daedalus and I can find them if we want."

"Interesting. We should take this prize from Terminus," Phaedra said.

"What is wrong with you?" Reginald said. "We need to get the constable. Thompson Sacripant has been murdered. Where is the rest of his body?"

"Terminus likely ate it," Phaedra said, receiving another look of horror from Reginald. "What? That is what demons do."

"So we are looking for gnawed bones?" Daedalus said, shaking his head. "Like what Husk and I found in The Swamp when we escaped the Mammon sisters. They ate children."

"Yes, witches will do that. Not this Madame Darke. She uses other methods to gain her magic," Phaedra said. "At any rate, you won't find the body you seek. Terminus will have eaten bones and all. It worries me that he has consumed powerful blood. He could summon assistance although Terminus is arrogant. He would not willingly ask for help, would never share power. It would, however, amuse him into manipulating another of The Hierarchy into doing something he wants."

"We are not taking that head with us, are we?" Reginald asked.

"Breathe, Reggie," Daedalus said. "I think best thing is to throw it into the sea."

"Let's find something to put it in," Husk said. "If we report it, Reg, it will cause a diplomatic nightmare for Ambriland. Best the emperor's family keep thinking Thompson ran afoul of other gamblers."

"I am leaving," Reginald said. "I have to go to the ball."

"It's all right," Daedalus said, holding his hand up to Husk and Phaedra's objections. "Go through the door, go straight down that tunnel. You'll come to some stairs, and they will take you all the way down to the shore. There are no doors or side passages to worry about. I will try to stop by later in the night."

"Us too," Husk said. "Have a drink at the Shark's Mouth. But Reg, don't say anything to anyone. Please."

"I am going to forget this ever happened," Reginald said. "For tonight. Tomorrow, I will kick some sense into you lot. Covering up a murder can't be the right thing to do. Isn't this Terminus dangerous to everyone in Ambriland?"

"He's dangerous to every mortal that has ever taken a breath," Phaedra said. "Telling them about him will not save them. They would not believe anyhow."

"Right," Reginald said. He turned and left, leaving the stench of his vomit to mix with the rising odor of death and decay amid the splendor of this treasure room.

"There's bound to be a sack or something," Husk said after Reginald had departed. "We will take his head to the cottage. I would like to ask Madame Darke and my patron what they think the best way is to dispose of him."

"A trophy like that will draw Terminus to us. We can't keep it with us," Phaedra said.

This way, human. I have found something.

"My cat has found something," Husk said. "What is it, Sariel?"

"How do you understand your cat so well?" Daedalus said as they turned down a darkened aisle with a heaped bundle at its end.

"Thompson resisted," Phaedra said, as they came to the body. "Your high cleric did not."

"He's still alive," Husk said, kneeling down to the slumbering form of Glorious Thierry, the high cleric of Ambriland. The old man appeared dead but for the faint rising of his chest.

"He will not wake," Phaedra said. "He is all but dead."

"It's impossible," Daedalus said. "I've just seen him. Glorious Thierry is at the ball. He went early. How is this possible?"

"You've seen Terminus," Phaedra said. "We must run. He will hurt those Urians. Their blood will call to him."

"What about Thompson?" Husk asked.

"Leave his head here," Phaedra said. "There's no time. Daedalus, take us to Rose Manor. Guide us out of here with all haste."

Once A Girl

A horn blared to announce The Barnacle Rose docking on Petit Gyo. No one outside the group had entered the little ship tavern to hear the tale. The Rooke could feel the tale being repeated in Smuggler's Cove, The Tin Green, Tem's Tavern, The Dark End of the Rainbow, and places he had not visited or given out tokens. The magic was working.

"I fear we may be trapped," Kentigern said. "We have to leave. The ship has docked."

Exiting the ship would require the group to go up a deck and cross a long distance through a crowd of dangerous people. The Rooke could see his companions all steeling themselves for the journey. He startled to see Freddie coming into the tavern from the galley exit.

"It's dark out though it be noon. Mt. Ambri has been spewing ash into the air," he said. "This will be no holiday."

"We should try to mix ourselves with everyone disembarking," The Rooke said. "Make it harder for anyone meaning us harm to do anything."

Millie and Freddie divided the group into two, with half going out the main exit and half out through the galley. Plans evaporated as a dozen men entered the isolated tavern from both entrances, led by a woman and three small children, the stink of sweet piss accompanying them.

Rat hissed, showing sharp teeth, and leapt forward, his lithe body scurrying forward, using fist claws as his weapon. Rat's speed saved Kentigern Dagan Leesh's life as a large man with a heavy, spiked club collapsed to the ground, dropping his weapon before it could split the old scrivener's head open.

"Rats, we must fight. They come to take us back to Hell," Rat said.

Rintyre leapt forward as Anwyn stepped out of the way of a knife-wielding toddler. "That's my nephew," Rintyre said as the green-eyed child turned on her.

The Rooke gasped. The child looked a perfect duplicate of Husk Grayvesone in miniature, the green eyes bright and emerald though flat and gleaming with malice. He moved toward the child as a blade hit him in the back of the calf. Another child, perhaps seven in age, snarled as it pulled its knife back for another go. The Rooke felt the poison as Kentigern grabbed and disarmed the child and turned him into the blade of Zac Grimm's sword.

No child fell. A smoke of black erupted to be covered with Tee Broome's robe. She threw it over the child as if extinguishing a flame. "I have antidote," she said to The Rooke.

Joel and Tavares fought like they were born to it, felling reveler after reveler. However, it was Millie and Freddie that cleared the danger with surprising ease. The Rat and his crew did much damage and soon had the woman cornered, snarling like animals at her.

"Cymbre," Zac said. "Rat, leave her to me."

"She is theirs," Rat said. "There is no saving the woman that you see. It is all demon now. The kind that cursed me and mine."

"Zac, no, it's not what you think," Cymbre said, looking at her fallen allies. "I had to. They'd have killed me. You have no idea the power a gutter baroness has. I didn't want any of this."

"I believe you," Zac said, stepping past Rat. He turned to The Rooke. "We can help her. We can use her to find out what this gutter baroness..."

Cymbre attacked. She pulled a pistol and fired. The shot grazed Zac's arm. He cried out and poked his sword through the woman. She gasped and looked at him, her eyes filled with dismay. Blood sputtered out of her mouth as she crumpled to the floor.

"She was all demon," Zac said, turning away, bleeding and

holding his arm. He was already bruised in several places from the fight. "It is like Rat said. Or this sword would not have hurt her."

Tavern XX:

This Sturgeon Stinks

The Pella women forsook marriage with men thinking to free themselves of the curse placed on them by the Queen of Hell after the fall of Alleysiande. It was their downfall and the ruin of many men.

The Idylls of Alleysiande, Vol XI. The Eternal Women of
Errapel
author unknown (translated by Hazel Kyran)

Petit Kyo

Rintyre pulled the bleeding Zac from the ship. The Rooke followed from behind. Cymbre Varian was dead, and there was nothing to be done about that. Tavares and Joel wrangled the small, snarling boy. He looked like a misbehaving child, nothing more.

This child had killed Ghita Mist, the wicker woman, a complex character who had done both great harm and given great aid to the world. In the end, The Rooke owed his life to the old woman. He staggered as he stepped onto the floating docks that would take him to Petit Kyo.

Tee Broomes pushed a vial in front of him, filled with a blue liquid.

"Drink, Rooke, or you will die," she said.

He took the blue liquid and felt a relief that came with a sharp cramp that resulted in him vomiting into the tide as they found the beach of Petit Gyo.

The island looked a bit of paradise. Almost no inhabitants at all. The Barnacle Rose would continue onto the Big Island in the evening which was hidden in a cloud of ash that rained down from the exploding volcano of Mt. Ambri.

The Rooke and his party would not be aboard. They would find another way toward their final destination. He pushed his way to the front of the party. There he took Aldo by the arm.

"We need to go to the west side of the island. It's not far. This is a very small isle. Freddie tells me that a ferry is there that will take us to Big Kyo. That is where we will finish this."

"I will give the child a potion to calm him," Tee said. "I learned so much from Ghita Mist before she…"

"Yes, you will have a much bigger job now, Tee. I hope you and Joel will remain at my side," The Rooke said. "You are our only healer. Have a look at Zac's arm. I would be surprised if Cymbre did not tip her blade with venom."

"I administered an anti-venom already. He wouldn't take anything for the pain, but the bullet wound needs stitching."

"We will see to that once we reach the Sturgeon. All the alchemy supplies you need are on this island," The Rooke said. "Although, the inhabitants may not realize it. Phaedra and Husk came here often to get supplies for her and the wicker woman. For Ghita."

This Sturgeon Stinks was an appropriately named dive bar on the beach. Few tourists came here. It was mainly fishermen and sailors and islanders. They all looked weary despite the heavenly setting. In all the blues and greens and white of the island, it was still hot. Outside of the steady sea breeze, it felt unbearable.

The Rooke settled himself at a booth in the back of the bar. Tavares and Joel put the sleeping child in a wooden booth. Rintyre put a blanket over him, smoothing his hair.

"Hang in there, Gabby," she said. "We will get you help."

"Keep loving on him," Joel said. "That is how to push the demon away."

Aldo and Kentigern brought food from the bar, mostly shrimp and fried fish. They distributed it along with tall mugs of ale and ginger beer. The Rooke summoned Taki to him.

"I need a map of Ambriland a century before The Evanescence. Can you do this for me?"

"I can, but I need pencils and parchment," Taki said. "I have lost mine in the fight. I had to run and hide."

"I grabbed your pack, Taki. Your maps and such are safe," Kentigern said. "Are you well, Rooke?"

"I am," The Rooke said. "Tee should have a look at that cut, Kenny."

"It's nothing," Kentigern said. "I thought we were all done for when we took down those two Spytes. Tee was quick to think in covering them as she did. To stop their venom."

"Good thing," The Rooke said, giving his old friend a pat on the shoulders. "Now, Taki, can you make this map quickly?"

"A map from before Ambriland's first destruction. Yes. I make map."

"I need two locations. The Swamp which was the estate of The Silver Swann. The Emerald Eye. They won't exist anymore, but I need to figure out where they would be if they were still about. When we go to the Big Isle, we will explore those locations and have our final piece of Ambriel's puzzle solved."

The tavern began to crowd, young locals, and sailors on shore leave filled This Sturgeon Stinks. The Rooke felt uncomfortable as he spied a number of children, worried they might be Spytes.

"I am going to tell a tale," The Rooke said. "Get Freddie and Millie to get us an exit when I get done. This will help us discover if Rintyre's nephew is salvageable. Hopefully, he will sleep through it."

The Gutter Baroness

The Rooke should have died on The Barnacle Rose. Young Cymbre Varian lacked finesse and subtly. She had lost the priceless magical box, several expensively made weapons, and her life. Good riddance.

Baroness Teriss Amber cursed a bit and entered the awful, common tavern on the far side of Petit Gyo. She thought of taking her knife to the throats of those in This Sturgeon Stinks. She could not risk it. She needed to retrieve little Jude. He was a weapon she could not afford to surrender to Cymbre Varian's careless ambition.

The child feigned sleep. She motioned to him from the door as the people's attention all went to The Rooke who exposed his red robes. Little Jude slipped under the booth and crawled toward her, smiling the whole way. He leapt into her arms as she whisked him out of the tavern.

"You look different, mother," he said.

"It will pass. I had to disguise myself," she said. "Let us be away."

"The Rooke still lives. His stories burn me."

"We will get him later. We have pressing business to attend to."

Time ran short. She took the Barnacle Rose to the main island as rain began to wash away the ash spewing from the volcano. She hoped her sisters had managed to arrive at the Imperial Bay Resort that overlooked Marinplaz. She loved its excess and luxury although this would be no vacation. She had to move fast.

Jude dragged behind the baroness as they entered the Imperial Bay Resort that glowered over Marinplaz. The grand hotel shot into the clouds in black glass and steel, obscured by the ash and rain. In the marble grand reception entrance, a familiar looking man knelt before Jude.

"You've dropped this," he said, offering the boy a smooth stone of some kind.

"Thank you," Jude said, looking up at the man as he whispered something in the boy's ear. Jude put the rock in his pocket. The baroness wondered if it were valuable in some way she did not understand.

"Jude, come," the baroness said.

"Your boy is lovely," the black and gray bearded man said, his brilliant bright eyes sparkling. The baroness sighed. Some high celebrated citizen, maybe one she had bedded in the past.

"He's not for sale. He is my son," she said, sharply. She had no time for this.

"Oh, no. I was not interested in…" he said and then smiled. "He is a good lad."

She took Jude firmly by the hand and headed toward their room in the penthouse on the sixty-sixth floor.

Teriss Amber's sisters awaited her there with a small host

in the penthouse suite at the top of the imposing black tower. The three women had to work fast, and they had not acquired nearly the infants necessary for the magic to do its work. They would have to trust to mundane means for a good many of their designs. The baroness did worry. The sisters had their hooks deep in Aerda, and many owed them favors.

"Hester, what kept you?" her sister, Inez, asked.

"Do not call me that," the baroness hissed. "Baroness Teriss Amber. Why can't you remember that you sick, little cow? We are the Amber family. It is what gives us our wealth and power in this time."

"We are alone. This suite is properly sealed. And it is who you are, Hester Mammon," Inez said.

The younger sister of the baroness looked old, withered, fat. Her magic had never been strong, and the old magic of the Black Swann had hurt her worst of all. Her older sister, Nell, insisted on that eloquent yet unremarkable look, the squat frame, the square shoulders, black hair pulled back in a severe bun, perfectly tailored suit dress down to the ankle, polished short-black boots with simple silver jewelry to go with her sleeve. She looked a school mistress to Hester. It suited Nell to stay in the shadows. Her magic rivaled Hester's, and she had to exercise caution when dealing with her older sister.

"Inez knows it, Teriss. We ran out of infants, and her magic is failing. She is frustrated, but she is a good girl and will not betray us," Nell said.

"I will find you more potion," Teriss said. "You will have your youth again, Inez."

"This one is young enough and has served his purpose," Inez said, eying little Jude who glared back at her.

"You would get no fear out of this one, so his blood is of no use to you, and he is mine," Teriss said. "Nell, what have you to report?"

"We found the heir. Grandson of Malcombe IV by his third daughter. The problem is he is only fourteen. The Three Councils have agreed to his succession. Too young for our original plan for him to marry you. We thought, a guardian with royal blood to prepare him for his duties. You."

"Will the three Councils agree?"

"Already done but it left us short in our magic for the moment," Nell said. "We have arranged for you to take custody of the boy, to guide him, and to perform the old ritual. To bind him to Lord Malfus. This boy never thought to rule. His grandfather disowned the boy's mother and yet the parents are dead. They both attended the Unity Conference in Aroghotto City. The boy has already been dubbed Lord Tombs and soon to be emperor."

"What happened to Aroghotto City?" Inez asked. "We left and then all of our hard work, all gone. Every one of my Spytes was there. And the infants I was promised had to be used for this Lord Tombs' ascendency."

"I am not sure. Some awful new weapon," Baroness Amber said. "All my best assassins were lost in that explosion or whatever it was. It took the entire city. I had to promote Cymbre Varian, and she has already failed me."

"She was not smart," Jude said, shaking his head.

"Cymbre was uppity," Inez said. "But useful. I knew when we made her that she would be difficult."

"Not as difficult as that child we lost years back," Nell said. "But she stayed true to the end. Odd that she fell to a party of weakling malcontent storytellers."

The baroness appraised young Jude, those startling green eyes, that dark hair, and perfect face. Jude Grayvesone was too famous. She could not remove him from her side. Her reputation would suffer if she discarded her child. She knew Bracken would come for him if she could not make the man dead.

"Jude and I will leave in the morning," Baroness Amber said. "Where is this young heir?"

"He is at his father's home. Castle Mal Tomb," Inez said, rubbing her hands together in delight.

"Where it all began," Nell said. "We have arranged an

airship. With the rain clearing the ash from the sky, it should be able to take off at dawn."

"Good. I will need a nanny for Jude. Cymbre is dead, and he gutted the one before her."

"Already handled. From the Elite Care Service. She will not be tracked, for privacy's sake. In case this one grows bored and guts her too. She will meet you at the castle," Nell said. "What of this Rooke?"

"Do we have any resources here?"

"Yes, a thin number. The four you see here. Fifteen in addition. Two Spytes, three Spiders, a couple of Scarlet Reds, a few of the usual minions," Inez said. "We could rally them."

"Do that. Make sure this Rooke and everyone he travels with never leaves Ambriland alive."

"It will be done. He is growing careless."

"Do not underestimate him. He is inching closer to a tale that will be uncomfortable for our schemes. He must die. As must my husband. And soon."

Jude looked unhappy in the little breakfast café of the Imperial Bay Resort. The baroness never had understood small children when there was no demon to control them. The one that kept Jude in check had gone dormant. It happened, especially in places like this, where the demon might return to Pandemonium to refresh its power. She felt souls being devoured, invigorating her.

"You don't like your breakfast?" she asked her stolen child.

"Why does daddy have to be dead?" Jude asked.

"He is not a good man. Jude. He hurt you. Remember? When you are asked by the IPD, you must tell them what he did to you."

"He didn't do those things. Mr. Piss did."

"Your daddy did it," she said, bristling. She hated that Jude called his master such a disrespectful name. She had never had a Spyte dare call its demon anything at all. "You are misremembering. Eat. We have a long journey."

"You are not my mother," Jude said in a whisper, his brilliant green eyes glaring at her with a bright soul. Impossible. "And my name is not Jude."

"Your name is Jude. You are my son. You are tired. I will give you something to let you sleep on the journey. We are taking airship to a place far away to the most splendid castle in all of Aerda. The oldest castle in all the world. It is the place it all began."

The boy put his fork down. Stubborn. He put his hand in his pocket, grasping something, a token he had stolen. He had shown it to her in the night when she asked about it. It was worthless, but the boy liked it a lot, even with the demon controlling him.

Maybe the demon would come back when he awoke without needing to repeat the binding. She would have her sisters prepare a sacrifice in any case. She could not have anything else go wrong.

The baroness picked up the child and carried him out of Imperial Bay Resort into a morning of ash and wet, a break in the sky appearing out over the Ambrien Sea as she boarded the airship.

Jude did not even acknowledge the orange and black ballooned vessel as he usually did. He loved flying. He slept, his hand firmly around the smooth stone, through the boarding, the takeoff, the landing. The demon never awoke.

The Tale of The Summer Ball

The soft cotton dress in white with the azure, silk sash did little to assuage Shanley's mood as she entered the ballroom of Rose Manor. Glorious Thierry was there in deep conversation with her father and The Silver Swann. Her mother was standing with several of her friends, all snickering at the six Urians. How Shanley wished she could dress like a Muddy girl, so natural and lovely.

The little girl, Lucie Tunvel, was dressed in a long, red frock with golden scales embroidered on it, a symbol of Ambriel's emerald eye on the shoulder.

"I love your dress," Shanley said to Lucie.

"Oh, thank you," Lucie said. "My grandmother made it for me. I've never been to a ball like this. We don't have them in The Mudlands. Grandmother says she wants The Emerald Eye to host such formal events so I must learn about them."

"We have dances. Not formally," Jesper Bagwell said.

Shanley surveyed all the attending Urians. They were all unusually beautiful she thought. Even the old men. Jesper's father looked a touch ill, but even so, those mismatched eyes made him remarkable. She had only ever seen cats with different colored eyes before.

"Shanley, would you care to dance?" Jesper asked her. "My brother thinks it would be good for me. Only I don't know how. I might step all over your feet."

"It would be good for you to actually notice people who don't have arms full of herbs," Trick said.

"That's all right," Shanley said. "I always have arms full of herbs. Jesper helped me so much with my garden this morning. But I am a terrible dancer as well, but we could try."

"We could break each other's toes. It'll be amusing if not a little painful," Jesper said. "I did want to ask you about the lavender you have cultivated. It is unusual."

"Oh, yes, it was my first attempt at a hybrid. With some lilac. You wouldn't think it would work…"

Trick Bagwell rolled his eyes and Xavier shook his head. Both children were dressed alike, in short suits of black and white, typical for the highborn of the islands. Trick had insisted on having his clothes match his new friend.

"Lucie, both Xavier and I will dance with you," Trick said. "Then you can decide who is better. We have a wager."

"I am glad you and your family are attending this ball. Xavier and Trick are such good friends now. Are you staying much longer?" Shanley asked Jesper as he led her onto the black and white marble dance floor as a small orchestra played a classical tune with a spinning rhythm.

"We are waiting for a ship," Jesper said. "Storms in the Marlinean Sea have delayed it. It might be my Aunt Delilah will have to take us home, but she can't until this ball is over."

"I am glad. I have enjoyed getting to know you and love the alchemy you have taught me."

"Yes, it is on that account I asked you to dance. The potions I have taught you for helping Xavier are not adequate for his continued well-being," Jesper said, spinning them away from the several other dancing couples. "And my father will never allow you to keep purity wyrms as you are not Muddy."

Shanley sighed. Of course, Jesper needed to talk about Xavier. He did not fancy dancing with her. She looked and saw River Swann and her half-sister, Siobhan, dancing, enraptured with one another.

The daughter of Emperor Alexan Sacripant had rejected River. The disappearance of Thompson Sacripant had been the excuse. Siobhan told Shanley in confidence, that in truth, the girl had been in love with someone else. River Swann did not seem upset in the slightest.

Tempest Redd, on the other hand, had been crying and crying. Shanley had discovered her in the washroom right before the ball. Shanley had wanted to help. When she asked Jesper if he had any remedies for the girl, he said there was no alchemy for curing a broken heart.

"The potion you gave my brother seems to work very well with his tea," Shanley said to Jesper.

"It wasn't a potion. My father administered purity graffing wyrms. That Phaedra of yours helped so your parents wouldn't see the wyrms. They suck impurities out of the blood. They removed the poison of the arryl weed and whatever is making him ill," Jesper said. "However, this is only temporary. Shanley, we can cure your brother. He would never need that noxious tea again, and he could play in the sun, sail the ships he loves so much."

"That's wonderful. My parents will forever be in your debt…"

"No, your mother was unreceptive. She would let your brother die instead of what we recommended."

"No. My mother can be horrid, yes, but she is not stupid. If you can cure him… What is it she objects to?"

"He would have to become Urian," Jesper said.

"Oh. No. She wouldn't like that. She wants him to attend Kingswell College in the autumn. She wants him to marry one of the Turien princesses. She wants to be royalty like my Aunt Astrid."

"And if Xavier joins us, he can never marry a royal. That is true," Jesper said. "We don't do royalty or rulers of any kind. Not like the rest of the world thinks. However, he can't marry anyone if he's dead. Your mother thinks her fancy doctor from the Flowery Kingdom has cured him. She knows nothing of your tea, the purifying wyrms, or Dr. Rege's careful treatment. Which is why we need you."

"What can I do?"

"Once Xavier is cured, he can still attend Kingswell College. He would come home with us. Get his spawning graff," Jesper explained, showing Shanley his bright blue tattooed bracelet. "When he joins Uriel's Covenant, his blood would be purified once and for all. He would have no disease at all. After, he would come home with Captain Robert Bracken onboard The Raving Parrot. He runs the coffee lanes for the Muddy."

"The Raving Parrot? That's a pirate ship."

"So is Delilah Sage's ship, The Shroud. This is Ambriland. It is a place of pirates. Shanley, your own father is a pirate. Or was."

"No, he's not. He's an admiral," Shanley said.

"A pirate admiral. Before King Charon made him admiral of the fleet which Ambriland's pirates could sink in a half minute if they came to blows."

"Why do you think my father is a pirate?"

"Because he was. Quite a famous one. That is how Delilah

Sage met him and had a baby with him," Jesper said. "It doesn't matter. Will you help us cure Xavier?"

"Oh yes, I will help. Thank you, Jesper," Shanley said as the music waned, and a slower tune began.

"Whatever is that smell?" Jesper asked. Shanley blushed, thinking he meant her. Then she caught wind of an unpleasant odor, like a rotten fruit covered in shit.

The odd Urian pappa, Goolsby Lamb, caught up with Jesper. "We have a situation," Goolsby said. "Sorry, miss, I need your dance partner."

Shanley stood alone in the center of the ball room as couples danced around her. She froze uncertain at what was happening. She spotted Trick Bagwell and Lucie Tunvel hurrying Xavier out the side door toward the family rooms. She started to follow when she spotted Phaedra and Husk entering, neither dressed for a ball.

The Silver Swann's odd monkey appeared out of thin air and ran up Pappa Bagwell's back. The monkey sat on his shoulder screaming and pointing at Glorious Thierry who began to cackle as he held up his cleric's scepter. Phaedra confronted him.

"Hello, Terminus," she said. "Leave these ridiculous people be. It's me you want."

"Phaedra. How delicious. I will destroy their priory. Let me taste you."

"Give it a go," Phaedra said, as the man reached to grab the woman.

Shanley could not grasp what she saw. The man caught fire but did not burn. He was repelled all the same. Noe jumped from Pappa Bagwell's back and produced a ball of fire from his butt, and tossed it at Glorious Thierry. What was happening?

"Shanley, we have to leave," Husk said, taking her by the hand. "That's not Glorious Thierry. That is a specter pretending."

"There's no such thing," Shanley said, absently.

"Yeah, um, ok, well, anyhow, he's gone mad then. Let's get you to safety," Husk said.

Shanley pulled back, going toward the action instead of

away. She could not understand anything that was happening. The Silver Swann threw out an orb of silver light or so it seemed to Shanley.

She heard someone yell. "It's a coup. Get River out of here."

"Face me, demon!" Sidon Bagwell said, standing with a bit of stick in his hand before the monstrous Glorious Thierry.

"You!" the monster yelled, its eyes turning into portals of horror and darkness as it faced Sidon Bagwell. "You cannot be. How? How are you together? Janus is defeated. How?"

"We are not so easily disposed of, nameless one," Phaedra said. "You are not legion. You are nothing, Terminus. You are not the end of us. You are simply over."

Phaedra moved toward the creature. It ignored her. Sidon Bagwell stood between Goolsby Lamb and Phineas Tunvel. The Glorious Thierry monster charged forward. Using some unseen force, it threw both Goolsby Lamb and Phineas Tunvel to the side with ease and drove a small knife into the Urian pappa's belly and twisted. Sidon Bagwell screamed, hitting the creature over his head with the bit of stick. He collapsed to the floor as Goolsby Lamb knelt at his side to shield him and staunch the bleeding.

Phaedra was there again. She embraced the creature again with fire. It turned, now burning, and melting into a stinking, silver-masked, dark robed ghoul.

"You cannot defeat me," it said.

"We will see about that," The Silver Swann said. "Begone. Back to the abyss with you."

She said some words Shanley had never heard. All went full black. And then, whatever it was, was gone. Sidon Bagwell lie on the floor, bleeding from his belly wound. Jesper sat beside his father, screaming for help. The Rose Manor was filled with doctors thanks to Xavier. They came to the Urian pappa's aid.

"Dad, you are supposed to cast spells with that staff," Jesper said. "Did you think hitting a specter over the head with a bit of stick would hurt it?"

"Didn't think it had a knife," Pappa Bagwell said, wincing as Goolsby Lamb and several doctors fussed over him.

"What has happened?" Shanley asked.

"I will explain it all," Husk said. "Although, you may not believe me. Phaedra, we need to leave."

"Terminus is not defeated," Phaedra said. "And we can't have all these people as witness to what transpired here tonight."

"No more killing, Phaedra," Husk said. "We will say Thierry went mad and then had a heart attack."

The Silver Swann collected her monkey and walked toward Husk and Shanley with Phaedra. "How did you know?" The Silver Swann asked.

"We found the body of Glorious Thierry. Alive but unconscious," Husk said. "And we knew he could not be two places at once."

"Terminus mimics," Phaedra said. "He can't possess a person who he does not mimic for a long while."

"Then we must end the life of the one he mimics. He is very close to having all the souls he needs to restore his full power," The Silver Swann said. "Take me to the body of Thierry, Husk. Shanley, help the Bagwells."

"My mother is going to be so confused," Shanley said.

"I have cast a spell to remedy the confusion. Husk is right, a simple heart attack. After all, Glorious Aldridge Thierry is dead," The Silver Swann said. "We will use the usual means to cover up Sidon's wounds. We will simply lie. You may find you have forgotten the events of this night in the morning, Shanley."

"I had such a good spell worked out," Phaedra said, giving The Silver Swann a pouting look.

"Let it be, Phaedra," The Silver Swann said. "Your magic is a bit too chaotic. Some still remember Sile Pyn. And memory spells are treacherous. Best to keep things simple."

And More Spytes

The Rooke surveyed the crowd as he removed his robes. So many had followed him, some from as far back as The Cross-Eyed Hag. He saw Freddie from the tin-sleeved thieves, Rat and Petra, black-ribboned despicables, and cautious imperials all mulling over the tales and the magic. Most of them did not have sleeves that would have allowed them on The Barnacle Rose and yet here they were.

Aldo and Kentigern stepped forward, giving him a thumbs up as they weaved in and out of the people gathered in the old tavern. The stink of fish had given way to an aroma of sea breeze and clean wind.

"There's a ferry to the main island," Aldo said. "We can leave in the morning."

"And SIN is back up," Kentigern said. "We will have to redouble our protections."

"What is the imperial narrative about Aroghotto City's fate?" The Rooke asked.

"They are blaming everyone and everything but the dragon," Freddie said. "No one saw your dragon. They say The Fistian Seat left before the attack, and so they seek him."

"Did you find your brother?" The Rooke asked.

"No, but I got a message. He is in Wyvern's Rest near The Dagger. He tells me Malcombe the Fifth is to be crowned. A child emperor. That could never go wrong."

"There's another Malcombe?"

"There's always another Malcombe, mate," Freddie said. "This happens to be the grandson of Malcombe IV. Lad was born Neville Tombs. Rest of the family died in Aroghotto City."

"How old?" Aldo asked.

"Fourteen. But don't look so scared, Aldo. Some elite baroness has been given the duty of looking out for him until he is of age. One we've all heard of in the celebrated circles of Aerda. Baroness Teriss Amber."

"Win some, lose some," Kentigern said as Aldo cursed under his breath. "Thought the dragon might have saved us some trouble. Damn."

"Let it be. We can only fight what is in front of us," The Rooke said. "Thank you, Freddie. You've been such a good friend to me and my friends."

Thiago, Anwyn, and Kostas were teaching a new bunch the game of Idylls & Grimoires while Zac and Rintyre looked on, both looking weary beyond words.

Rintyre sighed. "Let's get my nephew," she said, sending Zac over to get the boy from the booth where he was sleeping.

"What? Where did he go?" Zac said as he pulled a blanket up off the booth where the boy had been and found a bunch of rubbish masking the boy's absence. "He's escaped. Clever kid."

"Crap. With all of us here, how did he get away?" Rintyre said, pulling aside all the discarded clothing and blankets from the bench to make sure there was no child there. "We had him."

"It's all right," Rat said. "We find boy. We bring him back."

"No," Aldo said. "He is still not fully a boy, Rin. He's a Spyte. He's a killer. We will have him retrieved. But we will need specialists for this task."

"I don't know who these specialists are," Zac said. "But I'm going to be one of them. Rin, we will get your nephew. For you. For your sister and Bryter. And we'll get him clean."

"There have not been any such specialists since before The Evanescence," Kentigern said. "Erelahian knights no longer exist, my friend. We will have to use what we have to retrieve the child. But I agree with The Rooke, we can only fight what is in front of us. The boy is gone, and we have little time left."

"Well, how far can he have gone?" Rintyre said, looking at Aldo with disbelief. "He's four. Let's go look for him before we give him up."

They stepped outside into the evening sea breeze. The little docks were filled with old-style, wooden warehouses, windowless with large doors, one after the other. A stench carried from the dock.

"This sturgeon really does stink," Tavares Flaco said, intercepting the group. "And that Freddie fellow. Pretty sure he's a spy of some kind. He knows exactly who I am. Told me he has a signed shirt from my grassball days. No one like him would have gotten a shirt. He's not who he says he is."

"Oh, no. Not at all," The Rooke said, smiling like a cat who got in the cream. "He's The Fistian Seat. He has the mark on his right palm. And that gem under his shirt. It hides a slumbering dragon. Kostas recognized it, clever puzzler that he is. I think he knows that I know. Best no one else find out."

Tavares smiled full on, almost a look of delight. "Oh, the empires won't like that. Not one bit. Sly devil. Gerrard Frederic Al' Dhar."

"Rooke, why did you not tell us?" Kentigern asked. "That's big information."

"He is trying not to be discovered," The Rooke said. "And I wanted him to stay with us."

"Who is this brother he is looking for?" Aldo asked. "If that is Gerrard Al' Dhar, his brother is Konstantin Al' Dhar, the rightful Fistian Seat who was assassinated almost twelve years ago."

"Maybe he survived. They never found his body," The Rooke said. "No matter. The fire dragon has made The Fist an enemy of the world. We have some work to do. Tavares, will you gather the others and make sure everyone is safe. And let's keep an eye out for Rintyre's nephew. In case he tries to murder us again."

"Anything you say, boss," Tavares said as he started to turn away.

A dark-skinned child who appeared to be around ten years of age ran toward them from the dock. The Rooke recognized him as a Spyte as the aroma of sweet piss enveloped the party. The child laughed. He leapt like cat and raised a black knife.

Tavares moved with an unworldly speed, testament to his years as a professional athlete, and caught the child in mid-air a deathly inch from The Rooke's throat as Aldo snatched the poisoned knife from the child's hand causing the three men and boy to tumble to the ground together.

"He's slippery, this one," Kentigern said. "Hurry, get us inside. I'll get Joel and Tee."

Rat intervened, helping to secure the inhumanely strong Spyte, as Rintyre pulled open a warehouse door.

"How many of these murderous brats are there?" Zac asked.

"We are legion. You leave us be," the child said, its voice many voices all fighting to be heard.

The warehouse they found was filled to the top with heavy crates, reaching to the ceiling. Apart from the merchandise, it was empty, giving The Rooke and his party room to maneuver.

Joel pulled from his pocket his trinket. A broken onyx tower. The Rooke worried. The young man did not have the power of Sidon Bagwell or Dagan Leesh. He only knew the motions. The Rooke prayed the man had better faith than he.

"Do not ask its name," The Rooke said. "You want to bind it to a name of love."

"One that offends the demon," Tee said. "That will make it powerless, send it back to Hell, and restore an innocent child to the world."

Joel Broomes accepted the instruction. Tavares Flaco stepped up, knelt down to look the boy in the eyes and whispered. The Rooke heard.

"You might have been mine."

This sent the child into a rage. His face melted into a demonic visage as it attacked. It flung Rat and several of his party against a wall. It hissed at them.

"You belong to Hell," it hissed at Rat, trying to get at the emaciated young man. "You should serve me. Why would you fight me?"

"We don't like you," Rat said, standing back on his feet, shaking his head and somehow unbreaking his neck. The Rooke froze in horror. The Rat was not a living young man. He was a ghoul, no mistaking it. And yet, he had no odor of death, nor the mindless appetite for murder as all such creatures in his tales did.

The demonic child rushed at Rat, Tavares tackling him once more. It grabbed Tavares around the neck, began choking him. "Stab him," Aldo said. "Zac, stab him with your sword."

"I am not stabbing a kid," Zac said. "He'll die and then we can't save him."

Taki Toura took the sword from Zac in a blink and pushed it into the raving demon. It collapsed into a weeping child. "Your sword only hurt demon. Not child," Taki said. "It is one of Pharoah Sol's Judgement swords. How do you ever win games?"

"Taki, I reckon you would make a fair puzzler," Kostas said.

"A dangerous one," Anwyn said. "Can we have our box back now?"

Taki gave Zac his sword back, and pulled the puzzle box out of his pack and handed it back to Anwyn. "I should not be able to take it so easy. You are not careful enough."

"We should go," Aldo said.

"You should make sure demon stay gone," Taki said. "He will go now if you do ritual."

Joel began the ritual with a prayer in Asciendien. He spoke it perfectly, calling that great love the Urians went on and on about. He knelt.

"I need a name for him," Joel said as the child struggled and wept, clutching his head.

"Isaiah Rinaldo," Tavares said. "It is the name I would have given my son had Bittore and I not been convinced to sacrifice our child. We were going to call him Izzy. He would have been about this age had we not…"

"Murderer," the beast inside the child re-emerged, and hissed at Tavares. "You murdered your child. You did not love him."

"You are my son, and you are not dead," Tavares said. "You are loved, Isaiah. You are not a vessel for this demon."

The demonic presence disappeared without preamble, leaving a whimpering boy. His brown skin cleared, soft and radiant. His eyes filled with true tears. Joel stepped back.

Tavares Flaco picked him up and carried him away, hugging him as tears of joy and despair wet the bald man's cheeks.

"The demon will come back. This is a trick. It not see a way to win and so is hiding," Rat said to The Rooke. "You should bind that child."

"We will be cautious, Rat," The Rooke said. "Should we bind you?"

"No. I am a rat who is no longer fit for Hell."

Tavern XXI:

The Silver Swan Café

Children are wishes made by immortals.

The Idylls of Alleysiande, Vol II Metatron's Triumph,
author unknown (translated by Hazel Kyran)

Tiponi Harbor

The Rooke did not recognize anything as the ferry stopped in the opulent station of Tiponi Harbor. No swamp remained. Not as far as he could see. He lost his bearings as the group trailed into the mainland. The island seemed so much larger. And perhaps this was so as the last time The Rooke had seen Ambriland centuries ago, the volcano had been vomiting miles of magma, expanding the island toward the East.

He meandered down a well-manicured path of stone, under a canopy of flowers with many signs, directing tourists to various sights of interest, resorts, shops, and restaurants, the beach. Dark, ash-filled drops of rain polluted what would have been a beautiful garden path in the sun.

The Rooke saw the sign and pulled Aldo to have a look. The Silver Swan Cafe. He wondered if the imperials remembered how this name came to be.

"Seems a popular haunt," Aldo said. "We can grab a bit of something to eat there."

"There's a resort called the Malachian Monkey on the lake," Kentigern said. "I will see about getting us rooms there."

Tavares scratched his growing beard. "I wish Ghita had changed my face a bit more before she…" he said. "It's too stinking hot to wear a beard."

"We can't have you recognized," Aldo said. "Don't worry too much."

"We have to get my nephew back…" Rintyre said. "If this kid was around, I bet my nephew sent him. Or the thing, my foul stepmother, that controls the demon in him."

"We will find Jude," Kentigern said.

"His name is Gabriel," Rintyre said. "Do not call him that name. My nephew is Gabriel."

"We will help you," Rat said. "Phaedra will help. Gabriel is like a rat. He can choose to be good. He must convince the demon to leave."

"It is not so simple as that. He will need help, and Rin helped him," Joel said. "Your nephew threw off the demon, at least for a moment. He has a real chance."

"The demon did not stay gone. Gabriel will need rescuing in more ways than one," The Rooke said. "The child will need to go before The Relic before he can be returned to Carling and Bryter."

"Not sure that will do any good," Zac Grimm said. "They totally missed Cymbre."

"I am not sure they did," The Rooke said. "After all, a broken Spyte was on my list."

"Believe me, Rooke. She wasn't broken. She knew just what she was about," Zac said. "You heard the grandmaster. Joel, here, was the broken Spyte."

Kentigern raised a bushy eyebrow. "He might be on to something there," Kentigern said.

"It's hot and this misty rain does not help," Kostas said, yanking at his shirt. "I'm sweating like a pig."

"Well, if one is a pig," Anwyn said, giving him a playful nudge.

"Father, did you really grow up here? It must have been miserable," Thiago said, frowning.

"It wasn't like this," The Rooke said. "This was all a swamp. When I was your age, I thought it the most wondrous place in the world. But yes, it was hot. And magical. And horrifying. And wonderful. Let us get out of the heat."

Castle Mal Tomb

The ancient forest refused to retreat from the modern world. Phaedra felt the speed of the transport as it sped through the dark trees at a steady incline toward Aerda's oldest castle. She felt the dark magic of it, faint, bristling, expanding as the dragons stirred, releasing magic back into the world in heavy waves that fed the sorceress.

She remembered her previous body's death in the dungeons of Castle Mal Tomb when she defeated Emperor Malcombe II after The Evanescence. That should have been the end of Malfus, The Icari that gave Malcombe his power.

The demon had attached itself to the bloodline, passing to heir after heir through the centuries while Phaedra slept. Only one of that cursed line had survived the attack on Aroghotto City. And the youngster happened to be in the castle where Phaedra had fallen, leaving her grimoire tucked away in its vast library. This solved a lot of problems. Two birds. One stone and all that.

She prayed Malfus had not taken the remaining Absyrtus heir. She did not know if she had power to defeat him. She needed more time to marry her newly acquired flesh to her magic. She hoped that her cottage in Dusk Forest remained after so many centuries. From what she had gleaned, no one dared venture into the forest which gave her much hope.

The transport stopped abruptly where the trees gave way to a village beneath the mammoth castle, and the road turned from paved black to cobblestones. The driver turned around and spoke Chazir to her. She nodded. He would not go any further. He rambled on about how the village is cursed. The castle is forbidden. She would be in danger if she was lying about having business there. People don't go there anymore. And she should not either.

"I will be fine," Phaedra said, thanking him for his trouble, sending credits to his sleeve. She pulled her bag out and stepped away as the black, oval transport turned on its track and sped away.

She released the rats from the bag. They scurried away with their orders. Find a way into the castle where she would not be seen.

A neat and well-kept cobble path traveled through the forgotten village of Tombs, Old Chazir. It was a place of ghosts.

Not a living soul inhabited the shingled, white-washed cottages and shops. The fountain at its center sprouted clean water, and someone had planted roses around it. This place had been forgotten by the world and perfectly preserved.

In fact, it still appeared as it had the last time Phaedra visited. She might have entered the little bookshop to find the funny, little woman in her velvet suit fussing over a binding of a new edition. The bakeshop might have had fresh bread, patrons lining the window for the morning meal.

Phaedra had so many questions. She could not fathom how her final spell had evaporated the people of the village and caused the harrowing stories about The Dusk Forest that surrounded it. She wondered what brought the enigmatic Lord Tombs back and drove the old Absyrtus family away.

The castle had no sign of having been touched by the new technology of this world. It looked a picture out of one of those horror stories that old pirate, Fang Bracken, used to love scaring his pirate crew with a few centuries back. The castle had the history to go with it, one of both horror and triumph. Once upon a time, a good ruler brought a temporary light to this place. She felt both light and horror competing against one another as she approached the massive structure on the hill.

Emperor Alexan Sacripant tried to free the people of Aerda, back when she first met Husk Grayvesone, when she carried the body of Sile Pyn through a beautiful and stormy life. That old feeling of despair threatened her as she trudged across the mammoth bridge from the village into the castle, a hundred or more meters above the roaring river below.

The rats fanned out, delighted at finding food and dark places to roam. She rang the bell at the front door, not knowing what possessed her to do that. A white-haired man that reminded her sharply of Gerloch Nett answered the door, looked her over.

"Do you speak Acarian?"

"I do," Phaedra said, trying to think of a story to explain why she had come.

"Are you the nanny?" the man asked, his voice on the edge

of panic. "When the agency said they were not sure they could have anyone…oh, thank you for coming. The baroness is having a fit. She fired the last nanny the moment she arrived. That girl they sent only spoke Chazir. And her son does not."

"Sure, I am your nanny," Phaedra said, once more thinking that something was pulling at the cosmic strings in the universe. "However, I did not get details…"

"Baroness Amber Teriss is to look after Lord Tombs until he is old enough to be emperor…"

"I am to be nanny to Lord Tombs?"

"Only a bit. He will be in school or under the tutelage of the baroness. It's her son, Jude. He's four. And he's not a very nice child I am afraid," the man said, leading her up a marble staircase and down a narrow hall, through many passages until they came to a narrow back stair. He spoke at a breathless pace. "I can hardly blame the child. Seems his famous father was not good to him. And it's been an excruciating few months. For him. For the world."

"Yes, excruciating," Phaedra said. She watched a black rat ghost them, wishing she could make the things stop following. She hoped the man would not see them before she had a chance to gather them into her bag. She did not imagine rats were welcome in places like this.

The opulence of the castle had not changed over the centuries. The dark purples and blacks favored by Malcombe II had been exchanged for whites and blues. The gold filigree remained, lining nearly every sconce, every wall, every bit and bobble, every door. The castle shouted its wealth over the whispers of its secrets. Such was the way of castles.

"This is your room. I am sorry, I did not get your name," the man said. "The courier line is down. We are not on SIN, never will be. I can't get hold of your agency. But do not fear, I will make sure everything is in order. I see they removed your sleeve. That is good. We are not allowed sleeves here, but we are paid. Do not fear. It's hard for some to accept that you can live well without a sleeve."

"I am Mika, and I am aware that sleeves are unnecessary to life," Phaedra offered. "Should I meet these two boys this afternoon?"

"I am the valet. Hew Loren. Call me Mr. Loren," he said, giving a little bow. Phaedra wondered, for a moment, if she had flown back in time. This little man seemed a relic of ages well-past, an age that was dying when she first arrived in Aerda.

"Pleased to make your acquaintance, Mr. Loren."

"I have to return to my duties. I will let the baroness know you are here. The nursery is three doors down. The suite across belongs to our Lord Tombs. That is Emperor Neville....oh, I can't get used to it. Emperor Malcombe V he will be. Naturally. If you get lost, there are bells in most rooms. Ring it and I will find you."

Apart from a chill that came from both within and without, Phaedra felt she had stumbled on a brilliant bit of luck. She knew this castle. She could simply walk into the library, grab her grimoire, and disappear.

When she swung open the doors of the grand library, her elation subdued. The Tombs library was one of the largest in all of Aerda. And she could not remember exactly where she had stashed the little book. The ceiling reached high in a dome and the room could have fit most of the surrounding village. Instead of cottages and shops and fountains, the library was appointed in dark wood shelves running from floor to ceiling, floor after floor reached by spiraling metal stairs, all filled with books.

Voices distracted her as she entered to find a woman with two children, a teenager Phaedra could only assume was Neville Tombs, the heir apparent to the Chaziri Empire, and a beautiful, small child that looked Husk Grayvesone in miniature. He even had the eyes of lovely, emerald, green. Although not jeweled.

Phaedra recognized the woman. The magic she used to hide her decay did not fool the sorceress. Hester Mammon, one of the foul witches of Ambriland. The original gutter baroness and founder of The Spytes.

Phaedra hissed under her breath and prepared her deception.

She then felt a tremble of fury. The little boy, the descendent of Husk Grayvesone, would no doubt, be a Spyte. She would not have it. She would free this boy. She must use restraint. She could hear Husk Grayvesone across the centuries begging her to think before acting.

"Hello, are you the nanny the valet spoke of?" she asked.

"I am Mika," Phaedra lied. "I am told you needed a nanny for your son and Lord Tombs?"

"Yes. You have arrived just in time. I must go to an emergency meeting in Torr. I am to be the acting empress until Lord Tombs is of age. It is too dangerous for me to take these young boys," she said. "Do not worry, however, Mika, you will be safe here. Although isolated. But only for a short time. If you need anything, ask Mr. Loren."

She scarcely glanced at Phaedra as she swept from the library. The two boys both looked up at her. Neville Tombs was small for his age. He looked as if he might be related to the Roses, his curly hair, small nose, dark eyes beneath gold-rimmed spectacles. He was fair, and a bit meek without any of the harsh, sharp features of the Absyrtus line.

"I don't want to be emperor," he said as soon as the baroness was gone. "She says I have to drink this foul potion to get bigger. And I am to have tutors and will not be allowed to go back to school. I was never supposed to be emperor. My mother was disowned when she married my father."

"Don't drink the potion," Phaedra said. "You are fine as you are. And I think the time of emperors might be done. What about you, Jude?"

"I don't want to be emperor either," Jude said. "I am bored. And I am not allowed to kill you."

"We will find you something else for you to do then," Phaedra said. "Did you kill the last nanny?"

"No. I didn't kill anyone. Mr. Piss does all the killing," Jude said. "He's mean."

"He's pretend," Neville said. "Jude is an odd boy. Most four-year-old kids don't have homicidal, imaginary friends."

"Mr. Piss is a terrible pretend friend," Phaedra said. "Let's get you a better one. Have you thought about a pet? Maybe a rat or ten?"

"I don't like rats," Jude said. "I want a dragon."

"A dragon used to live below this castle," Neville said, not sounding at all like anyone who shared blood with any of the vile Absyrtus line. "There are stories about it. A silver dragon that could grant wishes. Only if you made the wrong wish, it ate you."

"Would it be wrong to wish Mr. Piss would go away forever?" Jude asked.

"I can tell you a story of a dragon if you like," Phaedra said, an idea coming to her. "This is a great library. There is a book called *The Oracle and the Monkey*. Do you think there is a copy here?"

"Probably," Neville said. "Only there are sixty-eight thousand, five hundred and ninety-three books in this library. The downstairs has another ten thousand. Children's books might be in the nursery. We could look there. But I have better idea."

Phaedra bristled. She wanted to get her grimoire and leave, and she had hidden it next to a copy of the children's book. She had been sure it had been in this library, and not in the one below. She must find it, and then there was the matter of these demon sought boys.

She liked Lord Tombs. He oozed charisma and intelligence and kindness. No sign of Malfus at all. In fact, the castle felt clean of the vileness she remembered when she had fought Malcombe II. More so after the baroness departed.

"What is this better idea, Lord Tombs?" Phaedra asked.

"Let's play secrets. Nanny Mika, it will help us all get to be friends, build trust, get to know one another. After all, the baroness has trapped us here together," the teen said, pacing back and forth as if it helped him think. "And call me Neville. I am not a lord or an emperor. I want to remain Neville Tombs."

"How is telling secrets a game?" Phaedra asked.

"We tell each other a secret about ourselves. Nothing dirty or anything. Something brilliant. Everyone has secrets," Neville said.

"Some secrets might be dangerous, young man."

"Worse than a four-year-old with a homicidal made-up friend?"

"You go first. What is your secret?"

Neville pulled a smooth stone from his pocket, a rooke's token.

"I got this in Aroghotto when a rooke traveled there when Nicholai Sacripant was emperor. You see, few realize, but the Sacripants are descendants of the Tombs. He was my cousin. It was a shame that my grandfather had him murdered. And that poor rooke got in the way. But I got this token at a place I was never supposed to be."

"I have one of those," Jude said, digging a gray stone out of his pocket. "I got it from a man in the island place. I told mommy I stole it. She likes it when I steal. I lie a lot."

"That's a big secret, Neville," Phaedra said, digesting Lord Tomb's revelation. It might be Malfus had not been able to get hold of this boy.

"I have a better secret than Neville," Jude said.

The three of them took seats on the floor despite chairs and desks being available that spanned the full length of the library. Neville and Jude placed their matching tokens on the floor before Phaedra.

"Both of you have secret tokens. The game is a draw," Phaedra said.

"No, that's not a secret. I have a token. That is all. I have a way better secret," Jude said.

"Let's have it then," Neville said.

"My name is Gabriel," Jude said. "And Baroness Amber is not my mother."

"A secret identity is great," Neville said, clearly believing Jude had made up his secret. Phaedra knew he had not. The little Grayvesone's Ambrien blood was shining through.

However, the demon was trying to regain control. Her rats

were keeping Mr. Piss distracted as he kept having to dislodge himself from rodent after rodent as they scurried between and under shelves, unobserved by the two boys. Phaedra wanted to laugh out loud.

"That is a fine secret, and we won't tell anyone, will we?" Phaedra said.

"Silent as the grave. Your turn, Nanny Mika," Neville said, a happy smile across the boy's face. He pushed up on his gold-rimmed spectacles. Phaedra liked him very much, resolving she would never allow Malfus to have him. Nor would she let Mr. Piss touch the Grayvesone boy again.

"I am not your nanny. I am Phaedra."

A beat. Neville laughed. "More secret identities," he said, clapping his hands. "But not very good that one. You're not a dragon. Tell us a real secret. You must have one, Nanny Mika."

"I am not a dragon. I am the sorceress, Phaedra. I can prove it. Give me your tokens, and we will hear what The Rooke's tale says, and then you can decide if you believe me."

The Tale of A Vengeful Specter

Husk admired the little window garden in the quarters he would take in his new position as house master of Shankly Hall. Phaedra bounced up and down on the bed as if to test the mattress.

Professor Estarte cleared his throat. "There will be fifty boys living here. First years so you will be starting out clean as I did. Ten of those are upper classmen to assist you, each in charge of four boys."

"I remember. I was one of those upper classmen," Husk said.

"I am sorry to put you out so early, but I am moving country to teach in Bal Turien. I will not have time to get you settled at the appropriate time. I am afraid the quarters are quite modest," Professor Estarte said. "And it will be difficult on you and your girl."

"Oh no, Professor," Husk said. "Phaedra and I are only friends."

"I have a bit of his soul," Phaedra said. "I didn't mean to take it, but we are bound. I live in the cottage with Daedalus and Reginald."

"Oh? You're making a joke?" Professor Estarte said. "I am afraid my Acarian after all these years is still not…"

"Nobody's Acarian is up for her sense of humor," Husk said, casting a glare at the girl.

"What joke?" Phaedra looked confused. "I am living in the cottage that you are leaving to live here with children. You are to protect these children, yes, Husk?"

"Yes, he will do well. The first-year students are lovely," Professor Estarte said. "The last year is heartbreaking. You will see. And house master is a prestigious position for a young professor."

"Not sure it helps my case for Dalmeade," Husk said.

"Most are not admitted to Dalmeade until they are older than me. Eight total years teaching, seven as a house master, and looking after young minds will put you in good stead with Dalmeade," Professor Estarte said. "And I have sent a letter of recommendation asking for an introduction and to allow you to begin the application process. It is a long and vigorous one that few pass."

"Would you not want to stay and do another seven years, Professor Estiarte?" Phaedra asked.

"I would if I were not getting married to a Turien girl. Being a house master is difficult with a family. You can only see them at week breaks and between terms although it is done. Is the rumor true that Siobhan Rose is to be engaged to River Swann?"

"It is a rumor that has not yet festered into fact. River is being pressured into it by his grandmother," Husk said. "Do not say anything, if you please, professor. My patron would be furious if she found out I said that."

"I am excited about it. River Swann and Siobhan Rose make a lovely couple. The wedding will give the islands something to celebrate should it come to pass. River and Siobhan will be better for Ambriland than King Charon. It is a bitter pill that Queen Sapphire's son is such a poor king."

"What is this wedding?" Phaedra asked.

"Phaedra, you know what a wedding is," Husk said. "Acarian is not her first language. She is from Daggera."

"Acarian is difficult to learn from Daggera," the professor said, picking up a box. "It was difficult enough from my native tongue of Esprite. You are doing well, young lady. I will bring you dinner when I come to get the last of my things. Go ahead and get settled. I will leave you my key this evening."

"What is meant by Esprite?" Phaedra asked, as Professor Estiarte left with a large box of nick knacks.

"It is the native language of Ambriland in actual fact," Husk said. "And Marlinea and several other lands in Aerda. I grew up bi-lingual as do most of the natives. Acarian, however, is considered a noble tongue and so most speak it."

"Interesting," Phaedra said.

"You know all these things, Phaedra," Husk said. "Don't you?"

"I forget things as I learn new things," she said, waving her hand to dismiss him. "This is not my world."

"Phaedra, stop touching everything. Help me unpack."

Phaedra fidgeted about the room, ignoring Husk. She picked up every book, touching everything Husk laid out which was not at all the help he wished her to give him.

"Why must you do this job?" Phaedra asked. "This room is too small. Your patron is wealthy, no?"

"I need to make my own way. There is a price when someone else pays for you," Husk said. "The Silver Swann has done more than enough to secure my future."

"You spend a lot of time worrying about this Dalmeade archivist position you covet. Stop agonizing over your future."

"I share your nightmares, Phaedra. You worry a lot about being reclaimed by The Icari and trapped in their hell."

"Of course, I do. Hell is a poor way to spend eternity. I wish a better ever after."

The little black cat, Sariel, followed Husk about his room which was now all in boxes as thunder filled the late afternoon. The last of the rainy season was at full force in Ambriland. Husk welcomed the breeze that interrupted the stifling heat of the islands.

"Damn, Professor Estarte will have to brave the rain to bring us our supper," Husk said. The cat purred. Phaedra's eyes flickered annoyance. She was nervous as a cat that was not called Sariel. Thunder rolled and the splatter of rain rose. "Is your roof at the cottage still leaking, Phaedra?"

"I repaired it," she said, holding up the bizarre journal that they had taken from Madame Darke's cottage. "And made it more to my liking."

Husk worried. The girl's magic was real and a bit unpredictable. "Should I even ask?" Husk said.

"What? It is vaulted and allows for lovely breezes from the sea. Reginald and Daedalus were well-pleased. I am liking living in that cottage. It seems a dream after being trapped in Pandemonium."

Sariel jumped on the bed and fixed his gaze on Phaedra. The little black feline was not particularly cat-like from what Husk knew of the creatures, calm and vigilant, never jumping at shadows like Captain Delilah Sage's ship cat, an overgrown orange beast called 'Terror'. Or constantly begging for cuddles like Daedalus and Reginald's cat, Sophie.

Husk removed Sariel from the corner of his bed. There was barely room for him. Husk began unpacking his own boxes, while Phaedra shadowed him. She was not being much use in helping him settle into his new quarters. She was curious, asking about every book, every article of clothing, all the things that belonged to Husk.

"Phaedra, stop gawking at my under garments," Husk said. "I suppose you'll want to go back to the cottage?"

"My magic isn't that strong," Phaedra said. "I can't stop this storm. I'll stay here with you. I want a nap. I will sleep on the floor so I will not tempt you."

"You do not tempt me, Phaedra. You terrify me. It's fine. The bed is big enough but don't set me on fire again. Try and keep your dreams to yourself."

"I didn't wish to set you on fire," Phaedra said. "Seems the Queen of Hell has placed a fire curse on me."

"What?"

"A fire curse. It's so that I cannot enjoy the pleasures of the flesh. If anyone tries to touch me in a lustful way or vice versa, they catch fire no matter the flesh I claim. Useful at keeping rapists away or chasing off a specter. Cruel should love come my way. I believe I was in love once. Before I was murdered."

"I was not lusting after you."

"You were having a lustful dream."

"I'll sleep on the floor."

The angry storm obscured the last light of the day while the rumble of thunder woke Husk from troubled dreams. Professor Estiarte had not returned, and he and Phaedra had fallen asleep.

Phaedra could not seem to stay out of his head even in her fleshy form. She felt like a real girl, smelled wonderful although he kept carefully to his side of the bed after being unable to find comfort on his hard-wood floor. He did not wish to be burned again.

The nightmares in which he traveled with Phaedra kept all lust at bay and terrified him to the soul. How cold and alien Phaedra's world appeared, all steel, glass, concrete, hordes of people living on top of one another in buildings that reached to the heavens, together and yet isolated.

Sometimes the millions of people that dwelt within this city became the rats that plagued Phaedra. In that cold world, she was a fair woman, fierce and determined, not a demon at all, but the rats chased after her.

In the nightmare, Phaedra turned on the rats which turned

into the people who transformed into hideous wraiths. All stopped in their tracks and started screaming as if in terrible pain. Husk could make no sense of it.

He sat up as a flash of lightening illuminated his room. Sariel hissed and vaulted from the bed to hide under it as wind and rain pounded the little window of Husk's slight dorm room. A scream from his nightmare echoed in his head and continued. No, this was no longer a dream.

"I am being hunted. It seems Terminus did not appreciate us stealing his host," Phaedra said, springing from the bed. "Foul echo horrors, so many. The demon that I saved you from has gathered them to come for us – your blood, my soul."

The cat stalked from under the bed, mewing and hissing all at once.

Terminus has enlisted the forces of Hell to capture an escaped soul. Hide, human, hide. Danger. Danger.

This all came out in Sariel's hissing as the cat leapt at the door. Husk trembled slightly. He was no fighter. He searched his room for a weapon. Nothing.

He grabbed his pencils and Phaedra's tattered journal he had taken from Madame Darke. He opened it and wrote Asciendien glyphs on a blank page.

Maz aan num holla

"Great love calls us. Why did you write that?" Phaedra asked, jerking the book from him. "You're not supposed to write in my grimoire."

Husk stared at the letters as others began to appear on the page, an ancient script he could not decipher. Wind blew through his window, breaking the glass and tumbling over the plant that held his wards.

Outside, someone cried out. He opened his door. A severed rat's head rolled past him amid hissing. A snake slithered into a vent, a thin brown thing. Lightning struck again, and staff members began to appear in the hall as the dorm steward, Weldon, came running from below.

"The storm has driven a bunch of rats and snakes into the

dorm. Thousands of them," Weldon said. "And the biggest fucking snake I've ever seen is wrapped around the exit. I think it's a swamp rattler. And it has two heads."

"We can't get out of here," one young man said, a new hire for the house kitchens. "And I've been bitten."

"That snake wasn't poisonous," a young steward said, giving the young man a kerchief to wrap his bleeding hand. "It was one of them fruit snakes, but there are vipers among them."

"The snakes are going to get up here," another said. "Get Hector. He's not afraid of snakes. He'll know what to do."

"Professor Grayvesone, you're an Ambrien," Weldon said. "Aren't your lot supposed to be able to charm snakes?"

Husk looked at Weldon, an Acarian from Pig's Spit. The things people believed about "all" Ambriens never ceased to amaze Husk.

"I hate snakes," Husk said. "Go wake up Hector. And call the reptile disposal unit in Marinplaz."

"We tried that already, but the dorm's courier line has been damaged by the storm. I can't raise a signal on it at all. How did so many get in?"

"Maybe the storm and bad plumbing," Husk said, wanting an explanation that did not involve hunting demons wanting to destroy him and Phaedra.

"Don't you worry, miss," Weldon said, addressing Phaedra. "We won't let the snakes get close to you."

"I'm not afraid of snakes," Phaedra said, cocking her head and giving Weldon a dangerous look.

"Go, Weldon. Get Hector," Husk said, sending the young man off. "We have a lot of snakes in Ambriland and the grounds this school is built upon was once an immense swamp. It's probably just a strange reaction to the storm..."

"Or an ancient warlock is trying to kill you and cares not a whit about how many others die with you. My rats will not be able to distract so many snakes," Phaedra said, whispering in his ear.

Uncertain, Husk crept down the main stairwell, holding a

lamp before him. He side stepped a snake busy swallowing a rat, its jaws unhinged. He grimaced, holding his breath and fear as he inched forward. The stench of wet death and reptile assaulted his senses.

Sconces flickered on the walls, and the narrow windows cast shadows of tree branches swaying in the wind, making claws of them with each flash of lightning. The few dorm staff left for the summer followed behind him, breathless and excited, a couple armed with sacks Hector had arranged to stuff the snakes into. Fabulous plan.

How little Husk's fellows understood danger and yet it drew them like moths to a flame. The giant swamp rattler, wrapped around the front door of the dorm, was visible from the top of the stairs. It was massive and two-headed, casting its shadow over the other serpents and the rats they hunted. Phaedra's rats were doing a decent job of distracting the snakes.

Half-eaten corpses of rats lined the narrow entry while others appeared in serpentine swollen bellies. Hundreds of them. The snakes clumped together full and listless, but not that swamp rattler. It could swallow a dozen of the rodents whole but seemed uninterested in them.

A double door with ornate handles, old and worn, served as the entry into Shankly Hall. Narrow glass panes decorated each side of the door, and when the storm lit the sky, Husk could see the two-headed snake clearly.

This is no natural serpent. I fear for you, mortal. Phaedra will bring you to harm, and I would not lose my guardian.

This came from the cat who slinked between his legs, hissing all the while at both rats and snakes. It was odd to see such a giant serpent with its body twisting in knots around the door handles as if to secure the double door so that no one could pass without disturbing it. Husk felt his breath caught in his throat. He wished for a weapon.

The bell chimed nine over the sound of rain and thunder. Another strike of lightning startled him as it revealed a shape outside the door, someone trying to come in. Husk rushed toward it without any thought.

He called out. "No, don't open it."

His voice did not carry over the storm. The swamp rattler unraveled in a flash as the door swung inward. The viper twisted around, revealing its full length as it uncoiled with both heads of dripping fangs faster than Husk could take a single breath.

The serpent struck the visitor in the face, leaving Professor Estiarte crumpled on the floor. Husk recognized his colleague in a second, but it was too late. Screaming echoed around Husk, running feet, all going up and away as the giant snake turned on him.

"No! You cannot have him!"

Phaedra's voice thundered, and the snake was thrown backwards, shattering glass as it hit the door. In a flash, Husk saw a masked figure rise where the snake had been. Terminus in his supernatural form.

Husk felt a surge of heat and wind radiate around him. Flames erupted from Phaedra's palms, gathering in intensity, and shot across the corridor. The snakes all burst into flames, even as several struck at his legs, one flinging itself to grab hold of his hand between thumb and forefinger. As he began to reel from the venom, he saw a ball of fire erupt from Phaedra's hand and burn the specter into nothingness.

All the while, hundreds of rats, some on fire, all squeaking and squealing descended on the body of the dead professor.

"Phaedra, it's dead. Stop this. You'll set the whole building alight."

"Terminus will devour this soul. I must stop it, or he will get more of an anchor here. I must try…"

Sariel chased the rats off the body of Professor Estiarte, but he would do no more. The black cat hissed and spit at the rodents as any cat might. Husk stood shaking, feeling he might faint there on the bottom of the step. He wobbled and the world spiraled away.

He envisioned the black cat turning into a shining, winged

man, holding a scythe, shielding him along with another winged figure bearing scales and a sword, along with Phaedra as both woman and dark apparition standing between a flaring light of warmth and comfort and an endless army of darkness.

Hold on, mortal. We will shield you until help comes.

This came from Sariel, not as cat, but as winged being holding a giant scythe, cutting a swath through rats and serpents. Husk wanted to turn and run, but he could not move. Blessed darkness took him, and he spun away from the chaos.

The Blame

The Rooke handed out another fifty or so tokens. He sat down between Aldo and Kentigern who had begun their own match of Idylls & Grimoires.

Zac Grimm stood up and pointed at Thiago.

"I won," Zac said.

"Not so fast," Thiago said. "You won the war. Not the game."

He put down the 'Maligned Beggar' card. He had kept it in his hand. Kostas laughed and Anwyn glared.

"That's not fair," Anwyn said. "I don't get how that one card overrides all the others played in the game."

"Did you even listen to the tales?" Thiago said, smiling. "You lot are supposed to be the game masters."

The Rooke wondered about that as well. Something was missing about this card. He took it from Thiago, feeling a subdued magic radiate from it.

"Well played," The Rooke said. "All of you."

"There is a slight problem," Zac said, lifting his now active sleeve. The livelies switched on to screens on the other half of the pub. "They are looking for us. An imperial librarian, an IPD agent, me…wow, we did not fool everyone."

Rintyre looked at her sleeve as it blinked to life. "We best hide. Won't take the wrong people long to realize we're who the empire are looking for."

"They can't think we are responsible for Aroghotto City," Joel Broomes said. "We were nowhere near the place."

"They think we are spies spreading lies," Zac Grimm said. "They said they will punish everyone responsible for 'bombing' Aroghotto City."

"Good luck with that," Thiago said. "Dragons can't be killed."

"And dragons don't exist by law and so will not be acknowledged. Not when there is an opportunity to blame enemies and kill them with the blessing of the people," Rintyre said. "Megdon and Chazir are blaming The Fist as they claim a witness left the the Unity Conference with the Fistian Seat before the attack. The Fist denies it. They blame rebels who are intent on bringing war to disrupt the empires."

"Then let us go find The Emerald Eye," The Rooke said. "Just blend in with the crowd."

"We have two more days," Kentigern said. "Let's grab beds at the docks. Maybe one of them is this Emerald Eye."

"And Tavares, keep an eye on that child. Do not let him slip away like Rintyre's nephew," Aldo said.

"I have him," Tavares said, his hand firmly gripped over the little boy's hand. "Let's get out of here."

Tavern XXII:

The Emerald Eye

In Ambriel's taverns of Salvation, all are welcome, their sins forgotten, the best part of their natures celebrated, their pain shared and lessened. One lost might here find a nourishing meal for an empty stomach, a soft bed for a weary body, companions for a lonely traveler, and a song for an empty soul.

The Idylls of Alleysiande, Vol 1 The Time Weaver, author unknown (translated by Hazel Kyran)

The First Salvation Tavern

The Rooke studied Taki's map of Ambriland again. He realized the location of the now defunct Swamp was not the same as that of The Silver Swann Café nor the Malachian Monkey Resort. Volcanic activity with the associated tsunamis had re-arranged the islands considerably over the last few centuries.

The Rooke reasoned they needed to go to The Emerald Eye where River Swann had first been given the 'Last King of Ambriland' card, and Thompson Sacripant had won the tournament. However, he could not make heads or tails of where that would be as Big Kyo had expanded with the constant eruption of the volcano that had once been at its center and was now at the far end of the island. Strange that. The Rooke could not imagine how a volcano might move.

"It should be right around here," The Rooke said, comparing Taki's map with the tourist book. "There's no inn at all where the Emerald Eye used to be, no sea cliff either and the inn bit was built into that cliff."

"Rooke, it should be obvious," Aldo said. "Wherever that first archaic is hidden will be shielded in magic."

"We have until tomorrow midnight," Kentigern said. "Let's go where the place used to be. Even if it's a piece of beach. We're out of time."

"What do we look for?" Kostas asked. "There are so many inns and bars and pubs all over the shore."

"We look for point on my map," Taki said. "It will be there."

"Look at all the inn and bar signs," The Rooke said. "The Emerald Eye's sign was a cat face with Ambrien, emerald, green eyes."

"Let's get hunting," Rintyre said, her eyes darting back and forth down the planked docks, along the rows of little inns and taverns along the shore. She looked transformed, dressed in a long, sleeveless, sheer, white island dress, sharply contrasting her pitch hair.

"Either we find it…" Thiago said.

"Or we all die," Anwyn said. "The fire dragon is watching us. I can feel it."

"Now, now, girl," Aldo said. "It's not the end. The dragons are calming and there is no telling what the cube will do. It will likely reset itself."

"It'll explode," Kostas said. "Like in the Second Cataclysm, and these islands will get blown away."

"If it comes to that," The Rooke said. "We will put the cube in front of that great black tower and flee."

"Black tower?" Thiago asked, looking down the docks across the bay. "You mean The Imperial Bay Resort?"

"Yes. That is where all the powerful visiting these islands are now," Kentigern said. "That is one of the most expensive resorts in all Aerda. It masks one of the Icarian black towers. One of them was destroyed in Aroghotto so there are only twelve left in the world. We stayed at one. The Glittering Raptor. Likely, the forces left will be rebuilding a thirteenth tower somewhere in the world, calling it a great hotel."

"Ta-She-Serra…I," The Rooke staggered. "I know what the first archaic is. Kentigern, you little wizard, you."

"What? What is it?"

"The twelve salvation taverns. They are the white towers that stand against the black towers. The Emerald Eye. That will be Ambriel's salvation tavern. We must find it. We must."

"The Emerald Eye is not a tower," Kostas said. "Is it?"

"All the salvation taverns are towers disguised as quaint little taverns, inns, and cafes," The Rooke said. "Let us find the first."

"How can we find something that is hidden in a place that no longer exists?" Anwyn asked.

"Have a little faith, girl," Tee Broomes said. "Let's go. Come along, Rooke. Where was it in the time of your tales?"

Memories as sharp as the heavy, wet heat struck at The Rooke. He sensed sand from centuries ago that had infiltrated his sandals between his toes, the feel of his white, linen shirt sticking to his back, the smell of the salt air lead him down the paved roads, black now with drawn lines for the steam carriages had once been sandstone and footed paths.

Tiponi Harbor was now a myriad of white stone, red-roofed and uniform buildings had once been simple sandstone roads lined with palm trees and tropical bushes until it came to planked docks filled with great sailing ships.

A single, planked pier at the very edge of the island graced the place where The Emerald Eye once existed. The modern pier was lined with windowed shops and people fishing seaside as it stretched out over the water, going nowhere. Umbrellas in bright pink, green, orange, and purple set next to long, white chairs peppered the artificially white sand beach blotched in black ash, a painted paradise over the real thing.

"Anything?" Tavares asked, holding little Isaiah by the hand. "A storm is coming. A bad one."

Thunder rumbled and tourists moved in a dance of folding chairs and beach blankets toward their inns and hotels, unbothered by falling ash but disturbed by coming rains. The once busy harbor which hosted mighty, sailed ships now had a small dock full of rented, recreational boats. Across the bay, under the shadow of the Imperial Bay Resort, massive, luxurious yachts pulled anchor as the promised storm inched toward the islands.

"Look, Zac and Rintyre have found something," Anwyn said. "Down the pier."

Rintyre trotted toward them, almost at a run, pointing back at Zac Grimm. "Come, we've found something. Can't be a coincidence," Rintyre said.

The group followed Rintyre down the pier. Zac Grimm sauntered toward them, pointing behind him at a simple fisherman's hut with a sign of a small cat, painted black with green eyes, pawing at fish leaping from blue waters. The lettering proclaimed it to be 'The Mandoras Bait and Tackle Shop", stating it had bait and hooks available for sale.

"Mandoras," The Rooke said. "Is this all that is left of The Emerald Eye?"

"This is the right place on the map," Taki said, holding up his map. "See. It is same place as the old inn."

"There's more. Here, at the side of the shop," Zac said, leading them to side of the ramshackle, wooden hut built at the far end of the pier.

The old wooden door into the shop was scratched and aged. Zac Grimm pointed out the carved rectangle in the door which matched the card Anwyn and Kostas had pulled out of Ambriel's cube.

"Kostas, Anwyn," The Rooke said. "Put the card from the cube here."

"Oh, I see," Anwyn said.

"See what?" Kostas asked, fishing the card out of his pocket, handing it to Anwyn.

The card fit exactly into the carving under the wrought-iron handle.

Nothing happened. Apart from the little Spyte child starting to growl and trying to pull away from Tavares. The tall man wrapped his arms around the boy and picked him up so he could not flee.

"It's all right, Izzy," Tavares said. "The storm scares him."

The company stood there for a moment, waiting. Rain began to fall in single, heavy drops. Lighting struck, sending sparks off the top of a metal-tipped lifeguard stand on the beach. The Rooke took a deep breath. Kostas gave the company an exasperated look.

"What's wrong with you all?" Kostas said. "Open the door."

Before The Rooke could react, his youngest son sprang forward, and the door flew open. There was no bait shop. The Emerald Eye appeared in full glory as they flocked in.

The polished pink, marble floors gleaned under colorful rugs, a high ceiling, a cool breeze bringing instant comfort, bright lights hanging from sheer, rounded lanterns of the ceiling, a wide reception area with passages into the immense tavern and one through to the rooms of the famous inn. The bamboo, hand-carved columns were rounded in the old style popular on the pirate islands, plants kept the place lively, and tall windows looked over the azure Ambrien Sea as lightening once more lit up the sky.

"Oh good," one of the employees of the inn said. "We need an entertainment. It's a big night tonight. Ah, it's you, isn't it?"

The Rooke tried to speak but he could not. He had not been wearing his robes nor had he summoned them. Yet, he saw them appear on his back as he stepped through the door. He looked at the person addressing him. A person from his past stood there, someone he knew to be dead. The Rooke opened his mouth to speak, and then saw. A resemblance to an old friend. Nothing more.

"You're The Rooke," the young man said. "Took you long enough. We've been waiting for you for centuries. Come, come."

The Rebel

*T*he rebel walked out of the Imperial Bay Resort that overlooked the beautiful azure waters of the Ambrien Sea to the northwest. He turned toward the tower behind him and saw black ash and orange flame rising behind it as the volcano raged. He made a gesture, a command, and the volcano went quiet, and a wind blew to clear the ash from the air.

"Sleep. Dream." He whispered. He took a deep breath, feeling whole apart from his missing name. He walked among the lost as they headed toward the tower. These lost souls did not see him, and so, he could not warn them.

The Hierarchy of Hell did not realize it had lost the rebel. Not that it had ever had him. Rebellion grew in that nether world of the dead and damned as it began to spark here, in this fragile and fading world of Aerda.

He glided toward the cliff's edge, looking down on the harbor below. He smiled and gave over Ambriel's Archaic, the twelve salvation taverns. Only eleven more marvels to pull from The Time Weaver's curious cube in order to elevate Creation in ways no mortal had ever imagined. He thanked his maker for this one chance, this slow miracle.

He bowed his head. The Rooke and his party would see a curse returned to the world to offset the extraordinary blessing of the taverns. Humans often misunderstood. The monsters, faeries, and extraordinary beasts returned was not an evil. It was a challenge. Beauty, possibility, and peril. A purpose. A test.

The rebel turned toward the path that would lead him down to the harbor. He ignored the grime, the ash of the quieting volcano, the pollution of the speeding transports that came up and down the tunneled road between the harbor and the awful black tower.

He sighed at time's cruel hand that had supplanted the lovely college and priory that once stood on the same land. No matter. If The Rooke continued, and the people wished, the dragons would awake to give them a clean slate on which to create instead of banishing this world into the hell it had earned.

He felt anxious to find the garden that would rise where Aroghotto City had once been. Phaedra, that mighty dragon, in her wrath had given the people of Aerda a great opportunity even if that is not what the dragon intended.

She had given Tem, the ice dragon, a place where he could heal from the wounds which he had sustained in Alleysiande's final battle at long last. The rebel, himself, had deep injuries that needed soothing after passing through Pandemonium.

The walkway that ran along the tunneled road was narrow. Few walked this path anymore, and none so much as looked at him until he reached the harbor. Thunder rumbled in the distance. Soft, cleansing rain drops fell gently cleansing the scars of the islands.

A small girl almost ran into him, running after her older brother. She looked up at him, her little dark eyes filled with joy and curiosity.

"Sorry, I did not see you."

"No harm done. You see me now. Why are you running?"

"A rooke has come. My brother and I go to hear a story. Would you like to hear a story?"

"I would. Where is this story to be told?"

"At the end of the pier, next to Mandoras Bait and Tackle," the girl said. "I have to go. There won't be much room and I want to hear."

"There will be plenty of room. Rest easy. You will have a place to rest, to eat, and to listen, and to dream."

He watched the children dart in and out of the tourists, the shops, until they came to the narrow pier at the end of the dockside. They did not see the cliffside rise before them, filled with lighted windows overlooking Tiponi Harbor. It had always been there, only invisible.

The dragon stepped before him in the illusion of a black-scaled dressed woman. She glowered as he extended his hand, giving her a ruby-like crystal. She lowered her head, shaking a bit.

"I told you to sleep," the rebel said.

"I am sleeping," she replied. "Thank you for this. It is most precious."

"It will stay with you regardless of what this world does."

"It will not replace the ones I lost in The Evanescence."

"Your children are as eternal as you are, Phaedra. They will wait here or in the Eternal Kingdom. Forever more. Now, my dear friend, let us go hear a tale."

"My children are in danger of damnation and manipulation. Until you have your name back, there will be no salvation."

"The sorceress who shares your name, keeps mine. So that your children will not be twisted into shadow dragons again. Have you seen the sorceress of Malachi?"

"I did. She stopped me cleansing this world in its entirety. I don't know where she is now. I want to find her as well. We have a bargain. She has lost her grimoire. And that is where your name is. I would help her find it if I could."

"You are a dragon. It is not your concern. It is mine. Now, come. Let us hear The Rooke's first tale in full."

The two settled down in the back of the rediscovered Emerald Eye as people gasped and exclaimed in delight at the massive pub and inn that was hidden inside the old fisherman's hut. He saw the little girl and her brother join friends, ordering food, and being delighted that there was no charge.

No one saw the rebel at all. The dragon was served as if she were any other woman. She tentatively tried some fish in a light butter and lemon sauce. She offered the rebel a taste.

The rebel saw a familiar man, no longer in a gold sleeve with a celebrated, red ribbon, dressed in simple island garb, a face filled with grief. He shook a young child.

"Isaiah, wake up," he said.

The rebel understood and wandered over to the distressed man. "Tavares Fabian Flaco, whatever is the trouble?" he asked.

"My son. He won't wake. I thought he was only sleeping. He's dead. He's dead."

"This is not your son. You and your wife sacrificed your child to Moloch," the rebel said. "This was the flesh of a Spyte, cruelly taken and used. Just as your son was."

The man held the boy to him, weeping inconsolably. Others in the magical inn remained oblivious, even those sharing a booth with him. The rebel propelled them into a small, private space.

"I didn't know. Everyone did it and celebrated when it was done. I wanted to take it back. Bittore wanted to undo it, but it was done," Tavares said. "I want my son. I want him back. My child, Izzy, he would be this age if I had not…if we had not…"

"Tavares, look at me," the rebel said.

The man gazed up at him, his eyes glossy with tears. "I know you," Tavares said, starting to shake from head to toe. "You were there, the night Bittore and I escaped. You saved us."

"You saved yourselves. And you might yet save this poor child's soul," the rebel said. "But it is no easy thing."

"Anything. I will do anything at all," Tavares said. "Only do not fault Bittore. I talked her into it. I love her so much. I only saw what she could do with her influence. I did not think we could fall…"

"No one ever does," the rebel said, smiling. "Will you agree to do my will?"

"What do you want?" Tavares asked. "I will do it."

"I need your help," the rebel said. He explained what was required as Tavares nodded, tears streaming from the man's eyes. All the while, the rebel kept his hand on the dead boy until the child took a peaceful breath. The eyes opened. The child looked at his father, not seeing the rebel.

"Did I miss the story?"

Tavares gasped, hugging the boy tight. "No, my son, no. You are here. Izzy, this is a miracle."

"What are you talking about, da?" Izzy asked, pulling out of his father's grasp. "You are so weird, da. I'm going to get some food with Kostas and Taki. They are my friends."

"How did you do that?" Tavares asked the rebel as the boy joined the others, as if he had always been there.

The rebel flooded Tavares mind with memories, making Isaiah a part of the last nine years and erasing the Spyte.

"I cannot say. I will tell you that Spytes may not enter a salvation tavern. It kills them as you have seen," the rebel said. "They must be redeemed first."

"Who are you?" Tavares asked, eyes wild, his will firmly resolved.

"I am who I am. Now do my will."

The Rooke came in mid-morning and began his tale, telling the fall of Alleysiande and the rise of Phaedra the sorceress thousands of years later. Such a marvelous tale which did not suffer much from the omission of the rebel's true name.

He drifted away as the tale ended, glancing at the painting that appeared at the back of the inn's tavern. It resembled the Idylls & Grimoire card of The Last King of Ambriland more than it did River Swann who had been the island kingdom's last monarch. The rebel felt tempted to stay, to hide in the inn attached to this salvation tavern. He dared not.

He could not save this world until he restored his name. Even if all the archaics were restored to Aerda, without him, The Hierarchy of Hell would win. A long battle lay ahead, and the rebel did not feel ready.

The Tale of Jabber and Liam

Dawn was a good way off when Husk first awoke in the hospital. Sidon Bagwell shared his room, still recovering from his wounds in his own battle with the terrible specter.

Feeling a small child, Husk felt afraid of the dark and wished to wake up the Urian pappa. He believed even as injured as he was, Pappa Sidon would do much better combatting Terminus than he had. He wondered what had become of Phaedra. He pushed himself up to find his black cat curled at the corner of his bed.

She is alive. And so are you. Terminus is gone. For now.

Normal cats did not talk. Or turn into winged and scythed creatures that fought armies of demons. Husk shuddered. He wanted to go back to the cottage. He tried to stand, but was overcome with dizziness.

"Sariel. I am so glad you are alive," Husk said. "How did you get in here?"

The cat did not answer. The spry, black feline leapt from the bed, across to the open window and disappeared into the night as the door from the hall opened, a light filling the room and being extinguished in short order.

The Silver Swann's monkey, Noe, scampered into the room, onto the bed of the Urian pappa, followed by the Bagwell brothers, Trick and Jesper. Husk pretended to sleep.

"Dad, dad, wake up," he heard Trick say. "Hurry, there's not much time. Jabber says we need to go. There is much danger. Goolsby and Phineas are waiting at the docks. Captain Sage has agreed to take us home on The Shroud. We can't stay here."

"Trick?" Sidon Bagwell said, his voice echoing his pain and

discomfort. "Kid, I can't walk. That knife tore my stomach muscles apart. What are you on about?"

"You can. You are almost healed. I have made you a potion," Jesper said. "Jabber, help me."

There was a flash of red light. Husk gasped as Trick turned to gather the small monkey in his arms. He had three eyes. One was red and glowing. Husk turned and saw Phaedra ghost past him. She turned a sharp eye on him and waved, uttering some Asciendien phrase.

"Wha…"

Husk found he could neither move nor speak. He watched as Phaedra opened her grimoire and uttered some spell or other.

"There you go. That will make it so no one will see us as we leave," she said. "Did your potion work, Jesper?"

"It did," Pappa Bagwell said, standing up. "I am not too sure about all this. It feels like kidnapping."

"It is the only way Xavier will live," Jesper said. "No one expects us to leave while you are still in hospital. And it gives us time to heal Xavier and return him home before his family melts down."

"I have sorted it," Phaedra said. "The Roses think they have approved for Xavier to visit his Acarian relatives. Which he will after you are done curing him."

The monkey scampered up Sidon Bagwell's side, hugging him. Husk thought it strange. From the first time his patron's monkey had seen Sidon, it had been obsessed with the man.

"What is it with this monkey?" Sidon asked, petting its head, and handing it back to Trick. "We can't take it with us."

"This is Jabber. He belongs to Janus," Trick Bagwell said, his third eye still glowing.

"Janus is gone. I will try to explain to your friend that it must stay with its mistress," Phaedra said. "It is not time for the monkey to join the sorcerer."

Noe hesitated in front of Husk. The monkey blinked and raised its forearm to wave a quiet good-bye.

"Jabber, let's go," Trick said. "We are almost done. You'll

need to go back to The Silver Swann like Phaedra said. It's ok. Everything will be fine. Maybe. Dad isn't ready yet."

"I will never be ready to have a monkey," Pappa Bagwell said, limping after the others. "We better get going. The fewer who witness this the better."

"Yes, it is imperative that Xavier Rose live," Phaedra said. "The oracle child proclaims him an Erelahian captain. He must live."

"The oracle child does not know anything anymore," Sidon Bagwell said. "He changed things back in The Mudlands."

"I know I did," Trick said. "But this thing is different. I know the Erelahian captains. That would not have changed when the Dirts attacked us. And Xavier will be one. If he lives. If he dies, we lose."

"If he dies, we make a new plan, Liam. We train up a new captain," Phaedra said. "Oracles are universally unreliable. I would assume it is the same with you from reading Hazel Kyran's *Idylls of Alleysiande*. They see too much all jumbled up in the time weaver's web."

"Phaedra, you are hurting my feelings. And don't call me Liam. That was my last timeline. I am Trick Bagwell now," Trick said, closing his third eye. "With any luck it is who I will be when I am finally allowed to die."

"I don't want you to die," Sidon said.

"You'll be dead before Trick," Jesper said, securing his alchemy set in his leather side bag, cleaning up his father's bed to make it look as if no one had been there at all. "You are way old."

"Dad is way immortal," Trick said. "I will die before him if it all goes well. If not, we will all be unmade. Which is way worse than dead."

"Trick, we really need to talk about this oracle business if this Xavier business doesn't go belly up," Sidon said, taking a bit of stick in his hand to use as a walking stick. The strange staff had a gem at its end, glowing red, a ruby, an invaluable gemstone it appeared. It glowed with a soft light.

"Dad, stop worrying. Mom will love Xavier. He can join Fox

Clan to get his spawning graff," Jesper said, holding the door open for them to leave. "That will heal him. We will have Xavier back before Ambriland can declare war on us. And you already know about the oracle bit. You just don't want to admit it."

Phaedra stood over Husk, whispered some words allowing Husk to move again. Husk watched them disappear, wondering if it were all a dream.

The morning rose hot and bright. Captain Delilah Sage set sail with the bulk of the visiting Urians, leaving only young Lucie Tunvel behind to apprentice to her grandmother as the next keeper for The Emerald Eye. Phaedra and Daedalus both rattled off the news of the day to Husk Grayvesone as he sat up in his infirmary bed after Dr. Rege had made a fuss over him.

"Never heard of anyone who survived eight venomous snake bites before. You look like crap, my friend," Daedalus said. "Shanley Rose is outside. She and Selkie Nett have made you some biscuits."

"The Muddy call them cookies," Phaedra said. "I call them delicious. I will gladly be fat to be able to eat such treats all the time."

"You didn't eat them all, did you?" Husk asked.

"No, I merely tested them to make sure they were a suitable gift," Phaedra said. "They are splendid."

"Shanley can come in and say hi. That's fine. Why is she being all shy?"

"She is worried you do not approve of her," Phaedra said. "And she much wishes for your affections. Although, I can't say why myself. You are such an average boy."

"As average as Ambriens go," Daedalus said. "I'll get Shanley. Phaedra?"

"I need a moment alone with Husk," Phaedra said. "Do reassure Shanley that I have no interest in kissing Husk."

"Shanley does not want to kiss me," Husk said, sitting up and inspecting his black and purple bruised hand. He pulled the sheet over him so as not to expose the other injuries. They burned but not so bad as they had.

"Shanley wants to more than kiss you," Phaedra said. "She wants to do things with you that were I to try, I think it might burn both of us out of existence."

"Phaedra, you must stop reading other people's thoughts. It is rude," Husk said, and changed subject before the dark-haired sorceress could continue. Phaedra had no filter, and she enjoyed Husk's blushes. "I had a dream that I suspect…"

"Yes, not a dream. Your cat is not a cat in the usual way, and Trick is an oracle. He lives backwards most times. He is living forward at the moment," Phaedra said. "And Sidon Bagwell is not who he seems. I hid his true name in my grimoire so that The Hierarchy may not have it."

"It didn't work," Husk said. "His name was Sidon Bagwell as you have just said. Is Sidon…"

"That was never his name," Phaedra said. "Not the name his mother, Imogen Vasilis, and his father, Gareth Janus, gave him."

"You believe that this Urian pappa is the lost son of the sorcerer, Janus?" Husk asked. "Phaedra, that mind of yours is out of whack. That would make him eons old, older even. No one knows how long ago Alleysiande existed if it all. It's impossible."

"Listen, scholar boy, last of Ambriel's people, you should know more than anyone still living that Ambriel weaves time and space. He does not have to be literally eons old. You know the children's tale. He was thrown forward in time only without his mother and half-sister. He came through with the oracle called Liam," Phaedra said, folding her arms in front of her and glowering down on Husk. "Sidon Bagwell is the son of Janus and Imogen. Hidden in time."

"That would make Trick the oracle of that children's book?"

"Yes, and now, you too, my odd scholarly friend, are part of that tale," Phaedra said. "Do not be so gloomy. We have saved more than one boy."

Husk did not wish to discuss being part of a myth further. He wanted a real life. With real people. Real love. Real ambition. He wanted to teach his subject. He wanted to become an archivist of Dalmeade so that he might earn the rare, privileged invitation to The Unapproachable Library. There, he could better understand the story into which Ambriel had weaved him.

"I think you're making fun of me, Phaedra," Husk said. "There's some joke I am not getting. About Pappa Bagwell. Or Shanley. I had the impression that Shanley quite taken with Jesper Bagwell."

"Maybe she was a little at first," Phaedra said. "The young man is pleasant to gaze upon. However, if a naked woman jumped up and down on his face, he would take no notice. He is a singularly minded man with too much interest in herbs and spices and alchemical formulae, and it is imperative he have offspring. A problem for another time."

"I suspect he notices girls, Phaedra. Or maybe its boys that interest him. He might be uncomfortable with intimacy. A lot of people are."

"And others fear their own fire," Phaedra said. "I will get Shanley."

Shanley hesitated at the door. She had a package in her arms, wrapped and neat. She gave Phaedra an uncomfortable glance and pushed the package into Husk's arms.

"It's biscuits of sea salt and caramel, and a book," Shanley said. "I thought you'd like...."

Husk smiled. "It's great. Are you alright?"

"Me? Good...ah...I was so worried," Shanley said. "I was terrified for you. I am so glad you are not ... that you are alive. Poor Professor Estiarte. I had him as a teacher, you know. I am so sorry that he died like that. They said a two-headed snake attacked him. I can't get over the horror of it."

"Me too. Thanks for these treats, Shanley," Husk said, taking one of the sweet biscuits. "They are delicious."

"Selkie Nett made them. I helped. A little," Shanley said.

"Xavier recommended the book. Said it would help you with Dalmeade."

Husk looked at the volume. *About Specter Level Grimoire Spells* by Tarana Holic. It was a banned book, but one that was studied in the Archives of Dalmeade. Husk nodded his approval.

"About Xavier? I hear he went to The Mudlands?"

"Yes, they can cure him," Shanley said. "He will join the Fox Clan. He will be back before school starts. He will be able to stay at Shankly Hall with you."

"Your parents are going to be…"

"Deceived. Aunt Delilah convinced them they are going to Acaria to visit our Aunt Astrid, the Duchess. Phaedra convinced my parents that Xavier was already healed," Shanley said. "To make matters better, he truly will be going on to Acaria with Captain Delilah and Siobhan after he gets through his joining. The Raving Parrot docks in Pig's Spit in the summer so it will be there to bring him home."

The conversation died. Shanley stood up, fidgeting with her dress as Phaedra exited the room, chasing after Sariel. Husk thumbed through the book. He held it up. "I really like this. Thank you," he said.

"Good. I hoped you would. I suppose you'll want to get some rest," Shanley said. "I…"

She started to turn away, then hesitated, leaned over, giving Husk a light hug and quick kiss, brushing his lips. It was pleasant although quick. Husk had no time to respond. The girl ran away so fast. Phaedra entered the room, Sariel firmly in her grasp. She smiled, looking delighted.

"I told you she wanted to kiss you," Phaedra said.

"So she did," Husk said. "And I didn't catch on fire or anything."

The Parting Glass

The closing bell rang as patrons of the Emerald Eye stood, clapping, and raising a parting glass as The Rooke took a humbled bow. The world had changed forever between his tales and the dragon that devoured Aroghotto City.

The painting that had stared at him came alive as the Last King of Ambriland stood up straight under his heavy crown, stepping aside to reveal a double-sided door, opening to a lighted passageway, that magical inn from the far reaches of The Rooke's memory.

Rintyre sat with her head on Zac's shoulder, pushing her glass against his and something like a smile on her radiant face. The two were joined in grief. He pitied Zac for the love he would never get from the girl who truly captured him. He had recovered from Cymbre Varian's deceit only to land in one of those tales that never ended well.

Kostas happily snored, lying out on a bench with his head to Anwyn's, both children sleeping as Thiago poked at his brother to wake him up. Taki played with young Isaiah Flaco, and that struck The Rooke as peculiar. Why did he allow Tavares to bring his child with him? Should the boy have not stayed back…?

Another thought intruded The Rooke's mind, in the way that stories did. Isaiah had been a Spyte without a name, now redeemed. That must be the magic of the Ambriel's salvation tavern. He could save so many Spytes if he could trick them into entering.

Kostas looked around wildly to find the ship in the bottle in his hand. He refused to put it down again, after having lost it back at The Glittering Raptor.

Kentigern clapped him on the back, pulling him aside.

"I've word from Talon. There have been no quakes for weeks. However, the valley is overrun with The Reliquary's citizens and rebels arriving by the boatload every day. Two new villages are being constructed. Bittore Rose has become quite the fixture at Tem's Tavern, telling your tales every night. She has added some of her own tales to her repertoire. I have told Gareth to ask Bittore if she would consider joining the Forge of Sentinels. I am not sure how Tavares will feel about that. Considering little Izzy and all."

The Rooke nodded. Vacationers lined up to pay their regards under the watchful eyes of Aldo and Tavares Flaco.

"Seems the fire dragon is appeased," Aldo whispered into The Rooke's ear.

"But for how long?" Kentigern said.

"Let us enjoy ourselves," Aldo said. "Go on, Kentigern, you've earned a moment here."

"The children are tired" The Rooke said. "They should get rooms and have a sleep."

"I will see to that," Tee said, giving her husband a gentle hug. "Joel, are you coming?"

"I made a new map of all the salvation taverns and where they were before the people go away," Taki said. "We can use this one to find the others. We must get the order right. I will work with Kostas and Ani to make sure order right."

"Thank you, Taki," The Rooke said. "You have saved us more than once. I am glad you are on our side."

"I am not on your side. I am on the Gnolgia side. If we restore your land, the Gnolgia get their kingdom back. We will protect our technology again, and the empires will not be able to enslave the people again. That is for the Gnolgia to do," he said, cracking a mischievous grin. "I am not meant to kill you provided we have common cause."

The Rooke watched Tee guide Kostas, Thiago, Anwyn, Taki, and Izzy into the inn. Some of the tin-sleeved thieves followed them including that young man, Freddie, who had helped them escape. The Fistian Seat in disguise. As best The Rooke could tell, well-over a thousand had found their way to the Emerald Eye from the previous places he had told his tales.

"It's all real," Aldo said. "And if the salvation taverns are real…"

"Yes, yes," The Rooke said, feeling joy well up in his lungs. "Then it all could be. Alleysiande might be restored. Or at least the bits of it that existed before The Evanescence."

Rat approached The Rooke after several patrons gathered their tokens. Fewer than ever wore sleeves. It seemed many had taken the time that the fire dragon had brought them to escape SIN.

"Rat, you and Petra already have tokens," The Rooke said. "Is there a problem?"

"We don't have credits. We wondered if you might provide us rooms here as the old man did for us before?"

"You can stay here at no cost or judgement. This is a salvation tavern," The Rooke said. "Go to that door as Tee Broomes and the children did. You and Petra and the others are safe here, welcome here."

"Petra was never a rat," the young man said. "I killed Chrysalis. That was me. And then I was a rat."

"You are no longer a rat," The Rooke said. "That woman there will give you a key to your own room. You will be safe here for as long as you like."

Rat had put on a few pounds and looked more boy than rodent, not a ghoul at all. His dark eyes were brighter, his skin seemed less scarred. As did Petra. The Rooke suspected that they would both remain sterilized without a miracle. Although, on this night, The Rooke thought that might be possible.

"Come on, let's go to our rooms," Aldo said. "I can't wait to have a proper night's sleep."

"I think I'll get a breath of air first," The Rooke said. "I want to see what the Emerald Eye looks like now. If it still appears to be a bait shack or if the full inn appears."

"You can't go outside here alone," Kentigern said.

The Rooke removed his robes and handed them to Aldo. "I'll be fine."

"We'll go with him," Tavares said, pulling Joel with him.

"We keep him safe," Joel said.

"Then we're coming too," Aldo said, giving Kentigern an exacerbated grin.

Outside, Aerda's full moon seemed to touch the rippling water of the Ambrien Sea. The Dragon Moon shone across the bay toward Marinplaz which glowed with its luxury resorts and cliffside manors of imperial elites.

"These islands are beautiful, no?" Joel said. "Even in the dark."

"This is Ambriland once more," The Rooke said. "Almost."

He walked toward the mainland, leaving the pier behind, toward the bars and little inns of the shore where vacationers were stumbling back to their rooms after a night's festivities, unaware of what had transpired at the end of the long, narrow pier.

The air smelled clean with the salty sea breeze. The rain had washed away all the ash, and the moon had the sky to itself, illuminating the refreshed white sands of the beaches.

The Rooke made to turn to see if the Emerald Eye had taken a new shape. Before he could fully turn, his gaze found a woman adorned in a scaled black outfit, too heavy for the heat of the islands, her piercing eyes, emanating both beauty and danger in equal measure. She was pointing toward the pier.

"I heard your tale, Rooke," she said, a clicking tone to her voice as if unaccustomed to speaking Acarian. Or at all.

"Did you enjoy it?" The Rooke asked, confused.

"I did," she said. "I have a question."

"All right?"

"Where is Phaedra the Sorceress?"

The Rooke assumed that Acarian was not her first language, that she was asking where Phaedra went after The Bagwells left the islands with Xavier Rose. He knew with his magic, she would have heard the tale in her own language, but it was not a perfect sorcery. He told it in Acarian and so she might have missed some nuance here and there in the telling.

"Did I not say? She remained in the cottage with Daedalus and Reginald while Husk took on his duties as house master of Shankly Hall at Kingswell College."

The woman said nothing. She stared at him as if he were very stupid. The Rooke realized in the same moment the assassins attacked that she was asking where Phaedra was at this very moment.

He did not have time to respond. The woman, with a force far greater than such a small person should have had, threw him out of the way of the assassin's knife.

Tavares pulled his sword and struck down two before The Rooke could yell. Aldo tried his pistol, but it was struck from his hand as a dark blade sought his throat and missed narrowly. The Rooke made to scream, pushing Aldo from the blade as the woman appeared in a flurry, fire erupting from some hidden weapon she had, burning Aldo's attacker to a blackened bloody crisp.

The Rooke fell to his friend's side, seeing blood appear at his throat. "No," he screamed. "No! No. Aldo!"

"I am not hurt," Aldo said, fiercely. "Much. I've cut myself worse shaving."

"That explains your messy goatee," Tavares said, parrying two assassins at once. Aldo had taken to punching their attackers, breaking one's neck with his bare hands in fury.

Zac Grimm appeared, dispatching the last of the assassins with his ancient sword. The young man smiled and then saw the blood. He dropped his sword.

"I wanted to throw this in the sea after I killed Cymbre," Zac said. "Glad I didn't. Don't want any more to die to these monsters."

"You did well, mate," Aldo said. "I think we got them all. You ok, Kenny?"

"I am good," Kentigern said. He took Aldo by the arm. "Let me look, mate. You are bleeding."

"It's nothing, old friend," Aldo said. "We have survived. But more will come. Rooke, you cannot stay out here."

A breathless moment passed and quiet fell around them as if some invisible force cloaked them from onlookers. Tavares smiled at Aldo, staunching the blood with a soaked rag.

"We have to get you off this pier," Zac Grimm said. "Rooke, what are you doing out here, idiot? We were safe inside but no way we can be safe out here. There were ten thousand listening to your tale tonight."

"Zac is right, Rooke. We should go inside. This remains Big Kyo. It is not Ambriland. Not yet," Kentigern said. "They'll be more. The only place we can hide is in the inn."

"Where is that woman?" The Rooke asked.

"What woman?" Kentigern said.

"The one that was speaking to me before?"

"There was no woman," Tavares said.

The Rooke stood up, shaking, feeling his jubilation interrupted with an awful fear. Both assaulted him causing an exhaustion that made him swoon. Aldo caught him up.

"Let's go, my friend," Aldo said. "The others be waiting for us."

The Rooke pulled away, stopped dead as he looked down the pier and saw no fisherman's hut. A song broke the midnight, the traditional melody once sung by Daedalus Sams, Husk Grayvesone, and Tempest Redd to end an evening at the famous inn. Those lost moments pulled at him. He looked up and centuries disappeared in a blink.

The Emerald Eye appeared as it had been before The Evanescence and The Subjugation, restored to full glory under the full, red Dragon Moon. The famous inn and tavern made new again, with light coming from the cliffside windows, greeting him with the promise of rest and comfort as reward for a quest completed. He looked back again trying to find the woman wearing the black scale suit.

He peered across the bay to Marinplaz. The full moon lit up the cliff where the priory once stood, revealing the Icarian black tower disguised as a resort, haunting and threatening. He knew that soulless revelers in the hundreds filled it while ordinary people only saw a grand hotel that they could never afford to stay in. Much the same as The Glittering Raptor, only far more menacing.

To ordinary people, the Thirteen Icarian Black Towers were instruments of temptation. Many ached to have their chance to enter the glowering tower on the cliff where the priory once stood. To the vast majority, this black tower and all the others, spoke of opulence and inexhaustible wealth and power. They did not see their doom. More tales would be needed to save them.

The Rooke turned his back on the tower so that it could not call to him and entered Ambriel's salvation tavern, The Emerald Eye. He recognized a young woman, the innkeeper, as if from a dream. Impossible but here she stood before him in the flesh. It was truly her as if time had never touched her from her young adulthood.

"We've been waiting so long for your return. Your room is ready."

She called The Rooke by his true name. He heard it although he could not repeat it. This was confirmation that he had indeed told his own tale over the last year. He swayed and nearly fell over.

Kentigern caught him. "Rooke, what is wrong?"

"I've done a horrible thing. I don't want to tell anymore stories," he said, remembering the tales that were to come. "I am such a fool, Kenny."

"We're all fools," Kentigern said, a cheeky smile, like the young man who laughed so easily in the years before Torres Rushie's name returned to him.

"What are you going on about?" Aldo said. "You're a damn hero. You saved my old hide. My wife and kids will be in your debt."

"No, that's not what I mean…" And then it was gone again. He could not remember anymore. He shrugged. "I would like to go to bed now."

"Come," Lucie Tunvel said. "You have earned a good night's rest."

Lucie escorted him and the others to the lifts where they would retire for a proper night's sleep. Tomorrow held promise of sun and good food with good friends and infinite possibility. It was enough.

The End

The Lore of Alleysiande
An Ordering of Events

The Fall of Alleysiande

Some truly believe a great continent, populated by magical people and mystical creatures, broken into 13 distinct rings once existed. When it disappeared from the world, Aerda became smaller. Much of the religion and mythology evolve around the stories of this fabled land. The events that removed Alleysiande from Aerda is collectively known as "The First Cataclysm".

1213 AA The Second Cataclysm

Something happened in the old Empire of Chazir, causing most of the people to flee or die. Some say a volcano with many earthquakes. The land became known as The Mudlands after as people who claimed to be descendants of Alleysiande stayed and endured the harsh conditions. The world referred to these people as "Muddy" as they did not seem to belong to the world.

8712 AA The Evanescence

Seventeen million people disappeared, leaving no corpses, no sign they ever existed behind within the span of a year. This included all the Urians and those who opposed The Three Infernal Empires.

Along with the people, all the fantastical and storied creatures, unicorns, faeries, goblins, wyverns, monsters of all sorts, also ceased to exist. Also, several places seem to have disappeared including the University of Dalmeade and the Unapproachable Library that was attached to it.

8726 The Subjugation

Emperor Malcombe Absyrtus II of Chazir was proclaimed the ruler of all Aerda in this year although The Subjugation began directly after Evanescence. The other leaders became his pawns, mere figureheads from that day forward. For the comfort of the people, three imperial Senates were formed for which elections were held in The Three Empires. The imperials refer to this event that crowned Malcombe II as "The Liberation Decree".

8914 The Common Uprising

Nicolai Sacripant is crowned emperor in a coup displacing Malcombe IV. He is aided by the uprising of the people of Aerda who wished to have the world separated into independent regions. Nicholai begins this process, granting independent power to fifty-seven nations.

8920 Assassination of Emperor Nicolai Sacripant and the Rooke, Steven Fowler

Both emperor and rooke died under the same assassin's knife. Emperor Malcombe IV retakes power and within 3 years has crushed all resistance to the imperial world order.

The Mythology of Alleysiande

There are 12 Sentinels of Alleysiande. They served as guardians, protectors, and the source of magic in that lost land. They are often referred to as Erelah or angels by the various religons of Aerda.

These 12 are divided into 2 groups, The Ascended and The Wayward. The Ascended left the world to return to The Eternal Kingdom (heaven, Nirvana, Elysium – pick your own vision), and the Wayward remained behind to try and remedy what creation had lost when Alleysiande fell. All are credited with creating their own people, the twelve Erelahian races.

The Ascended

Ambriel

Referred to as "The Time Weaver'. Ambriel has power over time and space. She made Ambriens which had various abilities. A few were called "world-spinners" in that they had the ability to travel to other worlds and other times. Most simply could see her weave, see that there were many worlds, could perceive all the possibilities. *She is also credited with the creation of oracles. This is disputed.

Metatron

Metatron is referred to as "The Scribe". He recorded the great events of creation and lent his magic to create the rookes as he departed the world. People with Metatron's gift could remedy an error made, and allow mortals to correct the damage of a misguided deed over time. He was also considered the Sentinel of Writers.

Sandalphon

The musician. Sandalphon shared his music with any who wished it. This music could restore a lost soul. His people are called Sandies. While they are incredibly rare, their gift is shared among most people.

Haniel

The Healer. Few have the true gift of healing, but they do show up now and again, even in the modern world. Haniel meant her gift to penetrate the entire population of Aerda. She never wanted it confined to Alleysiande where people were rarely sick or even injured to begin with. Some say, Haniel allowed in the corruption that took Alleysiande in her compassion. Her people were called "Hands" and could cure any disease by merely laying their hands on the afflicted.

Jeremiel

The protector of children. Sindians (as those who lived in Alleysiande were called) could live for a thousand years or more and so felt no need to have children for the first millennia of Alleysiande's existence. Jeremiel encouraged the Sindians to have children.

Children born in Alleysiande's first generation to those who were not Erelahians are all considered Jeremiel's people known as "Jems". They had the power to restore innocence to even the most corrupted soul.

The Wayward Erelah

Uriel

The High Sentinel known also as The Reconciler as it was his mission to reconcile the lost people of Aerda (the ones not living in Alleysiande) with the Creator, Ta-She-Serra.

Uriel did not create a people. Instead, he helped rescue as many Sindians as possible and made with them a Covenant. Any who held to the covenant would live free and under his protection provided they spent their lives doing what they could to restore Alleysiande back to the world. This covenant was marked by a living tattoo around the left wrist known as a "spawning graff" comprised of ancient runes which translated as 'Great love calls us'.

Over time, anyone could join this covenant. Those who did became known as "Urians". However, the world of Aerda despised these people, calling them mutts and vagrants and barbarians. They called the 'mutty' which later earned them the moniker of Muddy. Uriel's people all disappeared at The Evanescence.

Raphael

The Rain Maker. Raphael purifies and supplies water which is the source of life as far as he is concerned. He made created a single, immortal couple, The Dream Walker and Raine who produced a number of children. They and their children survived the destruction of Alleysiande and made their home in Mesa, Lux Verre until The Evanescence when they and all their progeny disappeared.

They were known as Mesians regardless of whether they had the water purification powers. The grandchildren of the Dream Walker and Raine and all generations were no longer magical. Perhaps being born away from Alleysiande and to ordinary mortals did not allow the power to propagate through the generations.

Malachi

The Sorcerer Prime. Malachi made Janus, the great sorcerer of Alleysiande who sacrificed himself atop the Black Tower in order to give hope to the future. It is hoped that Malachi made a spare. Janus had a son that was taken by his oracle and monkey on Alleysiande's last day. Little is known of what became of that child. Of all the powers ever granted to Alleysiande, Malachi's was most envied by the forces of Hell.

Mordecai

The Dragon Maker. Mordecai made the fire dragon, Phaedra, and the ice dragon, Tem. It is said these dragons made more dragons, beyond counting. On Alleysiande's last days, they pressed their children, untold numbers of dragons into gemstones and sent children on Mordecai's ship to hide them away.

Orifiel

Mother Nature, the Menagerie Keeper – protector of the natural world and animals of all sorts. She created shapeshifters called Igamie who were first spirit animals that could appear human provided they fed on humans every century or so.

Errapel

The Goddess, the restorer of Women. She made the Pella women who became known as Fishers due to the Fisher Dragons (a sea creature) that they commanded. Each Fisher born gave rise to such a sea dragon, an arrangement made between Errapel and Mordecai. These women survived the destruction of Alleysiande, believing they could use the women of Aerda to restore their lost land. They failed to properly understand mortal women. And were slaughtered for their failings.

Pedarial

The rock, the firmament, and protector of fertility. Considered the youngest and most innocent of the Sentinels, Pedarial created Pedarians who could bring fertility to even the most diseased and barren of lands or people. It is said, Pedarial is who caused the Wayward to remain behind after Alleysiande's fall.

The Icari – (aka The Hierarchy of Pandemonium)

There are thirteen of these suckers and each commands legions of demons. These all were once Erelah, angels, but they fell and became demons at the moment physical worlds were created. It is because of them that mortals exist, or they would not have been made to suffer and die. Some meant to rebel, to defy the Creator. Others were just a bit clueless and did not realize they would be damned and unforgivable.

Lecretia

The source of lust and desire. Represented by a sensuous woman wrapped in a large and horrifying snake, she is often called The Queen of Hell.

Shalchar

The Liar. Shalchar is considered consort to Lecretia and therefore, the King of Hell.

Bal'Ael

The Tempter. Bal'Ael loves debauchery. His legions make revelers. These things run about in human skin, often wealthy, always beautiful, and corrupt beyond mortal comprehension. Their temptation is difficult for any person to resist.

Malfus

Hell's Best Little Assassin, the Usurper. He wants to rule everything. Hell, Aerda, the Eternal Kingdom. He is often underestimated by his peers, by the heavens, and by mortals.

Abaddon

The Wrangler – he follows the Reckoners about trying to dismantle Ta-She-Serra's white horse rider in order to keep mortal worlds under Hell's management.

Beleth

The Instigator – he loves to cause war among mortals. He sews discord and acquires mortal souls by promising and delivering revenge.

Moloch

Devourer of Innocence. Moloch thrives on inspiring people to sacrifice their children to him. He's really good at it.

Forcas

The barrister. He brings law and order and justice. Not really. He wields power like a club – loves using order to bring about oppression. He is the twisting of justice although before he fell, he was meant to be its embodiment.

Kokabel

The Faerie Goblin – he/she (never stays the same gender for more than a minute) made faeries and sprites and goblins using the same power as the Sentinels – twisted people into those creatures – corrupting them and their magic. Although, Kokabel could never take the free will of those creatures and so they sometimes defy their maker. Poor Kokabel. Gets no respect at all.

Ose

The spy and finder of secrets. He is big on the blackmail -what better way to take a soul? Coerce a mortal to do something terrible and then keep it secret as long as the mortal stays true to his new, demonic master.

Phenex

The trickster – is as like to trick a good person as one of his fellow Icari. No one trusts Phenex nor should they. He never tells the truth, and he never lies. He's a mess.

Vassago

The poet, pretentious and literary, sibling to the sentinel, Sandalphon. Was in love with Kokabel and so followed him into Pandemonium. Collects souls by granting fame. He wishes to not be damned although understands that is not possible for him.

Azazel

The rage. Azazel went mad when he fell from the Eternal Kingdom. He is a very, very angry energy and uses irrational hate, fear, and rage to separate mortals from their souls.

A Word on SIN (The Sleeve Imperial Network)

All sleeves are made of metal and make a thick bracelet that holds onto a rectangular screen at a person's wrist. Each sleeve has a ribboned band, cloth, leather, or jeweled. The metal and the ribbon indicate social status. Some bands have engravings which further clarify the person's standing in the empire.

The most common sleeves are steel. These are worn by at least 70% of the population and are given the greatest variety of ribbons. A copper sleeve indicates the "acceptable level" and is the second most common sleeve. Rose gold, silver, platinum, gold, and palladium are all rare, given to the most elite of citizens.

Acknowledgments

For my daughter who pushed me to that first writer's conference and made me take my writing seriously. Thank you, Kate.

Once more I must mention my cousin, Elizabeth, who gave me that rather indelicate shove which made me stop with all the excuses. I needed that.

For Janet Reid, one of the most generous people in publishing, and her Reef of Reiders. What would I have done without you? You gave me the courage to press on and the tenacity to finish despite the harrowing odds pitted against us.

For Jeff Somers and his brilliant *Writing Without Rules* which made me laugh. And made me finish all the stuff I started. Also, funny. And cats. His cats. They helped too.

For my brother, Mac, who was there first and has never let me down. Not once through all the trials and tribulations of our lives.

For my nephew, Alan, and our long talks about history, and his incredible breadth of knowledge that helped so much in my research to give the world of Aerda life.

For my editor, Tolly Maggs. His enthusiasm made those difficult changes easy, elevating the tale to better than I could have imagined. I really appreciate the time taken and the patience in helping me see where this could be better.

For Jori Hanna, helping me put this book out in the world with her skilled guidance, infectious enthusiasm, publishing knowledge, and her amazing cover art. Thank you.

To the entire crew at the school district who put up with my madness all these years. For lending me your names, your stories, your wisdom, your inspiration, and your patience. Cy, Austin, boss Ryan P., Granville, Vicky, Amanda, Steve R., Josh R., Josh M., that other Josh, Daniel, Denise, Sheryl, Morgan, Evelyn, Jeanna, Bill R., Bill G., Jim G., Michelle, Chris, Cosandra, Diana, Greg, Kim, Rebecca, Susan, Tim and Tim again, Myra, Jackie, Trey, Rick, Keith, Hector, Dale A, and dude Dale,

Sheila, Sherry, Ryan A., and the other Ryan, and all the rest of you that have come and gone through the years.

For my beta reading crew; Rose, Carly, Claire, and cousin, Kate. My fellow Carkoon visitors who read through early chapters while I was still exiled amid the kale: A.J., Melanie, Lennon, and Brenda. You got the journey going.

For my dad, a writer, and his unpublished book, *We Have Always Known There Was An Eden*. His stories started me on this journey, building in me that want to return to the garden that I had seen and somehow lost before I ever touched it. And for my mother who nurtured a love of books in me that opened new worlds for me through all the darkest nights of my life.

To my cousin, Jere, who gave an eight-year-old kid *Lord of the Rings* and unwittingly created a life-long obsession with fantasy.

For the guys in Rooke; David, Jimmy, Andy, and Steve. You'll never know how much that music of our youth inspired me. Thank you for those great nights, playing those ambient venues all over our town. Truly magical. You have no idea.

There are more people to thank than my brain can load up right now. However, there are more books to come. Thank you all.

E.M. GOLDSMITH (probably) resides in a bunker at an undisclosed location. She is a master gamer, a life-long fantasy enthusiast, an avid reader, and a storyteller. She is a software engineer for a large school district. Her spirit animal is a pug. She is a die-hard Liverpool FC supporter, never to walk alone. She is a pirate born too late, a fallen soul seeking salvation, and on her best days, she is a dragon.

Connect with her at www.emgoldsmith.com